after the

Rain

Drifters, Book Nine

SUSAN RODGERS

*"We sometimes think we want to disappear,
but all we really want is to be found."*
To the Harbourfront Players of Summerside, Prince Edward Island.
'My own little Drifters gang.'

Contents

Prologue

The Sawyers had a rule.

At West Point Grey Academy, where Emily-Grace attended grade two and where David was a Junior Kindergarten student, the children were to be left alone to fend for themselves on the playground and in the classroom, just like any other kids, despite the presence of personal hired security provided by their parents. Yeah, the family had a history that required extra vigilance and eagle eyes in the interest of the children's safety, but Emily-Grace and David only understood this on a peripheral level. The kids on the playground didn't understand it at all.

So far this year, David was doing okay in JK. He was little, just four and a half. For the most part he was a happy-go-lucky child. His sister, Emily-Grace, was the more sensitive quiet one, and grade two, for her, was an exercise in frustration. For one, the Sawyer kids were late starting this year. It was already mid-October. Schooling for much of the last few years and the beginning of this year had been carried out in small classrooms on the sets of the children's parents' films, or on airplanes and buses during their mother's big tour a year ago.

Since starting school two weeks ago, Emily-Grace's belly hurt in the mornings, got a little better Friday evenings, and steadily ached worse on Sunday nights. Today was no exception. It was Monday, and Daddy was walking Emily-Grace to the playground to wait for the entrance bell. Together they had already taken David into the school, since he was littler and his teacher always met the kids inside by the classroom. Emily-Grace had helped her little brother with his coat and his cute blue Paw Patrol knapsack. Like any

1

good sister, she hung them both up on the hook underneath the name *David*, which was drawn on yellow poster board and decorated with shiny stickers of cars and trucks.

There was never any trouble encouraging David to go into his classroom. He loved school. His teacher was a sandy-haired man with friendly eyes. Emily-Grace wished he was her teacher too because he always took David's hand and had lots to say about good things like going to the Vancouver Aquarium over the weekend and meeting the new Beluga whale baby, who he said was so small and always swam by its momma.

Daddy's hand was always a bit sweaty when he walked Emily-Grace back outside to where she was supposed to wait with her classmates for the entrance bell. He either talked a lot or not at all, depending on whether or not she responded, she supposed. Usually she didn't say much, just answered his questions with a word or two. He asked silly stuff anyway, like *Hey, that girl is smiling at you, is she your friend?* Or *Did Momma put that yogurt you like in your lunch today?*

Now, Emily-Grace heard his knees crunch as he knelt before her on the grass and adjusted her coat, zipping it up a little tighter against the cool breeze off the Pacific.

"Have a good day, sweetheart," he told her, snugging her pink Disney princess backpack up a bit so it lay more comfortably against her back. She wanted to beg him to stay with her but she couldn't bring herself to ask. For one, none of the other daddies were staying, nor were the mothers, who all walked by Emily-Grace's daddy and smiled shyly. Even the ones who were parked way at the other end made it a point to walk by Emily-Grace's daddy every day and smile their stupid smiles at him.

To his credit, at least, he ignored them. Before he ever left his daughter, Josh Sawyer always stayed on bent knees and faced her for an extra few moments.

"Emily-Grace," he was saying today with that worried, sad look that just made her belly ache worse, "it will get easier. I'm sorry you had to start late this year. You can tell the kids all about Australia, about the koala bears we saw while I was working there. They'll love that."

She didn't answer but Emily-Grace knew her daddy could read the fear in her eyes. After a minute while she just stared at him and ached for him to stay, while she pushed the tears down somewhere deep inside, he sighed heavily, leveraged his hands on his knees, and got up to go.

Big Dan was waiting just beyond her daddy. With his head down and his keys, which he'd retrieved from a pocket, dangling from one hand, Josh gave Dan a friendly clap on the shoulder as he passed.

Emily-Grace watched as her daddy turned around at the metal fence. She frowned as he waved at her, and she didn't bother waving back, although she wanted to.

When it drove away, the King Ranch pretty much pulled Emily-Grace's tender belly along behind, the ache was so bad now.

Big Dan. The other kids knew he was her 'friend' but they didn't get why he had to go to school with her. Sometimes it was Susanne who shadowed Emily-Grace and David. It just depended on the day and what activities the kids were up to in their classrooms, like if they went on field trips to Science World, for instance. Sometimes both Susanne and Dan had to come to the school. Always, one of them was on the playground when Emily-Grace was outside. They just weren't allowed to say anything, to interfere at any time unless, Emily-Grace's momma had told her, there was special reason to. Momma never said what that special reason might be, but Emily-Grace knew it had something to do with the sad time when she, David and Momma were locked in the little house a few years ago.

I wish you could interfere all the time, Emily-Grace said silently to Big Dan now, who met her wide, fearful eyes and gave her a tiny smile. It was a quandary; her whole life was a quandary. *I want you here and I don't want you here,* she thought. *Like Daddy. You're my only friend. But none of the other kids have grown-up friends who come to school and who only talk to you when you are ready to be driven home or to meet Momma or Daddy.*

At six years old, almost seven, Emily-Grace knew about bullying and about kids that could be mean. She knew this because there were always a half-dozen kids on the playground who rudely questioned her about Big Dan and Susanne, and whose parents were curious about her parents. These kids asked a lot of questions and passed a lot of judgments. Already they had mean nicknames for Big Dan and Susanne, and for Emily-Grace herself, who was quiet and shy and who always clung to her knapsack and stared at the ground while the others said these things unbeknownst to Dan or Susanne.

Today was going to be a bad day, Emily-Grace could already tell, because it had started with Dylan knocking over her orange juice at breakfast, which got the sticky stuff in her cereal and all over singer-dolly, who was lying by Emily-Grace's cereal bowl. Momma got breakfast while Daddy got David dressed, because David was being fussy over which jeans he wanted to wear (one pair was black and the other was faded blue denim, and Emily-Grace secretly wanted him to wear the black ones because Jacob wore black jeans a lot). So when the juice got knocked over, Emily-Grace's momma didn't get cranky like Daddy might have. Instead, she just smiled at Dylan and picked him up so he wouldn't get the juice all over himself. She got a cloth from the sink and talked to him while she mopped it up, never even noticing that the juice got in Emily-Grace's cereal, so Emily-Grace had to eat it anyway, although Momma was good about promising to give singer-dolly a bath, at least.

Now, on the playground, Jordan Lewis' mother was dropping him off. When his mom left with a hug and a wave, Emily-Grace found herself the object of his sole attention. He opened his big mouth and immediately said, "My mother said your daddy was in jail before. And that he should have stayed there so your mother would still be living with some singer."

Emily-Grace couldn't help herself. Her jaw dropped open and she said, "Why?" It came out as a frantic squeak.

Jordan was a big kid for his age. He always wore work boots and played superhero games at recess, pretending he was Spider Man or Superman or one of the Teenage Mutant Ninja Turtles, much to the detriment of any kids who happened to get in his path while he was saving the world, because he usually just steamrolled them. Emily-Grace, so far, only got his verbal abuse though, because she was quick on her feet, thanks to lots of group and private ballet lessons over the last few years.

The kid couldn't wait to tell Emily-Grace why his mother thought Josh Sawyer should be locked away. He was so excited to tell her that his voice got all loud so more kids could hear this disgrace. "Because he beat up your mother. She was even in the hospital. Your daddy is not a nice guy, my mother said."

"No, he didn't." Emily-Grace was struggling to remember what happened during the sad time a few years ago. Could this be true? Her momma did cry an awful lot back then.

Puffing up his chest, Jordan walked closer to Emily-Grace. "My mother says your mother is crazy, that she is with the wrong man."

And the right man is…

Emily-Grace didn't have to question just who the right man was, although she was too young to understand the ins and outs of adult relationships. "Jacob," she found herself mumbling as she stared up at Jordan's accusing eyes and leering grin.

Jordan continued his torment. "My mother said your daddy is a loose cannon."

"I don't know what that is," Emily-Grace replied in a whisper. "I don't know if my daddy is that."

She was afraid to look up at Big Dan but Emily-Grace could feel his eyes on her. With all her might, she wished that he could tell her what a loose cannon was, and whether her daddy was one. The tears that had been threatening since her momma woke her this morning were hovering near the surface now, but Emily-Grace swallowed them away. No way was she going to cry in front of Jordan, and there were other kids around now too, all feeling a self-righteous pity for Emily-Grace, whose daddy, they now knew, was a loose cannon, whatever that was.

When the bell rang a few moments later, Emily-Grace let the kids walk past her towards the school while she stared at the ground. The teacher, Miss Catlyn, called her name but she couldn't bring herself to turn around. She couldn't make her feet move at all.

Clutching the straps of her knapsack tight enough to keep herself from floating away and disappearing, Emily-Grace, with an aching heartache, looked up to meet Big Dan's kind gaze, and was surprised and a little frightened to see the look on his face, which seemed to her to be a mixture of anger and sadness.

Please, she begged him silently as a tear escaped her right eye and snaked its way downward, *please please please can we just leave?*

But the Sawyers had a rule. The kids were to deal with their own crap when it came to other kids. Emily-Grace knew this.

The teacher strode towards her, calling her name, but now cranky Miss Catlyn's voice was not only the mad kind, it was the *loud* mad kind.

Dan got to Emily-Grace first, which surprised her. He bent and hugged her tight, and since she knew he wasn't supposed to touch her at school, his gesture scared Emily-Grace. But at the same time, it felt so good, so safe, to be in his trusted arms. Letting go of her knapsack straps, she hugged him back.

"Don't you worry about that boy," Dan told her, while he wiped her tear away with a thumb. "He is just repeating things he doesn't understand."

"But my daddy..."

Emily-Grace didn't get a chance to finish asking her question. The grouchy teacher, a woman who always wore her blonde hair in a tight bun and who made the kids do a ton of stupid worksheets every night, was suddenly at her side.

As she grabbed Emily-Grace's hand and dragged her towards the school, Miss Catlyn spoke over a shoulder to Dan. "I realize you are responsible for the safety of this child, but you are not to interact with her at school. I'm fairly certain you're aware of that, sir."

Emily-Grace heard Dan mutter, "Yes, Ma'am," and shuffle his feet, which was something he never did, ever. Twisting her neck around, she watched him for as long as she possibly could before the teacher got her to the door.

But then it was time to go inside. Dan would be taking up a post outside the school for the day so he could watch her door and David's door. Emily-Grace would be alone all day, in the classroom where she knew nobody, with kids who whispered and laughed about her, and with a teacher who wouldn't let her talk to the one person she considered a friend.

But she was used to pushing the sad feelings down deep into her belly, so she did that, but she did not hear a word the teacher said all day and it got her into trouble more than once. At recess, she stood alone and shivered, and aimed her eyes towards Dan's sedan, on the big guy himself, who was standing and leaning against it, his arms crossed. She was grateful, because his eyes were telegraphing strength to her, but she knew he couldn't do a thing about the army of kids Jordan conjured up around her. So she stood there and took the abuse but couldn't answer the questions, which were all about her daddy and jail and meanness and hitting and beating and hurting her momma.

She knew all Dan was allowed to do was watch. What she didn't know was that he ached for Emily-Grace as she planted her feet, knuckled her hands into fists, and locked her Jessie-blue eyes on him.

The Sawyers had a rule, and Dan had no choice but to follow it.

Chapter One

"I'm just saying we can do our own thing, you know, not follow the Joneses or whatever that old saying is about keeping up with your neighbors. It's our wedding; we can make it happen in whatever way we want, that's all. It doesn't have to be some big extravagant affair where we're expected to invite half of Hollywood."

Grabbing a pillow, Jacob rolled over onto his belly, scrunched up the pillow, and shoved it under his face. Wrapping both arms around it so his elbows jutted out, he turned his scowl towards the floor-to-ceiling window wall in the bedroom so his new fiancée couldn't read more into his thoughts than he was willing to tell.

A heavy sigh tinged with more than a little impatient exasperation accompanied his movement, but he didn't utter it. A feminine arm reached over his back at the same time layers from a blonde bob cascaded over Jacob's exposed cheek, which was red and robust after a good sleep well earned from the vigorous nocturnal activities he and his girl had gladly partaken of in celebration of Jacob's whispered proposal on the beach the night before.

"Jacob, I'm not saying our wedding has to be the next big thing. But it's got to be *some*thing, you know?" A petite turned up nose and dancing jade eyes entered Jacob's frame of vision, followed by rose-pink lips and the gentle thud of a naked body. "We're only going to be getting married once." The upturned lips did an about-face, ending up upside down. "Our families, at least, need to be there. And my girlfriends. JP, Katrine, Charlene…your Scots buddies. They'll be upset if you get hitched without giving them the opportunity for a three day bender."

Feigning frustration, Jacob couldn't fight the small grin that poked its way through the grey clouds of his mixed-up thoughts. Even losing the view of perpetual sunshine and gently lapping waves, now obscured by his wife-to-be's cherubic cheeks and glowing eyes, didn't manage to annoy him. His eyes flickered thoughtfully as he pondered his good fortune, and the grin turned to a full-fledged jaw-cracking smile.

Talia. She was a dream. This life he was living was a dream.

In the two years since she walked into his life as a backup singer, something hard in Jacob's soul had finally let go. That old ache of loss was still there, it would always be there. But it was less acute these days, replaced by a bubbly good-natured blonde who giggled like a child at movies when everyone else was crying, who laughed outright, her head thrown back and popcorn suspended in one hand, when the action hero kissed the leading lady. Talia was irreverent, kind, easygoing, understanding and patient. Best of all, she had music in her; from her neon pink painted toes on up, throughout her body, and imbedded in her soul. So what if she'd left Jacob's stage shadow and skyrocketed to the top of the country music scene? She was more of a crossover artist, anyway.

An impish, dimpled grin, and a jubilant playfulness inherent in the sparkling green eyes staring at him now, cemented her appeal.

Now, Jacob lifted his right arm from its hiding place underneath the pillow, and drew the pretty blonde close for a swipe of his lips across her softer pink ones. Closing his eyes as he did so, he lingered there until a gentle quiver alerted him to Talia's need to laugh. She swiped at a lone long curl that fell rogue beneath his chin before she spoke.

"You need a shower, pretty boy. Your hair is dripping salt."

A low *pfffttt* escaped Jacob's lips. "I don't see the point. This body's hitting the beach before noon." Rolling over onto his back as he stated his intentions, Jacob eased Talia's head onto his shoulder. "I'll shower before dinner. I swear." Sucking in a breath he added, "Maybe."

"You swim, I'll be sending emails."

Alarm crept up Jacob's body. The earlier frown returned. His thoughts telegraphed themselves across to Talia instantly.

She pouted. "Let me enjoy this just a little bit, okay Jacob?"

A quiet voice spoke. "You know the drill. We have to run this by Deirdre, and by your team too, so they can mobilize the PR minions."

"So they can cushion the blow to your fans."

Jacob's eyes widened. He fixed a cool stare into Talia's searching eyes. "Huh. And none of your adoring rednecks will blink an eye."

"Sure they will. They'll be tweeting lots of hearty congrats and raising glasses of champagne. Yours will be threatening suicide." Raising her fingers as quotes, she joked, "Jacob Ryan's marrying a country singer. God help us."

"Raising brews, you mean," Jacob retorted with a laugh, referencing the champagne. "At tailgate parties where the chief entertainment is bonfires fueled by torn up lobster traps."

"Only on the coast. Cowboys throw rotten fence posts on their fires. That they rip apart with their bare hands, by the way. Those guys don't need tools."

"Yeah, that's because they *are* tools. Country music. Yeesh."

"Ha ha. Funny guy. You can pretend you hate the whole 'got a flat tire on my pickup' shtick, but I know who my number one fan is. As of last night I do, anyway." Talia swatted lightly at the bare chest before her but couldn't avoid sharing a tiny grin with her man, who smiled widely back, his blue eyes flickering happily in the lazy morning light. "I'll call my manager asap. And when will we tell the illustrious Madame Keating? Before or after you play with the dolphins?"

She was greeted with silence. Raising her head higher off Jacob's chest, Talia gazed emphatically at the new frown blooming beneath the beloved cobalt eyes, which were now avoiding her by trying to focus on the pale, airy cathedral ceiling of their resort suite.

"Okay, I get it," Talia said pointedly. "Once Dee knows, Jessie knows. And you're not sure you're ready for that. For her to know."

Shoving her aside, Jacob rolled away from his gal and perched on the opposite side of the bed with his back to her. Yawning, he stretched out his arms, his back muscles rippling with the effort.

Talia continued. "She'll be thrilled when she hears, anyway. And Josh will do a happy dance around her."

When all he could hear was the lapping of the waves, Jacob twisted around and faced his mussed-up blonde. She was sitting now, too, one knee bent on the bed and the other leg draping over the edge onto the floor. A slight warm breeze wafted in from the half open patio door and breathed in whispers around her just as the sun peeked out from behind a cloud, so that Talia's skin glowed from behind. But her smile was gone, replaced with a slightly anxious grimace that did nothing for her rosy cheeks.

While twisting her fingers around and around each other, Talia spoke again. "I get it. So if we have a big wedding we have to invite Jessie and Josh and you're not up for that. We have to invite them because we'll need a hundred bridesmaids and a ring bearer, who will be your son Dylan, of course, and we'll want a flower girl, who would of course be Emily-Grace since I don't have any little kids on my side of the family. So suddenly our wedding becomes you wishing you were standing on the altar next to Jessie."

"Oh, for God's sake. Tal, last night under the moon, on the beach…that magic was about you. About us. Not about my old girlfriend."

"Who just happens to be the mother of your son. No biggie. The woman who…broke your heart."

"Most of us don't make it through life without the occasional smashed-up heart, Talia. Makes for great songwriting." Stretching across the bed, Jacob laid his head in his fiancée's lap.

Caressing his curls, moving them back so she could see her man's cheek, Talia forced a small smile, then lifted her other hand so she could run the backs of her fingers sensuously over the Celtic cross tattooed across his back.

"I like them, Jacob, they're an awesome couple, really, but if you're not comfortable with Josh and Jessie coming, my mom can watch the kids while we're saying our vows. Emily-Grace is six now, she's a grown-up in little girl shoes anyway. Her parents don't need to be there if you don't want them there."

"Dylan'll turn the place upside down." Thinking about the fancy shindig Talia apparently wanted, Jacob groaned. "I just think we should do the church stuff quietly, on our own somewhere, like maybe here on the beach with JP and your friend Tabatha as witnesses. Then we can have a drunken bash when we get back home."

At her silence, Jacob looked up into pensive green eyes with endless depths that instantly turned his soul inside out. He almost moaned with relief at her captivating presence in his life, and instantly begrudged the earlier angst at the thought of Jessie finding out about his impending nuptials. At the thought— no, the wish—that the news would hurt her somehow.

A gentle voice broke into his reverie. "I want the dress, Jacob, and the planning and the cake and the music. And tons of friends and family to share our amazing special day with."

A slow exhale made its way up to Talia. "Can we talk about this later? Can we just enjoy it for now? The whole 're-gonna-be-together-forever' thing?"

"The whole 'til-death-do-us-part' thing? Yeah," Talia whispered, bending down to brush her lips across Jacob's ear. "Okay. All right. But tonight, we talk. And then we call Deirdre."

"And now?" Jacob stretched again, a long, hard stretch that rippled his abs this time, and that achieved the desired effect of teasing his adoring girl. He urged Talia closer.

A quick smile lit up her cheeks again, and Talia squealed when Jacob pulled her down on top of him. No answer was forthcoming, at least not a verbal response, but soon Talia's body spoke for her.

They got to the beach before noon, but barely.

That night, Jacob called Deirdre.

Chapter Two

"Do y'all ever do any work? You're always sittin' around the island drinkin' tea and gossiping about the Vancouver Canuck next door."

Because she'd hung around with Jessie on the tour last year, Kayla had picked up the singer's old Charleston habit of saying 'y'all.' In fact, she'd picked up a lot of Jessie's habits of late, the most important being Jessie's way of seeing the world, and of wanting to make a difference in her own small corner of it.

After she bounced into La Casa's bright, sunny kitchen, Kayla dropped a heavy packet of brown-paper wrapped posters on the kitchen island. They landed with a loud *oommpphh* and enough wind-power to send an abandoned tea towel over the granite edge onto Deirdre's new terracotta floor.

Jessie reached down to scoop it up. "The hockey player next door just got traded to Tampa. Dee's devastated."

"Carlotta's devastated," Dee corrected her. "She's trying to raise a good old Canadian grandson." Retrieving a teacup from the cupboard, she placed it in front of Kayla, who settled into a high butter-soft Italian leather stool next to Jessie. "Carlotta spends more time at the rink with little Eric than his parents do."

"Apparently hunky number nine next door loves fresh biscuits," Jessie explained to her bubbly sister-in-law. "Carlotta met him at the rink when he volunteered with Eric's hockey team, strategically questioned him on his love of baked goods, and dropped some off the other day. She took Eric with her and the boys ended up scrimmaging in the guy's driveway. She's hoping her grandson will get the hockey bug, but she's got a fight on her hands."

Leaning conspiratorially forward, Dee spoke in a low tone so Carlotta, who at the moment was on her hands and knees racing cars in the nearby playroom with Dylan, wouldn't hear if she chanced to wander back to the kitchen. "Eric wants picks on his skates."

"Hmmm?" Kayla asked, wrinkling her eyebrows together. "Meaning?"

"So he can jump." Jessie's eyes twinkled.

"Oh! Okay, oh!"

"Carlotta took him to see Kurt Browning's latest ice show."

Clueing in, Kayla surmised, "So he wants to be a figure skater. That's pretty friggin' cool. Kurt Browning's a fantastic athlete. I'll never forget his sexy 'Brick House' number."

"The old Commodores tune?"

"That man can move." Kayla drew a hand in front of her face to illustrate the smooth glide of Kurt Browning's funky moves. "And on skates, too. Yeeouch. Eric sounds like a kid with style. 'Shake it down, shake it down, shake it down, shake it down, y'all.' Or something like that. You just gotta love funk."

Laughing, she reached a glittery nail towards the posters. Ripping open an end of the brown-paper wrapping, Kayla eased one out and held it up to Jessie, then steered it around so Deirdre could read it.

Scanning the catchy, vibrant graphics, Dee reflected aloud. "B boyz. I can't keep up. I'm getting old." As if to cement that truth, she absently rubbed an elbow. Jessie touched her arm and the two women shared a small smile.

"It's a really fun style of dance, Dee," Jessie explained. "It's kind of like the old breakdancing that emerged on the streets years ago. It's a perfect way to engage some of the Downtown Eastside youth."

"It's based on gangs, isn't it?" Deirdre asked. "Don't they do some kind of battling?"

Kayla jumped in. "It's a safe way to express conflict. Dance is a great communicator." Turning to Jessie, she grinned. "I can't thank you enough for helping me out with this project, Jess. I love having you home. I love having Josh and the kids home."

"I love *being* home," Jessie replied with a wry half-smile. "Although you know your brother. Guess where he is today."

"Hopefully resting, after what I heard about his last film. Is it true that he actually got hit across the back with a real log during some fight scene in the river?"

"He's an action junkie. And that comes with the territory."

Dee cut in. "But it shouldn't have. The actor who hit him thought the log was a prop that would break, but it wasn't. Josh is lucky he wasn't more badly hurt."

"You'd think two cracked ribs would teach him to slow down, huh?" Jessie quieted as she reflected on her husband's frightening accident.

Looking closely at her, Kayla frowned. "Scared you, did it, sis?"

"Meh." Jessie wrapped both hands around her teacup. "I can't worry myself sick every time Josh goes out the door. I just have to cherish him when I'm with him. Otherwise I'd lose my mind." This time, Dee was the one to reach out and offer a comforting touch. Staring at the teacup's gold rim, which caught the overhead light and glinted prettily, Jessie continued. "Anyways, Josh is fine. Sore, but okay. He took Emily-Grace and David to school just after eight, and drove down to Robson to meet with Charles and Charlie."

"About…?" Kayla was only half interested. She was studying Jessie, who seemed a little down today. Jessie's shoulders were hunched and her eyes were still trained on a now empty cup.

"About a new television series. A contemporary western, this time. It's something Charlie's been developing for years."

"Which will involve horses. I see. Josh'll be over the moon. Jess, are you okay? You're a little green around the gills."

Finally letting go of the teacup, Jessie settled back into her high chair. "I'm good, Kayla. Everything's great, really. It's just…" She looked up at Dee, trying to let loose the emotion that an earlier chat had unleashed like melting snow from a beaver dam on the first warm day of spring. "Jacob and Talia are getting hitched. It's great news, it really is. It just kind of threw me, that's all."

"Good 'ole Jacob finally popped the question, did he? He decided to snatch up the reigning Queen of Country before some love struck duet partner of hers sneaks in and drags her off in his pickup truck, huh?"

Dee spoke up then. "Talia is a perfect match for Jacob. She'll be a good mom to Jessie and Jacob's monster child."

"Dee, really!" Jessie's glare towards Dee was half in jest, though. She managed a smile.

"Jessie and Josh's kid, you mean," Kayla added softly. "From what Josh tells me, Jacob doesn't take Dylan a whole heckuva lot."

"He takes him when he can. He wants to." A slice in her gut brought a new grimace to Jessie's tired features; worry crisscrossed her cheeks with reckless abandon. "Between his schedule and Talia's, it's tough, that's all. And ours," she added wryly. "This business kinda sucks for the kids. We're all over the map with them."

"Jessie, honey," Dee started, as if they hadn't had the same conversation a thousand times already. "The kids are doing fine. They've got more love coming their way from everyone around them than a lot of kids get in their lifetimes. You've got duplicate toys at some of your locations, and you stick to a routine as much as you can. They're okay. Really. They're learning to adapt to change. It'll help them in the long run. You'll see."

"How does it work when Jacob takes Dylan, then?" Kayla asked pointedly. "I mean, does Dylan go with him okay?"

"Are you kidding? That little guy may be all rough and tumble when it comes to keeping me and Josh on our toes, but let's not forget who his biological father is." Jessie leaned forward and twisted around a bit to better face Kayla. "Dylan does great when he's in his comfort zone, but he's still just a two year old living a crazy lifestyle. He likes having Momma and Daddy close by. And by that I mean me and Josh, not Jacob. Dylan wants bedtime stories he's used to, and familiar toys that help him feel cozy and safe."

Kayla's frown telegraphed her understanding as Jessie went on.

"This is the thing, Kayla. Jacob rarely takes Dylan without taking Emily-Grace along too. And if it weren't for her—and let me tell you, it's never a problem to get her out of the door, because Jacob is Emily-Grace's everything—Jacob would never be able to peel Dylan off Josh's body. It's never me that hands him over," she added with a begrudging grunt, "because Jacob prefers to keep some distance between he and I. It's just…well, it's easier that way. So Josh either flies the kids to Jacob or they arrange to meet up when I'm not around."

"And David?"

"My darling middle child wouldn't dream of doing overnighters away from his overprotective parents. He can barely get through a whole day at Junior Kindergarten. Emily-Grace has a hard time leaving him. She makes sure he's got his teddies and bedtime stories lined up on his bed before she goes, because he tends not to miss them until bedtime, and with Dylan around, they could be anywhere."

She drifted sideways for a minute, pointing at Kayla as she spoke. "I once found Bunny in the toilet. After a visit from the plumber, may I add, who had to pull the toilet up to find out why it wouldn't flush. Gave him a scare, I'll tell you, and me too, before we realized the brown fur we saw wasn't the real thing." Back on track, she added, "Anyways, David is a momma's boy, and I'm glad of that because I'd lose my mind if I had to be away from all three kids at once. It's hard enough letting David and Emily-Grace go to school."

A wistful sadness passed through Jessie's eyes at that, and she purposefully lost eye contact with Kayla and Deirdre, who gave the moment the reverence it deserved, accompanied as it was by unbelievable memories of a kidnapped family a few years earlier.

"They're at a private school though, right? West Point Grey Academy?" Kayla asked. "You can do distance learning when you need to be away, so you can take them with you when you're working?"

"Yes, thank heavens, it's the same school Emily-Grace started at for JK just before she turned five, and so far they've been accommodating, but we're trying to arrange our schedules so only one of us has to be away at a time. As much as possible, anyway. So the kids can have some continuity. The last few years have been nuts."

Kayla set down the poster in her hands and leaned her body into Jessie's for a hug. "It sounds like all of you are doing the best you can to make things work, Jessie. Dee's right. In the long run, the kids will thank you for it. And so will Jacob."

"I hope you're right, Kayla. Our kids are our life. I just…I wonder what will happen when Talia and Jacob start having kids of their own, that's all. I mean, it's hard enough now. When Dylan becomes no more than an occasional visitor in the Ryan household, what's it going to be like for him, trying to fit into another family?"

"He won't be alone, if Emily-Grace continues to accompany him."

"Emily-Grace would move in with Jacob and Talia if she could. Trust me on that one."

Wrinkles knitted across Kayla's brow. She squirmed a little in her seat as Dee sighed and left the room to wander down the hallway. A playroom crash and a loud cry from Carlotta was her cue to give the younger women a few moments alone.

Kayla spoke quietly. "Okay, I get that Emily-Grace has had her struggles. She's such a quiet little thing. She's doing okay, isn't she? At home?"

"If by okay you mean she is settling in to grade two, she's eating, she's sleeping, well yes to all of those things, although she still has the occasional nightmare."

"As does her mom, I hear," Kayla added tenderly. She shrugged at the surprise coloring Jessie's already concerned expression. "Despite the crazy time zones you two are often in, Josh and I do manage to connect on occasion. He told me."

"I'm okay," Jessie stated rather matter-of-factly. "Really, things are mostly good, Kayla." She backtracked a bit. "The odd bad dream sneaks in once in a while. That's all. Usually around the times Jacob takes the kids."

"Understandable. Really."

"It's just, well, it's harder than I thought it would be. Letting them go. I'm glad for Emily-Grace because she simply worships Jacob, and Talia's a dream with her, at least according to the bit I can get out of Emily-Grace when she comes home, but the visits have made things a little tougher on the home front. That's all."

"With Josh."

"With Josh."

Jessie shoved herself out of the soft leather and made her way around the island to the kettle. She refilled her teacup and spoke with her back to Kayla, her voice floating up on the thin line of steam still emanating from the kettle. "He's an amazing dad, Kayla, he really is. And for all intents and purposes Josh has made Dylan his own. It's beautiful to watch them together. Josh reads to him at night, almost always with David on the other knee. But there's no room there for Emily-Grace, and even if there were, well…Well, the thing is, Emily-Grace most times would rather read to herself. I sit with her a lot, but she makes it fairly clear where her allegiance lays."

"She wants Jacob?"

"He was her safe place during a very bad time. And Talia is a gentle princess. I doubt they discipline Emily-Grace, ever."

"But her daddy does."

"Barely. You ever look into her big blue eyes? There's so much sadness there, still. When she comes back from her visits with Jacob, she's all but unreachable. She curls up in bed with her dolls on her lap and stares out of the window, wishing she were anywhere but with us. Heck, Emily-Grace does that when she comes home from school."

"She's only six, honey. She doesn't understand."

"That's the sting of it. She doesn't, but Josh does."

"Oh." Kayla gulped past the sudden sticks in her throat. "Oh, I see."

"At least she still lets me in sometimes. When she's lonely, I think. But she barely tolerates her own daddy. The more time she spends with Jacob and Talia, the more she pulls away. I can't see that getting any better when she hits her teen years. Kill me now."

"Not even remotely a good choice of phrasing, Jessie. Seriously."

"Aw, you guys gotta lighten up about all those old threats."

"Do we. Uh huh. I mean, nuh-uh. Or let me put it this way. No fucking way."

"The bad times are done and gone, Kayla. We just need to continue to focus on putting the pieces back together."

"Look, Jess, the wedding will come and go, although I know it won't be easy for you." Hesitating, she added a post-script. "Honey, I know what Jacob meant to you."

A subdued wince was Jessie's response.

"What he means to you," Kayla amended.

Dismissing the difficult truth, Jessie waved an arm in the air. "I miss him, Kayla. That's all. I miss his friendship and the music we used to make together. I'm glad for him and Talia, I really am. What's the alternative, wishing for him to be alone and sulky all the time?"

"He's hooked himself up with a country singer, aren't they always sulky? They sing about sulky stuff."

"They sing about life, silly girl." Jessie leaned both elbows on the island and faced her sister-in-law. "At any rate, I'm just glad he's not alone. But hearing this today just brought forth a lot of old, sad memories, that's all. It hurts."

A small smile creased Kayla's lips. Reaching forward, she took Jessie's hand in hers and gave it a gentle squeeze. "What's life without a few challenges, huh, Jess? If it were perfect all the time you'd have nothing to write songs about."

"I need about five lifetimes to write all the songs life has bestowed on me."

"Well, throw some of them my way. I'd just as soon use a few of yours than have to fight the copyright police for the workshops."

"All right. Will do." With a half-smile, Jessie drew in a big breath. "Enough of my worrying and whining. Show me this poster again, and tell me what the latest is on your newest little project."

"Little! I wish! Okay. Well, first things first, Jack Deacon has agreed to loan me his assistant to help get organized and do the outreach to the youth on the Downtown Eastside. As you already know, we're modeling the workshops on Jack's acting workshops. And he's offered the same space. I'm going to see it tomorrow."

"So you're drawing in the at-risk youth from the neighborhood." Another sad smile worked its way into Jessie's countenance.

Catching the melancholic tone, Kayla looked up. Her voice was softer when she spoke again. "Yeah. You bet."

"Good on you, Kayla. That's great."

Jessie's reward was a glow direct from Kayla's heart to hers. Then Kayla continued. "I'll touch on all styles of dance, but mainly for the basics. Most of the workshops will be based on B boyizm because I believe it's a style these young people will relate to, at least at first. We'll incorporate some live music into it, too, using some of your band—thank you—and, well, artists like yourself and maybe even Jacob at some point if we can convince him to take part when he's in the city. The workshops will run all winter minus a month or a bit more off at Christmas, with the focus of doing a multi-city tour across Canada in the spring."

Sitting back, she beamed.

"It's really great, what you're doing, Kayla."

"I need some time at home. I need to get to know my niece and nephews again."

"So when Emily-Grace goes off the rails at fifteen, she'll have a sounding board."

"Ha. So when Emily-Grace goes off the rails at fifteen I can take her for her first tattoo, you mean."

"God help me."

"Or maybe we'll do that when she's twelve." The remark was accompanied by a wink, which generated a genuine laugh from Jessie.

At that, small footsteps came running down the hall. A small boy with long dark curls flung himself into Jessie's arms. Laughing more openly, she gathered him up in a big bear hug. Instantly, the tension in Jessie's shoulders deflated as her smile grew wider.

"You are my light, little fella," she crooned into one tiny ear, which made Dylan giggle and wiggle. He leaned back then and pointed to the counter behind his mother.

"Cookie," he demanded as Carlotta and Dee settled around the large island.

"Just one," Jessie told him, accepting a ginger snap from Dee's outstretched hand and placing it in Dylan's. "Then if you're still hungry Momma will carve you up some apple slices."

But Dylan didn't manage to finish his ginger snap. Resting his head in the cozy nook of his mother's neck, he dropped off to sleep while the women continued to discuss the logistics behind Kayla's new dance workshops. When the sun soaked the south-facing windows of La Casa with its usual mid afternoon warm glow, reminding Jessie that she'd agreed to pick up David and Emily-Grace at school, it was time to go.

"Come for dinner," she proposed to Kayla as she planted a gentle goodbye peck on her sister-in-law's cheek. "Josh needs to see for himself that his baby sister's hair is once again blonde and ponytailed. He totally won't believe me."

"I can do dinner," answered Kayla with a new light in her gentle Josh-like eyes, as she followed Jessie out to her SUV. "But the hair will just be a tease. I'm getting it dyed again tomorrow."

"Um…?" Jessie shifted Dylan from her body to his car seat, fastened him in, and grinned slyly at Kayla. She planted a hand on one hip. "Let me guess?"

"Don't even try." Leaning forward, Kayla whispered into Jessie's ear. "Blue. For the duration of the B boyz workshops. Seems to fit."

"Ah ha," Jessie chuckled, shaking her head. "Maybe I'll join you. I've never gone blue."

"Liar. I saw the new Marvel film."

"That was temporary. A semi-permanent."

With that, Kayla popped a helmet over the aforementioned blonde tresses, hopped on a hot pink electric scooter, saluted, and motored off down the lane.

A final wave to Dee and Carlotta, and Jessie was right behind her, thoughts of what to cook for dinner racing through her brain, and sad memories of the old painful days with Jacob soaking her heart.

Chapter Three

$\mathcal{A}$ low rumble announced Josh's arrival on their street long before he turned into the driveway. It was a perfect early fall day on the west coast, and Jessie wasn't surprised that he'd apparently switched off his King Ranch for the classic red and white Harley at some point during the day, and gone for a spin. With relief, as she yanked chicken breasts out of the freezer and popped them into the microwave to thaw, she reminded herself that her husband was out for a ride simply to cherish the wind blowing through his half-helmeted long hair, and not to avoid her, which was the case not all that long ago.

"Kids," she called over her shoulder to her three small children, who were spread out in the adjoining living room, Emily-Grace on the leather couch with a pile of books at her side, David and Dylan rolling around vintage cars their Peterborough cousins had sent them via snail mail in the spring. "Daddy's home."

Immediately, the two young Sawyer boys made a dash to the sliding glass doors, their mother shadowing them so she could manipulate the lock and then stand back to watch the cherished reunion. Emily-Grace remained on the couch, and Jessie couldn't help but notice that she was shrinking lower into it, a tiny scowl marking her diminutive features.

Josh was whistling as he stepped lightly down the flagstone stairs. The small iron gate clanged itself shut after he passed through. His happy greeting was muffled under the sounds of two small giggling boys he scooped up and held close.

Smiling widely, Jessie stepped across the back deck towards him, and reached for the black motorcycle half-helmet dangling from Josh's fingers.

She caught his eye when she took it, and noted her hubby's twinkling chocolate-eyed gratitude, which she knew was meant for this, one of life's near-perfect moments. Both she and Josh tucked the little homecoming away in their memory banks for some grey day down the road.

"Have these little monkeys been good for Momma today?" Josh teased as he drew David closer and planted a kiss on the small cheek. Dylan was supposed to be next, but he squealed and wormed his way down so he could run inside and grab a painted red wooden fire truck to show his father.

David planted both hands on Josh's stubbly cheeks, focusing his attention away from Jessie, who gently laid an arm on Josh's black-leather clad elbow and leaned in for her own kiss. "Daddy, come play cars wif me and Dylan."

"Give me a few minutes to take off my boots and I'll come play, okay buddy?" Josh was wincing a little as David moved in his arms. Jessie grasped her son's small waist and set him on the floor. He skipped off to play, hollering loudly at Dylan to leave his cars alone as he went.

"You need to take it easy, Josh," chided Jessie quietly as she helped remove the thick motorcycle jacket. "You need to give those ribs a bit more time to heal."

He didn't answer.

Wondering why, looking up at Josh after she hung his jacket up on a hook, Jessie followed his glance to their daughter on the couch.

Sidling forward, Josh bent to brush his lips against Emily-Grace's forehead. The little girl didn't resist him, but she didn't acknowledge him, either. Instead, she simply wiped a palm against her forehead to try to move a few stray strands of fine blonde hair, and sniffed quietly as she did so.

Josh dropped carefully down beside her and placed an arm around the bony shoulders. "The Velveteen Rabbit again, huh?" he asked her as Jessie watched, absently crossing her arms over her belly and shifting her weight to one foot.

Emily-Grace flipped the page.

Josh tried again. "Did you do any reading at school today, Emily-Grace? Is that your favorite thing to do at school?"

"Today was painting day. And math." The words were spoken with an air of childish exasperation, clipped and final.

"Did you bring a picture home for me and Momma to see?"

"It's drying."

"What'd you paint?"

She didn't even hesitate, firing a blow with a sullen impudence far beyond her six years. "Me and David and Dylan and Momma and Jacob."

Other than dropping her arms to her sides, Jessie couldn't bring herself to respond. Nor could Josh, but he did manage to catch Jessie's eye before he sighed heavily, and eased himself up off the couch. Jessie blinked away a quick unease before noticing that her daughter fixed her usual sad gaze on Josh's back as he moved away. The small knuckles were white on the sides of the book as Emily-Grace slouched deeper into the big couch.

"Well. I guess she told me," Josh managed as he moved past Jessie, touching her elbow as he passed.

Silent, Jessie bit her lip as her daughter's eyes moved upwards and met hers. But instead of sending a scalding look of reproach in the child's direction, Jessie simply let her shoulders sink. Emily-Grace buried her nose back in her weather-beaten book.

"Dan said it was a bit rough for her at school today. Playground stuff. Sit," Jessie demanded, after turning to Josh. "Give me your foot."

"I hope she adjusts soon. Leaving her there in the mornings just about kills me," Josh answered. Reaching down he said, "I can handle it." A quick wince caught him off guard. Relenting, he sat back and rifled long fingers through his layered hair. Jessie bent and unzipped one boot, wiggling it off his foot with practiced care.

"Betcha loved the bumps," she tried, attempting to infuse some lightness into the air.

"What bumps? This is B.C., not P.E.I., where muddy potholes swallow up whole families."

"Wish I could've gone with you. Where'd you go?" Graceful guitar-playing fingers wiggled Josh's other boot.

"We'll get Kayla to watch the kids this weekend, Jess, okay? Now that we're all in the same city for once? You and me can take a ride up Cypress and find that rest stop we used to go to." He winked, and Jessie's cheeks pinked up.

"So where'd you ride today?"

He shrugged. "Just up to ROAM for a coffee, and then I cruised around the Endowment Lands for a bit. I needed a few minutes to clear my head."

"After the meeting? How'd that go?" Jessie moved Josh's discarded boots aside and settled her body down next to his on the wide chair, being careful not to jar his still sore ribs. From their vantage point across the room from Emily-Grace, they watched as she traced words and tried them out with a quiet whisper and a despairing sigh.

"It was good. Mostly. Jonathon was there."

"Oh. Hence the drive, hmmm?"

"Yep." Deflating a bit, Josh turned his face towards his wife. Closing his eyes, he breathed her in. *Lavender,* he caught himself thinking. *Comfort. Home.* "At least he showed up."

"He's been okay, Josh. Don't be so hard on him."

"Personally, yes. I give him kudos for not alienating me entirely. But professionally is a different story."

"He's just kicking himself in the ass for letting you go, back then. Steve's awesome, but there was no way his golden boy charm could carry *The Wyatt Boys* on its own. It's Jonathon's own fault the series was cancelled, not yours."

"'Course it was my fault, Jessie." Josh's lips were buried in her hair. It seemed today was just a day for bad memories to fight their way through the muss of everyday life. Despite the success and renewed happiness of the past few years, bad stuff still had a place in the collective memory of the Sawyer household.

Jessie twisted her fingers around her husband's and turned her face towards him so she could brush her lips against his, and instill in him some courage and strength, for she could see that he was faltering here, today. A heavy sigh from the depths of Josh's toes confirmed it.

"Babe," she murmured to him. "Whatever Jonathon's dragons are, they're his to slay. We have enough of our own."

"Emily-Grace is one," was the whisper that came back to her. Josh's eyes were still closed, but he lifted one tired hand and placed his fingers underneath Jessie's chin, then kissed her softly.

"Well, yes, but…there's something else."

Josh's eyes wafted open and peered into Jessie's solemn pale blue gaze. "What is it?" he asked quietly, a little bit afraid.

Jessie hesitated before responding, wiggling a bit in the wide armchair as she pondered what to say. After all, this newest problem was likely nothing more than a vivid imagination at play.

A gulp escaped her lips. Looking down, she twisted both hands now around her husband's fingers. Gentle pressure from Josh settled her a bit. "It's just that…well, Jacob and Talia, that's all. They've announced their engagement."

Pondering that, Josh glanced over at the two young boys now happily zooming cars around and underneath Emily-Grace's suspended toes. "I guess that's a good thing," he said, a tinge of uncertainty in his voice. Eyes narrowing, he looked back over at Jessie. "Isn't it?"

Like a waterfall, Jessie's anxiety poured out. "Josh, it's just that, if you decide to do this series, it's a long haul. Six months, at least, hours and hours and hours a day. And it's not just the time. It's another *Drifters*, right? Of a sort? Horses and stunts and lots of physical stuff? Not to mention you're supposed to be playing some guy who lost his wife, some guy who is on a gloomy journey to find the light again. I just feel like we're going to have enough challenges here at home with the kids without having to go down some dark road…again."

"And that's all got to do with Jacob how?" Tense, Josh was frowning now, and his grip on Jessie's fingers was tighter.

Pushing him away, she stood, which startled the kids. Emily-Grace watched her, the small blue eyes silently affirming what the little girl's soul knew, which was that her daddy sometimes brought tension to their home.

Jessie watched her for a second, computing that, then turned back to Josh and spoke in a subdued tone. "We need you around, Josh. To help us navigate the troubled waters when they come. Jacob marrying Talia is a harbinger of trouble."

"Why." It wasn't a question. It was an insistent demand, colored with an envy Josh tried unsuccessfully to bury.

"Because these children love Jacob, that's why."

"Do they."

"Yeah, they do. And we don't need them filling their need for an absent daddy by jumping into Jacob's arms."

"And Talia's. God bless the little country queen." His sarcasm was biting.

"I know what you're thinking, Josh. So stop giving me the hairy eyeball."

Josh couldn't hide a small smile at that. But he managed to pull up a serious countenance again by biting his lip and fixing his eyes briefly on Dylan. "Okay, little miss psychic. What am I thinking?" he asked her.

She turned a little circle before answering, stooping to pick up a tiny blue ambulance so her foot wouldn't accidentally squish it. As she stood, Jessie flailed an arm towards Josh. "You're thinking that I'm jealous of Talia. Because she is everything I'm not these days."

"Country superstar, blonde, gorgeous, about to marry pop royalty. Yeah, I see where you get that from." Josh grinned.

Pouting, Jessie planted her feet and stared at her husband. Unbidden, tears crept into the diaphanous eyes Josh loved.

Quick to notice when he crossed a line, Josh jumped up with a tiny, "Ouch," and faced his wife. "Hey," he started. "Choosing to slow down a little to be with your kids—and your husband, I might add—does not reduce your standing in the world of music. Or in the acting world. And," Josh reminded her, "we agreed we would do the best we could by our kids. If that means letting Jacob be the good guy while we maintain as much stability as we can manage at home by disciplining the kids, then so be it. Jessie," he added, "Jacob did right by the kids when neither of us could manage it. If anything, he deserves to have them when he can. And for the record, I'm not abandoning you and the kids to go off the grid for six months. You'll come with me when you're available, and we'll set up tutoring and a great big playroom on set. Best of all, we'll live at the Alberta ranch, since the series is shooting in Calgary. We'll be together. Okay?"

Her pout grew deeper. "You took the job already."

"No, actually I didn't." Josh studied his wife's defeated shoulders. "But I'd like to."

"And Jonathon? I'm assuming he's coming on board as Exec Producer? Since when did that become a thing?"

"Since Charles and Charlie begged him to help get them some producing

28

street cred, because Charles, Mr. Music, has never exec produced a TV drama on his own and Charlie has never, let's face it, produced at all."

"And Jonathon is still Canada's pride and joy."

"Despite my attempt to sink him, however unintentional it was, yes," Josh admitted ruefully. "He is a magnet for funders, unlike most of Canada's talented pool of wanna-be producers."

"You like the part, huh?"

His wide smile was infectious. Jessie let her lips turn up, just a wee bit at the corners.

Josh answered honestly. "I love the part, Jessie. It's challenging, and it's steady work, which means at least some semblance of continuity in our lives. And it's the lead. Charlie's happy to play a supporting role since he'll be up to his eyeballs in writing and paperwork."

"But the kids. School."

"We'll get tutors, and we'll make sure they have play dates with the kids of other cast and crew, like always."

"Kayla'll be pissed."

His eyebrows wrinkled. "Why?"

"She was counting on having me here to help with her Downtown Eastside B boyz project. And she's coming over for dinner, by the way, to see you and chastise you for messing around with martial arts champions in rocky riverbeds."

A diabolical grin crisscrossed Josh's face. "Cool. Let her." A hand lifted to absently rub his side.

As Jessie looked down to spy a tiny pink-cheeked two year old tugging her pant legs and gazing up at her, she heard Josh's voice add a few last notes to their conversation.

"And Jessie?"

"Um-humn?" Bending down, Jessie scooped Dylan up and snuggled her lips into his baby fresh neck and chest.

"You might be able to still help Kayla. A bit, at least."

Surprised, she turned. "What?" Her eyes narrowed. "The new show is being shot near Calgary. In Alberta. One province away from Kayla and her workshops. Isn't it?"

"It is. But it needs a soundtrack." Josh looked a little red-faced at that. "And Charles plays favorites, or so the media accuses him on occasion."

"Which we would record in Vancouver. So much for being together. Liar." Jessie snuggled Dylan closer.

Kayla's scooter approaching in the driveway sounded like a sewing machine. It didn't have a lot of power compared to the Harley, unless one counted de-escalating a potential fight.

Josh stepped closer and reached out a hand to ruffle Dylan's dark curls. The little boy leaned over and dropped into Josh's arms for a cuddle.

"It's just for a few songs, Jessie. Vancouver's a hop, skip and a jump away from Calgary."

"That's what they all say," Jessie sighed. "Before the shit falls out of 'er."

"Music," Josh said, "will set you free, Jessie. You'll get back in the studio and maybe do some guest spots acting on the show, we'll have some continuity for a bit, and we'll be fine. Deal?"

Against her better wishes, Jessie groaned but added a quiet, "Fine."

A vibrant voice from the direction of the sliding doors cut into her worry, but not before Josh pressed his forehead against hers and whispered, "You worry about worrying, did you know that?"

Grimacing, Jessie turned to Kayla, who stood at the door and threw out her arms, from which dangled jellybean emblazoned bags from a candy store in Vancouver's Pacific Centre.

"Who wants candy?"

At David's happy squeal, Emily-Grace's silent wonder, and Dylan's sleepy but curious eyes, Josh and Jessie rolled their eyes at each other, wide grins now creasing each other's face. Kayla's bouncy presence was always a light.

Josh leaned into Jessie and nodded towards his baby sister. "You're worried about Jacob and Talia spoiling the kids? You might want to leave the kids with me when you leave the shoot to come back to Van."

Marching towards his sister, Josh gathered her into a big hug, which essentially resulted in Dylan squirming between them. "Who is this gorgeous blonde? Where's the purple-haired sister I know and miss?"

Kayla's happy eyes met Jessie's over his shoulder. Sure as rain, there had been enough to worry about in the Sawyer family over the last many years.

Now was a time for hope, in small packages and in a myriad of very ordinary family ways.

Easing forward, Jessie snuck under Josh's arm and joined in the hug, which soon included David as well. Momentarily, small little girl arms wrapped themselves around Jessie's waist, and she looked down to spy her daughter peering up at her from underneath long eyelashes.

"Sweet girl," Jessie murmured with a smile, and reached down to draw Emily-Grace into their circle of love.

Chapter Four

After dinner, Josh settled himself at the kitchen island with Emily-Grace to help her do a worksheet from school. Kayla and Jessie chattered amicably, Jessie washing pots and pans while Kayla dried. Dylan was cranky, ready for his bath and bed, but Josh pulled him up onto his lap and gave him paper of his own to color while Emily-Grace worked. David sat on the counter by Kayla so he could show her the family's secret hiding places for serving spoons and the like.

Both women's ears perked up when they heard a pencil fly across the room, hit the front of the stove, and roll to a stop.

Emily-Grace's sharp voice was swollen with fury. "Stupid Dylan. Stupid Daddy."

Josh was silent with the exception of a slight scratching sound as he rubbed his jaw with a finger and forefinger. His eyes were locked on his daughter's knuckled fingers, which were, at the moment, ripping her homework to shreds. Clearly surprised, he didn't try to stop her.

"Emily-Grace?" Jessie asked, her lips working to find the words to get to the bottom of the temper tantrum without having a tantrum of her own over the child's blatant bad mood and outright disrespect, which were both not exactly commonplace in the Sawyer household.

Careful to ignore Kayla's eyes, Emily-Grace looked up at her mother. "Daddy picked up Dylan and so Dylan wrote on my homework." The pearl-blue eyes were floating.

"I'm sure your teacher will understand, honey." Jessie dried her hands on Kayla's towel and leaned over the island. She tried to put the pieces of her daughter's homework back together, but with one fell swoop Emily-Grace swept them onto the floor. They settled there like confetti after a wedding, still and large and quiet, yet not forgotten.

Recovering his senses, Josh pushed back his chair and set Dylan on the floor. Immediately, the two year old started to whine. Extending his arms to Josh, he begged to be picked back up. Kayla dropped her towel on the island and skirted it, scooping up the baby of the family and expediently whisking him and David upstairs for bath time.

"Emily-Grace, I'm not entirely sure what brought this on, but this is not how little girls honor their teachers. Bringing in torn-up worksheets is not an option." Josh bent to pick up the scattered pieces, then stood and laid them before his daughter on the island, while Jessie sidled nervously away to fetch a roll of tape from a nearby drawer.

Instantly, the youthful arm flung itself sideways again, sending the paper bits back onto the floor. They floated on the air before they landed. Each torn piece may as well have been a rock when it hit this time, as an angry, confused silence filled the room.

Josh moved to speak, but Jessie caught his eye and shook her head. She nodded towards Emily-Grace. The little girl was sobbing now, both elbows on the counter and fists shoved in her eyes, beneath which thin trails of salty tears were snaking their way downward.

"Sweetheart," Jessie started, bending over so she could be eye to eye with her troubled daughter. "Do you want to tell me what's bothering you?" From her peripheral vision she could see the usual nerve on Josh's cheek twitching, which was not always a good sign, since over the years it had become a fairly consistent sign of rising blood pressure.

"Daddy," the child whispered. "He shouldn't have picked up Dylan."

"Daddy was just trying to comfort Dylan, to keep him quiet so you could work, honey."

"Daddy shouldn't be picking Dylan up at all. He's not even his daddy. Jacob is."

A shock wave flitted down Jessie's spine and into her toes. Eyes darting up to Josh, she watched him pocket his hands in his jeans and suck in a breath. He avoided looking at her and instead kept his vision focused clearly on Emily-Grace. One ankle turned over on its side, and Jessie watched him count slowly to five, and then to ten, as Trudy had taught him years ago when his temper threatened to climb too high.

Emily-Grace was too young to understand the ins and outs of biological fatherhood. But apparently she was not too young to escape the teasing of kids at school. She was not a talker at the best of times, but once Jessie sent Josh upstairs to help his sister with the boys, she pulled her six year old onto her lap on the couch in the front room, and urged the truth from her.

As she did so, Jessie realized with a sense of dread that Jacob would have to play an even larger part in the conversation here, tonight. The media was everywhere these days, and the Sawyer family was a constant target of speculation and wonder in the celebrity-crazed world. Like it or not, Jacob was, on some level, an extension of their family.

"Okay," Jessie said, inhaling slowly as she snuggled her teary daughter in close. "First of all, we've talked about Dylan before. You remember when we lived with Jacob, right? You know that babies need to grow in their mommy's tummies for a while, and that when Dylan first started growing, you and I and David were living with Jacob. Follow me?"

"And now we live with Daddy so he watches out for Dylan the same way he watches out for me and David," Emily-Grace sighed. "But Momma, today a kid at school said that Dylan should be living with Jacob. That he doesn't belong to Daddy."

Okay, way to break my heart, thought Jessie. *Way to break my daughter's heart.* She sucked in a breath and rallied. "Sweetheart, Dylan belongs to Daddy as much as he belongs to Jacob. The kid at school doesn't understand because he doesn't know us. He doesn't know Jacob and he certainly doesn't know Daddy. He doesn't know how much love they both have for all three of you kids. You're all so lucky to have so much love around you!" For effect, she snuggled her daughter in tighter, wrapping her in a cocoon for extra safety and warmth. It worked. Emily-Grace settled into the crook of her mother's neck, her movement accompanied by a big exhalation.

"The thing is," Jessie continued gently, tenderly wiping strands of hair off her daughter's forehead and cheeks, "kids sometimes say things they hear their parents talking about, even when they don't really understand.

Because sometimes it seems like the right thing to say, even when it isn't."
She was floundering, and paused for a moment before continuing. "Emily-
Grace, you know that our family is different from a lot of families. We've
talked about this before."

"Because of yours and Daddy's work."

"Yes. Because a lot of people see our movies and hear my songs, so they
know about us. It makes them feel like they really know us, which makes
them think they know what is best for us. So people say things that sometimes hurt. That are not always the truth. Because the thing is, they don't
know us at all. Not really."

"Why, Momma?" The pale eyes were staring at Jessie's hand, which was
wrapped around Emily-Grace's smaller one, a thumb gently moving back
and forth to offer what comfort it could.

"I don't really know, sweetheart. All I know is that it's not always easy
being in the spotlight the way we are, and I wish to Heaven I could protect
you from the people out there who don't understand. Who will try to hurt
you kids with their words." *And their actions,* she thought, as her own tears
threatened, memories of a dark, damp basement coming back to haunt her.

She adjusted Emily-Grace on her lap, which resulted in the little girl's
gaze finally meeting her mother's tender expression. "Emily-Grace, the best
I can do is try to prepare you for the people out there in the big old world.
To prepare you for growing up. And for starters, let me just tell you that the
best way to respond to kids who say things that might hurt is to tell you to
look at them in a different way. They're not trying to be mean, honey. They're
just confused. You are a strong little girl with so much love in your heart.
You come from love, sweetheart. So much love! So you need to give them
love back, even when they try to hurt your feelings."

She laughed as the splashing sounds of two happy boys drifted down
the stairs. Kayla's cry of, "I'm sinking, I'm sinking!" wafted downwards too.

"She's got the red boat," Emily-Grace mused with a small smile.

"She does indeed," grinned Jessie, aching to go join her youngest two in
the simplicity and innocence of bath time, and dreading the years ahead,
which meant exposure of her children to yet more worldly unpleasantries.

"My teacher's gonna be mad about my homework, Momma." The small fingers were wringing together now. "Miss Catlyn's the meanest teacher ever."

"We'll tape it from the back. I bet she won't even notice."

At that, Emily-Grace moved to get off her mother's lap, but Jessie called her back. "There's one more thing about Jacob we need to talk about tonight, Emily-Grace. Just one more minute, okay? And then I'll help you sort out that worksheet of yours."

"Are we gonna go live with him again?" The lift in her shoulders and the hopeful light in her eyes almost devastated Jessie.

"No, kiddo, no." Then, curious, Jessie switched gears for a moment. The opportunity was too good to pass up. Rarely was Emily-Grace in the mood to share her thoughts and feelings. Jessie took advantage of her openness. "What about Daddy?" she asked, perturbed at her daughter's sudden perkiness at the idea of living with Jacob. "Aren't you happy here with Daddy?"

A confused glimmer of love and fear crossed Emily-Grace's pink cheeks. She thought about the question before responding, and Jessie felt sick for prying into her daughter's heart and soul in a way that felt somewhat deceitful. But she listened closely.

"I would just rather live with Jacob, that's all," was the simple response. "With you there too."

"Why?" As she asked, Jessie focused her eyes on wiping back more loose strands of her daughter's hair, for fear of what the child's pale blue gaze might reveal.

"Because when we had Jacob instead of Daddy, there was always music. I miss the music. And because Dylan ought to live with his real daddy."

"Even though Dylan messed up your homework?"

"Well, Jacob probably wouldn't let him."

In a few years she'll be adding the DUH in there, thought Jessie wryly. *Yeesh. Just-about-seven, but going on sixteen.*

"And…what about me? Where should I live?"

"You would live there too."

"And Talia?"

"She would go home."

"David?"

"With us."

"Daddy would be lonely without us." It was a whisper. *Please tell me you would at least miss your own daddy.*

"Well, Jacob is lonely without us now."

"He misses you kids. And I know you miss him. But he's coming back to Vancouver soon, Emily-Grace. You'll see him soon."

"We should live with him again and not just visit all the time. Daddy could visit us instead."

"Honey…"

"What, Momma?" Emily-Grace traced the chest embroidery on the red plaid western shirt Jessie was wearing.

"Sweetheart, you know about being married, right?"

"Yes." The shoulders crumpled. "I forgot. You and Daddy are married. So we have to stay here."

"And the thing is…Jacob and Talia are getting married too. They just decided."

She was met with silence while Emily-Grace computed exactly what that meant, and how it would filter down to her own little world. The small fingers stopped their tracing, and the sea-pearl eyes peered hopelessly up at Jessie.

"Momma, the boy at school said Daddy is not a nice man. I want to go live with Jacob and Talia since they will be married. And I want to take Dylan and David with me."

That floored Jessie. She froze. Her voice, when she finally found the nerve to speak, was quiet and subdued, and a slight tremor gave away her growing fear. "What do you think, Emily-Grace? Is your daddy a nice man?"

"Most times," was the answer, which erupted in sobs and hiccups. "It wasn't really his fault Dylan scribbled on my homework. Was it, Momma?"

Ignoring the question, Jessie cuddled her daughter close and whispered in her ear. "Daddy is very special, Emily-Grace. He had a hard time once, and he paid very dearly for it. He made some mistakes. But honey, we all make mistakes. All of us. Your daddy…I love him very much, and I know you do too. And Daddy loves us back. So don't you let anyone tell you that he is not a nice man. He, Emily-Grace, is the *best* man. Ever. And don't you ever forget that, okay? Okay, honey?"

It was Emily-Grace's turn to wipe her mother's tears away. She traced one as it fell down Jessie's cheek. "Why are you crying, Momma?"

"Because I'm a sucker for your daddy, and it hurts me to see anyone hurt him, that's why. Now let's stop all this mushiness and get that homework taped back together before it gets too late for you to have a bath."

Easing herself up off the deep, low couch, Jessie hung on to her daughter and headed for the kitchen. Like a monkey, Emily-Grace held on tight, until Jessie passed the entry to the stairs. She let her down when, startled, her eyes locked on to Josh's. He was sitting on the stairs, having evidently listened to the conversation between his wife and child, Dylan's sippy cup in his hand.

Jessie didn't have to ask what he heard. Slouched and silent, Josh's forearms rested on his thighs. The endless moist eyes were as sorrowful as they were the first night he and Jessie met.

As Emily-Grace ran to grab the bits and pieces of her homework, Jessie stepped towards him, but Josh got up and made his way back upstairs.

With a sigh, Jessie followed her daughter into the kitchen and taped up the worksheet. They muddled their way through it together, before heading upstairs to bath time and bed.

Chapter Five

*T*wo days later, as she motored her electric scooter down Hastings Street, Kayla pondered the newest challenges that had come, unbidden and unwanted, into the life of her brother's oldest school-aged child. Sliding into a tiny parking spot, she settled the scooter, tapped the code from the meter into the parking App on her iPhone, and looked both ways before crossing the street. Despite the ever-present sadness in her niece's pale eyes, she pushed thoughts of Emily-Grace away for now.

Because Kayla had a meeting. And she was nervous.

Pushing open the glass door of Jack Deacon's rented space on East Hastings Street, she took a deep breath for courage.

I'm a dancer, she scolded herself. *I can't expect to know how to handle administrative stuff right from the get-go.* She was excited about the B boyz workshops, but that didn't keep nerves and uncertainty away. It was easy to think about the dancing and the spring tour, at least from the stage's point of view. It was a heck of a lot harder to consider the paperwork that had to be done to get them all there.

Paul, as usual, helped. Her cute boyfriend's easygoing nature had the power to instantly relax Kayla, especially when she was being outright annoying with her worries about whether she could handle street-hardened students, or how to even start booking theaters for the spring tour.

"Wish you could be here today, buddy," she thought absently as she scanned the large open space before her for signs of the dapper, silver-haired Jack Deacon. "I could use a boost."

Paul, a lawyer, was in court for the day, though, so Kayla would have to deal with her nerves on her own. Jessie would have joined her, but she and Josh were taking all three children to the dentist for check-ups. Their time at home in Vancouver together was sporadic at best, despite each other's best efforts to remain in the city as much as possible, so appointments were generally plentiful when both were available to wrangle their busy children.

"I can handle this. I can handle this," Kayla muttered to the semi-darkness in an attempt to calm herself down. "Law of attraction. I am queen of all things workshoppy."

Clipped footsteps moved down a set of stairs at the widest open end of the space. Realizing she was silhouetted against the glass door and window, Kayla craned her neck around in search of a light switch. A dim body moved past her and she heard a click.

"My apologies, Miss Sawyer," Jack Deacon offered graciously as the room was quickly flooded with light. "I came in the back way. My assistant usually gets the lights when she unlocks the front door."

As if on cue, an impeccably dressed woman swept towards them from Kayla's right, a Starbucks coffee firmly grasped in one raised hand.

"Ah, Mandy, please say hello to Kayla Sawyer. Kayla, this is Mandy, my personal assistant and your new helper." Jack leaned conspiratorially closer to Kayla, who couldn't help but notice a comforting spicy aftershave scent hovering about his very distinguished three quarter length double-breasted cashmere coat. "My wife wants me to slow down. But I won't for long, only as long as it takes for us to have a few months off to do some things around our home, and maybe take off for a week or two to cycle around Tuscany. Might as well keep Mandy busy in the meantime."

"A second honeymoon." Mandy winked at Kayla as Jack beamed alongside her.

As the woman's empty hand clasped Kayla's warmly, the dancer took a moment to size up Jack's assistant. Mandy was maybe thirty-five, Asian, perhaps of Chinese ancestry according to her elegantly sculpted cheekbones, porcelain skin, and exquisite deep-set eyes. Thick dark hair fell in shiny, healthy waves down between her shoulder blades, resting on a silky grey sleeveless top, which was tucked neatly into a black knee-length pencil skirt.

The woman's handshake was firm, the almond eyes alight and welcoming, yet sharp and focused.

"Kayla," Mandy said kindly. "Jessie's sister-in-law."

"Yep, that's right," Kayla enthused, burying her fear and avoiding glancing down at her ankle-high slouchy leather boots, which barely covered striped red-at-the-top grey wool socks over bright print leggings. "Or Jessie's dancer. Or Josh's sister. Take yer pick." She swallowed, and shoved both hands inside the deep pockets of the baggy brown leather aviator jacket Jessie gave her after the last tour, a replica of Jessie's own, which she had worn endlessly on tour and about which the dancers teased her mercilessly. The teasing had only ended up with all the dancers being given similar jackets as parting gifts after months of touring. A miniature embroidered oval crest over the left pocket was the only thing distinguishing the gifts from Jessie's own flight jacket. It simply stated *Jessie Wheeler, Light 'n Love Tour*, in tiny red and white stitches.

"Well, Kayla, not everyone can say they're talented enough to make Jessie Wheeler's dance troupe." Mandy nodded at the crest. "And I have a feeling you're about to emerge from these workshops very much in your own skin with new accomplishments for this city and our country to celebrate. It's quite the project you've taken on."

Steeling herself upright, Kayla relaxed slightly. From the corner of her eye, she noticed Jack's lips turn up a bit at the corners. His eyes were his good-looking son Charlie's eyes, serious but aloof, sparkling and alert.

"Come," he directed her, placing an arm gently around his visitor's waist. "We'll show you the space."

It didn't take Kayla long to lose her fear. Easily, she was soon swept up in the grandiose vision that inspired her workshops in the first place. Giving that vision a concrete visual reference helped immensely. Jack's space was large and roomy, each wall painted a base white with swirling abstract floor-to-ceiling murals rendered overtop in primary colors. The floor was a rich pale hardwood, original to the 1920's era brick warehouse, sanded and stained to bring out the lovely, rich grain. There was a stage at the far end, from where Jack had originated earlier. It was entirely painted black, walls too, and opposite it, near the East Hastings entrance to the space, was a technical booth for sound and light techs, as well as to accommodate a stage manager. Above the stage were rows of stage lights. Chairs were stacked in a storage room off the main area. Close by were glassed-in offices. Opposite those was a lounge area, complete with a kitchen bar (non-alcoholic—water, juice, coffee and tea only) where participants could hang out. Not far away along the same wall an electric fireplace sat cozily bordered by a few comfortable couches and chairs.

Overall, the space was comfortable and openhearted in tone. Kayla's body was electric with excitement. "Part of the aura," she said aloud to Jack and Mandy, "is the fact that this is where Jessie was discovered, right? This is where she performed when Charles and Dee first spotted her? Acting in some play?"

"Jack found her down the street first," Mandy affirmed with a convivial smile. "Although he often gives the Keatings all the credit, kind man that he is." Mandy touched Jack's elbow when she said that, and let her hand linger there, which struck Kayla as odd. She pushed the thought away. Jack was known to be a stand-up guy, a married man who lived for his wife. No way would he be anything but faithful to Lydia.

"Phew," enthused Kayla as she stood at the door where she would occupy an office. "This is such a relief, having you guys on board, I mean. And having this space to work in. I can hardly wait to get going on this project. When do we start? I've already got posters to direct interested participants to their social workers, who will do the screening."

"How's your Monday look?" Mandy was keen. She won Kayla over with her enthusiasm and genuine interest in pleasing Jack. "Nine a.m.?"

A hand shot out, practically without Kayla's brain even engaging it. "You got it," she grinned widely. "I'll bring the coffee."

Jack, too, shook on the deal, and the three amicably parted ways.

Over her shoulder as she strode back across the street, Kayla noticed a young First Nations girl leaning against the building, sucking on a smoke. She was dirty, her jeans worn in all the wrong places, and her dark hair, hanging long underneath a beige wool cap, was limp and thin. The girl's eyes were locked on Kayla.

You're just what I'm looking for, mused Kayla as her frame of vision widened to include the entire charismatic building. *But can you dance?*

Before puttering away, as she zipped up her jacket, Kayla gave the place one last look to lock in her memory banks for later. The sun was bright overhead; it lit the front face of the building so it almost glowed, as if to drive home the point that this was a place where *good things happen*.

The workshops had a home.

And Kayla had a purpose.

～ ～

While Kayla was touring the Deacon space, Jacob was meeting with another of Vancouver's show business elite. Two of them, in fact. Deirdre Keating was paying a rare visit to her husband's towering offices on Robson Street just so she could catch up with Jacob, who seemed to spend less and less time in the Vancouver apartment he still kept on Southwest Marine Drive, and more and more time with Talia, well, wherever she might be. Sometimes that included the luxurious sunny 3500 square foot corner flat Talia bought six months ago in Nashville or, like last week, a vacation spot in some exotic part of the world. Other times they met up on the road, either at Jacob's engagements or at one of Talia's.

Occasionally the couple went off the grid to one of Jacob's father's houses, strewn along the south like plastic houses from the board game Monopoly. Tom Ryan's outspoken political ballads had won him fame, but there were dissenters. Over the last few years, the songwriter had found himself faced with more than one threat of assassination. He was afraid to sleep in the same bed for more than a week.

Talia wasn't with Jacob today, and as Deirdre greeted one of her star entertainers with a hug, she knew from his MO over the last two years that Jacob would only be in Vancouver long enough to sort out some business, then he'd quickly cut and run. Jacob wouldn't want to see Jessie. Despite their occasional contact at shows they still did together, like the tour they'd agreed on, or at awards shows or fundraising concerts, where they remained civil in a guarded sort of 'miss you' way, they were not comfortable hanging out for any length of time. Hurt still reigned between them, the kind that sucked in the breath with remembrance, the kind that, like falling leaves in fall, had left parts of their souls empty and bare. There were things Jacob couldn't let go of, despite Talia's calming presence in his life (or was it Talia's distracting presence, he sometimes asked himself?). The biggest of these, besides the loss of Jessie herself was, of course, the absence of the children in Jacob's everyday life.

Now, Jacob moved into the meeting room without taking off his denim jacket. He dropped into a chair near the end of Charles' boardroom table, loosely crossed one faded black-jeaned ankle over the opposite knee, and drummed his fingers on the highly polished mahogany.

Deirdre, greeting her husband as he strode into the dimly lit room, felt sorry for the combination of nerves and sorrow lining Jacob's face. With a graceful flourish of both palms against her creamy tailored skirt, she lowered herself into a deep tan leather seat opposite Jacob, and waited for Charles to drop a thick file on the table and start the conversation.

"How's Talia?" was the first thing out of the producer's mouth, which he fired across to Jacob without looking at him. Charles opened the file folder instead and started rifling through, accenting his search with a series of light grunts that telegraphed annoyance.

Jacob glanced up at Deirdre before answering. The elegant woman, both hands neatly folded in her lap, was studying him with an air of tenderness and concern.

"Talia's great," Jacob managed, shifting slightly as he spoke. "She would have liked to come with me, but she's shooting a new music video tomorrow and needed today for prep. I've learned that sometimes it's better just to stay out of her way when she's working."

At that, Charles finally looked up, and peered up at Jacob from beneath dark-framed reading glasses. His hands remained on the file, but they stilled. "She's very driven."

"She gets off on the ride. And she did it without you two," Jacob added lightly. "Blows my mind."

A tiny grin sent across to Charles managed to relax Deirdre. There was something warm in Jacob's eyes when he talked about his new fiancée. It was a cherished look, an acceptance of joy, finally. It cascaded through his eyes like a dancing light, but sobered and dimmed with, Deirdre understood, memories of happier meetings in this room with Jessie by his side.

"Talia was well on her way before she backed you up in Seattle, Jacob," Charles decreed. "But let us know if she ever decides to change teams."

"Meaning genre or management?" A wider grin accompanied the wise remark.

"Genre's hardly a thing these days. Country music's more than ninety-per-cent determined by where the artist lives. Tell her to sell the place in Nashville and move to L.A. Not that she needs any help to rocket up the crossover charts any faster," Charles added, starting to rifle through the files again. "Now where's that schedule?" he muttered. He reached for an intercom on the phone to his right. "Magda, can you bring me in a copy of the details for the shoot in two weeks? Jacob's schedule for the Children's Wish Foundation video shoot?"

"I emailed that to you last night," Deirdre reproached him. "Just pull it up on your phone."

At Charles' scolding rebuke, she sighed and nodded towards him, while speaking to Jacob. "The old man's not into technology. It's a wonder he makes magic happen the way he does."

"It's the minions, Dee, as you never fail to remind me," answered Charles with an air of detachment. "I wave my arms and they push the buttons." He looked up at Jacob again, and met the young singer's honest cobalt eyes, which were fairly striking amongst his usual neglected three-day beard and longish curly hair.

The file folder dropped to the table and Charles sat back, lifting a thumb and forefinger to absently caress his pale lavender silk tie, which sat in slick sophistication against a usual white tailored dress shirt. "Jacob," Charles asked. "Why don't you come to dinner tonight? We'll invite Jessie and the kids. You can spend some time with Dylan."

"Thanks, Charles, but I'm flying back to Nashville tonight. I did mention it…the jet…" Jacob squirmed, a sudden thought of Charles' mental health dashing across his mind, seeing as the man seemed a bit forgetful here, today.

Relief spiraled over his features when Charles responded. "No, no, I'm aware of your plans, Jacob. But you said yourself that it's best to leave Talia to herself when she's working. Stay here. It's just one night. The kids miss you."

"I'm making plans to see them again, Charles. It's all good. Josh is meeting me here when we're done, to sort a few things out, after he and Jessie do the dentist thing with the kids." A tiny but forceful pang zipped up his stomach then. The dentist. He, Jacob, would likely forever be excused from taking his son to such regular appointments. But the thing is…he didn't want to be. In his mind he disappeared for a second as he wondered how his rambunctious two year old was handling the poking and prodding of a dentist.

Deirdre noticed. She reached a hand across the table. "Jacob," she intoned quietly, "Dylan could benefit from seeing his father on a spontaneous visit. He misses you, and so do we. Please stay for the night. Carlotta will cook whatever you want. Fajitas, maybe."

"Fajitas are Jessie's thing, not mine," Jacob snapped, a little more emphatically than he meant to. Backpedaling, he switched his legs around, swiveling slightly to face Deirdre so as to avoid Charles' immediate hard stare. "I just mean…it's Jessie that always liked the fajitas."

"You're getting married, son," Charles broke in after a moment of uncomfortable silence. "We'd like to be a part of that, if we can. Of yours and Talia's lives."

"Yeah, well, I appreciate that, but Talia's life is insane right now, and as both of you know, so is mine. Good luck catching up to us, other than with business."

"Maybe you should let us catch up to you, honey," Dee said softly, in the mother-like tone she reserved for those closest to her, meaning Jessie and Jacob, for the most part, and sometimes Josh when she could find it in her heart to try to trust him again. "You can't outrun the past, Jacob."

A haughty *pffft* escaped Jacob's lips, which he uttered while staring at the edge of the expansive luxe table. "I'm doing okay. I'm running along just fine." He straightened, effectively ending the homey reunion with the power couple he worshipped, and turned the meeting into work mode. "Uh, guys, can we just get moving on this stuff? I'd like to head back to Nashville before dark."

Magda chose that moment to knock and enter with a newly printed schedule. The dark-eyed beauty's movements were a saving grace in mitigating the sudden hurts that filled the room. Charles pressed on, firming up Jacob's already long-planned schedule for the next few months, but the meeting was stilted and formal.

Jacob took lunch alone down on Robson while he waited for Josh who, according to a hasty text, was running a half hour late. Snacking on a chicken shawarma sandwich wrapped in foil, Jacob leaned one foot against the red brick of a store across from the Keating Building, and watched the assortment of people who called Vancouver home make their way up and down the busy street. For the most part, nobody noticeably recognized him, which Jacob appreciated, but then again the folks who worked and lived in this area were too engrossed in their own lives, and in their phones, to stop and stare at the young jean-clad man eating lunch across from the building where he'd recorded the songs that made him a star.

One man, however, surprised him.

Matt snuck up on Jacob from the side, a white grande Starbucks in one hand. "The prodigal has returned," came his warm friendly voice, which immediately turned Jacob's head.

"Matt," Jacob enthused sincerely. "Geez, it's good to see you, man. Looking dapper as always." Careful not to drip the messy sandwich's contents onto his friend's pristine blue wool pea coat, Jacob gave his old security a gentle hug, which was more than Charles and Deirdre got upstairs a few hours earlier.

"You too," Matt agreed with a clap on Jacob's shoulder. "Are you going up to see Charles?"

"No, been there, done that," replied Jacob casually. "I'm waiting for Josh." Eyes widening a little, he looked past Matt. "Is he with you?" He didn't need to add *Is Jessie with you? And the kids? My son?* Suddenly Jacob felt ready to bolt. He swallowed, and dumped the last of the shawarma into a nearby round metal garbage bin, licked his fingers, and turned back to face Matt, planting his feet wide apart as he did so.

"Big Dan's with them," was Matt's simple response. "He watches over Emily-Grace and David at school, most times. He and Susanne take turns; today was Dan's shift. He went along with Josh and Jessie to the dentist. Tailed them, I mean." Glancing around, his voice shifted to a more serious tone. "You're taking a chance."

Jacob shrugged and settled back against the brick wall. "Don't take this the wrong way, Matt, I appreciate what you guys have to do, but I sure got tired of it fast. I get now why Jessie always, well…" The words faded away.

"Miss Independence, huh?" Matt leaned back against the brick next to

Jacob and took a swig of his chai tea. "You must be finding life equally challenging with the Queen of Country, though."

"Ha. You can say that again. Her security's nothing like you guys, in fact not much is like it used to be. You guys were family. Always, Matt. All of you with the exception of—"

"Morgan," Matt cut in. Sobering, he added, "I hear you."

"Talia's security is all business. It's always 'Mister Ryan this, Mister Ryan that.' But in some ways we both kind of like it that way."

"It's easier to build walls than to take them down, Jacob."

"Ah, Matt, you too? C'mon, man, cut me some slack here, will you? I'm doing the best I can. I'm here, aren't I? About to meet up with Josh again? I mean, I'd rather shoot heroin up my veins than have to adhere to his fucking wishes about when I get to see my own kid."

"Easy, Jacob. I know how unfair all of this has been for you. I just want you to be happy. We all do."

"I am. I'm happy. Talia's a true light, Matt, she's the real deal. We're getting married, in fact." He added that part as if he just remembered it. Still, the truth of what his future held lit up Jacob's eyes and eased away the sadness that coming back to Vancouver always wrought.

"I heard. Congratulations." Matt's warm handshake was genuine. "And when you're ready to have more children, you call me. Kids need bodyguards they can relate to, not ex-military in black pants and camouflage jackets."

A hearty laugh was Jacob's response. "We will for sure, Matt. Hey, why don't you bring your ladies down to Nashville for a visit? I'm sure you could use some time off from guard duty. Come for a holiday, whatever."

"Maybe I will," Matt smiled. "My daughter would love it. She'd be the envy of her friends."

"Katy was the envy of her friends the moment the other kids realized who her father works for, Matt."

"She's been teased too, though, Jacob. Jessie's kids are getting it at school now too."

That perked Jacob's ears up. "What?" he asked, incredulous. "What do you mean? How? They're just little kids."

"They started back at school with big kids."

"Yeah, West Point Grey Academy. An expensive private school that I'm sure Jessie and Josh pay a fortune for in order to keep their kids insulated from the kind of shit celebrities have to deal with."

"Emily-Grace is in the second grade. She's on the playground with older kids. She's growing up fast."

"She grew up fast, you mean. From the time she was two."

Both men were silent and reflective then, until Jacob cut in with, "What's going on?" He couldn't picture his beloved Emily-Grace suffering from the heartless cruelty of other kids. She'd already suffered far too much.

Matt pointed his coffee cup towards the Keating Building across from them. Behind its tallest floor was a crystalline blue sky with not a cloud to mar the perfection. There were new leaves at the men's feet, yellows and crimson reds that had fallen from trees planted along the Vancouver sidewalk. They crunched when Jacob moved. It was a perfect day.

But Matt wasn't pointing at the sky. He was gesturing to a silver Lexus SUV that had just pulled up to a metered parking spot. The driver's side door opened, and Josh stepped out, unaware of the presence of Jacob and Matt across the street until Jessie, too, got out. She exited the passenger side door, and was about to remove the children from the car so she could wander down to the Starbucks on the corner and wait for Josh there.

But then she stilled, placed one hand on the hood of the SUV, and absently rubbed the sweaty palm of the other against her jeans. Her gaze was trained over Josh's shoulder, towards the other side of the street. Her expression was sober, where moments before her head was tipped up in laughter as Josh teased the kids while they drove downtown.

Josh turned.

It took him a minute to take in both Matt and Jacob, and respond. It wasn't a surprise to see Jacob—heck, Josh was expecting to see the guy, that's why he was here. But it was always nerve-wracking to see Jacob and Jessie respond to each other in that forlorn way that hurt both so deeply. That cut them both so raw to the core.

It didn't help that Emily-Grace, at that moment, spied Jacob too.

Jacob and Matt both vaulted upright when the SUV's door whipped open and she bolted out. If she hadn't cried out Jacob's name as she jumped to the asphalt, Josh wouldn't have turned and instantaneously—roughly—grabbed her arm, preventing her from leaping into traffic.

A heartrending, terrifying skid accelerated the fear, as Josh hauled his daughter into his arms and whipped around to shield her, with no concern that the car careening sideways towards them might hit him instead.

The scary moment passed and the car, a small Mazda sedan, carried on its way, its middle-aged Korean driver waving a fist at the Lexus as it moved on.

Jacob and Matt settled, and stayed put on their side of the street when it appeared a nasty accident had been avoided, although their hearts were racing. Jessie had cried out, and now, both hands over her mouth, was skirting the front of the SUV towards Josh and her daughter, glancing into the Lexus first to make sure David, at least, was still sturdily braced in his car seat.

Josh was losing it.

Rearranging his grip on Emily-Grace so that both of his hands were wrapped around her small biceps, he lifted her rather ungraciously onto the hood of the vehicle. "You know to look both ways, Emily-Grace!" he yelled. "What the hell were you thinking? Jesus Christ! What the hell were you thinking?!"

Shaking uncontrollably, he raised his right hand to her cheek and made her look up at him. There were tears of fear in his eyes, but Emily-Grace only saw anger. She shrank from her father, and melted into her mother's arms when Jessie was close enough.

Josh let her go, but he circled himself around in front of the SUV after closing the side passenger door. Both hands on his hips, he paced until he could settle somewhat, then he looked up to meet Jessie's frightened eyes over the back of his little girl, who was clinging hard to Jessie, trembling, her face buried in her mother's shoulder. Reaching out, Josh laid a hand on Emily-Grace's back but she shrank from him, a tiny strangled mewl escaping from her lips as she moved.

Jessie reached out to Josh and touched his arm. She took his hand and pulled him towards her, and he accepted the gesture and let his lips brush her forehead, but then he spied Jacob again, with Matt, tense and frightened and, no doubt, witness to Josh's inability to comfort his daughter.

"Fuck," he muttered angrily. "Jesus Christ."

At that, Matt gestured to Jacob and they made their way across the busy four-lane street.

After having approached the Sawyer family, Matt went around to the sidewalk side of the SUV and greeted Dan, who had pulled up behind the Lexus, as he was removing David from his car seat. Dylan was sound asleep, so for the moment they left him.

Emily-Grace was sobbing by now, but she knew Jacob's green apple scent and his gentle touch, and so when she felt his strong hand on her back she melted away from her mother and into his soothing embrace. He held her while she cried, burying his own scraggly cheeks in her little girl essence, and then his eyes drifted upwards to meet the pearlescent blues of the woman he would always love.

Their connection was always instant, always generated from their toes to their hearts and minds on an electric blue current that zapped its way firmly home by zipping between them. Jessie swallowed, and nodded a stilted 'hello' to her old lover and best, best friend from days gone by.

God I miss those eyes, she thought as the memory of letting him go a few years earlier, after the unreal night when Nadia died, flitted across her addled brain.

God I miss this child, thought Jacob as he built a thicker wall against the power Jessie had to crush him. It was getting easier to push her away, because he had Talia now to ease his hurts and make life rich and full. But being in Jessie's presence still disarmed him, almost completely, and without mercy.

Matt and Josh were watching, one a little less surreptitiously than the other, although Matt was doing his best to engage Josh in a chat with David about the visit to the dentist so as to give Jessie and Jacob a minute.

"She scared the crap out of me," Jessie managed to say to her old song-writing partner. She bent to her daughter and whispered in her ear. Jacob fought against the familiar aura of lavender that encircled him but, in the end, he gave up and breathed her in, closing his eyes as he did so.

Josh noticed, and the nerve on his cheek twitched, but his heart was finally starting to slow down after the scare they'd all just had, so he bit his lip and tried to focus on David's explanation to Matt about the visit to the dentist.

"Baby girl, you scared Momma and Daddy," Jessie was whispering as she rubbed Emily-Grace's back. The sobs were slowing now, but the arms wrapped themselves tighter around Jacob's neck. "You need to look before you cross the street. Okay, honey? You'll remember that for next time, I know you will."

Inadvertently, Jessie rubbed Jacob's bicep with her left hand. She looked up into the sadness his eyes always telegraphed, right from that first day when they met in the old dark Scots pub. "She's okay," she told him. "She just got a fright."

Unable to respond to Jessie, because he needed to gather his wits from the far reaches of the street to where they'd disappeared, Jacob focused on the child in his arms, who he hadn't expected to see that day, and whom he hadn't seen for about two months. "Sweet girl," he murmured, "don't be mad at your daddy. He was just scared for you."

Emily-Grace finally spoke. "You're my daddy. I want you to be my daddy." Raising her head, she wrapped a strand of Jacob's curls around her fingers, again and again, a movement reminiscent of her mother's nervous habit. "I want to live with you."

"Oh," Jacob smiled wistfully. "That's the best compliment a girl ever gave me!" He looked up to meet Josh's regretful stare. "I'm gonna talk to your daddy right now and sort out some time we can spend together, okay sweetheart? You'll get sick of me, we'll spend so much time together. We'll make cookies like we always do and eat every last one in front of your favorite Disney movie."

Jessie's heart ached at the treasured memories of their cookie-baking days together, but she pushed her own hurts aside to study her daughter. With the exception of Emily-Grace, they were all trying to let the past go here. They had to. Still, she wanted to fold herself into Jacob's arms just for old time's sake, just to read his soul so she would know he was okay, but she knew she couldn't. Taking the high road, she wiped out the elephant that, at least to her, was not yet on the table.

"Congratulations, Jacob. Really."

His gaze from beneath her daughter's fine darkening-blonde ringlets was unreadable, but Jacob managed a small, "Thank you."

"Talia's really done it, huh? She's beating me on the charts now."

"Guess I got the better woman in the end, huh?" Jacob's curt reply was delivered with a taste of poison and a toss of his dark curls.

"Ouucchhh," was Jessie's honest but confused reaction.

"What'd you expect, Jessie? You knew it would only be a matter of time before someone else unseated you from that throne of yours. 'Specially since you're so busy with all of these kids these days. Momma time must really cut into your creative time." The ache twisted deeper in his gut as the pink lips he loved to kiss parted in surprise. Jacob's eyes narrowed as he bent towards Jessie and lowered his voice to a throaty growl. "The momma thing probably really slows down the raunchy sex too, huh? Although I kinda recall you telling me that Josh isn't really into some of the more, would you say, risqué stuff that we liked, huh?"

Staunchly, Jessie planted her boots, crossed her arms, and nodded towards her daughter. "Really, Jacob? Uh, little girl here? Can you keep your nasty comments to a 'G' rating?" Biting her lip, she added a quiet post-script. "I thought we were okay…is this how things are going to go?"

"Hey, I'm just calling it like it is. You made your choices. Suffer the consequences." He shifted Emily-Grace in his arms, and she sighed and buried her chin in his shoulder again, facing away from her mother and simply staring up the street.

Tears pricked Jessie's eyes, but she ducked her head and chewed on one corner of her lip while she thought about what to say. She could hear her middle child nattering away behind her, accented by Matt's occasional chuckle or Dan's deep voice, but Josh was silent. His eyes bored into her back, though. She knew he was watching this unplanned meeting, in fact she could feel him ready to vault forward and rescue his wife and daughter from the only man who ever threatened to take them away, if you didn't count Morgan, their old security, that is.

"This little girl adores you," is what Jessie finally said to Jacob, trying to turn a corner on the awkward conversation. "She needs you in her life. Go upstairs with Josh and figure out some dates for visits. And please, Jacob… just remember that these children are not pawns to be played off against Josh and me. They have lots of love for everyone."

"I see that," retorted Jacob darkly. "I'm glad Josh makes the kids so happy that they want to live with me."

SUSAN RODGERS

"He's a good man, Jacob." It was hard to get the words out. They stuck in Jessie's quickly closing over throat like new sticks on a beaver dam, keeping the terror inside. "You know that."

"Then why is she afraid of him?"

"She's not. Josh got a scare and his reaction frightened her. And she heard things at school that upset her, that didn't help when Josh lost it just now. That weren't true."

Small pitchers have big ears. Emily-Grace raised her blotchy cheeks and met her momma's eyes. "They were true, Momma. You told me they were."

Closing her eyes, because she could feel Josh's agony at hearing that for the second time, Jessie swallowed and stored up some strength with a hefty intake of breath. "Baby girl," she said, "we also agreed that people make mistakes. Now come with me so Daddy and Jacob can make plans for you and Dylan to do some visiting."

"No."

"Sweetheart, please. Come with me, we'll go down the street to Starbucks and I'll treat you to one of those kid-sized frappes you like."

Cutting in, Jacob said, "After the dentist, huh? You're such a good mother, Jessie."

Storing up her nerve to growl at Jacob, Jessie spied a soft humor and a tender smile. "You dork," she sighed, somewhat relieved.

She watched as he bent his lips to Emily-Grace's ear. "If you give me a few minutes to talk to your daddy, I'll come down to Starbucks to see you after. I'll bet you won't even have finished your sugary drink when I get there."

"You promise, Jacob?"

"I promise, kiddo. You are one of the great loves of my life." Jacob's throat was scratchy when he said that, and he didn't look at Jessie as the words were uttered, but even David fell silent as the group absorbed that simple statement.

Jessie touched his arm again. Jacob looked up, and it was everything he had in him not to lean forward, kiss her, hold on and beg her to take him back. Only the thought of Talia made it easier to let go, but his arms were going to feel awfully empty without either of the Sawyer women in them.

"Dork," Jessie whispered again, softly this time, trying to still the ache in

54

her heart. She only had to twist around to meet Josh's eyes to see an equal pain. And as always, the ache for Jacob lessened as the steady one for Josh burned bright.

"Can I see Dylan?" came a quiet voice.

"Yeah! Yeah, of course," Jessie said, hunkering up her shoulders. The littlest boy was sound asleep, snoring even, with bits of drool drying on his chin. "He would sleep through an earthquake," she teased. "Just like his dad."

Even Jacob was uncomfortable with that reference, but Josh took it well. Still, he wished he were anywhere but here at this time, with his daughter angry at him and his wife lost once again in Jacob's powerful aura. He pocketed his hands and waited, toeing a crack in the sidewalk while Jessie and Jacob admired the child Josh was raising as his own, who was conceived at a time when it seemed there was no hope for, well, pretty much anything.

In a few minutes Jessie finally stroked her youngest son's cheek and eased him out of the car seat and into her arms.

"Leave him in the seat," Josh admonished. "Let him sleep or he'll be a tyrant later. Jacob and I can manage him."

"Nah, you guys need to sort things out without this little monster raising hell," she said to him. "He's due to wake up," she turned to Jacob, "and it's never pretty." Grinning, she eyed Matt and winked at Dan. "What are you doing for the next half hour or so, handsome?"

Laughing, Matt scooped David up to ride on his shoulders, and sidled off down the sidewalk with Jessie, Dan, and the kids, although Emily-Grace ran back to Jacob for two last hugs before he disappeared inside the Keating Building with Josh, where the guys could use Charles' fancy new boardroom table to meet in private.

Upstairs, the guys settled in and pulled out their iPhones. Their iCalendar Apps were opened and studied before either began to speak.

"I'll be in L.A. for at least fourteen days," started Jacob, lowering his head and peering closely at the small screen. "I may have a short break after that. Not sure yet."

"I suppose one thing about having Charles and Dee sort out yours and Jessie's schedules, they leave holes to accommodate the kids." Josh shifted his weight, and didn't notice that the silence greeting his comment was anything other than Jacob studying his own calendar until Josh looked up and caught his eye.

Jacob sat back on the soft leather chair and chewed thoughtfully on a fingernail.

"What?" Josh asked, unsure why the air around them seemed to have suddenly chilled.

"I just don't know about that break, that's all," Jacob said honestly. "Talia's got some dates coming up that I know she wants me around for." He rifled a finger through his hair and knuckled a pen Charles left on the table earlier. Clicking it rhythmically against the table, he waited.

With his thumb and forefinger, Josh rubbed the stubble on his chin. He frowned at Jacob, but gave him the benefit of the doubt.

"After that, then," he tried. "Middle of November, after Emily-Grace's birthday. Or come for her birthday, maybe."

"Yeah, I dunno. Maybe. Actually, I'm pretty sure we're in Europe then. Vienna, Berlin, Paris. Not sure where else."

Josh's phone clattered to the table. "So what was the point of this little exercise then, Jacob? Meeting here today. Were you, I dunno, just hoping to get a glimpse of Jessie?"

Throwing Josh a few well-placed air daggers, Jacob refused to rise to the bait. But he kept hitting the pen against the table until Josh rather delicately, considering the way his blood pressure was rapidly rising, removed it from underneath the callused fingers.

"I'm supposed to ask you if Emily-Grace can be a flower girl," Jacob finally threw in, the words spoken carefully and without expectation.

"Yeah, of course," Josh answered, forcing his nerves to cool. "She'll love it. We'll love it. Congrats, Jacob. Talia's awesome. When? How soon is this big wedding happening?"

"Not soon enough for you, eh buddy?" Jacob's eyes were razor sharp as they took in his adversary's bitter discomfort.

"Honestly?" Josh stuck with the hard truth. "Tomorrow wouldn't be soon enough for me. Although does it really matter? When, I mean?"

"You bet your ass it matters. I'll be taking my vows seriously."

Josh's eyes flashed. Somewhere in his body a low hum started. Not rage, just…a warning.

Jacob lowered his pouty stare to the table. "New Year's Eve, we're thinking. Maybe."

"You sound real sure about that, Ryan."

"Oh, fuck off."

"All right, all right. I'm being an ass." Josh threw his hands up in a truce. "We'll bring the kids and help you celebrate."

"Uhhh…"

"What? I just assumed you'd want Dylan there too. And maybe David?"

"Dylan can be the ring bearer, Talia says. So, yeah. But…"

"Oh. I see." Josh raked his fingers through his hair and sat back. He studied Jacob, who was wholly averting his gaze. "You don't want Jessie and me at the wedding. I'm thinking she will want to be there, to keep an eye on the kids."

The cobalt eyes darted up and met Josh's liquid browns straight on. Jacob laid his thoughts flat on the table before them. "I don't want Jessie at my wedding, Josh. Nor do I want you there, for that matter. Especially not you, actually."

"We got to let that shit go, Ryan. We're raising kids together. We need to show them we're all okay."

"We're not, Josh. We're not all okay, and we never will be."

My life is a dream, Jacob told himself then, sitting at the fancy boardroom table across from Josh. *So many men would give their left nut to be where I am in my career. And to be with whom I am about to marry. What the hell's my problem?*

"All right. Fine." Thoughts of Emily-Grace's recent rebellions crossed Josh's mind. The small blonde body absorbed into the comfort of Jacob's embrace earlier on the street was enough to settle Josh into considering more seriously Jacob's side of this less-than-ideal co-parenting scenario the families would be faced with for the next several years.

"You know Ryan, I accept my part in hurting you. I accept that Jessie still loves you, and that on some level she always will. I accept that we're all better off if the two of you see each other professionally but not personally, whenever possible. But don't cut her out entirely, okay?"

A low thunder accompanied Jacob's backwards movement on the swivel chair. He stood. "I admire this false bravado or whatever the hell you're throwing at me, Josh, but with the exception of places with lots of people around, I sure as hell can't see you much ever wanting Jessie and me in the same room together. I think in reality that scares the hell out of you."

"I'm not scared of anything, Jacob. I trust my wife, implicitly and without fear." Echoing his movement, Josh rolled backwards too, and rose. "And I know she needs you in her life. For the kids."

"She made her choices." Jacob's voice was thick, as if his tongue was swollen with all the tears he left unshed over the past few years.

"Those choices were hers. Not the kids'."

"What kind of game are you playing, Sawyer?"

"Jesus, Jacob, make this easy on me, will you? Why do you always have to fucking carve my heart out with a dull knife?"

"It's Emily-Grace. Am I right?"

A heavy silence marred only by the occasional murmur of voices in the hallway, or crisp hard-soled shoes passing by, filled the room.

Finally Josh acquiesced. "Look. Jessie's been having these moments of panic. Like, thinking you're going to move on and leave Dylan behind. And it seems that Emily-Grace comes with Dylan, as far as you and our son are concerned."

"Leave him behind? Why? Just because I'm marrying Talia?"

"Think of it this way, Ryan. Where you and Talia go, your kids will go. It's going to get harder to ship ours off to you, with school and after-school stuff like Emily-Grace's ballet, and we don't want to lose that connection with you. I already feel like we're losing it."

"I'd think it would be easier for you to just let me go." A slight arrogant guffaw cemented Jacob's thoughts, which were less than charitable.

Josh sent him a look of utter hatred, but he quickly replaced it with something more amenable. Silently, he thanked Trudy for the tools to help his temper abate. "You want me to say it? I'll fucking say it. Jesus."

"I'm waiting."

"My girls are indebted to you. Hell, I'm indebted to you. I'm trying to do the right thing here, which I sure as hell can tell you is one of the hardest things I've ever done. They need you in their lives, Ryan. Dylan fucking needs you, only he doesn't really know it yet. Hell, David needs you, because as they all get older they're going to need each other more and more. And I'll tell you one last thing, Jacob, but only because I've learned the hard way that relationships that count are worth saving. And that's that you need them. You need Emily-Grace and Dylan, and by extension you need David and you need Jessie."

"I can't, always," is what Jacob said then, the words tumbling over each other like snow in an avalanche. "I just can't, Josh. I'm trying, but it's easier to just go away and forget about them, you know? It's easier to hide. It's easier to let them go."

"So you do that by burying your head in the sand down in Nashville? And lose yourself in celebrity and tours and films and booze and whatever the hell else comes along? So you can forget about what really matters?"

Jacob started backing away, a few steps first, slowly, but he stopped when he reached the door. "I know what you're trying to say, Josh. But I'm not you, and I will never—be—you. You want to know why Emily-Grace wants me? Because she knows that too." He pointed a finger at his long-time rival as he spit out that final bullet and shot it straight into Josh's already torn-up heart. "I get that Jessie is too blind to ever see that. For whatever reason, which I will *never* fully understand or accept. It kills me that you're raising those kids instead of me. That you've got Jessie and I don't. But every time I come here, to this godforsaken west coast hippie city…"

He stopped and waved an arm fruitlessly in the air. "I feel the dagger in my heart twist harder and harder. I hate it. I hate how it feels, I hate coming here, but even worse I hate having to walk away. So yeah, there are times I want to just let them all go. Because, like you, I know it's not going to get any easier. And there are times when I want to hang on, because sometimes I get this grandiose notion that when you fall again, and you will, because you're weak, I'll be standing by to pick up the pieces. But not for Jessie, anymore, no, not for her, because I can't handle that kind of heartache anymore. For the kids. For Emily-Grace, who needs a steady rock in her life."

He turned to go, but as he grasped the handle and motioned to turn it, Jacob had a final thought. He fired it at Josh while half-twisting around, a look of almost peaceful knowing on his face. "I'll bet that's why you're asking me, isn't it? To stay involved with your family? Because you need this rock—me," he gestured to himself, "more than anyone."

At that, Jacob turned the handle and pushed open the door.

Charles, in his office down the hall, started to call out to him when Jacob strolled by, but the guy's hands were shoved in his jeans pockets and his head was down, so Charles bit Jacob's name off quietly instead.

He shoved back his chair and glanced down the hallway in search of Josh as, at the opposite end, Jacob pushed past Magda at her new glass desk, shoved open the door and, in the foyer, punched the down button on the elevator.

Josh wasn't moving. But he looked up at Charles when the imposing man entered the boardroom. With both hands raised at his sides, Josh spoke. "He's wrong, Charles. This time he's wrong."

With no clue what Josh was talking about, but his intuition and sixth sense kicking in, Charles just nodded. "I know, Josh. I know."

He rested one strong hand on the door handle, for balance and for strength, swung gently around on his heel, and left Josh alone with his demons.

Chapter Six

"For God's sake, Josh, you must have said something to him."

A large red and white striped pillow hit the ground at Josh's feet. He and Jessie were in their bedroom in their modern, boxy home in the UBC neighborhood, yawning and stretching and taking the large pillow shams and assorted stuffed animals—Tedsy, of course, and the tiger Josh bought Jessie at a flea market years ago—off the bed so they could climb in and snuggle up. But Jessie was in a foul mood, which started the moment Josh had wandered down to Starbucks and met her, Matt, Dan, and the children after his meeting with Jacob.

"I can't believe Jacob would just leave the city without keeping his promise to see Emily-Grace. He barely even glanced at Dylan, for that matter! So obviously you pissed him off with some stupid nugget!"

At Josh's silence, Jessie stopped railing and, with Tedsy in her hand, wheeled around to look at him. Immediately her temper cooled. Setting the broken, armless teddy bear on a nearby white wicker chair, she sighed and made her way around the bed to her stricken husband.

"Josh, I'm sorry. I'm being a bitch, I know that. But Jesus, what reason did Jacob have to break his promise to Emily-Grace? She's inconsolable!"

"Like I don't know that, Jessie? Seeing as I get the brunt of her anger these days?" Josh pushed Jessie away from him and spun around to sit on the edge of their big bed. From his vantage point he could see a cargo ship off in the distance, here in Vancouver from some exotic distant port to deliver fertilizer, maybe, or oil. It was long and rusty looking, and Josh figured the sailors on board would be some glad to be reaching safe port tonight. He wondered how long they had been riding the open seas, and whether their journey was idyllic and serene, or over rough waters. He sure as hell felt he and his family were back on rough seas these days. And always, always, always, it seemed Jacob was a fairly big part of the problem.

"So what happened, then? Why did I have to spend the last five hours trying to settle my daughter? Why was she so friggin' angry that I had to send her to her room, huh?"

"What, you didn't like playing 'bad mom' for once? Maybe you should do it more often so you and I can at least be on a level playing field with her!"

"Josh, what the hell?" Groaning loudly, Jessie dropped her butt down next to her husband. Taking his warm hand, she took another tack. "Look, it's obvious something happened today, that's all I mean. You came home with no dates and no plans for the kids to meet up with Jacob, and he bailed on Emily Grace. That's all. I'm not accusing you of anything, I just want to understand."

"It's late, Jessie, go to sleep. I'll talk to Charles tomorrow and see if he'll speak to Jacob on our behalf."

"So you did piss him off! What the hell!" Jumping up from the bed, Jessie was about to launch into another tirade when a small voice opened their door and peeked in. Jessie's glance towards the door alerted Josh to the fact that one of his kids was likely there, so he twisted around.

It was David. The little boy yawned widely as his daddy rose up and banana'd around the foot of the bed to pick him up.

"What's up, little buddy?" Josh asked him. "You're supposed to be dreaming about talking puppy dogs right about now."

"Emiwy-Gwace is cwying again." A sleepy hand came up to rub tired eyes.

"Agh," Jessie complained. "I thought she was finally asleep. C'mere, little guy. Let's go tuck you back in." To Josh she said, "I'll lie down with her. I'll see you in the morning."

"No sex, I take it. Or am I not raunchy enough for my wild wife?"

Before sniping back at him, Jessie caught a playful glint in his eye and couldn't help but allow a tiny wry grin to escape. "Dylan naps around two. That gives us about an hour tomorrow before one of us has to run out to West Point Grey to pick up the kids."

"We could have an hour and a half if we ask Dan to drive them home."

"If Dylan stays asleep, you mean. The little tyrant."

At the door, she paused. Despite his attempt at good humor, Josh was despondent. His shoulders were sinking and his eyes were questioning and moist. With David tucked into her shoulder, Jessie walked back to him.

"Babe," she whispered, "I'm sorry I lost it. And I'm sorry you're not exactly welcome in Emily-Grace's room right now. But this is parenting, apparently. It's not always sunshine and roses."

Drawing her to him, Josh pressed his lips against Jessie's forehead. He stayed there for a moment and breathed her in.

Their fingers lingered in each other's until Emily-Grace's sobs grew loud enough to rip them apart. On her way out of the door, Jessie tossed a few last words over her shoulder. "You're still not off the hook, though, husband. I want to know what the hell happened today. With Jacob, I mean."

When she was gone and the door *shuffed* closed behind her, Josh sat down on the bed again, but this time he was facing the door. "Nothing like feeling shut out of your own house," he grumbled to himself. "By your own daughter." Cursing Jacob, he wondered how this would all end. Maybe it would be easier to just let Jacob go off and live his own life. Let him marry Talia and take his leave of the Sawyer family. Dylan could grow up with Josh as his only known dad. He would be just fine. And so would Emily-Grace after a time, even during the rebellious teen years because, Josh told himself, he would always be there for her and eventually his constant love and support would win her over.

The overall problem, Josh knew in his heart, though, wasn't about the kids going with Jacob at all. The overall problem was Jessie.

She was the one who needed Jacob in their lives. Judging by her infuriation tonight, she was the one incapable of letting go.

In Nashville a few nights later, Jacob wandered up to Talia's Bridgestone Arena dressing room door and stuck his head inside, but the lavish white room—delicately scented with multiple fresh flower arrangements, its back wall lit from floor to ceiling with muted blue lights—was jam packed with people. Most were loud and obnoxiously drunk, and the men, due to wide-brimmed cowboy hats some wore like crowns, obscured his vision of Talia.

Leaning against the doorframe, Jacob stuck a hand in the pocket of his brown leather jacket and pulled out his cellphone. Tapping on the Twitter App, he scanned the left column for trending tweets. Talia was at the top. The first thing that crossed Jacob's mind was *I wonder if Jessie knows.*

Talia had cleaned up that night. They were at the country music industry's biggest awards night of the season. She walked away with Best Everything— single, album, music video, you name it. Talia was the latest sweetheart of the country music world, and was quickly rising to the top ranks of the pop charts as well. She was on fire, and the whole world knew it.

Spying her man across the room, Talia, who was at that moment guzzling champagne directly out of a bottle, paused before shoving her way around people to cross over to Jacob. Beaming, radiant, when she got to him, she stuck her arm out to offer him the champagne, and he took it. While Jacob's head was thrown back, with his lips parted and the champagne generously flowing through them until he almost gagged from the sweet, bubbly beverage, she silently appraised him.

Raking her glittering eyes over the typical black jeans, cowboy boots, black skintight dress shirt open at the neck, all topped by the leather jacket, she shivered. His presence completely disabled her. The casual way he leaned against the doorframe and stayed on the perimeter of the celebration, eyeing it with his usual dissociative puppy dog wonder, made him a perfect target for rescue.

"My God," Talia crooned to him, as she leaned closer and pressed her hand against the back of his left thigh, "let's skip the party and just go home. Please?"

His smile encouraged her. Talia sank deeper into the saturated baby blues and let her body fall against Jacob, who tipped the bottle back for one more drink before bending forward and whispering a sweet, "Congratulations."

Suddenly a petite body careened between them, and wrapped itself under Jacob's arm.

"Kelly," demanded Talia, who was stunning in a low cut mid-thigh bell sleeved gold embroidered Vera Wang, and brown leather embroidered cowboy boots to match, "this man is mine. Find your own."

"I lost Michael about four doors back," Kelly swooned, high on great music and pleased as punch for Jacob's girl, "someplace between the mandolins and the banjos. There might be a guitar or two in there somewhere as well."

Sure enough, as both Jacob and Talia cocked their heads to listen, music floated below the high pitch of the jubilant crowd. Kelly grabbed the champagne bottle from Jacob but stayed tucked under his arm, much to Talia's amusement.

"I won't see him until dawn," Kelly protested, with an eye roll thrown in for good measure. "Unless I land in his lap around three, that is. Then he'll be forced to acknowledge me."

After taking a hefty swig, Kelly offered the champagne back to Talia, but country artist Kenny Chesney beat her to it, thrusting another celebratory bottle into Talia's hand and crushing her towards him for a congratulatory hug. Swept up in the excitement of the biggest night of her life thus far, Talia let Kenny—a star with the career longevity she craved—steer her back into the room, where a rousing cheer welcomed her.

At the door, Kelly and Jacob watched, both unable to wipe the wide grins off their faces.

Kelly pointed the bottle towards Talia's back. "She's a keeper, Jacob."

"She sure is," he responded, shoving thoughts of Jessie and the children away. "Don't worry, I'm not letting this one go. Ever."

"Wise choice," Kelly agreed. "So when your career tanks, you can just sit back and let Talia rake in all the glory. And all the money."

"And what'll I do," Jacob teased, "sit back and write campfire songs?"

"Nah, you'll be too busy taking care of the kids." Immediately she closed her eyes. "Oops. That was my usual insensitive clone speaking, not the real Kelly Kelly." She poked him in the ribs. "I'm sorry, Jacob. I'm a thoughtless bitch."

"Nah," he replied, still smiling despite her unintentional slip, which threatened to crush the joy right out of his heart, "I'm the thoughtless one. I should've been thinking straight back when you told me to stay the hell out of Jessie's life after she and Josh split. Then I wouldn't be spending my days missing kids that were never mine in the first place."

"Dylan's as much yours as Jessie's, honey." Kelly offered the champagne back to Jacob. "Sex Ed 101."

"Not so much," Jacob said, squeezing her a little tighter. "He isn't. Biology notwithstanding. You know why, Kel? Because Jessie was never fully mine, so the way I see it, neither's Dylan." *Or Emily-Grace,* he breathed quietly to himself. *Or David.*

"Heartless," pondered Kelly as Jacob deposited a chaste kiss on the top of her head before leaving her to move through the crush of the crowd to be by Talia's side. But in all honesty, she knew what he said rang true. And here tonight with Talia, Kelly's old *Mystic Nights* co-star seemed genuinely happy, at least as happy as Jacob ever seemed to be. *Because the thing about him is,* she told herself, *there is always a layer of hurt in Jacob Ryan's ever-watchful dopey melancholy eyes. It clings to him the way shadows cling to the moon, sometimes bright, and sometimes dim.*

Tonight the hurt was vague, so vague in fact that it all but disappeared, and the reason was the effervescent, beautiful, sweet and kind Talia who, at the moment, was as lost in Jacob's soul as he was in hers.

Kelly resolved to milk the party for all it was worth. But first, she pulled out her iPhone and snapped a photo of the lovers. She didn't bother to run it through Instagram to pretty it up. Instead, she texted it straight to Jessie.

"See what you're missing, Jessie?" she whispered to the image as it sped off to Vancouver. "Your poor puppy is finally happy. He doesn't need you anymore."

Kelly pushed her way into the overcrowded room, yanked a new champagne bottle off a tall side bar, and jumped up on a creamy Italian leather sofa situated against the far wall. Holding the bottle above her head she hollered, "Three cheers for Talia!"

One, she told herself, *is for Talia's wins tonight.*

Two is for seeing the light in Jacob's eyes.

Three...is for Jessie and Josh.

Smiling happily, Kelly shoved her phone back into the pocket on the side of her mini-dress. When she checked it later, the message to Jessie remained unanswered.

Jessie was re-watching Talia's live performance on YouTube when her phone bleeped. Already she'd played the song six times, pausing more than once on close-ups of Talia to study the dimpled face and peaceful, happy jade eyes Jacob apparently wanted by his side forever.

"I hope you're happy together," she frowned as she reached for the phone. "I mean that. Sincerely."

Tapping on Kelly's text and using her thumb and forefinger to zoom in on the photo of Jacob and Talia, Jessie noted that the message had no supporting narrative, but it didn't need it. The image spoke volumes for anyone curious about whether the couple were truly in love. A small smile was lighting up Jacob's eyes as he and Talia held onto each other; it was a look Jessie knew well. The only thing missing from the image, if it was Jessie instead of Talia in Jacob's arms, was angst beneath the surface in Talia's joyful eyes as she beheld her lover. The angst was always there in Jessie's eyes. Because when she was with Jacob, a very big part of her heart was missing.

She was wise enough to recognize that, and grateful enough for her life with Josh today that Jessie was able to close the image and send Jacob and Talia muted good wishes.

But before she let Jacob go, she zoomed in closer on his lightly whiskered face so she could memorize the sparkle in the blue eyes she missed. It was that image that took root in her heart, haunting it more and more each passing day with weariness, and with a yearning Jessie was at a loss to grasp.

Chapter Seven

*T*he first day for participants in Kayla's Jessie Wheeler and Jack Deacon sponsored workshops was one of those dreary rainy Vancouver fall days that chilled the bones and sold a lot of hot coffee. Soup sales were also up in the city on that day, which was a Monday just after Emily-Grace's seventh birthday.

After kissing Josh and their children goodbye, Jessie took the Lexus down to East Hastings to give Kayla a hand and to help ignite continued interest in the workshops. Josh was to drive Emily-Grace and David to West Point Grey Academy, and Dylan to Dee and Carlotta in North Van, before meeting Charles, Charlie and Jonathon at the Keating Building on Robson to go over plans for his new series.

Jessie was running late—it seemed everyone in Van was driving to work today instead of using the Skytrain and buses. "I caught every red light," she called to Kayla as she dropped her Aviator jacket over the back of one of the chairs in the office her sister-in-law was using in the Deacon space.

Jumping up, Kayla popped a coffee pod in the office Keurig. "Here," she said momentarily, handing over a steaming mug as Jessie settled into the chair next to the one where the jacket lay. "How was your weekend? After Emily-Grace's party, I mean. That was sheer chaos."

"Fine," was the short answer. Then, shrugging, Jessie added, "You missed the worst part. The boy who has been giving her trouble at school showed up late. Like, fifteen minutes left, late. His father's as much a bully as he is, apparently. The dad couldn't wait to tell us how many awards Talia won at the CMAs. Listed them all, in fact. In front of Emily-Grace. And Josh.

Which wouldn't have been a big deal except…" She sighed and wrapped both hands around the mug.

"Ummm…so why was it a big deal?"

Jessie uncrossed her legs and stared at the mug. "He started by staring at Dylan and saying, 'Oh, so that's Jacob Ryan's kid.' Which of course led to Talia." Re-crossing her legs, Jessie took a sip of the hot coffee, looked up at Kayla, and said, "You should have seen this guy. He totally couldn't wait to tell us everything he knew about Jacob and Talia. Standing there by the other parents with a bad military crew cut and an Armani suit, on a Saturday."

"Um, so maybe he was working?"

"Whose side are you on?"

"You forget who you are and who you're connected to, Jess. For these people, you and Josh are interesting diversions from everyday life."

"Objects of curiosity, you mean. Circus sideshow freaks."

Yanking her iPhone out of a pocket in the Aviator jacket, Jessie tapped on her photos App and opened the pic Kelly sent the night of the awards show. Tossing the phone on the desk, she gestured towards it so Kayla would pick it up.

"Even Kelly's out to get me. Look."

Chuckling at Jessie's obvious anxiety, Kayla fell lightly into her chair and took a good look at the picture. She handed the phone back across the big wooden desk to Jessie. "Kelly's motives are never the same as those of the rest of the world, Jessie. I'd think you'd know that by now."

"So what the hell was she trying to prove, Oh Wise One?"

"She was trying to prove that Jacob's moved on, that's all. That he's doing okay and you can stop getting so uptight over him."

"I'm not—"

"Oh, yes you are. And don't think Josh doesn't notice."

"Josh knows where he fits, Kayla. He knows he's everything to me. The last thing he's worried about is Jacob, except where Dylan's concerned, that's all. And Emily-Grace, too," she added with a frown.

"Well then, that's a good thing, isn't it? So why are you so upset?"

"I don't know!" Jessie's voice was a wail. "I guess because I don't need reminders of sexy Jacob's puppy dog eyes sent to me from wherever the hell in the world he happens to run off to and hide in!"

Kayla spoke softly. "You've got a constant reminder of Jacob in your life, Jessie. And I've got news for you. The older Dylan gets, the more he's going to look like Jacob and remind everyone, you and Josh included, that Josh is not his father."

"Jesus, Kayla. Josh *is* his father, or at least one of them as far as we're concerned. Jacob is starting to make more and more excuses to remove himself from Dylan's life, anyway. Your amazing brother is the guy doing the potty training and rocking the little monster to sleep, not Jacob."

At that, the main door to the space opened with a loud *whoosh*. It seemed all of nature was trying to get in. As the door closed, forcing the wind and rain to remain outside, high-heeled boots staccato'd their way across the mostly empty space towards the offices.

Mandy stuck her pretty nose in, smiled widely at Jessie, and thrust out the hand that was not carrying a floral ceramic Starbucks travel mug. With a final spiteful glance at Kayla, Jessie rose and accepted the greeting.

"Hi, Mandy. Long time no see."

"Jessie. I was wondering when Kayla would get you in here."

"She just needs a hand to hold on to for a day or so," Jessie replied, looking back at Kayla and ending their discussion with a small smile. "She'll do just fine on her own."

"Well, we're glad you're here. Jack plans to give you ladies and your helpers a few hours to get the bugs out before he drops in to say hello."

"Speaking of helpers…?" Jessie raised her eyebrows at Kayla, who immediately checked her iPhone for the time.

"I told them 8:30," she explained, "to give me some time to fill you in on the schedule." She shoved a paper across the desk towards Jessie, who bent and took it. "That includes Paul, by the way," Kayla added. "He promised to drop by to help us assess the students and find worthwhile occupations for those who might not be quite so, shall we say, light on their feet."

"So some of the students will participate more in the live music than in the dance, right?"

"Right. Although initially everyone will have a chance to learn the various dance styles. We're doing this to maximize the self-esteem of these mostly twenty-somethings. So those who can't dance can focus on the music. We'll bring the band with us to open our shows and to play a song here or there. Some of the participants, I'm hoping, will be multi-talented and will choose to dance as well as play in the band." She shrugged. "It just gives them more to hang on to, you know? In terms of self-esteem and chances for success?"

With a swish of her shiny black hair, Mandy piped up and spoke to Jessie directly. "We found the participants through various Downtown Eastside agencies. There's a good mix of guys and girls, more girls, but that's okay, at least we have a few guys. They're all aged eighteen to twenty-five, all from different cultural backgrounds. They were interviewed and screened for suitability, and all have sworn they are not using."

"Will you be screening them for drugs?" asked Jessie, slightly uncomfortable at the blatant reminders of her life on the streets, which started her blood pressure pounding in her ears as an all too familiar old fear started running through her mind.

"No," was Kayla's quick answer. "Look, Jess, you and I have been around enough of the bad shit to last us fifty lifetimes."

Josh, thought Jessie sadly, suddenly wishing he was coming here today as well. Sometimes she just wanted him close by, so she could touch him and hold him and tell him she loved him. He was trying so hard these days—staying clean, supporting her, loving and caring for their children despite the challenges they faced.

Kayla saw the dark memories flit across Jessie's melancholy eyes like a raven in flight. Reaching for her hand, she allowed her lips to curve upwards despite her stress on this monumental first workshop day. "I just mean that we'll know if some of the group are using. We'll know."

"I expect so," Jessie answered quietly, twisting her sleeve around a finger.

"They'll be fine." Mandy's declaration lent an air of authority to the discussion, washing a calm over the room and adding confidence to Kayla's nerves. "We'll help them, right? That's why we're here, isn't it?" Raising her travel mug, she saluted the girls. "Here's to Day One. Now give me a few moments to grab the list of participants and get this sugary espresso into me. Then I'll come join you two and we can go over our day."

Shortly, Paul and the two helpers Kayla had hired from a local dance studio arrived. Paul was quick to grin widely at Jessie, and she couldn't help but get caught up in his enthusiasm. Cute as a button, with his own casual flair, he stripped off a vintage fifties era grey canvas jacket to reveal a white undershirt and red suspenders, which he'd attached to grey flannel pants. Peeking out from beneath the hems were comfy canvas Vans.

Eyes alight with mischief, Jessie reached forward and yanked an unlit cigarette out of his mouth. She held it up like a trophy. "And this is…?"

"I'm quitting." Paul yanked it back and shoved it between his lips.

"Since when?" Kayla asked, clearly unaware of her boyfriend's plans.

"Since I plan to learn this dance thing too." Paul tapped his chest. "I've got to keep the lungs clear. Cardio."

"I hear you," Jessie laughed, recalling her own addictions and secretly longing for a smoke. "So you'll suck on that one until it gets all soggy and droopy?"

"Too much information," Mandy smiled, resting a hand for a moment too long on Paul's arm as she passed by on her way back into Kayla's office. "Although shouldn't it be the other way around?" She winked at Jessie. "Or should I ask what's all soggy and droopy before I go jumping to conclusions?"

"Women," was Paul's tongue-in-cheek carefree answer, as the glass front door blew open. Twisting at the waist to see who was coming in, he touched a hand to a grey fedora he wore atop his longish waves of dark hair. "Sex. Is that all your kind ever think about?"

Raucous laughter followed him to the door to greet the two helpers, Cheyenne and Sharlyne, who Jessie was fairly certain she would get mixed up throughout the duration of the fall and winter program, since the girls were identical blonde twins, matchstick thin and rosy-cheeked.

Just before nine a.m., the workshop group started to file in. Some were immediately excited to see Jessie amongst the welcoming committee, but others, walls of life securely in place, seemed completely unphased by her presence. She watched them with a mixture of sorrow and hope, for each of them were shades of her in one way or another. They were runaways, prostitutes, druggies, youth with no chance at life because of conflict at home, or youth with no real home, or only a succession of foster homes, until life on the streets seemed the most tenable option.

72

The last of the group to arrive shuffled in late at 9:40, just as Kayla and Mandy were ready to organize the gang into four smaller groups. The girl was without a doubt one of the youngest and, it was quickly apparent, the most hostile. Kayla recognized her as the aboriginal girl she'd seen lounging against the glass window at the front of the space that long ago day when she first met with Jack and Mandy.

Casey had sauntered in with the wind and rain, slouching with all the sincerity of a die-hard lifetime street dweller. Instead of saying hello, she stood to one side chewing on bubblegum, her hands shoved in the pockets of oversized dirty, baggy jeans that were held up by a length of rope tied tightly around her small waist. It was cold outside, but today only a thin loose black T-shirt worn over a grey tank top protected Casey from the elements.

She didn't speak. But Casey did fix her gaze on Jessie, and the look she fired in her direction was pure hate. Confused, Jessie narrowed her eyes to challenge the new girl, but couldn't help withering slightly.

Kayla spoke, and tried to bring the late addition into the group with a forced non-judgmental detachment. "Casey," she affirmed, as she consulted a clipboard she'd tossed earlier onto a plastic orange chair. "Am I right?" At the same time, she wondered how this youngster got into her program. The others seemed at least somewhat interested, and more so as they talked about what to expect for the next many months, including the excitement of going on tour. This Casey girl was clearly downright antagonistic, according to the darkness in the non-expressive eyes Kayla could barely see behind the loose waves of damp silky black hair cascading in front of her face.

"What if I am?" Casey spat out, as Jessie sucked in her breath and shifted her stance to take in the girl more closely.

Kayla expected some hostility from the range of hard luck personalities in the room, so she took Casey's rudeness and lack of respect with a grain of salt, while Mandy silenced a few snickers from a nearby Filipino boy with a hot glare. Shooting a quick glance in Jessie's direction to gauge her response from Casey's outward chill, Kayla was almost surprised to see, in her famous sister-in-law's countenance, a grim-faced tense alertness.

Interesting, Kayla thought, before she waved an arm in the general direction of one of the groups off to the side and told Casey to join them. Paul was in charge of that particular group; pulling a chair up, he flipped it around and straddled it so he could face his five subjects with an air of relaxed abandon.

"Go wherever you want," Kayla told Jessie twice, because Jessie was still eyeballing Casey, oblivious the first time she was given the instruction. Not surprised, Kayla watched Jessie start moving towards Paul's group, but then stop and consider where to go when Mandy got there first.

"She sure likes to touch people," mused Kayla to Jessie quietly, as they watched Mandy squeeze her chair close to Paul and delicately rest fingers with perfectly white-tipped French-manicured nails on his arm.

"He doesn't seem to mind," Jessie teased, changing course and starting off towards a group setting up near the stage at the back of the spacious room. "Try having my man," she grinned sourly. "Women are always trying to touch him."

"Many women on the planet *want* your man," Kayla retorted. "Why, for the life of me, I cannot guess. To me he's still the little kid that once chased me around the block with a worm dangling from his fingers."

"Josh must've been some cute when he was little, huh?" Jessie's eyes lit up. Wisely, she chose to bypass the worm reference. "Did he look like David?"

"You mean did he have long blonde hair and sweet expressive brown eyes? You bet. Was he adorable? Did my friends hang with me so they could be near Josh? Hell, yeah. Even when he was four. Have fun with your group, Jess. Tell Cheyenne—"

"I think it's Sharlyne."

"You sure?" Kayla squinted. "Oh, maybe. Well, anyway, tell Chey-lyne or Shar-enne she has half an hour before break. Then we'll do some dancing and try to ferret out the club feeted sort from the more hopeful sort."

"You got it," agreed Jessie, with an amicable touch on Kayla's arm as she moved away.

Settling in with her group, she was relieved and happy to find most of the gang animated and excited. A look over to Paul revealed that he was doing his best, but that he was struggling to get Casey to participate. The young girl was sitting on the furthest edge of the small circle possible, staring at the floor in an unfriendly silence.

After the break, it was quickly apparent who the most promising dancers were. Kayla and the twins ran the group through some simple moves that engendered a lot of laughter and more than a little pushing and shoving. Casey slouched on the sidelines and watched.

After a bit, Jessie considered approaching her. Stepping away from the dancing, she was hesitant, unsure how the girl might react, but she sidled over anyway. "You want to give this a try?" she asked. "They're having an awful lot of fun. I'd be happy to help you."

The invitation was greeted with a low grunt that Jessie took to mean 'no,' but she tried again. Maybe Casey just needed a little private work on the side to help build confidence and to lower her walls.

"Coupla steps?"

"Up yer ass," slipped out from between Casey's dry, cracked lips, as she shifted her stance to lean away from Jessie.

A tall black girl with straightened gossamer hair passed by on her way back from the ladies' room. "Give up on her," she said to Jessie. "She don't got much to say 'cept poison. I don't know how the hell she even got in this program." Moving off to the center of the room, she started parroting Kayla and the twins in some basic B boyz moves.

"You know, I get where you're coming from." On the sidelines, Jessie spoke to Casey with her arms crossed, watching as a female dancer bumped into Paul and landed on the floor in a heap of giggles. "I lived on the streets too. I got a break right here in this building."

"Yeah, that's how you like to tell it, I hear," spouted words from the belligerent lips. "Everyone around here treats you like some kind of hero. They're real good at ignoring the truth of who you really are."

A sharp spike radiated up Jessie's spine. "So…you mind telling me who I really am?" She stole a sideways look at the girl in the dirty clothing next to her.

"I don't need to tell you. You already know. I've heard you say it." The dark eyes encompassed Jessie, their angry vendetta flashing across the surface.

Jessie's answer was all but inaudible. "Thanks for reminding me."

"You screwed Jacob Ryan because you couldn't stand to be alone, and then you took his kid away from him so you could go back to sleeping with a guy everybody hates. You're a slut." Her voice raised, Casey started walking away from Jessie who, from a standstill, tracked every step with hopeless desperation and embarrassment.

Casey had one more arrow to fire from her arsenal. "You're the last person any of us want to help us. Because none of us want to be anything like you, hurting others so you can just take care of yourself. You oughtta give Jacob Ryan back his kid. I see heartache in his eyes every time he sings. Bitch."

"So do I," murmured Jessie to herself, hugging her arms tighter around her belly. Eyes moist now, she looked up at the others in the room as the weather snuck in again, leaving rain and dead leaves in its wake as Casey shoved open the door and stormed away. "I see the heartache too. And I hear it."

As luck would have it, Paul had stopped the music just as Casey burst into her tirade, so everyone in the space was witness to Jessie's newest humiliation.

Kayla twisted around to Paul and signaled for him to continue. Tiptoeing across the room to Jessie, she spoke carefully as the music bloomed again. "You know better than to let her hurt you, Jessie. She's an angry kid whose only mission is to storm over everyone in her path."

"I know," Jessie managed to smile. "But somehow I think I'm done for today, okay Kayla? Do you mind?"

"Oh, honey," Kayla tried. "Please don't let her get to you. Stay for lunch, at least."

But Jessie just shook her head and strolled across the room to retrieve her jacket from the back of Kayla's office chair. Her throat was tight, and she didn't trust herself to speak past the tufts of cotton now wedged in there, threatening to asphyxiate her in front of all these hopeful young wannabe dancers.

Outside, Jessie turned left at the doorway, hoping to lean against the brick and gather her wits instead of leaning against the glass window, which would leave her feeling even more exposed than she already felt. But the brick was taken. Casey remained, her back against the brick, one knee crooked against it, and a hand raising a smoke to her lips.

Jessie froze and rocked back on her heels, surprised to see her still hanging around. As the wind blew her hair every which way, and as the last bit of rain chilled her to the bone, their eyes locked.

"You know," Jessie managed. "Jacob's a big boy. He knew what he was getting into." *Why am I explaining myself to this angry girl?* she asked herself. *Why do I care what she thinks?*

Casey's answer was an obnoxious shrug and a deep puff on the smoke. Averting her eyes, she focused on a blinking pink neon sign across the street, seemingly unconcerned with Jessie's defense.

"You shouldn't pass judgment on things you don't understand," Jessie whispered loudly, before spinning on her heel and walking away. Before she left Casey's illuminating presence, she grabbed the cigarette from her fingers and started sucking on it, inhaling deeply. With a heightened sense of relief, Jessie gave in to the head spin that washed over her.

Casey didn't bother protesting. A new smoke was lit within the minute, as Jessie's back faded off amongst the homeless and destitute of Vancouver's Downtown Eastside.

Chapter Eight

At home that night, Jessie's silence disturbed Josh, but not as much as the faint odor of cigarette smoke that clung to her. Curious, he casually stuck a hand into a large front pocket of her aviator jacket and pulled out a pack of smokes. Half the pack was gone.

Even Emily-Grace noticed. "You smell like Jacob," she said to her mother in the kids' bathroom later as Jessie helped her snuggle into warm flannel pajamas.

The remark only brought a new onslaught of anguish, but Jessie touched her daughter's cheek and said, "I know. I'm sorry, sweetheart. Momma had a few cigarettes today but I promise I won't have any more, okay?"

"Cigawettes will make you die." David, on his belly pretending to swim in the nearby tub, pouted his opinion. "The smell makes me sick."

"I like the smell," breathed Emily-Grace. Leaning forward, she sniffed her mother's neck. "Jacob," she sighed.

"Oh, Lord," moaned Jessie under her breath. "C'mon, David, time to get out. Momma will read you and Emily-Grace a story tonight while Daddy settles Dylan."

Later, with the two older children nestled beside each other in Emily-Grace's bed, their small faces tucked into a picture book about undersea life, Jessie started down the hall to check on Josh and Dylan. The littlest Sawyer had been fussy that night, as if he, too, sensed the presence of Jacob in the home by virtue of the smoky aura encircling his mother. Or maybe he'd just caught her anxious vibe.

Now, though, as Jessie peeked into his room, the two year old was peacefully staring into Josh's eyes, seemingly relaxed and openly curious. A worn brown teddy bear was receiving a good twisting around and around in Dylan's small fingers. Music filled the room—a ballad. Jessie caught her breath. It was the ballad she and Jacob had recorded together that crashed Twitter the day it was released. A love song. Josh was playing Jessie and Jacob's love song. Why?

Just outside the door, she paused to listen, her heart in her throat for the second time that day as Josh balanced Dylan on his lap and spoke to him.

"You remember that guy who took you and Emily-Grace a few times over the last year? One time, he took you camping in Prince Edward Island. You had ice cream every day, and got to put your toes in the Atlantic Ocean, according to your big sister. Jacob and Talia played guitar and you all sang campfire songs. There were a few grownup friends around who probably always wore black," Josh added, referring to Talia's ever-vigilant security team.

Jessie peeked while Josh adjusted their youngest on his lap, and she touched her heart with a sigh when Dylan giggled in his big-eyed baby way and re-focused on his daddy.

Josh continued. "Well, that guy is super busy these days. So busy in fact, making music and being in love, that he's lost his focus. So he's not really doing a very good job of planning another visit with you kids. But the thing is," and Josh's voice got quiet, so that Jessie had to lean in to hear, "he misses you. I know he does. And so one day he will make plans to see you again. But for now," Josh cocked his head to listen to the love song, which he had seen played live for the very first time on one of the hardest nights of his life, "I will remind you of him. I will tell you about him, and I will play his music for you the same way I know your momma does. I hope this is okay with you."

As if he understood what he was being told, Dylan gurgled and smiled and repeated one of Josh's last words, which he often heard from the mouths of Emily-Grace and David. "Okay," he said with a wide-eyed smile while juggling the teddy bear.

Josh laughed while, outside in the hallway, Jessie covered her mouth as a silent tear trailed down her cheek.

She had to laugh next, though, at Josh as he rocked Dylan. "Now, on to another important issue. We need to do better on this potty training thing.

And I hope, little guy, that this is truly the only real challenge of your entire life."

Jessie crept away, and sat in the hall hugging her belly until she managed to get her emotions under control.

When Josh joined Jessie in bed later, he found her sprawled on her side facing the large glass patio door, staring out at a sailboat gaily surfing the evening waves. Still fully dressed, she had submitted to a good cry, which was obvious from the red blotches on her cheeks and the damp pillow underneath her.

"All right," Josh said softly, running the backs of his fingers down one sad cheek as he curled his body in behind her, "would you mind telling me what started the waterworks and got my girl smoking again today?"

A few choking sobs cleared their way forth before she spoke, and Josh couldn't help but smile tenderly when his wife's voice came out all pitchy and high.

"Somehow I figured Kayla would have already alerted you," was the fretful answer.

"She tried," replied Josh matter-of-factly, "at least I guess she did. My phone was rather noisy in my meeting today. I shut it off and I guess I forgot to turn it back on when I rushed out to get the kids at school and, you know. Forgot to dig it out again. So...what happened, little one? I take it the workshops were not what you expected." His brow furrowed. "Is Kayla in the same shape you are?"

"No, I don't think so, she was having fun, I think," Jessie said, rolling around and reaching for Josh's waist so she could pull him in close. In his ear she murmured, "I just got reminded of my mistakes today, that's all."

"Which ones?" Josh asked, and then chuckled as Jessie pushed him away and swatted him. "C'mon, baby girl, we all make mistakes. Throw the first stone, you know? Don't be so hard on yourself."

"I just..." She cornered right. "Josh, I heard you talking to Dylan. And I heard...you played the ballad. Jacob's and mine. For Dylan."

Before he responded, Josh pondered what he'd said to their little boy. He touched his wife's cheek. "I'll never forget what Jacob did for us, Jessie. I know what he lost. I'm not going to let him lose his son too, just because he's sad and scared."

"Do you think he'll come around again?"

"Oh yeah, for sure. Of course he will. But right now…" Josh shrugged.

"He's in love," Jessie answered for him.

"Crazy in love, I think. Again," Josh added wryly.

"I'm happy for him."

"I am too. And one day he'll come for these kids again."

"I hope so. Josh?"

"Mmmm?" He snuggled close and closed his eyes, but blinked them open after Jessie spoke.

"I'm in love too."

"Hmmm?" He frowned. "I hope you mean…"

She swatted him again. "Of course I do! Yeesh! With you. Dork. I love you. So much."

Josh didn't answer, at least not with his voice. He took what was handed him while the children slept, despite the faint smoky scent of his often troubled wife who, now, was every bit as keen to express her love for her husband through the wonder of touch.

Then they slept and, refreshed, woke to a fresh pink dawn, and three small children burrowed between them, all arms and legs and cherubic, peaceful faces.

"We're so blessed," Jessie whispered to her sleepy husband, as he smiled and wiped sweaty wisps of hair from Emily-Grace's forehead.

"Yeah," was all Josh could manage, brushing his lips carefully against his wife's forehead so as not to wake their perfect babies and burst the dreamlike bubble his life had become.

～⌒⌒

In Nashville, Talia finally managed to coerce Jacob into sitting down to go over wedding plans. They were almost buried in large fan-topped cushioned rattan chairs pulled up to a matching round glass-topped table in the sunniest, coziest pale room in Talia's large condo. Light gauzy curtains wafted in on the warm breeze from the open sliding glass doors. On the table was a pretty clear glass jug adorned with hand-painted sunflowers, filled with the iconic sweet tea that Talia insisted on making pretty much from the day she moved to Nashville, since it seemed like the 'in thing' to do in the south.

She filled a glass for Jacob as he wriggled his chair in closer to the table.

"So, New Year's Eve," she reminded him. "Here in Nashville. My parents will fly down some time after Christmas."

"How much is this shindig gonna cost?" Jacob teased.

"As if," she laughed. "One thing we'll never have to worry about, Jacob, is money. You and me are good to go in that department."

"As long as we don't forget how lucky we are, Tal. We owe it to everyone else whose dreams will never come true to at least be grateful for what we have."

"Of course. Jacob, I'm already starting to sort out where I can make my money most useful. I'm thinking of starting a music school in my hometown. So kids with not a lot of opportunities in Seattle have a place to go after school and on weekends. So they've got something for themselves they can focus on."

"I'm in. If you want me to be."

"You know I do. I'll gather some folks together next week and we'll sort out the details. But today," her wide-eyed smile and two cute dimples vanished, which was Jacob's cue to sit up straight and pay attention, "we talk about our wedding."

"Only if we get to practice for the wedding night after we're done."

The dimples reappeared, along with a sweet pink blush Jacob adored. Gracefully, Talia rolled her eyes and tossed her blond layers. "Is that really all you ever think about?"

"What else is there?" With a twinkle in the cobalt eyes, Jacob grabbed the iPad in front of Talia and used a finger to scroll down the page she had open. "Don't we have a wedding planner to do this stuff?"

"We do, thank you for paying enough attention to notice, but these are things you and I need to decide before I meet with him again."

"Him?"

"Him. He's the best in the city. First things first, Jacob…" She peeked over his shoulder, clasping his arm as she did so. "Okay, so do you care about the cake?"

"All I really care about is the entertainment. And the wedding night." Jacob let the iPad fall to the table.

"We've established that." A pretty smirk lit up her eyes. "The wedding night part, at least."

"Yup."

"Okay, so I'm going with a red velvet marble, then."

"A red velvet marble what?" Puzzled, Jacob wrinkled his brow.

"It's a cake, redneck."

Jacob slapped the table and leaned back confidently, as if he'd just signed an international peace accord. "Deal. One down. So who is available on New Year's Eve to play?"

"For us? Take your pick."

"You're gloating. I thought we said we weren't going to gloat."

"Just a little, Jacob. All those singing lessons…callused fingers…" She drifted off.

A happy chuckle told Talia that Jacob completely agreed. "Just a bit, then. That's all."

"So what about Maroon 5?"

"I figured for sure you'd want country. Tim and Faith, maybe?"

"They're old school. And no. Sting?"

He frowned. "Talk about old school."

"Come on! *Fields of Gold*. He's sophisticated and classic."

"No to *Fields of Gold*. And to anyone who wrote or ever sang that song. That includes weird guys on YouTube playing toy cats."

At her confused look, he hunkered up his shoulders and said, "It's a thing. I've seen it. Only I think the song was *Somewhere Over the Rainbow*, maybe." Raising his hand, Jacob pawed thoughtfully at the itchy whiskers on his chin.

"Jacob—focus!"

"What? Okay. Where were we? Oh. I draw the line at *Fields of Gold*."

"Fine. Ummm…Jessie?"

"Yep. Conversation closed. Now—"

Roundly cutting him off, Talia figured this was as good a time as any to bring up Jessie and Josh, and the case of the blues Jacob seemed to be carrying around with him since his last trip to Vancouver. He was so blue, in fact, that some nights she wondered that he even remembered proposing

marriage, so disinterested did he seem in the wedding planning. "Are we…
still going to have Emily-Grace and Dylan in the wedding party?"

"Ahhhhh…" Jacob sat back and turned his head away from his fiancée.
She touched his arm. "Jacob, you need to see those kids. They need to
be at your wedding."

"Fine, Talia. But as far as sorting out their travel plans and wardrobe,
would you mind if I left that up to you?"

Hesitant, Talia nodded. "Sure. Although I thought you and Josh were
doing okay handling travel and stuff."

"For a while, yeah sure, we were doing okay."

"What changed?"

He didn't answer. Instead, Jacob stared at the painted sunflowers on the
glass pitcher, wishing he felt as sunny and happy as they appeared. He tried
not to picture real sunflowers, which only had a short time to shine before
they crumpled and dried up and turned to seed.

"Did you have a fight?"

"No, Talia. Look, I don't want to get into this right now, okay? Let's just
stick to wedding plans."

"Did something happen with Jessie? Is that why you're upset?"

"Jesus, Talia, let it go, will you?"

Shoving back her chair, Talia eased herself up. She took a few steps before
stopping near the open window. Looking out at the street, she crossed her
arms before speaking.

"I'm marrying you in a few months, Jacob. It's kind of a big deal, to me at
least." Wheeling around slowly, her jade eyes glistened as she spoke. "I need
to know you're one hundred per cent in this with me."

Groaning, under his breath Jacob cursed women and their constant need to
hash everything out all the time. Pushing himself up from the table, he made
his way over to Talia and took her in his arms. "Tal, I'm *seven* hundred per cent
in this with you, okay? Or more. And you will never need to be concerned about
Jessie, ever. She and I were done long before Dylan was even born."

"So why were you upset when you came home from Vancouver, then?
What happened? You need to share these things with me so I don't think
you're going to jump out this window one of these days!"

Grinning slightly, Jacob leaned forward and peered downwards. "Uh, Tal, we're on the third floor. The most damage I would do is maybe break a leg or two. Maybe an arm."

"You know what I mean."

"No, look." Rifling a hand through his unruly locks, Jacob moved away from Talia and wandered over to the baby grand piano she'd had set up in the southwest corner of the narrow room. "I saw them all together. That's all. The whole damn sweet, perfect family. Jessie and Josh and their three little kids, one of whom is supposed to be mine. I haven't seen them all together since the Seattle concert you backed me up for. They were around some for the tour last year, but I stuck to seeing Jessie on stage as much as I could and managed to avoid the whole Sawyer fairy-tale."

"I see. So I guess that sucked."

In response, Jacob plucked out a few sad notes on the keyboard. He ended with a loud cataclysmic *crruunncchh*. Placing his hands on his hips, he turned and faced her, his chin slightly raised in defiance, as if he were daring her to say the wrong thing and piss him off further.

But he didn't count on Talia's capacity for kindness and understanding. Making her way to him, she wrapped both arms around his waist and smiled into his fuzzy cheek. "Jacob, you and I are going to have the most beautiful family some day. And Dylan and Emily-Grace and even David will be a part of that, you'll see. When they're older and their parents piss them off, they'll be running to us all the time."

A sweet smile beamed up at Jacob. He couldn't help but soften. "Somehow, hearing you say that, it feels like it could actually come true," he murmured. "You're really something, Talia, you know that?"

"I do. I know it. The five CMA awards on my bedroom mantel have a tendency to remind me just how perfect life can be." Giggling, she wriggled further into her fiancé's embrace.

"You don't need any awards, Talia. You're an amazing person without them." *And you're sweet and happy and untroubled and perfect,* he added to himself, although Jacob couldn't keep a sharp knife from scissoring into his abdomen when he thought it. Squeezing his eyes shut, he wrapped both arms tightly around Talia's shoulders and silently apologized to Jessie for thinking it.

Then he thought *Jessie was right. I'm way better off without her and her constant suffering.*

And finally, finally, he actually felt like he believed it.

Chapter Nine

It took Jacob coming back to Vancouver to get Casey back into the workshops, although Kayla did some serious considering before reaching out to the troubled teen again. In the end, she found her lounging against the exterior brick of the Deacon space on the Friday before Jacob's expected visit.

Taking a deep drag from a smoke, Casey met Kayla's curious eyes the second Kayla parked her scooter and bounded onto the sidewalk. Head turning the slightest bit possible, Casey followed her movements towards the glass door even after Kayla swung it open. And she watched her let it go before going inside, so that it silently closed while Kayla took a few steps backwards and planted her boots across from Casey.

Casey let the hand with the cigarette drop to her side. She maintained Kayla's hard gaze.

"You know," started Kayla, turning one slouch-booted leather ankle over onto its side. "I'd almost think you hang out here just hoping to get invited back in."

Casey couldn't help herself. She eyed the dancer's trim form and brightly patterned leggings with barely disguised jealousy.

Continuing, Kayla added, as Casey took another drag and insolently blew the smoke in Kayla's face, "I have to admit, I would have considered it last week. Inviting you back in, that is. Except that we're a month in now, and you've missed too much. You'd be too far behind."

Taking a few skipping steps backwards, Kayla twisted around and reached for the glass door again.

"I ain't missed shit."

"Pardon me?" Unable to stem her curiosity, Kayla stopped and eyed the unkempt young girl again. Silently she wished Casey would move those long locks of hair away from her dark eyes so Kayla could look into them and see what demons the girl was protecting.

"You heard me."

"I ain't heard shit," mocked Kayla, not unkindly.

"Well, for one thing, ain't no one in there knows shit about the B boyz thing. Includin' you."

"For one thing, huh?" For the second time, Kayla let the door close. She faced Casey as a homeless couple in their sixties strolled by pushing tied-up bags of clothing in squeaky-wheeled grocery carts. The man, long greasy grey hair shoved behind both ears, kept his eyes on Kayla's tight Yoga-dance butt as they sidled past. "That makes me think there's a second thing. You saying 'for one thing.'"

"There is." Casey finished her smoke and let it fall to the pavement despite the presence of a metal outdoor cigarette receptacle Jack had installed years ago.

Kayla pointed at it. She kept her arm outstretched and taut as a slow grimace curled her lips downwards, until Casey succumbed and picked up the still smoking cigarette, then shoved it into the receptacle's grainy sand, all the while holding Kayla's gaze.

Huh, thought Kayla. *There may be hope for this one after all.*

"You need someone on skins."

"Is that right?"

"I been watching." The small girl gestured to the large window. "You got lead guitar, bass and keys, but you ain't got no drummer. And every band needs a drummer."

"I see." Kayla paused, uncertain. "Know where I can get one?"

"That depends." Casey fished for another cigarette from a packet she withdrew from a deep, dirty pocket of the oversized jacket she'd pulled into use for the day.

"On?"

The firm-lined mouth worked for the words, but it seemed they were hard to voice. Two girls from the workshops buzzed happily by, calling out friendly greetings to their dance trainer as they passed. Apart from frowning at Casey, they ignored her.

Finally Casey spoke her mind. "I hear Jacob Ryan's gonna be here."

Kayla's eyes narrowed. She pocketed her hands in the zippered hoodie she'd tossed on before leaving hers and Paul's small 1940's clapboard home in the idyllic, cozy tree-lined Dunbar neighborhood. "You don't seem like the type to like Jacob's music."

Casey's heart rate picked up at the same time her body perked up. "You know him, don't you? I mean personally. Because of Jessie Wheeler."

"Seriously? You're a Jacob Ryan fan. You strike me more like the vintage Pink Floyd type. All angsty and dark and serious."

"Jacob's dark."

"I suppose he is. He's pouty, at least."

"Is he pouty for real?"

Is there light in those eyes? Kayla wondered, trying to peek underneath the unruly hair. "If you want to know, you need to come back to the workshops. You play drums?"

"Do I play drums." For the first time, a genuine smile lit up Casey's dark cheeks. She swiped a bit of hair out of her eyes. Immediately, Kayla relaxed. The girl's gaze was suddenly, surprisingly, lit from within.

"Don't bother lighting that," Kayla grinned, reaching forward to haul open the glass door again. "You can't smoke indoors." Holding open the door, she smiled widely as the girl stepped inside. Behind Casey's back, Kayla threw Mandy a 'thumbs-up' sign.

Casey twisted around as they walked. "I just don't wanna see Jessie no more. I'll stay if Jessie don't come around."

"Jessie's on her way to Europe for some shows," answered Kayla. "She'll be gone all next week. You don't have to worry."

Casey stopped. "You booked Jacob for when Jessie would be away," she deduced.

"Aren't you the wise one. You're damn right I did."

"They must really hate each other."

"Ha. On the contrary, Casey. Now, take off that jacket and let's get to work. All right?"

"All right. Gimme some sticks."

At Kayla's raised eyebrows, Casey slipped off her outer layer. A light step and a serious grin preceded her way to the drum set waiting idly in the far left corner of the open stage. She dropped onto the low, round black leather stool behind it, and rolled up her sleeves.

～～～～

"Unbelievable," Paul said to Josh and Charlie at La Casa later that night, where the gang was gathered for a spontaneous Friday night pizza dinner so Kayla could help Josh gather up the children for the drive home while Jessie was away. Josh and Charlie had been in North Van all day, working with Jonathon and Charles to go over casting and other details for the new series, which was tentatively scheduled to start shooting in March.

Paul continued. "The kid looks twelve. I don't know how she can see a damn thing through all that hair, which almost completely obscures her face when she's drumming, but shit! I don't know where she learned, but that girl has some serious training. I'd even go so far as to call her a prodigy on the drums."

At that, Paul sat back and waved an arm in the air to accentuate his point. The guys were perched around a miniature vintage wooden table that Deirdre had found at some exclusive children's store; each adult male butt was uncomfortably ensconced on a small, hard, wooden chair. Each guy also had a tiny teacup in front of him. David was serving or, really, bossing. He had Dylan setting the table for the men. Josh couldn't help but grin at the little guy's leadership skills, although he and Charlie had exchanged one hard, knowing glance earlier when David demanded Dylan turn the tiny plastic cup handles to face out on the right hand sides.

The guys' easy smiles grew wider at the instruction, "This way, Daddy," which was accompanied by David aptly demonstrating how to hold a pinky finger out to the side.

"Dee," Josh had mouthed to Charlie afterwards. "It's not like he knows these things on his own."

"Charles," Charlie had tossed back at him with a laugh. "The things Stella doesn't know about etiquette aren't worth mentioning."

Now, Josh and Charlie were rather incredulous at what Paul was telling them. "Casey could have her pick of bands, she's that good," Paul was saying as he wrapped up his commentary on the day's biggest surprise.

"Maybe Jessie could give her a few songs to do," Josh started, until Kayla stuck her nose into the conversation.

She was sitting on the floor against a wall with her arm around Emily-Grace. The child was reading to her from a favorite well-thumbed dinosaur picture book. "She hates Jessie. That will never happen."

The three guys were silent as the shock of that comment settled in.

"I'd ask why but I'm guessing I already know," Charlie mused quietly, taking a pretend sip from the cup David was pushing at him. "Umm, good," he added, to the little boy's delight.

"Casey doesn't know Jessie," Kayla added when she saw the stricken look on Josh's face. "Obviously."

"It does seem like Jacob came out better on this one," Charlie muttered, peering up at Josh from beneath serious eyes. "I'm sorry, buddy."

"Don't be." Josh sat back and avoided everyone's stares by glancing towards the hallway, from where he could hear Ulysses and Charles entering with likely more than a few pizza boxes in their arms. "I'm just sorry I'm the cause for any hard feelings against Jessie. She doesn't deserve that."

No one answered. Uncomfortable, Josh scanned the room. "Don't any of you blame Jessie. What happened had nothing to do with her."

"Josh," Kayla urged, as Emily-Grace looked up at her daddy. "Not the time, bro."

"It's never the time," Josh said carefully, eyeing his daughter. "So I'm making it the time. What happened to our family was beyond our control. Jessie went to Jacob because she needed him. Because I lost my shit for a while."

"Cool it, Josh." Adamant, Kayla put her hands over Emily-Grace's small ears, but the child pulled them away and kept her eyes locked on her daddy's.

"No, Emily-Grace needs to hear this, Kayla."

Paul and Charlie stared at their teacups, Paul twisting his around while Charlie rhythmically raised and dropped his.

Inhaling deeply, Josh focused his gaze on his daughter. "Emily-Grace knows I was the bad guy. If she hears anything bad about her beautiful momma, ever, she knows to let it go. Right, honey? You know we've had some rough times. But us Sawyers are tough. We're getting better every day." An implacable stare and a frozen body was all Josh got from Emily-Grace. It was as if the child went on freeze-mode when the bad days threw themselves back into her life, gutting her belly and putting her mind on hold. Kayla glanced down at her. *Is she even breathing?*

Josh forced himself upright, knocking his plastic teacup and tiny plate over and upsetting David as he did so. Dylan picked up the pieces, which wasn't lost on Josh. *Just like your dad,* he muttered to himself. He thrust an arm out towards his daughter.

"Grampie's back, sweetheart. I can smell the pizza. Come get a slice with me."

But Emily-Grace forced her gaze back down at the colorful dinosaurs parading across her page. She shrugged off Kayla's arm, and traced a finger over a T-Rex.

To break the uncomfortable silence that followed, Charlie leaned over and scooped up Dylan. Overjoyed, Dylan roared happily in his arms as Charlie stood and held him upside down. "I sure hope our new baby's a boy," he mused. "I've had enough of ballet and the color pink."

"Uh, gender neutral toys are in right now, Charlie," reminded Paul valiantly as he too stood, after throwing Kayla an apologetic look for all the bad stuff that had suddenly entered the usually happy well-stocked La Casa playroom. "Capiche?" He nodded at David, who stood statue-still between his father and sister, a white plastic kettle in his hand.

"This generation's going to be so confused," was Charlie's wise retort. "C'mon kids, let's go get pizza. You like pizza, Dylan?"

Paul scooped up David and they left the room. Dylan's happy laughter was soothing as it trailed behind him, but then all that was left in the playroom was the sound of a little girl softly murmuring to herself.

"T-Rex cannot do Yoga very well. His arms are too short for chaturunga. T-Rex cannot do Yoga. His arms are too short for chaturunga."

Despite herself, Kayla chuckled and looked up at her brother, who stood beyond the table, the edge of one lip curled down, eyes moist. "Since when does T-Rex do Yoga at all, Emily-Grace?" she asked the little girl.

"Momma showed me on Facebook," was the quiet answer that, in some ways, both Kayla and Josh were happy was forthcoming.

"Of course she did," smiled Kayla, leaning sideways to kiss the top of her niece's blonde ringlets. "I'm going for pizza. You come too, sweetheart, whenever you're ready."

As she passed Josh, Kayla sent him a look of caution. "She just turned seven, big brother. Keep that in mind, okay? She's still a little girl." And she left the room.

After a moment, Josh wandered over to his daughter and knelt down before her. "Maybe you and me can watch that minion movie you like, Emily-Grace? We'll get some pizza and put the boys to bed early, then you and me can make some popcorn and watch the movie together."

"I want Momma."

"Momma has to do some shows. She'll be home before you know it."

"Usually I go with Momma. I like going with her. Grammie went."

"Grammie is Momma's manager. She takes care of Momma on the road."

"So does Jacob. I want to see Jacob."

Ouch. "Jacob is not doing these shows with Momma. He won't be there."

"I just wish Momma wouldn't go away and leave me all the time."

"We're doing our best, Emily-Grace. You're in school now and this is a short tour, just a few cities. We thought it would be better if you stayed home this time." Trying to touch her backfired, as Emily-Grace just pulled away and stared at her toes.

"I want Momma."

"I wish I was with Momma too, honey. I really do. I wish all of us could have gone with her this time."

The small eyes were floating. Every time his daughter captured him with those pearlescent miniature Jessie-eyes, Josh crumbled. Now was no exception. His daughter's angry, wounded stare telegraphed that she was one step away from a complete and utter meltdown. Josh knew this, because he was suddenly feeling the exact same way.

"Baby girl," he tried, shifting his weight because his knees were protesting, "we need to work this out, you and me. We need to find a way to be friends again. You and me were always best buds, remember? Even after…even after all the bad. You're everything to me. You know that, right?"

"I. Want. My. Momma. And I. Want. Jacob."

Charles chose that moment to stride into the playroom. His sudden presence was a break in the untenable silence, in the silent fury twisting itself around and around in the pretty little room like a tornado looking for a place to land.

Emily-Grace tossed her book roughly aside, jumped up, and moved quickly towards him. Charles made the mistake of asking her to stay the night. "Carlotta will make us pancakes in the morning. Deal?"

Throwing a hard look back at her father, Emily-Grace took her grampie's outstretched hand and nodded. "Okay," she agreed, before her small footfalls echoed down the lonesome hallway.

Easing himself up and then down onto one of the small chairs at the little table, Josh grasped a soft brown teddy bear abandoned in favor of the tea party. Focusing on its plastic eyes was the only way he could keep from having a total meltdown, there at La Casa, in a place where, for far too long, he had not been welcome.

"Jesus, Jessie," he whimpered to the bear, as if it could send his wife a telepathic message. "What a fucking mess I've made."

Softly, Kayla had padded back to check on her brother. Now, she moved into the room and bent down next to him. She took the bear from his hands and, with one hand, held it aloft. With the other, she lightly rubbed Josh's back. "I thought we established that this was not your mess, Josh," she offered, a grain of truth in her voice that eased Josh's angst a little. "She's getting older, that's all. She's at an age where she's trying to make sense of her world and it confuses the hell out of her. You absolutely will lose this battle if you take every little thing Emily-Grace says and does personally."

Josh stood, and Kayla rose with him.

"I will lose this battle if every time I try to get near my daughter someone else gets in the way," Josh said, gesturing with a flailing arm towards the hallway. "I was hoping to have this time while Jessie is away to try to break down some of Emily-Grace's walls."

"You'll have all weekend, and all next week," determined Kayla. "But for tonight, you'll have to share her with the rest of us who love her." She smiled. "Come on. Pizza's getting cold, big brother."

But she was wrong. Things in Europe didn't go quite as planned. On Sunday night, long after Jacob flew into Vancouver on a private chartered flight with Talia and many of her nameless burly uniformed security officers alongside, Jessie and Deirdre landed gracefully back there as well, in the Keating jet.

Chapter Ten

Before flying back to Vancouver, on Sunday morning Jessie, Deirdre and Matt flew from London, England, across the channel to Paris, France. They were driven directly from the airport to the historic Olympia Theatre, so Jessie could do a sound check for the evening show. She wasn't the only artist involved—she was a last minute addition to a 'Needs for Children' awareness tour, taking a spot vacated by Taylor Swift, who ducked out because of a scheduling conflict. Josh had encouraged the trip—six cities, ten days.

"You need this," he had told her. "You need to get out there and be around grownups for a bit. Me and the kids will be fine."

Initially hesitant, she had agreed.

After the sound check in Paris, Jessie retreated to the hotel for a rest before it was time to head to the venue for the show. Skyping her family was the first thing she did when she got to her suite. Boots and jacket still on, she had the iPad ready before Matt and Deirdre were even through the door behind her.

Afterwards, bundling up her iPad in its leather case, Jessie sighed and turned to Dee. "Being away from them just does not get any easier."

"Of course it doesn't, honey," Dee answered carefully. "It's hard for most people. But for you…"

"Don't remind me," groaned Jessie, as she stood up from a ladies' antique secretary desk, then pivoted and collapsed backwards onto the nearby king sized bed. "I just wish this little mini-tour would speed up and be over."

"Is everything okay at home?"

"Sure, yeah. If you count Josh constantly trying to break down Emily-

Grace's seemingly eternal bitter mood, then everything is fine. She's seven going on seventeen."

"Charles said she was great with him and Carlotta Friday night and yesterday."

"Of course she was. La Casa is neutral territory. It's her safe place."

Nudging his jacket off his shoulders, a designer black leather bomber he picked up in London, Matt interjected. "Jessie, we have about two hours before we have to leave for the Olympia. Should we order food? Or go down to the restaurant?"

"Or would you rather Matt and I leave you to rest?" Deirdre asked casually. "We can have something ready for you just before we go."

"Matt, we better order in or I'll have to stand in front of you and fight off hordes of sophisticated Parisian women I know will be craving looks at those ripped abs I know you're hiding."

A glint in Jessie's eyes had Deirdre shaking her head.

Jessie adopted a low, sultry voice as she continued teasing her good friend. "It's the innocent hazel-grey eyes, the oh-so-touchable jeans, although I won't say where," she winked at Dee, who laughed and wagged a warning finger at her girl. "Add the black leather for that wild, rough element all the women want these days…Oh, and let's not forget the adorable hair. Spike, the ladies are all over you. I think that redhead in the elevator woulda stripped right down for you in front of us if you'd given her the time of day." Jessie sprang up to a sitting position and hovered cross-legged near the edge of the bed. Pointing a finger at Matt, she shot him a wicked sideways grin. "Maybe you should go find her. She's probably waiting in the lobby hoping you'll make an appearance. Unless she's on her way to the spa to tidy up her Brazilian, praying you'll show up in the bar later."

With a screech, Jessie ducked when, after he hung up his jacket, Matt fired an empty water bottle at her. "Easy. Down boy," she laughed, admiring the way his chest and shoulders filled out his white button down shirt, and ignoring his embarrassed blush. Eyes twinkling, Jessie bit her bottom lip and gave Matt one more appraising look before she turned to her manager. "I'd better get something into me now, Dee. What do you guys want? Crepes? We're in France!"

At their easy smiles, Jessie couldn't help but light up, right from the inside of her soul to the tips of her fingers. Gone were the days when she desired the company of no one. Gone were the days when she self-medicated with Jim Beam and funky smokes. Gone was the old sadness. The only real challenges that remained were uniting Josh and Emily-Grace, and Jacob and the kids.

But after the relaxed two hour break in their schedule—which was spent eating and goofing around and discussing everything from Josh and Charles' new series to Kayla's workshops and tour plans for the spring—once the little group was back in their sleek black SUV limo for the ride to the venue, all hell broke loose. Literally.

The first thing that alerted Jessie and Deirdre to the presence of nefarious activity was Matt's quick reaction to sirens and emergency vehicles, which started streaking past them a kilometer from the historic Olympia. Their driver pulled over to let the speeding vehicles pass, and just when he started out again, more appeared on the horizon. So he, like the drivers of the other vehicles on the street, pulled back over and stayed put to let them pass.

Matt tapped on the window that divided the passengers from the driver and the tour escort. As it rolled down, Jessie and Dee quieted their conversation about a new offer Jessie had for a film that would go to camera soon after Jacob's wedding on New Year's Eve, and tilted their heads to listen. The tour escort, a Caucasian black-ponytailed thirty-something in an expensive tailored suit accessorized with discreet silver and diamonds that rivaled Deirdre's flair for elegance, had an ear bent to her phone. And her face was an interesting shade of avocado green.

When she ended the call, she spoke rapid French to the driver, a quiet, sophisticated greying man of African heritage, who gasped and yanked off his chauffeur's cap before bending over at the waist and sucking in deep breaths. His repeated curse shocked Jessie and Dee into stunned silence, but Matt's blood pressure shot up instantly.

"What is it?" he demanded. More lights and sirens careened by, forces of reckoning and salvation on what was becoming a very dark day in the history of an oft-troubled city, if one took in Paris' collective past over many centuries.

"There—been—a—a shoot. A—shooting," their escort told him in halting English, almost afraid to meet the eyes of the star in her care.

"Where? How close to the Olympia? How bad?"

"Sir, it bad. It just 'appen. Weapon, uh…'ow you say? Automatique, uh, weapons."

Deirdre, who was sitting across from Jessie so that her back was to the front seat, cried out and moved across to sit by her girl. She took her hand as all of them tried to sort out the implications of a shooting that could possibly be terrorist related…or, perhaps, just the beginning of terrorist activity in the city. And they were about to do a big show…Jessie would be on stage…

Matt didn't hesitate. "Turn the car around as soon as you can, Monsieur Avadian. Jessie won't be doing the show tonight."

Jessie would have laughed at Matt's attempt to say the man's name with the proper accent on the French prefix, Monsieur, but this wasn't the place or time. Their driver was now sobbing, his cap clutched in his hands. He seemed to be wringing it out although, with the exception of his tears, it wasn't wet.

"Oh God, Dee," Jessie whispered as she watched him, spellbound, a slow serpent of fear now inching its way up her body. "It must be really bad."

Matt was poking at his iPhone. He had navigated to Twitter. Now, he looked up at Jessie, his face stricken with fear. "It's bad," he told her, knowing she would find out the truth momentarily anyway. "It's at the Olympia."

"Wh-what?" Besides the initial panic of *Omigod, we are on our way there,* a messed up flurry of scattered thoughts zigzagged through her brain. First was *Who was shot? The people lining up to see my show?* Second was *How many? Were there children?* The next was *Josh. I need to let Josh know I'm okay.*

"Oh, dear God," Dee was saying over and over. "Dear God." There were other performers on the bill tonight, and celebrities slated to be in the audience. She clutched Jessie's hand with a trembling desperation as tears started to fall down her cheeks.

Looking past Dee at Matt, Jessie met eyes filled with a grateful fear. She swallowed.

Matt leaned forward and laid a hand on her knee. "We're going home," he told her, as she entwined her fingers in his, reaching for the strength she knew she would find there. "We're taking you home."

Able only to nod in stunned silence, Jessie let her fingers trail away from Matt's and focused past him to an array of yet more emergency vehicles roaring past. "There are a lot of them," she whispered as a high-pitched buzzing in her head ferreted out the anxious fast French of their tour escort, who was finally receiving some action from their driver. Good thing, too, because just as the man put his hands back on the wheel and turned on the blinker, Matt was poising to jump over the divider and start driving.

Jessie knew what he was thinking. *Was I a target? Am I a target?*

"Josh," she mumbled to Matt as the car started to pull back out into traffic and Matt settled. "Please text him." She couldn't even if she could muster her shocked fingers into moving. Deirdre was not letting go of Jessie's hand, and the woman's eyes were closed, her lips moving in quiet prayer. *Gratitude?* wondered Jessie numbly. *Or is she saying prayers for the dead and... their families?*

She copied the driver's earlier position and buried her head between her knees as Matt nodded and sent an urgent text to Josh, and one to Charles.

━ ⁓ ⁓

Josh was negotiating his kids through Vancouver's Science World, one of Emily-Grace and David's favorite spots to visit in the west coast hippie city, when the text came in. Since he was expecting Steve and Charlie to arrive imminently with their kids (Steve had two boys now, and Charlie would have his daughter Stella, Emily-Grace's dark-haired dramatic best friend, with him), he shifted Dylan to his other arm and fished his cell out of his jacket pocket in case one of his friends was texting him to say he was running late.

The text chilled him.

Jessie fine, incident at Olympia before our arrival, will call later. Going back to hotel then flying home

"Jesus Christ," he cursed as an icy fear constricted his throat.

Steve wandered up behind him, his eleven-month-old youngest, Cole, in a stroller pushed by Charlie's elegant, yet feisty and confident Stella, who immediately hugged Emily-Grace. Charlie was right behind them, chatting with Steve and Sophie's oldest, Caleb, who was now three. The two girls showed off their newest toys, miniature stuffies from an online Penguin game, as Steve and Charlie read the terror in Josh's eyes.

100

"What?" Steve asked, not sure he really wanted to know.

Josh shoved the iPhone's screen in his face.

Charlie angled his head to look. "They're coming home?"

Steve grabbed the phone and navigated to Twitter. Charlie followed suit with his.

"They have four cities left," Josh managed. "This can't be good."

"She's okay," Steve reminded him, eyeing the kids to be sure they weren't paying attention. They weren't. David and Caleb were chasing each other in little circles around the guys, and the girls were in their own little penguin world. Dylan, however, was wriggling and whining, begging to join the fun. Josh set him down, and placed both hands on his hips. He glanced up at Big Dan, who was lurking nearby.

Holding out his own phone, Dan strolled over.

"Sorry, gang. This outing's over. Let's go."

Josh ignored the directive. "Why hasn't Jessie texted me or called me herself? Dan?"

"I'm sure she will the second she can, Josh. I trust Matt. She's fine. Let's go."

Charlie spoke next. "This just happened, Josh. I'm guessing there's some urgency to getting her to safety. Matt's got her. Come on, let's take the kids to your place."

"Susanne and Ulysses are on their way, Josh," offered Dan. "They'll have the place secure before we get there. Just in case…" He scooped up a running Dylan as the little boy ran past. "C'mon there, big fella. Let's go."

Momentarily stunned, Josh just stared at him.

Steve shoved him, hard, as he grabbed his youngest son's stroller and whipped it around to face the entrance of the geodesic dome that was Science World. "Josh, kids, come on." His voice was high-pitched, urgent. Passing Josh back his phone, he pulled his own out of a deep pocket. He sent a text to Sophie, asking her and Jane, who thought they were about to enjoy an unencumbered day of church, brunch, and then shopping on Fourth in Kitsilano, to meet them at Josh and Jessie's place.

Forty-five minutes later, everyone was safely assembled in the UBC house. Visions and memories of the abduction of Jessie and the kids had left Josh somewhat immobile, although he had managed to pilot home the Lexus, which he was using to accommodate the kids' car seats. Now, though, he barely made it into the first floor washroom before emptying the contents of his stomach. Emerging afterwards, the fear in his eyes turning them dark and damp, he faced Emily-Grace who, being the intuitive little thing she was, immediately accosted him.

"Why didn't we stay at Science World? I wanted to stay at Science World. You promised we could stay all day. Me and Stella are so mad at you right now."

"Oh, Jesus," Josh answered. All of the kids had been near impossible to wrangle and coerce into car seats. The guys had no choice but to force them and to tune out their vociferous complaints. Josh was not in the mood to stand accused again. Not now, while he was waiting to hear from Jessie. Deciding the only way to put the ki-bosh on what appeared to be the onset of a serious mood, he grasped his daughter's arm and gently urged her towards the stairs leading to the basement media room. "Sit," he demanded.

She did, on the third stair. "Something happened," she said, as the other guys started rooting around for snacks to distract their busy offspring before sending them to the upstairs playroom. "I know it did. Otherwise why would Susanne and Dan and Ulysses and Grampie all be here? Why did we come home? Is Arnie coming too?"

"Arnie's coming over later, I think, if I know this crew. Emily-Grace, you know why you need to have a grown up friend with you at school. And why Dan or Susanne or sometimes Matt or Ulysses, or Arnie, come places with us."

"To keep us safe."

"That's right. So sometimes things get a little crazy in the outside world and it's just better for us to be in our own house where everybody can keep an eye on things."

"What about Momma? Where's Momma?"

"Momma's in France. You know that. We Skyped with her when we got up this morning." His stomach clenching, Josh couldn't help but avert his eyes towards his phone. *Ring, goddamnit. Ring.*

He ached to try calling Jessie, but Emily-Grace needed answers first. And would Jessie even answer?

"I hate all this." With fury and frustration, Emily-Grace threw her well-loved singer-dolly down the stairs. The new penguin stuffie tumbled to oblivion by her right side, forgotten. The small yarn-haired doll that in some ways resembled Jessie with her guitar lay on her back on the floor below them and stared blankly up at the low ceiling.

Josh shivered, and looked back at his daughter.

"I have to tell you, sweetheart, sometimes I hate it too. And so does Momma. But sometimes it's necessary."

"Other kids don't have grown-up friends that follow them everywhere. That go to school with them."

"Stella does, and so does Caleb sometimes, at pre-school."

"Not like with us. Not all the time!" Angry tears threatened as Emily-Grace turned her ankles inwards and crossed her arms.

By now, Josh was starting to panic. His breathing quickened and he felt his stomach threatening to erupt again. "I'm on your side this time, Emily-Grace, trust me. But right now I have to tell you, I'm pretty darn glad Momma and Grammie have Matt with them."

A new terror took hold in the little girl's eyes. "I want to Skype Momma again." The voice was a timorous whisper, the small fingers lost as they tried to twist and twist and twist something that was no longer there. Emily-Grace reached up for a ringlet and started twisting that instead.

"Unbelievable," murmured Josh to himself as he watched her and wondered what it was that had disappeared from Jessie's arms as a child to jump-start the same anxious behavior. Reaching for the small hand, he drew the fingers to his lips and kissed them. "So do I, baby girl. How about you go play with Stella for now, and keep an eye on David, Caleb, Cole and Dylan for us grown-ups, and I will try to get Momma on the computer again. Deal? I'll call you the second I reach her."

The small lips turned downwards. Emily-Grace pulled her hand back from her daddy and folded her arms across her belly. She didn't move. The anger in her eyes flashed up at Josh like a lighthouse beacon on overdrive.

"I need a few minutes to try to reach her, sweetheart. Okay?"

A heavy sigh was the break he needed. He stood, and gently urged his daughter upright as well. "I can hear the kids going upstairs. Why don't you go show Stella the new computer Momma and I put in the playroom? You can play Penguins."

At that, Emily-Grace finally moved, but she went downstairs instead of up. To Josh, the simple movement of retrieving singer-dolly was like reawakening Jessie. *That better be a good sign,* he told himself as Emily-Grace pushed past him and disappeared upstairs.

The timing was right. Suddenly Josh's cell was ringing. The call display read *Jessie.*

Afraid to breathe, he took the call, bypassing everyone and heading quickly out to the much quieter back deck. Pacing, he shoved a finger and thumb against his damp forehead and called her name into the phone.

"Jessie! What the hell—"

She was crying. His heart sinking, Josh dropped to one of their bright summer chaises, not bothering to push a few dried leaves aside as he did so. They crunched under his weight. He trembled, but not from the cold.

"Are you okay? Are you hurt? Is Dee okay, is Matt? Jessie, please tell me."

A few quick sobby inhales later, she told him what she knew. "Everyone's fine, here at least. Not so much at the Olympia. Josh, gunmen opened fire on people waiting in line to see us sing. To see *me* sing!"

"I know, I know," Josh soothed her, wishing to hell he hadn't encouraged her to do the tour. "Twitter…you know…"

"We don't know how many…yet…but they got them, we think. The gunmen." Even saying it was incredulous and unreal.

"Where were you? Were you backstage? You're not still there, are you?"

"No, no, we were on our way there. We were about a kilometer down the road. We didn't hear…we didn't see…" New sobs overtook Jessie's attempt to continue speaking.

"Thank God," whispered Josh. "Thank God."

"We're…back at the airport. Dee's with me, and Matt's talking to the pilot of the jet. He isn't letting us on until there's a full security check."

Letting that sink in, Josh groaned. *Yes, Emily-Grace,* he moaned inwardly, *sometimes I hate this too.* But he had to be strong for his wife. He knew Deirdre would not be any help to Jessie now, or at least not much. This new tragedy was unbelievable and unbearable.

"You'll be fine, little one," Josh told her, sounding more confident than he felt. "Let Matt do his job and just come home."

"I…will…" came a choking sob. "We'll be home as soon as we can get there, Josh."

"I need you to come home," he added remorsefully. "I was crazy to suggest you take that skinny singer's spot in the first place!"

"Are you calling me fat, husband?" The attempt at a joke was weak, but it was something.

Josh caved a little inside, but he was too overcome to take the bait. "Let me get Emily-Grace," he finally suggested. "She needs to hear your voice."

"I need to hear *her* voice," was the quiet response from far away in France.

"I love you."

"Love you back."

When their daughter took the phone, she crawled into a large child-sized playhouse and gathered herself up into a ball before she put the phone to her ear. Josh felt the air move at his side, and looked up to spy Steve watching her.

"Jessie?" he asked.

"Yeah."

"She's okay?"

"Physically, yes. But this will set her back."

A warm hand on his shoulder was Steve's way of acknowledging that the attack on the venue where Jessie was supposed to be playing at this very moment was likely going to set all of them back. But how far?

"Sophie and Jane are here," he said. "Do you want to come down and say hello?"

"Give me a sec," said Josh, his gaze not drifting from his daughter.

"You got it. We'll be going through your refrigerator when you're ready."

A low chuckle emerged from Josh's throat. "Thanks, Steve," he said.

"You got it, buddy."

Emily-Grace wrapped up her call with a sweet, sad smile. Josh heard her say, "I love you too, Momma," before she hung up. After a moment, he crawled into the small playhouse and scrunched up his knees alongside hers, on the opposite side.

She handed him his iPhone.

Then, the tears flowed freely. Emily-Grace crawled into her daddy's arms and buried her fine blonde ringlets in his chest.

Chapter Eleven

A warm body slid next to Josh at dawn the next morning. He was lying on the leather sofa just inside their front room, where he'd sat for most of the night waiting for Jessie to come home. Dan was on security duty; the big Scandinavian was yawning when Ulysses dropped Jessie off at home. Matt had escorted her down the back way and delivered her into Dan's care on the back deck. Arnie was parked in the driveway. Charles wasn't taking any chances. Until they found out who the target was at the Olympia in Paris, he would see that security for the entire Sawyer family was once again on high alert.

"Hey, Dan," Jessie had waved as she advanced towards the big guy, who rose from a chaise as she approached. Gathering her into a big hug, over her shoulder Dan had met Matt's serious eye.

Jessie had turned to hug Matt goodbye before she left the men to discuss the terrifying events of the last many hours, which seemed to have once again spun their lives into a vortex where none of them wanted to go.

"Matt, you sweet, handsome, sexy good friend. I love you to pieces. Now get Ulysses to take you and Dee home. Then go home yourself to Julie and that beautiful teenager of yours."

"I'll be back before noon, Jessie. Don't think of going anywhere, any of you. And for God's sake that means the kids too. There will be no school for Emily-Grace and David until we have some answers."

Saluting him just as a wide yawn almost cracked her jaw in two, Jessie uttered, "Yes, sir, sexy handsome Matt, sir."

But he could see the fear and worry in her eyes, so he didn't chastise her as he usually would for seemingly not taking his wishes seriously. Matt knew damn well Jessie was taking him seriously. She had learned the hard way to listen. And to obey.

Jessie had turned to Dan again. "How was it here today? Ummm, yesterday." She scratched her head. "What day is it? What time is it here?"

"It's almost five a.m., Jessie. Charlie and Steve were here with their families until about six. Charles stayed until Ulysses insisted on driving him home so he could get some sleep, although I bet he fell asleep in his study, in his leather chair, I might add."

"And…Josh?"

A gesture towards the sliding glass door behind Dan was her answer. "He's okay. He needs to see you for real, to know you're okay."

"Ahhh," said Jessie, new moisture forming over her eyes at the sight of her husband curled up on his side on the big couch, a soft white blanket wrapped around him.

Matt allowed a small upturn of his lips at the expression on her face— tender, sweet, genuine deep love. Letting his eyes drift back over to Dan, he saw that the big man was also somewhat awed by the love he saw in the diaphanous blue eyes.

Blushing as she realized she had zoned out in front of her security, Jessie had dipped her eyes to the deck floor and waved behind her at Matt and Dan. One toe in front of the other, she had made her way inside and eased down next to her husband.

Wiping the usual rogue hair away from his cheek and gently urging it to settle behind his ear, she smiled at him as he blinked his eyes open.

"Jessie," he grunted, propping himself up on one elbow. "You're home. Finally."

She tried to answer but couldn't. At the Vancouver airport, she and Matt had quizzed Ulysses on what he had learned about the day's events. Dee had remained silent, the horror too great to bear. Ulysses told them seven people were killed and twelve remained in hospital, nine of those in critical condition. Two gunmen had carried out the carnage on the street as people stood in line to see Jessie and the other artists. One of those who had died was a seven-year-old girl.

Now, Jessie fell apart under the weight of that knowledge. It seemed like her body would rip itself in two, the sobs coming in deep, powerful waves that hurt so much she thought she might actually break. She was home now, in a place that was safe. In a familiar embrace, on a soft leather couch. Josh was the one person she trusted beyond all others to be witness to such great pain. He held her tight to him, his big arms wrapped tightly around her quaking body, his tears commingling with hers, his pain absorbing hers.

From just beyond the sliding door, Matt couldn't help but find himself riveted. Always when Jessie was with Jacob, there had been an extra little wall between them. As desperately as Jacob tried, he could never quite scale it or erase it except, perhaps, with music. When they played together, Jessie and Jacob were always intimately connected in and around each other in a soul-way Matt knew Jacob longed for even in the deep bliss of sleep. But the wall Jessie kept between them never quite disappeared. Sometimes, watching them in the old days, Matt had thought it might. But now, spying helplessly on Jessie and Josh, he was reminded of why it never did.

These two, husband and wife, parents of three gorgeous children, actors and singer, were connected from the day their eyes first locked onto one another. Somehow that day, in the garbage outside Charlie's club, they became one and the same. What was that old Emily Bronte quote? 'Whatever our souls are made of, his and mine are the same.' That was Jessie and Josh. They were always touching one another these days, always parting with longing that said *I wish we would never have to part*. What would they become as their children grew, as they greyed and grew stooped and eventually had to part forever? Dust? Two heavenly united souls?

Matt had no clue. But what he did know now, as he watched his sweet friend give her pain over to the man she loved and cherished above all others, was that he was witness to a love so real that it had to have come from the Divine. And that knowledge, as he swept around on his heel and gestured for Dan to walk him to the flagstone walk at the far end of the deck, was what carried Matt forward as he walked away. For walking away from Jessie was never easy, and was always made worse when the tides of life drew her down into unbearable abysses. She was his charge, his friend, and often his light, as she was to others around her as well. And now, too, her children were light, each their own special little being that adored their mother, that gave off their own lights simply from being around her.

Matt knew Jessie had a spell, hell, he'd always known that right from the first time he looked into those tragic eyes. Was it all her, the spell? Or was it transferred onto her by virtue of her fame? *Well, yes, it's her,* Matt thought. It was her sometimes naïve, hopeful personality, her way of looking at the world without jaundice. The spell was Jessie's essence, the way she processed the many hurts that had come her way, and that often threatened to sink her once and for all. A lot of what made her special came from her music, as well, which took Jessie to the same surreal place it carried others who heard her play, who watched her grieve on stage.

Would someone want to hurt her? Yes, there were those who wanted to hurt her long before Jacob Ryan became famous and got soaked up in the hearts of lovelorn women all over the world. There were many more now, over these past two years, who made no secret on Twitter and Facebook, and in blogs worldwide, that they hated Jessie for hurting Jacob the way she had. *For using him,* their angry words said. For going back to Josh.

Would someone hurt her by going after her fans? Maybe.

Dee's whispered words at the back of the jet while Jessie slept were right. This was going to kill Jessie.

～～～

She surprised them all.

"I'll be okay, babe," Jessie murmured to Josh two days later. "I'm just going downtown. I'm losing my mind holed up in here."

He was on his way out, but was hovering at the back door while he waited for Emily-Grace and David. It was early morning, and Josh was driving them to school before meeting Steve and Charlie at Charlie's parents' place to help wrangle an ornery horse. "I don't want you leaving here, Jessie," he said. "Not until we know more."

"We know what we need to know now, Josh," she countered gently, grabbing the kids' coats from their hooks. "It wasn't about me. It was never about me."

"What makes you think that? Just because some radical militant group claims the attack was about all of the artists involved? That does not preclude you, Jessie."

She took another tack, switching her weight to her other leg as she did, for effect. "If the terrorists wanted to hurt me or any of the others, they would have forced their way backstage."

"They wouldn't have had a chance. They made their point the only way they could have."

"They could have shot me while I was getting out of the car." This was spouted hotly, as bright sparks of anger suddenly rose to the surface of the wounded eyes Josh cherished.

Letting his hand drop from the door, where he was leaning, he made his way back over to her. Taking his wife in his arms, Josh spoke tenderly, wiping a loose strand of hair away from her cheek as he did so. "Jessie, I don't want you thinking stuff like that. Isn't it enough that we've already been scared out of our wits? We're not going to get past this by considering what *might* have happened."

Roughly, she shoved his hand away. "We can't avoid the truth, Josh, that on many levels this attack was definitely a message to me. What was the message? 'You spread pornographic moves and lyrics through music and dance, and therefore contribute to the downfall of the world's youth.' I don't do that. My music is about love! But we both know my past, don't we, Josh? And so, apparently, do these terrorists."

The nerve on Josh's cheek twitched, but he kept his cool. "Their communications were clear, Jessie. The attack was not focused on you. It was planned long before you even joined the tour."

"True, but I'm sure the terrorists were thrilled when they heard I would be part of the Olympia show. If we had listened closely, we probably would have heard them cheering. Just think, 'Oh, Jessie Wheeler's coming, righto, remember those pornographic photos she did? We have our poster child!'"

"Jessie, you're only driving the nails in deeper by thinking that way." Taking a few steps back, Josh let his fingers linger in hers until he had no choice but to let go. "I have to go. Stop thinking bad stuff. Focus on the good."

She threw up her arms. "What good? All those people, Josh! A child Emily-Grace's age! I can't stand it." Blinking, fisting her hands, she stared at him until he stopped moving and simply watched her, his face downcast.

"You know something? Me or the other artists could have been shot, but we weren't. But we still could be."

Gritting his teeth, Josh turned his head. When he locked her in his sight again, he was pale. "Jesus Christ, Jessie," he growled. "You can't be worrying about this. We've got security, so much in fact that it's bloody impossible to try to do anything or go anywhere half the time."

"Would you just listen? That's what I want to tell you, Josh! There's no point in being afraid. Hell, I've been afraid of dying enough times in this singular lifetime of mine that I could hole myself up in fear in a corner for the rest of my life. I'm not going to lie to you, I am scared—I am. But I need to live my life, as I've told you many times before when we've had this very same conversation, and on those grounds I refuse to let the cowardly actions of some hypocritical zealots take my freedom!"

"Those other times, Jess, the targets were—" Biting his tongue, Josh choked back the words.

"I know," she stammered as her eyes brightened and dimmed like a light powered by a fading battery, "don't you think I know, babe? I thank God every day that you and me both are still here. But, Josh—innocent people in Paris died, and more will likely be dead by the time this thing is put to rest. So do I have a right to freedom, you ask? To go out and live my life? Every right. Every right, Josh, to honor these people. Which, by the way, means another trip to Europe. I've already told Charles and Matt. We're leaving as soon as we can get organized, in a day or two."

"No. No way!" Josh's heart sank, along with his hopes for having his wife safely close by for the near future.

"Yes way, babe. Josh, I need to go to the hospitals. I need to see the people who were hurt, to look them in the eye. To meet the families of the people who were killed. That little girl was the age of Emily-Grace! I can't stand it!"

"So you need to do something, I get that, Jessie, I do, because I know how much you care. It's me you're talking to. But baby girl," Josh walked back over to Jessie and placed his hands on her cheeks, forcing her to meet his terrified gaze, "you cannot assuage your guilt about this horrible thing that happened that was, by the way, completely out of your control and, as I said, likely masterminded long before you were ever even involved, by putting yourself back in harm's way! And not just you, by the way. You'll be taking Matt and Charles with you for sure, and maybe even Dan or Susanne."

Apprehensive, Jessie straightened. "Arnie's coming with Matt."

"So what if something happens to them? Matt's already paid a heavy price on the job! Julie will be beside herself. She won't forgive you for this, for taking him back there."

"I need to do this, Josh. I need to go. Everyone's on board. I'm not forcing anyone to come along who doesn't want to."

Dropping his hands, Josh circled angrily. "You're not going. Jessie, this one time I am putting my foot down and saying no. You will not go back to Europe until we both agree that it's a safe option."

"Seriously, Josh. Exactly who do you think you're talking to here?" The blue eyes flashed in quiet furor.

"I know exactly who I am talking to. My wife. My rebellious, stubborn, selfish wife. And I am putting my foot down. You will not set foot on the Keating jet. Or on any other jet, for that matter!"

"I most certainly will. And you, dear husband, will not stop me."

"Jesus fucking Christ. You're out of your goddamned mind."

The impasse was great, and it had no clear resolution that could possibly make both parties happy. Small footsteps behind Jessie made their way to her, so she twisted and bent and hauled her daughter up for a big hug. Emily-Grace was really too old to be carried, but she wrapped her legs around Jessie anyway, laid her head on her mother's shoulder, twisted it partway around, and met her father's furious eyes.

She spoke with a quiet wisdom far beyond her barely seven years. "Daddy, I will go with Momma. I will take care of her and see that she is safe."

At that quiet proclamation, Josh's eyes widened. As his frightened gaze drifted up to Jessie, he shook his head wildly. "No," he whispered. "Just...no."

Quaking with anger, he moved to leave, but Jessie vaulted forward, her daughter in her arms, and grabbed him by his vintage shirt collar. Gathering it quickly into a clump so she had a grip on him, she hauled her husband roughly towards her.

"I love you, you big dork. I love you beyond belief, and so does your daughter. Don't you ever leave this house angry, or without kissing your wife a proper goodbye."

Emily-Grace's seven-year-old giggles and cries of *yuck, gross* were tinkling bells of light after the harsh words tossed between them, and Jessie felt Josh soften as she held him close.

"Please don't go back to Paris," he begged her, his breath warm in her ear as he pulled her as close as he could against his chest with their daughter sandwiched in between. "Please, Jessie. I'll lose my mind."

She didn't answer and, instead, turned his cheek back to her so she could brush her lips along his stubble.

Dan approached outside. "Josh?"

"I'm coming," was the definitely less than thrilled answer. "Emily-Grace?" Josh lifted his daughter out of Jessie's arms and grabbed a delicate arm to tuck into a sleeve of her coat. "Where's your brother? Do you have your lunch?"

David came running for his coat, and Jessie helped him into it. With a final hug and kiss, she handed Josh the kids' backpacks and turned her middle child to face the door.

With a last backward look over his shoulder, Josh, with the two oldest Sawyer kids alongside, strode over the back deck to the flagstone path. Each child had their own bodyguard today, and extra security would be in place at every door to the school, because Josh and Jessie felt the kids needed their 'normal' school routine, yet were desperate for whatever security they could manage, at least for the first little while until things settled somewhat.

Arms crossed, Jessie watched them go, sighing and turning back into the room the instant her family's backs could no longer be seen.

Dylan was playing at Jessie's feet. Matt wandered in and scooped him up. "I hear we're going out today," he said to Jessie as she walked away to start clearing the breakfast dishes. "Can I ask where?"

"The workshops," was her disheartened answer. The verbal sparring with Josh had drained her. Looking up at Matt, who made her smile when he ambled into the kitchen behind her with Dylan hanging over one shoulder, the little boy laughing hysterically in a two-year-old fit of giggles, she added wistfully, "I need this, Matt. I need to get out, to keep moving."

"You should know by now that you can't outrun this thing, Jessie," he told her wisely, finally hoisting Dylan back around to his chest. "Constantly moving is not going to make the anxiety go away."

"I know, Matt. But you know me. I need some music. I need to move my body. I'd just as soon deal with the anxiety without the benefit of pot or booze. So Kayla's workshops seem like a safe bet." Placing a cereal bowl in the dishwasher, she added, "Josh is as pissed as I thought he would be about the Paris trip."

"Can't say I blame him." Matt set Dylan down and passed Jessie a couple of orange juice glasses. She lined them up like soldiers. They sat upside down and dripped onto the plates in the rack below.

"Matt?" Almost pleading, Jessie trained her soft eyes on him. Leaning a hip against the dishwasher door as she closed it, she said, "You know you don't have to come on this trip, right? I would never intentionally put you in harm's way...again."

He was close to her, just a few feet away. Forcing her eyes lower on his body, Jessie took a step towards him and laid a palm against his shoulder, where a bullet meant for her had been absorbed but had exited cleanly, thank God. But...what would the chances be of Matt surviving another bullet?

Gently, Matt bent his left arm up and laid his hand over hers. He couldn't help himself—with the fingers of his right hand, he touched her cheek.

When Jessie met his gentle hazel-grey eyes again, she saw only tenderness and love.

"I'm here for you. Always, Jessie."

She swallowed. "It's your job, Spike. You're paid to be my shadow. But there are lines in the sand you don't have to cross if you don't want to."

Blinking, he removed his hands from her. Regarding Jessie with mutual respect and admiration, Matt allowed a small smile to form on his lips. "My job, is it?"

Ducking her head as a pink flush colored her cheeks, Jessie mumbled, "As if. Matt? You know you're my best friend, right? You're everything to me."

She let her hand fall to her side but he wrapped his fingers around it and gathered her close for a friendly hug.

"Technically, when all is said and done," he ascertained in an attempt at sounding businesslike, and failing miserably since he couldn't keep emotion from leaking into his voice, "I suppose I'm just an employee. But Jessie, I wouldn't dream of you going back to Paris without me. Arnie feels the same way. You are such a gift to us. Your music is a gift. Let us give back, okay? And know that both of us consider it an honor to watch over you."

"Thank you, Matt." Jessie squeezed him tightly, and took a second to bury her face in his neck. Inhaling his familiar spicy aftershave, which commingled with the gel Matt liked to use in his hair, she sniffled. "I don't deserve you. I don't deserve any of you."

"You've got that backwards, Jessie. Just so you know." Releasing her, he beamed and nodded at Dylan, who had opened a drawer and removed almost all of the Sawyer family Tupperware. "Check this out."

Dylan was sitting on his butt, hammering his fists on each upturned plastic container. "Dwums," he announced proudly. "Like Momma has on stage wif her."

"Well, I guess we know what Dylan will be playing when he gets older. Jacob will be crushed." Matt couldn't resist crouching down and playing a few of the drums himself.

Frowning, Jessie crossed her arms. "I'll never find the proper lids to match all of those containers again. Friggin' Tupperware. Come on, Dylan," she ordered. "Let's go see us some real drums, buddy!"

Turning back to the sink, she grabbed a green and white striped dishcloth and wiped it over the countertop on the kitchen island. After rinsing the cloth, she squeezed excess water out of it and hung it around the base of the faucet. Touching Matt's elbow, Jessie brushed her lips against his cheek. Scooping up Dylan, planting a kiss on his soft little boy cheek, she handed him to Matt and strode towards the stairs, so she could run up and brush her teeth, and pack a bag for her son. Five minutes later she emerged back downstairs and waved to Matt.

"Day's getting on, buster. Let's roll."

Following her with Dylan in his arms and a happy light in his eyes, Matt closed and locked the door behind them, and they were off.

Chapter Twelve

*J*ack and Lydia Deacon owned a large estate in Southlands, an exclusive Vancouver neighborhood populated by multi-million dollar homes, many of which were on large acreages to accommodate barns and corrals. Josh's drive out after dropping Emily-Grace and David off at West Point Grey Academy, where he patrolled the school himself to ensure the expensive security he and Jessie paid for was in place, would have been pretty if he could have relaxed enough to enjoy it. It was early December now, and Southlands came second only to the Point Grey neighborhood for foliage cover in Vancouver. In some places, mystical leafy branches even arched across the road.

But twice, as the morning's heated discussion with Jessie played back and forth in his brain, Josh slammed a palm heavily on the steering wheel of the King Ranch, ignoring the gorgeous crisp reds and yellows and greens that almost seemed to be waving in order to get him to notice them. His obstinate wife, her chin raised in defiance and an expression of quiet fortitude settling onto her face, paraded over his retinas again and again in stubborn insistence, as if to say *how dare you challenge me?*

It was fear, Josh knew, that sucked his innards dry when he considered supporting Jessie's wish to fly back to Paris. Fear, that constant enemy that challenged them seemingly endlessly, had come back to haunt them. Everpresent but somewhat pushed aside these last few years, it was accelerating again, stealing their blissful nights and threatening their sanity. Already Josh and Jessie had paid a heavy price for their work. They paid it every day, in fact. The bleak terror earned by their collective past never seemed to leave them; it stuck to Josh and Jessie like honey and sliced bananas stuck to peanut butter.

Now, as he stood by the Deacons' Olympic sized equestrian corral, admiring the array of Arabian horses Jack collected the way ordinary folks collect dogs, cats and hamsters, Josh's brooding silence attracted a hard fist to the left bicep from Steve, who planted a foot on the lowest rail of the quaint split rail fence, and bent his elbows over the top.

"Ouch!" fumed Josh, rubbing his arm. "Was that really necessary?"

"Lighten up, Sawyer." Steve was chewing gum. He blew a thin pink bubble that burst immediately. "We've got a job to do. Whatever little fight you and Jessie had over you wanting sex and her turning you down—again—doesn't have a place in the company of these great beasts. Life is bigger here."

"She doesn't turn me down—ever."

"You're shittin' me."

Josh shoved him sideways. "Sounds like you need to up your game, buddy. And why would she turn this down?" Gesturing to his own body, Josh tried to grin, but Steve knew the undercurrent of Josh's serious mood had nothing to do with sex. He watched as his friend's attempt at jocularity quickly upended itself into a frown.

"What?" he asked, his stomach tightening as he waited for Josh to speak.

Josh settled back against the rail and melted his chin down onto his hands. He stared at the fine horses jogging past. "She's going back to Paris."

"When?"

"ASAP. Soon."

"Whatever the hell for? Did she forget to steal the hand lotion from the hotel?"

In answer, Josh just groaned and buried his forehead.

Ahead of them, the proud Arabians danced by, their manes and tails held high. Sprays of sandy dirt sprouted from their heavy hooves each time they hit the ground; they were physical odes to the Deacons' great wealth every bit as much as the 7000 square foot grey brick Victorian revival abode, in front of which Josh had pulled up in the King Ranch twenty minutes earlier. To get around the house to the corral, he had passed a 12000 square foot barn which held, he knew, at least twenty-five top rate stalls.

Jessie must have loved coming here in her Charlie days, he caught himself thinking. Jack and Lydia were a gracious couple that, despite their great wealth, were always friendly and seemingly down-to-earth. Even now, as Steve rather dazedly settled in next to him at the rail, Josh could see Jack wandering casually past the outdoor pool towards them. Jack was leisurely clad in a herringbone blazer overtop beige slacks—definitely not riding attire. Josh couldn't help but wonder how often Charlie's father rode these beautiful beasts. Had Jessie ever ridden them? Did these magnificent creatures ease her loneliness, which Josh knew was acute in those days? After she met him, but was still with Charlie, did she…think about him as she cantered around the corral?

She might have been thinking about me, Josh thought with a wry half-smile. *But she was riding horses like that one, not these fancy pants animals.* In a corral adjacent to where the Arabians pranced, a wild-maned muscled chestnut galloped alone, stopping and skidding every once in a while to stare back at the men. Its eyes were searching, seeking; even from across the corral Josh could sense the horse's loneliness and confusion. It was new here, which was the reason Charlie had asked Steve and Josh to drop by. The horse had come from a troubled background of abuse and neglect, and a lifetime of riding meant only to collect trophies.

Yep, that's the one Jessie would have picked, Josh decided. Retrieving his iPhone from his jacket pocket, he selected the photo App, and zoomed in and snapped a picture for her.

"Boys," called Jack in greeting as he got closer. Immediately, he tuned into Josh's thoughts. Pointing across the Arabians at the lone corralled chestnut, he said, "Jessie would've had that one eating from her palm. She always went for the ones that were hurting. No interest in the real prize."

"Y-yeah," responded Josh, as his face flushed red. "You still hanging onto that old fantasy, Jack? And you with a new grandbaby on the way?"

"Jessie and Charlie were never quite right for each other, Josh. Charlie liked the Arabians. He still does."

"I'm not sure how Jessie would take that, Jack," stuttered Josh, as Jack winked at Steve.

"Take it any way you like, son. Just take care of what you've got for the rest of us, okay?"

Paris. Jack was referring to Paris. Josh could sense a worried relief in the older man's kind eyes. Jack almost seemed to be challenging him. Josh pointed to the chestnut that, at the moment, was bucking and kicking its fury at being enclosed and stared at. It was almost as if it was quite intentionally sending a message to its newly arrived owner.

"See that beautiful creature?" Josh asked Jack, as Steve leaned closer so he could eavesdrop. "Ain't no one gonna tell it what to do. It's got a mind of its own."

"Just needs a little lovin', that's all, Josh. Delivered with a firm mind and a whispered tenderness."

"Is that all. Just how well do you know Jessie, Jack?"

At that, a wide grin broke out on Jack's wrinkled, handsome, movie star face. "Who says we're talking about Jessie? Last I knew, we were chatting horse talk. Come on. My spoiled son just texted Lydia. He's at Elysian Coffee on West Broadway. He can't go a day without a handcrafted six-dollar drink. It'll take him another half hour to get out here by the time he parks the Porsche and updates his mother on the status of our expected new grandbaby."

As they approached the troubled horse, Josh found himself lost in its gaze. The horse still pranced and bucked a little as the men drew closer, but its snorting and pawing was more contained and, instead of using the entire corral, it stayed in a twelve foot area near the men, who stood a few feet back from the rail and watched it.

"She's just scared," Josh murmured quietly, so as not to frighten the horse further.

Behind his back, Steve and Jack exchanged glances. Was he still talking about Jessie...or the horse?

"What did you say her name is?" Josh asked Jack in a low husky voice as he stepped carefully closer.

"Blue," offered Jack, with a confidence he didn't feel. This horse was on the way out, as far as he was concerned. He'd only taken it in the way he took in Jessie all those years ago, because something 'soul-level sad' compelled him. Even now, he felt guilt at the thought of letting Blue go, but heck, what would be the point of keeping an angry horse he'd never ride? The Arabians were more Jack's style. This one was just a sad orphan.

"Hey there, pretty girl," he heard Josh saying and, if there was ever any question as to why Jessie loved Josh, it was quickly answered now in the tender voice that had the horse pricking its ears forward to listen.

Raising a hand in warning, but a little too late, Jack sucked in a breath as Josh bent to climb through the fence. "Son, don't," he started, but if Josh heard him, he gave no clue. Jack couldn't bring himself to look away, and he wondered why Steve wasn't also calling out to his friend in warning. Instead, Steve was still and silent, and calmly watchful.

Once inside the fence, Josh faced the troubled horse and held his arms, palms up, gently out to the sides. He never lost the horse's gaze. "Blue," he said softly. "That's a really nice name." Standing quietly, his denim jacket open a little, his jeans falling enough over his brown boots so they dragged on the dirt, from the back Josh looked like the cowboy he was at heart, and not the Oscar winning actor at once despised and loved for being someone not everyone understood. Somehow, intuitively, Josh ascertained that this gorgeous wild creature with the white blaze on her forehead and soft, limpid eyes almost covered by an unruly forelock, was also misunderstood.

Holding her gaze, he waited until Blue stopped in front of him before he spoke again. "You just need a friend," he whispered. "You're lonely. You're tired of being used."

Pawing the ground in front of Josh, Blue snorted and tossed her head. It wasn't a nod, per se, but to Steve and Jack, two men who had been around horses all their lives, it seemed like one. The horse took a tentative step forward. She brushed her nose against Josh's chest. Steve and Jack didn't dare breathe. Josh stayed still, but he smiled, sadly and only slightly, as the big animal assessed him. Inside, he felt like crying. The fight with Jessie, the constant worry and fear for the safety of her and their children...the insane madness of Paris...and now, a stunning creature whose frightened, moist, soulful eyes spoke to him...told him...that there was, and always would be, injustice and pain in the world...

It was all too much. He was glad he had his back to the men, because Josh didn't want them to look into his eyes and spy the secrets of his soul. He didn't want them to know how much it hurt to look into eyes as hurting and damaged as his. *I thought I was over all that bullshit,* he found himself thinking. *From two years ago, from before, from my dad's abuse, from the loss of my mom, from the descent into the Black Death before...before Jessie.* Strange, how this soft-nosed beauty in front of him had the power to draw up all the old hurts. It was as if she saw him bucking and kicking and running and crying out just as she had earlier.

"Beautiful girl," Josh managed, his throat crackling from the tension of all the old memories washing over and through him. "I'm so sorry." Slowly then, as the horse bowed her head just the tiniest bit, Josh reached out to her. "Blue," he murmured as she let him touch her nose, then the white blaze; as she let him trail his fingers tenderly through the wild forelock no groom dared even touch. "It's okay now. It's all gonna be okay."

And with that, the horse looked up at Josh once again, meeting his eyes for just a moment before she tossed her head, reared up in what may have been a salute, and trotted off around the corral. Now she, too, appeared proud, holding her head up high and frolicking for the men, for Josh, as if a new trust was born, and the anger was now set aside.

"What the hell was that?" came a surprised voice from behind the three men.

Turning, Josh climbed back through the fence and set his eyes on Charlie, who held out a tray of lukewarm coffees.

"Nothing special," shrugged Steve, as he accepted a beverage. "Just Josh, aka Billy from *Drifters*, doing a little horse-whispering. No biggie."

Clearly, Jack and Charlie were both astounded at what they'd just witnessed—at the already noticeable transformation of the wild horse. Josh studied the toes of his boots, not yet all the way back in the present, soulfully speaking. Part of his soul was still in the corral with Blue, acknowledging all the old demons that it seemed would never go away.

"Just when I think I have you figured out, Sawyer, you do something stupid to remind me what a douche I am." Charlie let a light flicker over his eyes as Josh finally looked up, somewhat surprised at the comment. Changing tack, Charlie gestured to the corral. "Jessie would love this horse."

"I hear she's for sale." Finally feeling a weight leave his shoulders, Josh leaned an elbow on the top rail.

"Who, Jessie or the horse?" laughed Steve, earning a solid punch in the arm from Josh.

"I'll take her," Josh said, angling his head towards Jack. "I hear our family will be spending some time at our ranch, come March. We could use another horse."

"You serious?" asked Jack. "Maybe you just caught her at a good time."

"It was the carrot in your pocket," Steve joked. "Cause it sure as hell wasn't that musky after shave you wear."

"Emily-Grace will love her."

Jack and Charlie instantly recoiled. Steve rolled his eyes.

"Don't you let that beautiful child anywhere near this beast," Jack warned. "Ever. An abused animal like this will always be unpredictable."

"You got that right." Toeing a hole in the dirt, Josh grinned, finally feeling a bit like his better self.

"I'm so confused. Are we talking about Jessie or the horse?" Steve teased, picking up on the earlier conversation.

"Why didn't she come with you today?" Charlie asked, curious. "She'd love watching her cowboy work with this horse."

"Just think of the sex you'd get tonight, Josh," Steve winked, elbowing Josh so that his coffee spilled over the rim. "I bet the spell'd last all week."

"Told you already, buddy," Josh chuckled, "I don't need any special charms. I get sex whenever and wherever," he waved a hand at Steve, "I want."

Charlie frowned. Steve grimaced. Jack laughed and clapped Charlie on the shoulder. "How do you like them bananas, son?"

"My wife's eight months pregnant," answered Charlie. "How do you think I like them?"

"Wherever?" tossed in Steve, trying to sound casual.

Ducking his head, Josh sipped his coffee. Serious again, he caught Charlie's eye and answered his earlier question about Jessie's whereabouts. "She's as stubborn as ever. You think she'd listen to me? Nope. I don't think she should be going anywhere public yet, but Jessie wanted to drop in on Kayla's workshops to see how things were going and, I gather, to do some dancing. I'm hearing they're having a lot of fun down there in your space on Hastings, Jack."

A serious silence came from Jack's corner. He tilted his head and looked up through knitted eyebrows at Josh. "Jessie's going down to the workshops today?"

"Yeah. Why?" Suddenly Josh let the hand with the coffee fall to his side. "Is everything okay down there?"

"She was supposed to be away all week, Josh. Am I right?"

"Yeah, until some diabolical deranged idiots changed her plans for her. Why?" Shifting his feet, he tensed.

Steve and Charlie watched in silence, curious, as Jack worked his mouth for the right words to say. "It's just that Kayla's brought a few guest instructors in this week, Josh."

It hit Josh a full ten seconds before it hit the other two guys. But it was Steve who voiced it.

"Jacob," he announced in a grim voice. "And Talia?"

At Jack's nod, Steve reached over and yanked Josh's cell from his pocket. He held it out to his friend. "Call her. No way is she going to be in the right head space to deal with seeing Jacob and Talia today, Josh."

Staring at his phone, Josh started to punch in his password, but then he stopped and dropped the phone back into his pocket. "Nah," he said, thoughts of the earlier fight with Jessie rampaging through his brain again. "She's bringing Dylan with her. Maybe seeing Jacob will be just what she needs."

The words were greeted with a nervous silence.

"What?" Josh asked. "Jessie's a big girl. And what she needs today is music. Regardless of whatever else she and Jacob mean to each other these days, one thing they will always share is music. But I gotta tell you, I'm gonna kill Kayla for not telling us." He sniffed in the crisp morning air, and wiped his nose. "Come on, boys. Let's get to work."

Depositing the empty coffee cup back in the tray Charlie had set on the ground at their feet, Josh swung around on his heel and ducked back through the fence rails. Blue stopped her dancing and watched him move. Then she stepped lightly over to her new friend, and buried her nose in his chest.

Chapter Thirteen

Forty-five minutes after they left the house, Matt slid his latest shiny Audi into a curbside metered parking spot behind Kayla's pink scooter. Both he and Jessie were silent, and both locked their gazes on the glass door of the Deacon space.

Puzzled, Jessie spoke first. "Matt, did you…?"

"No, Jessie, I didn't. When would I have had time?" Matt gestured behind him to Dylan, who was muttering happily to himself in the car seat behind them. "Your little monster didn't give me a moment's peace."

"Hey! I'm the only one allowed to call my kid a monster. Capiche, Casanova?" Grinning stupidly at her son, who reached out a hand and grabbed Jessie's proffered fingers, she continued. "So why then, are there two uniformed security guys outside the workshop space?"

"I don't know, Jessie, but I think we'll find out before I let you go in there, okay?" Reaching for the ignition, Matt started the vehicle again, planning to drive to La Casa, from where he would contact Jack Deacon, Mandy, or Kayla, whoever answered first. He groaned indignantly when he saw Jessie whip open the passenger side door.

She stuck her head back in. "Matt, I'd think more security would make you happy. Come on, let's go check it out."

Against his protestations, she opened the back door and retrieved her son from the car seat. Together Jessie, Matt and Dylan made their way across the street and into the dance space, to the amazement of the two uniformed security officers they passed by, one of whom spoke into a lapel mic as they entered.

But Jessie's impulsive nature didn't win her the day, this time. Instead, she let Dylan coast gently to the floor when her eyes adjusted to the dim light. Inside, on stage, his back to her as he faced a full back line band lineup, was Jacob.

A loud, "Oh, shit shit shit!" cued everyone to look to the left of the darkened space to spy Kayla with both palms pressing against her mouth. Then they all looked to see where she was staring. Jacob, in his usual lazy slow puppy dog way, was the last to look.

He almost sank to his knees. Relief? Fear? More relief than fear here, today. Because he had heard the news and seen the footage of the desperate carnage outside the historic Olympia. And he, like Josh, needed to see Jessie to know that she was okay.

Although he knew she wasn't. Because, well…he knew her.

His eyes drifted downwards to the small child reaching his arms upward and crying for his mother to pick him back up. But Jessie wasn't moving. The child with Jacob's startling cobalt eyes and waves of curly dark hair pleaded loudly until a set of strong male arms reached down and picked him up—the steady, reliable Matt.

Jessie was too lost in a new chaos to react. This one threw her in a dozen new directions. *Kayla, you lying, conniving bitch; Jacob; Oh shit, is that Talia?; Jacob; How long has he been here? How long is he, um, staying?; Kayla, I'm gonna fucking kill you; Kayla, did you ask him to come because you knew I was supposed to be away this week? Too bad people got killed and I had to come back home!;* Then a quick, remorseful, *Oh that was a shitty thought, where the hell did that come from?;* and then a final, mournful, teary-eyed, *Ja-cob, were you even going to see the kids while you were here? Cause I didn't hear anything about it; Here, in Matt's arms, is your son, remember him? Our love made him. Remember?*

It was a lot to process, but Jessie was saved by Paul who, at a desperate gesture from Mandy, who always, to Kayla's chagrin, seemed to be at her hipster lawyer boyfriend's side when he was present—which was more often than Kayla originally thought he'd be, since he had a day job—started the workshops moving again with a loud call to a good looking long-haired long-faced tattooed guy at the central microphone. Jessie recognized the guy immediately. He had played guitar for her many times, on stage. She groaned when she saw the keys player—Christian. She hadn't needed the band with her in Europe. A back line band was provided on her tour, and besides, she was only supposed to be doing three songs.

She bit her bottom lip and tried not to cry here, in this very public venue. The worst kick was when she spied the drum set on stage and, behind it, a ferocious glare from the silky haired spiteful girl—Casey, was that her name?—who obviously decided to show up at the workshops again because Jessie was supposed to be away.

Matt heard her murmur *Et tu, Brute?* in Kayla's direction as the dancer approached.

"Jessie," Kayla pleaded before she was even twenty feet away, as the participants turned back to the guy at the mic, who seemed to be doing some sort of 'introduction to being on stage' shtick. "Don't be mad."

"Fuck—you."

"Aw, c'mon, Jess! You knew we were having Jacob here at some point!"

Jessie twanged a fake arrow between her sister-in-law's eyes. "Didya think I couldn't handle it, Kayla? Or…no, I get it. It's crystal clear now. Jacob didn't want to see me. Or his kid. That's not really a surprise."

"Jessie, you know he finds it hard to see you. It's not that he doesn't want to, according to Talia, it's just hard for him. He's not all that ready yet."

"Oh, getting to know Talia now, are we?" *Jesus, you Sawyers*, she thought bitterly. *Two major blowouts with two Sawyers in two hours. Lovely start to my day.* "What, did y'all go out for drinks? Easier without little kids in tow, isn't it?"

"Cut Jacob some slack. He's—"

"I don't care what he is. Tell him to grow the fuck up and take some responsibility for his son."

Jacob was approaching now, silently padding up to them on tiptoes despite the pointed black boots he wore that dripped the hems of the usual black jeans overtop.

Matt saw his eyes land on Dylan, but also saw him force them away onto Jessie, so he moved away a little with the child in his arms, to give the two some space. Talia approached Dylan, and smiled sweetly at him.

When Jessie looked over, her furor increased when she saw her country star/crossover rival lift the child into her arms. It hurt worse when Dylan stopped fretting and lovingly looked into the young woman's wise, loving, sparkling jade eyes.

Swallowing back her bitter torment, Jessie faced Jacob head on. "I'm surprised the whole fucking city isn't here. Every goddamned little fan-whore in it."

"Jesus, Jessie, settle down, will ya?" Taking her elbow, Jacob steered his ex gently towards Kayla's office.

For her part, Kayla threw up her hands and let him go, but she and Jacob locked eyes before she did so, and a slight tremor at his bad boy good looks escalated its way up her body before she looked away. "Damn," she muttered before making her way over to Talia, Matt and Dylan as, up front, the workshop participants refocused on their instructor.

Once in the small office, Jacob quietly closed the door and eyed Jessie with a mixture of fear and undisguised worry.

Shivering under his scrutiny, which hurt tenfold because of the hold he would always have over her, Jessie glanced away. With a guttural choked grunt, she grabbed a nearby basket full of cell phones and held it up. Questioning eyes faced Jacob, the basket held aloft at Jessie's side. "She took their phones?"

He shrugged. "No pictures or video. I couldn't care less, but Talia…"

"Yeah, I counted her security. A dozen in here, in total? Coupla strong looking women, too, that's good! Counting the two behemoths out front? Or is that six each…? Guessing the women are on your team."

"She's a…well, a little freaked out over what happened in Paris."

"Aren't we all."

"Damn it, Jessie." Jacob stood on high alert, one hand shoved in his jeans pocket so he wouldn't inadvertently reach out for her, while the other scratched nervously at some nondescript spot beneath his nose. He repeated that maneuver three times before Jessie grabbed his arm and demanded that he stop.

"It's fine," she almost gasped, choking on her words and throwing her arms out to the sides. "I'm fine." Because she knew that was what he wanted from her here, now. She could sense it in his eyes, in the way Jacob bared his soul to her through their haunted, worried windows to his soul.

It seemed the doors were open then, the old thin wall a little thinner. And so Jacob removed his left hand from its hiding place in his pocket, and grabbed Jessie's elbow. He pulled her as close to him as he could, and held her while she trembled and struggled not to lose it.

When she finally pulled away, removing her lips from where they'd landed next to his warm neck under the familiar curls, she whispered her sorrow with her own troubled eyes, and swiped annoyingly at the mist collecting beneath them at the same time. "I'm going back over," she said. "Tomorrow, hopefully. To see the place, you know, to...lay it to rest."

"Are you. Josh must be thrilled."

"You and him can swear at me behind my back while I'm gone, while you're visiting with the kids."

His silence pissed her off, but on no level was it a surprise to Jessie.

"I don't get it, Jacob. You were doing great with them."

"Was I? I haven't got a clue what to talk to Emily-Grace about, or what the hell to feed my own son. Talia and I just need to start fresh."

"With your own kids."

"Hell, yeah." The shoulders, in the old blue plaid shirt Jessie loved on him, which she wondered if he wore just to remember her by because she used to wear it to bed, sank deeply. "Josh is raising Dylan. The kid's got a daddy, despite your husband's less than stellar reputation."

"Oh, babe," Jessie whispered, clearly seeing all the hurts rise to the surface again. "Dylan belongs as much to you as he does to Josh. He's not going away. And if it's any consolation, Emily-Grace is still treating Josh like a leper these days. The kids at school are apparently Jacob Ryan fans. They can't stand me, and they can't stand Josh. And they love to remind her."

"Good."

"Sadist. It makes you happy to know Josh and Emily-Grace are suffering, does it?"

"No. It makes me happy to know you are."

"Fuck—you."

"Fuck you back."

"Damn it!" Jessie dropped into the nearest chair. "You know, Jacob, I've had a real hard coupla days. I kinda just need to somehow turn this day around. I had a huge fight with Josh, I'm super pissed at Kayla, and now you're here to remind me of everything I've done wrong in my life. I wonder if I'm dreaming…" She pinched herself and immediately yelped. "Nope. Not dreaming. Nor am I having a nightmare, although it's the same thing to me anyway." Shoving her legs over the side of the chair, Jessie tilted her head sideways and stared at him.

Jacob was staring right back, but he'd leaned back against the wall now, in his usual Jacob stance with one knee bent and the foot against the wall. Biting the side of his lip, he shoved his hands back in his jeans pockets.

Jessie groaned loudly.

"What?" he asked her, as he shrank into himself and tried not to melt in her presence.

"You fucking kill me," she murmured. "You break my heart, Jacob Ryan."

"Point taken. Glad to be of service." He fidgeted. "Why?"

"Because, doofus. Things were so messed up when we were together. But what was the one thing we did right?"

As if on cue, Dylan's joyful voice rose from out in the main room. His sounds were almost always cheerful.

"He's a really happy little boy," Jessie said softly. "Busy as heck, but he's happy. He knows he came from love."

"Love. Is that what it was? Felt more like pain to me."

"Yeah, well, whatever it was, it made for good songs. Eh?"

"Go fuck yourself." Jacob reached for the door handle, but he couldn't make himself leave. He chewed on an offending lip and turned his head back towards her. "Jessie," he said quietly.

She let her gaze drift back up to him.

He continued. "I'm so fucking glad you're okay. I couldn't have…I couldn't have gone on…without you…"

She swallowed past a bitter new fire in her throat. "Yeah, you would have. You have Talia now, Jacob. And I want you to know I'm glad for that."

"So'm I," he whispered back. "But that doesn't change a thing between you and me."

One of the phones in the basket started ringing, playing some old jazz tune as its ring tone. Jessie, relieved to have a moment to gather her senses, waited until it stopped before she answered Jacob. Her voice came out thin and drained, despite the attempt at sounding hopeful. "Sure it does, babe. Don't you see, Jacob? It changes everything."

A hard knock came at the door. They both jumped and Jessie, who was super on edge anyways these past few days, cursed.

Grateful to have a moment to look away from Jessie, to remind himself that Talia came with a big red bow and not a worn out old armless teddy bear, Jacob nudged open the door with his toe. The blonde twins, Cheyenne and Sharlyne, were standing there.

"We got voted," Sharlyne started, "to ask you all to sing."

"No way are you leaving here without singing. None of you," added Cheyenne. "Talia too."

"Lovely," mouthed Jessie to Jacob when he turned to look at her in a nervous, surreal, questioning sort of way.

From Jacob's perspective, singing with Jessie would be almost like making love with her again. In fact, in some ways, it had often seemed like that was exactly what they were doing on stage when they performed together, so incredible was the high of sharing music and the mic with her.

She knew it. After a moment to process Jacob's feelings on the subject, Jessie's eyes lit up.

"All right then," drawled Jacob to the girls, to their utter delight. "All right."

Chapter Fourteen

"No," stated Jacob, as he stared from the edge of the stage to a frizzy-haired girl slouching in a plastic orange chair below. "The ballad's off limits."

"Wuss," said the girl as above, in her usual spot at Jacob's right, Jessie bit her lip and tucked the fingers of both hands into her back pockets.

Anxious, she glanced over at Jacob, who seemed to be looking anywhere but at her. So Jessie twisted around and caught Christian's eye instead. The suave, stylish master of the keys was still sitting on the straight-backed chair he'd pulled up to the grand piano an hour earlier.

"You pick," she told him. "Pick something upbeat." *No love songs,* she demanded of her soul. *Stay on safe terrain.*

Using her heel to spin back around, Jessie's eyes caught Talia's. The country star was taking it all in, her fiancé and his old flame skitterishly trying to sort out what to sing for this ragtag mop-topped crowd of dancers, but she seemed totally cool with it, which caught Jessie by surprise. Talia was watching the goings-on with an air of easy acceptance it seemed as, nearby, Kayla was vigorously chewing her nails.

"How about *These Blues?*" asked Christian, with a nervous twitch of his butt on the chair as he did so. Being caught by Jessie here with Jacob and Talia was mortifying to him, despite the fact that he often accompanied other artists. Just not…these artists, per se, at least not since Jessie's split with Jacob. He hoped he wouldn't be replaced as Jessie's main keys player.

The song was safe enough. Jessie tossed her curls and fixed her gaze on Jacob, who finally looked her way. "Good?" she asked him, her heart clenching at the sight of her old flame and singing partner standing once again to her left.

132

Lifting his hollow body guitar over his shoulders and settling it into place, Jacob shrugged. "Whatever," he said in an attempt to sound unconcerned, the puppy dog eyes like those of a Bassett hound, sad and forlorn. "I really don't care."

Prick, thought Jessie, as she looked forward and picked out their son amongst the small assembled crowd, which was easy enough to do since only a few folks—including security—were standing at the back, and the only one small and fast moving in the semi-darkness was quite obviously Jacob and Jessie's two year old.

The first strums of Jacob's guitar energized the room immediately. Despite the bad start to her day, Jessie felt her heart lift immediately. Things got better when her voice had company—Jacob's harmonies were a balm for the soul. By mid-song, there was no way the new dancers could stand still. Momentarily, the chairs were shoved aside in favor of room to move, and soon Kayla was leading the fray.

They stuck to safe up-tempo tunes for a good half hour before cries of, "The ballad, the ballad!" started to piss Jacob off. Tearing off his guitar, he shook his head and started to move away, but Jessie's voice stopped him.

"Okay, all right, take it easy, you heathens," she admonished the small audience. "How about we do a different slow song? Not one of ours." She turned to Christian. "*After the Rain*, okay? Jacob?"

At Jacob's noncommittal shrug, Christian led the way into the well-known Blue Rodeo tune with his usual gentle touch and easy dramatic flair. Wiping sweat from their brows, the dancers lined the walls and sprawled in the orange chairs to watch. One of the twins picked up Dylan and started to waltz happily in slow circles.

On stage, the song was transformative to the two hurt souls of the artists performing it. Somewhere mid-point Jacob could no longer ignore Jessie to his right. Slowly, his eyes trailed along the black floor of the stage before drifting up to meet hers. As Christian did some improvisational phrasing, Jessie ran a forefinger along her top and then her bottom lips, following the nervous movement up with a hesitant grin.

The music lifted them up and away. Jacob's heart grew lighter, and he finally offered a gentle smile back.

At the back of the room, Matt and Kayla were standing together now, with Talia in her own little world ten feet away. All three were spellbound at the limitless capacity Jessie and Jacob seemed to have to come together in perfect harmony, no matter how long their onstage absences were, and despite the lack of rehearsal. As expected, their special talent was in mesmerizing their audiences with ballads. This safe Blue Rodeo tune had everyone—including the artists themselves—spellbound.

Casey was watching too, from the far corner between Mandy's office and the craft table, where not a soul noticed her, since everyone's eyes were locked on their unplanned entertainment. "You bitch," she said under her breath to Jessie even though there was no way Jessie could hear her. With fists clenching and unclenching at her sides, she unsuccessfully fought a rising blood pressure as Jacob and Jessie recreated their old magic on the small stage. But she couldn't bring herself to leave. Like everyone else in the room, she was riveted at the glorious sadness of Jessie and Jacob's musical connection.

As the last chords of the tune faded into the dark corners of the big room, Jessie let her fingers drop from the microphone. Crossing the six feet to Jacob, she gave him a gentle squeeze. "Thank you," she whispered, soaking up the green apple scent that, to her, encircled him like a rainbow. "I really needed that today."

Unable to help himself, Jacob hugged back. But he had nothing to say. Instead, he let go, and then moved a finger up to nervously wipe his top lip before removing the guitar from his shoulders. About to set it down, he glanced toward a set of expensive shiny western boots marching up the stairs to the stage.

Talia. He'd almost forgotten she was there.

"How about I do one with you?" she asked, a confident smile lighting her face. Long, sparkly gel polished fingernails wrapped themselves around the neck of Jacob's guitar to stop him from dropping it into its plush velvet case. The overhead stage lights caught the warm flecks in Talia's green eyes. Dimples on her rosebud cheeks, and a comfortable peace she telegraphed to him, passed through Jacob. The tension in his shoulders visibly dissipated.

Lifting the guitar again, he placed it over his shoulders one more time, then sucked on his lip, ducked his head, and pivoted slowly around to face

Jessie, with Talia directly behind and beside him, her graceful fingers proprietarily around his waist. Suddenly he felt a surge of strength in facing Jessie who, he could see by the way she was rubbing sweaty palms against the hips of her jeans, was struggling just the littlest bit to comprehend the unexpected power Talia seemed to have over him, to calm him the way Jessie herself once could.

Talia tossed her blonde bob and smiled at Jessie. "Sing with us," she encouraged generously.

"S'your turn now." Jessie's nervous hand movements stopped as she moved forward. Lightly, she touched Talia's arm as she passed by. Moving to the back of the room, Jessie took a deep breath and watched Jacob move into position next to his fiancée.

"Can't see him playing country," Kayla breathed to her as she sidled up beside Jessie, arms crossed. "This should be good for a laugh."

"She's crossover," Jessie mouthed back to her. Inside, her stomach was churning. The nefarious events of the weekend were still fresh, snipping and biting at her gut like hungry piranha. Watching Jacob sing with the woman she felt rivaled her in many ways was engendering a new anxiety she hadn't expected to have to face today. Matt, always ready, willing and prepared to be the rock she needed, moved to her side. With Kayla on one side and Matt on the other, and Dylan having the time of his life in the arms of one dancer after another, Jessie prepared herself for the usual wrenching pain to slice her in half.

But something unexpected happened. Slowly, as Jacob followed Talia's lead in a rousing country rock anthem that completely re-energized the room after Jacob and Jessie's slow Blue Rodeo tune, her arms stopped squeezing her belly. On stage, Talia was wholeheartedly bringing Jacob into her song by capturing him with her eyes and never letting go; he played the guitar with a grin and a zest that brought everyone's moods up out of the fear and uncertainty of recent despicable world events, and out of the grim circumstances in which most of the assorted runaways and drifters and past drug addicts in the large space had found themselves in the past few years. But mostly, the song, which the pretty Talia sang with a booted foot keeping time and a wide smile beneath an upraised arm, which pumped the air with equal time, lent an infusion of hope to Jessie, who watched the scenario in front of her bring a sincere healing to someone she deeply loved.

Too long the vision in her head of Jacob, when she allowed him to occupy her thoughts, was one from that long ago time when she let him go. The pain in his eyes that night, after the Nadia crisis finally came to a head, had stayed locked in her heart. Her visit to his dressing room at his father's concert, after she and Josh had reconciled, was another bad memory. It was the night she'd told him she was expecting his child—a child that would, for the most part, be raised by her and Josh. *What a kick in the ass,* she knew. *No wonder so many of our fans splintered off and decided they hate me.*

This new vision of Jacob was one Jessie resolved to tuck away in a safe place in her heart. Would it replace the old agony? Nah. Of course not. Jessie kept her pain in her soul; like a sponge absorbing water she soaked it in and let it dry inside her, let it meld into the crevices and bones and skin so that it was always a part of her. Sometimes, when it felt like the outside world was raining bad stuff that tried to get inside her, the sponge got wet again. On those days, at those moments, the old pain seeped right back into Jessie's heart, pumped there by an inability to set it all aside, to let go.

Jacob was now letting his glance land on Dylan who, somewhere about halfway in between where Jessie stood and Jacob played, encouraged by his thrilled dance partners, was throwing back his small head and laughing. The biggest surprise of the day was that Jacob started laughing along with him.

Amazed, Jessie looked wide-eyed over at Matt. Hands easy and relaxed on his hips, Matt's handsome features were glowing in the semi-darkness. Lit by peripheral bleed from the stage lights, a gently acknowledged peace was settling over him. Catching Jessie's surprised glance, he let his eyes land on her, too, and a happy smile formed on his lips. Matt didn't need to speak, but his eyes narrowed playfully, and he gestured towards Dylan and Jacob.

To Kayla's bemusement, Jessie hooked an arm around his and laughed wholeheartedly.

Unobserved in the far corner, Casey's waiflike figure was moving to the beat of this new Jacob. Unable to help herself, bits of the lyrics of the familiar tune made her mouth move, and her experienced wrists casually and rhythmically maneuvered the Vic Firth drumsticks she clutched in each talented hand. In her mind, Jessie's despicable presence was now replaced by this new power couple that were lighting up the stage for all of the assembled hopefuls in the room.

A half hour later, Talia wrapped an arm around her man's waist and gaily bid the group 'so long.'

Before they said their good-byes, Jacob lifted Dylan into his arms.

"He's got the Ryan charm," Jessie murmured to him, holding Dylan's fingers as she did so. Dylan played with Jacob's flannel blue-plaid collar and peered up at him with curious two-year-old innocence. "He's trying to figure out why he feels so connected to you."

"Do you think he's got music in him?" asked Jacob, meeting his own eyes—the smaller, not-yet-tainted-by-the-world version—and wondering how much this child intuitively understood.

"How can he not?" Jessie determined. "Didn't you see him dancing to you and Talia?"

"Hardly," Jacob grinned, a quick light dancing across his eyes. "His feet barely hit the floor."

"There's something about Ryan men," Jessie teased. "Women love to hold them in their arms."

A raw chuckle found its way to Jacob's surface, and he shifted Dylan to his other hip and shifted his wondering gaze from his son to his ex. "I hope you're jealous as hell."

Jessie's genuine laughter lit up the room. "Of course I am. You know I am."

Jacob's voice softened. The baby blues Jessie loved took on a serious tone. "Are you happy, Jessie? Finally?"

She didn't answer right away. Instead, Jessie tucked her thumb into the curve of Dylan's small fingers, and let a slow smile spread across her face. "Y-yeah," she told him, tilting her head to one side. "Deliriously, actually."

"He's a lucky guy."

"He wouldn't have said so this morning."

The next bit was harder to say. Jacob fixed his gaze on Dylan's small belly, scrunched up his eyebrows, and pulled down on the little guy's shirt while he spoke. "Is he a good dad?"

"He plays your music for Dylan when he puts him to bed. He even plays him our ballad. So he knows, you know?"

Surprised, Jacob looked back up to Jessie. The surprise faded quickly though, and was replaced by thoughts he couldn't bring himself to voice. But Jessie knew what he was thinking, the way she felt she always knew what the men close to her were thinking.

"Dylan's here, Jacob, just waiting for you to make time for him. So, for that matter, is Emily-Grace. She's desperate to be with you."

His jaw working, Jacob deflated. "I will," he promised. "After the wedding. This month is a little nuts, with the usual Christmas crap, parties and stuff, and all the planning. You know." He shrugged.

"Okay," she agreed. "But promise me. You can't let Josh have too much influence over him. He'll have Dylan riding horses and on the motocross course when he should be practicing piano." She winked.

"As long as he doesn't play hockey." Jacob juggled Dylan and lifted up one arm so Talia could slide in underneath.

"Not much chance of that," Jessie frowned. "It's hard enough keeping the two older ones in school, much less fitting in Emily-Grace's regular ballet and piano lessons. And we're moving to the ranch in March, for Josh's new series. We may end up having to hire a private dance teacher for Emily-Grace."

"Speaking of the kids," Talia asked happily, "can you bring them to a fitting today, for their wedding outfits? Since we're in the city and all."

"Ummm…sure, I guess. It'd have to be after school, though. The kids get out just after three."

"We figured that." At Jessie's questioning look, Talia beamed and gestured towards Kayla. "Me and Kayla. We booked a designer's place downtown that does fittings for weddings."

"Okay," Jessie answered, a slight nervous tremor to her voice. "Can you text me the address?"

"Sure, I'll get the number from Kayla."

"We might be a few minutes late. David'll be starving and Emily-Grace will want a drink."

"No worries."

"They like stuff from ROAM coffee, up near our house. It's a ways from downtown. So…it'll take us a while. If that's okay."

"It's fine, Jessie. Really. Just come when you can."

"You'll be there, right Jacob? I can't bring Emily-Grace in to see Talia and not tell her you're in the city too."

"Sure you can," he said coolly. "Just tell her Talia is here on a gig."

"Word's gonna get out that you were here."

Talia interjected. "With your permission, Jessie, we'll take the kids for dinner, okay?" Jacob started to protest but Talia placed a slim finger over his lips. As he groaned, she added, "We can take them right from the designer's shop. We'll have them home by six thirty or seven."

"Oh? Oh. Okay. Um…"

"Is there a problem? Does Emily-Grace have ballet or piano?"

"No, she doesn't, not tonight. And that would actually be a help, because tomorrow, um, Paris, you know." Jessie regained her equilibrium. "I'm hoping to be leaving early, if Charles and Dee get things sorted today. But this guy," she nodded at Dylan, "well, he's a handful. And that's his cranky time. I'm not sure you'll want to have both him and Emily-Grace for dinner."

"He's Jacob's son, Jessie," Talia encouraged easily. "We'll be okay. Might be good for him," she teased, as Jacob backed away a little, annoyed. "David too, if he wants to come and if you and Josh are comfortable with him joining us."

"Um…I'll leave that up to David, okay? He likes to have either Momma or Daddy close by."

"Sure. You got it."

With an apprehensive swallow, Jessie eyed Jacob. He frowned back at her, but managed to stem his sudden attack of nerves at having all three young Sawyer children alone with he and Talia for a few hours by steering the conversation in another direction.

"Where are you shooting your new film?" he asked.

"I'm not sure," Jessie said. "Um, Talia, the kids' security will have to go along, okay?" To Jacob she said, "It's looking more and more like Belgium, at the moment." She ran a trembling hand through her large curls.

"Ouch," offered Talia. "Not to the security. We have tons at our disposal. To being so far away."

Jessie's gaze shifted to her. Jacob's woman did have a very agreeable aura. She smiled a little wistfully. "They would prefer Dan and Susanne, or Matt if either Dan or Susanne can't stay on after the school day. They know them, right? Your guys and gals would be, um, a bit scary to little kids."

"Okay. We'll have lots, then. Security."

"Fine. Okay." To Jacob, Jessie added, "I'll only have to be away for about six weeks. It won't be too bad. In the meantime, I've got a wedding to look forward to, right?"

At the awkward pause that followed, Jessie just shoved her thumbs in her pockets and raised and then lowered her shoulders. "Oh. Ah. I see."

Jacob met Talia's reassuring eyes before glancing back over at Jessie. "Just the kids, okay, Jess?"

A hard crunch on her bottom lip bought Jessie some time while she considered what to say. "Jacob," she entreated softly. "Talia...please. I'd like to be at your wedding." As if to express his opinion, Dylan laid his head against Jacob's big shoulder. Without losing Jacob's gaze, Jessie reached out a hand to rub her baby boy's back. "Dylan's saying please too. He wants his momma there. Please."

Talia made a motion to move away and give the old lovers their privacy, but Jacob forcefully grabbed her hand so she couldn't leave. She stared at a crack on the floor.

Jessie turned an ankle over and felt a hot flush rise in her cheeks. Her voice was barely audible. "I know you don't hate me."

His pouty lips parted, but Jacob shook his head. "No," he finally said. "I don't hate you, Jessie. How could I, I still—." At Jessie's shocked expression, he shrugged casually towards Talia. "It's okay, she knows. She knows how I feel...about you. And kudos to Talia, she thinks you and Josh should come to the wedding. But I don't intend to be saying my vows to the woman I'll be spending my life with in the presence of the woman I thought I would be spending my life with."

"Talia," Jessie tried, wanting and needing to set Jacob's feelings against some kind of frame of reference so Talia wouldn't storm out, as Jessie might have, had the situation been reversed. But she stopped when she saw a peaceful acceptance settle over Talia's fresh complexion.

Talia helped her out. "Jessie," she started. "Jacob and I had this talk a long time ago. He tried to piss me off enough to get me to leave, but there's this thing I've learned about loving this man." She leaned forward and clasped Jessie's hand, then whispered conspiratorially, "He doesn't let you in. You have to push your way in there and plant a great big fishhook in his soul to keep him from swimmin' away. Ain't that right?"

"I don't…I don't know, I—"

"I know that wasn't your experience with him, Jessie. The two of you gravitated towards each other like steak to the barbecue." Talia smiled at her redneck metaphor, and Jessie swallowed, but visibly relaxed. Talia continued. "But after you…" She glanced sideways over at Jacob, who stared at his toes and shuffled his boots uncomfortably. "Well, honey, nobody had a chance with him without doing some serious baitin' and fishin.' It was like goin' after a big ole salmon. But now…well, now I think I've got my hook sunk in him pretty deep. And I intend to keep it there. Part of my strategy is in not wasting time lost in the past. I'm focused on growing the future. And I've learned, over the past few years, that the way to do that is to just love this guy. It's that simple."

Mystified, Jessie withdrew her right hand from her pocket and tentatively reached out to touch Jacob's scratchy chin. Slowly, she eased his gaze upwards so he had to look at her. He didn't try to fight her, or pull away.

"Are you happy, Jacob? You look happy with Talia. And why not? You should be. This woman is freaking amazing."

A small smile made its way to the surface, forcing itself through Jacob's cool demeanor. "She *is* amazing," he agreed. "And her new single is stomping all over your latest." Leaning over, he nudged Dylan back into his mother's arms.

"Ah. Since I'm clearly no longer a threat then, why don't you let me come watch you marry this superwoman?"

"Because," Jacob answered, grasping Talia's hand tightly as he started to move away, "I'm starting a new chapter in my life, Jessie. Talia and me are starting a new chapter. As she said, it took us a while to get here, to a place where I could love her back. Where it no longer hurt to breathe. So I don't need the old pain staring me in the face on my wedding day, despite how far

I've come to get past it. To get past you. And personally," he nudged her hard as he passed, "as much as I'm glad you're okay after Paris, I think it's really shitty that you're even asking to come." Just past her, he stopped and turned his head to the right so he could whisper in her ear, "Let me go, Jess. I'll try to do better with the kids. But as far as you go…let me be. It's so much easier when you just let me be."

Unbidden moisture formed in Jessie's eyes then, and she hugged Dylan tight as the child snuggled his arms underneath his belly, and tried to sleep.

Talia pulled her hand away from Jacob's, and he moved on without her.

Trying to recover her senses, her voice choking a little with emotion, Jessie spoke to her. "He's so tired," she said, nodding slightly at Dylan, but Talia got what she was really saying.

She touched Dylan's small cheek. "He sure is," she said softly. Then, looking up at Jessie she added, "It'll get better, Jessie. Things will get easier as time goes on, I swear."

"Wow," Jessie said, raising a hand from under Dylan's butt to wipe away a lone tear. "Didn't you hear about what happened in Paris, Talia? Hanging onto anger just results in explosive violence."

"Oh, honey. Please don't compare what Jacob's feeling to the horrific acts of misguided terrorists."

"Then show me that he's over all that crap that once was *us*."

At that, Talia smiled in her sweet honey-infused way, stepped back, and held her arms open wide. "Here you go, sweetheart." There was no malice in the words. Instead, the gesture was meant to be a reassurance, of sorts, for Jessie's benefit. And it was.

Jessie smiled. "You know what I think, Talia?"

"What, honey?" The country singer was aglow.

"I think you are every bit as amazing as Jacob makes you out to be. And I think he is damn, damn lucky to have you."

The smile evolved into a steady wisdom and peace. Talia placed a palm over her heart. "Don't take this the wrong way, Jessie. But I've fought hard to get him to see past you. And now that he's for the most part on my side, I am happy to tell you that I'm the lucky one."

Talia reached forward and encompassed both Jessie and Dylan in her arms. "Love's worth fighting for, right?" Letting go, she squeezed Jessie's arm as she started to move away. "You might be interested in knowing… I learned that from you. See you at the fitting in a few hours, sweetheart."

A new power took hold that day, and it was called hope. It affected everyone in the Deacon space with its ability to raise spirits through music and love and friendship, and it held true long after the lights went down and the security alarm was set.

On the way back up to the UBC house, Matt gently probed Jessie for her thoughts.

"He'll be okay," she told him, laying a hand over his and smiling. "And for some reason, Matt, that's helping me be okay."

Chapter Fifteen

"She told me I was very brave," Jessie said to Josh as she dried the non-dishwasher safe dinner dishes for him while he washed. "At the designer's." Glancing downwards, she eyed the screen on her iPhone for the umpteenth time. It was clear; there were no new texts from Jacob or Talia about the kids, who were currently at IHOP gobbling sugary pancakes for dinner. "About going back to Paris, I mean." Dropping the towel against her belly, she added, "She's the only one who said that to me. Out of everyone."

"And what does that tell you, Jessie?" Josh peeked over at her, all rosy-cheeked after their pre-dinner lovemaking, which they'd made sure to fit in prior to starting dinner, despite Jessie's need to grab her iPhone on the nightstand the second she started to come down from a delicious orgasm.

"It tells me that she's one helluva woman, that's what it tells me. She understands my need to go. Or maybe she just wants to get rid of me." Guffawing at that, Jessie picked up a pot and absently wiped the towel over it. "She really loves him. And the feeling seems mutual, as far as I can see."

"Not even close to being funny," Josh grimaced, referencing Talia wanting to get rid of Jessie. Swiping a handful of soapsuds, he deposited them on Jessie's nose.

She grabbed his hand and twisted him around so she could plant a tender kiss on his lips. "I'm going up to start packing," she murmured. "Since Charles finally gave me the good-to-go for tomorrow. Or maybe you want to join me in the bedroom? According to Talia's estimate, we have another half hour to ourselves."

"Making up for lost time?" he teased.

"Well, it's either that or answering emails, and I'd just as soon snuggle with People magazine's 'sexiest man of the year' than deal with those."

"That was last year." Josh's cheeks bloomed pink with embarrassment. "Charlie was so pissed."

"Steve was relentless. He still can't let that go."

"Come on. Leave the dishes. Let's go upstairs."

Josh didn't need more encouragement. When, later, they finally dashed downstairs to meet Jacob, Talia, and the kids, both he and Jessie were flushed from a hasty shower.

The children were wired. Susanne and Dan, who felt compelled to stay late on security duty, so strong was their care and concern for the little Sawyers, ushered the two oldest down the flagstone walk to the back doors. Hand in hand, Jacob and Talia took up the rear. Dylan was in Jacob's strong arms, happy as a clam.

Hanging onto a colorful plastic takeaway cup from iHop, with a red lid and a crinkly straw, David rushed towards his father's arms the second he stepped in the door. Josh bent to scoop him up. "What you got there, buddy?"

Jacob shifted an excited Dylan over to Jessie. He was wiggly, so she set him down and he ran off to grab a toy to bring back to show Talia, with who he seemed quite enamored.

Emily-Grace immediately grabbed Jacob's hand and sent her mother a disparaging stare. "I want to stay with Jacob."

Josh, who was only half-listening to David rattle on about his unplanned and exciting adventures, dropped his gaze to her, then darted his confused eyes up to Jacob, who simply stood in place and shrugged.

"You've probably got some homework, Emily-Grace." Jessie reached for her daughter, but the seven year old had her mother's obstinate nature. "It's already late."

"Jacob can help me."

Trying to make light so as to dispel the buildup of pressure in the room, Jessie tossed in, "Jacob doesn't know math. He's a musician, remember?"

"It's not math," came back Emily-Grace, raising her small chin in defiance. "I have to read a story, that's all."

Jessie bent to her. "Sweetheart, Jacob has promised to come get you again soon. But for now, we have homework and bath time ahead of us." It broke her heart to see tears welling up in the small blue eyes.

"Why?" asked Emily-Grace, clinging hard to Jacob's hand. "Why can't I live with Jacob?"

That simple sentence, spoken in front of everyone present, had the power to crack Josh's heart in two at the same time Jacob's swelled arrogantly. Josh couldn't force his eyes away from Emily-Grace. He hid in the comfort of his four-year-old's small arms until David wiggled down to join his brother.

Emily-Grace looked away from her mother and up at her hurt and bewildered daddy. "I want Jacob."

"Okay," Josh nodded, his throat choking with emotion as the rest of the room went silent. Even Dylan and David seemed to be watching closely to see where this standoff would go. "If it's okay with Jacob. Go."

"What?" Jessie was aghast. "No. Sweetheart, Daddy's just joking."

The small shoulders were shaking now as Emily-Grace leaned into Jacob and laid her cheek against his fingers. She held her daddy's gaze.

Pleading with Jacob, Jessie stood and reached for her. Emily-Grace cried out and pulled away.

"Jacob," Jessie begged, "please. Give us a hand here."

Relenting, Jacob finally bent to Emily-Grace.

She had to force her eyes away from Josh. Many years later, as an adult, she would still remember the pain she caused him on this day.

"Emily-Grace, this is your home," Jacob said. "I promise you we will spend lots of time together right after the wedding, okay? You and me and Dylan, and maybe even David if he's up for it."

"Tonight," she insisted stubbornly. "You and me can go to Science World tomorrow."

"I have to work tomorrow, pretty girl," he told her. "With your Auntie Kayla, remember?"

"I can dance. I can come and help."

"I know you can, kiddo. In fact, I'm sure you're a way better dancer than most of Kayla's crew, but for now you need to go to school."

"Please, Jacob. Please." The small face leaned in to his, forehead to forehead.

146

Emily-Grace was always Jacob's weakness. He had nothing to add, nothing to say, which would ease whatever old hurts this child clung to.

Finally, Josh could stand it no longer. Striding forward, he caught her off guard, grabbed her around the waist, and twisted her around so he could carry her away from Jacob. Her screaming trailed loudly behind her all the way up the stairs, behind Josh's heavy footsteps, which moved quickly up the stairs and stopped at the door to Emily-Grace's room. Still screaming, she started pounding on the door that her father closed behind her, wailing on it with all the might her small fists could muster, as Josh held tightly onto the knob so she couldn't escape.

Downstairs, a white-faced Jessie faced Jacob, feet a hip's distance apart, her body shaking.

"He won't hurt her, will he?" Jacob whispered, as Talia tried to direct the young boys into playing cars on the floor while Dan and Susanne tip-toed quietly outside.

"No," Jessie answered softly, trying to block out her daughter's screaming and praying that Josh, too, wasn't silently crying. Yet…she knew he was, on the inside. She could picture him standing there, one big hand on the door-knob, and hurt pouring over and through him like bitter cold Vancouver rain in winter. Jessie could feel his pain, and it was acute.

To Jacob's credit, he didn't rub it in. "What is it about him that she can't stand?"

"It's not…that's not it," Jessie attempted wildly. "She loves him like crazy, Jacob. Didn't you see the way she was looking at him, daring him to save her? It's all the old shit, that's all. Most of her earliest memories are about him. About aching for him when he wasn't available, both when we were missing, and then when he was so…lost."

"She's terrified," Jacob murmured, "of losing him again."

"Yeah. Only now it's not just him, babe. It's you too."

An *Oh, God* moment passed over Jacob then. His lips parted and he nodded, just slightly. Upstairs, the agony continued, unbelievably becoming louder and louder as the futility and frustration of a little girl's pain escalated.

Jacob's eyes went from dark to light and then to dark again. He swiped the back of his hand over his mouth and licked his lips. "C'mon, Talia," he ordered. "Let's get the hell out of here."

"Jacob…" Jessie begged. "Please. Don't shut her out. She needs you."

"Does she?" Locking his eyes into Jessie's, Jacob was not immune to the heartsick confusion he spotted there. "I don't need her, Jess. Not like that, not anymore. I need a new life, one that I've fought hard for. Tell Emily-Grace I'll see her at La Casa for the Boxing Day shindig, and then at the wedding. After that…I dunno…if it's going to be like this every time, I just don't know. Okay?"

Mouthing a silent *I'm so sorry* to Jessie, Talia got up and crossed the room to Jacob. Taking his hand, she started to lead him outdoors, but he turned back to Jessie as he moved. "Your world is as fucked up as ever, huh Jessie? Why the hell doesn't that surprise me?"

"Fuck, you can be cruel, Jacob," Jessie countered, balling up her fists. "Seriously?"

"Just tellin' it like it is," he said, still unable to turn away from her. "The agony of Paris will suit you just fine."

A gasp from Talia stirred Jessie into action. She gave him a shove, and he threw his arms up in capitulation and started backing away. Jacob's last sight of her as he slapped the doorframe on his way out was his old gal licking her lips and stubbornly wiping tears away.

"You fucking bastard," Jessie breathed to his back, wanting to pull him close and comfort him, and at the same time wanting to slap him.

Dan and Susanne were waiting close by. Susanne stepped back into the room and waved a teary Jessie upstairs. "Go," she insisted. "Me and the big guy will keep an eye on these two. They need to burn off some sugar before bed anyway."

Nodding her thanks, Jessie pivoted around slowly and made her way to the stairs, Jacob's hard, angry stare sneaking into a dusty corner of her mind to hide as Josh's bent head came into view.

Letting go of the door handle to his daughter's room, Josh turned away from Jessie and, without a word, brushed by her into the room where they'd twice made love earlier in the day.

Sensing freedom, Emily-Grace threw open the door and tried to dash by her mother, but Jessie was quick. Grabbing her daughter around the waist, she lifted the thin, writhing body and carried her into the pretty pink bedroom she and Josh had decorated for her for her sixth birthday just over a year ago.

"Emily-Grace, this has to stop," Jessie said, plunking down on the bed and forcing her daughter down onto her lap. "I know you're confused. I know it hurts to see Jacob go, but it hurts Daddy so much when you talk to him that way. He loves you so much, baby."

The small body shook as Emily-Grace cried. "I want to go with Jacob, Momma. I know you're not taking me when you go away again. I just want to go stay with Jacob."

"Why not Daddy, honey?" The small body was still shaking, but Emily-Grace's hiccupping slowed. She wrapped her arms around her mother. "Why don't you want to stay with Daddy? Because of the kids at school?"

"It's not just the kids at school, Momma." Emily-Grace struggled to get a grip, to explain to her mother why it hurt so much to be a Sawyer child who *remembered*. Finally, she said what she felt. "It's everyone. It's the teachers, it's the big kids, and it's all the people who were staring at us kids at the restaurant tonight. When Susanne took me to the bathroom, a lady tried to take my picture. She asked Susanne why us Sawyer kids were having dinner with Jacob and Talia. She thought maybe Daddy was messed up again, she said. Is it true, Momma? Is Daddy messed up again?"

"Oh, baby," Jessie said, dissolving into fresh tears, and holding her daughter tight. "Why did you have to grow up so fast, huh? Do you even know what that means? Messed up?"

"It means Daddy can't take care of us. That's what it means. He drinks beer and goes to sleep and doesn't wake up. And you are going away again, and you are not taking me and David and Dylan. I'm scared, Momma. I'm so scared!"

Resolving to have a chat with Susanne the second she got the opportunity, to get to the bottom of the curious woman in the IHOP restroom, Jessie rocked her daughter back and forth.

"Sweetheart," she breathed into the blonde ringlets, "Daddy is just fine. He was sick for a little while, and yes that made it hard for him to take care of us, but he is just fine now. He takes very good care of all of us, and he is trying so hard to stay fine. You know all those meetings he goes to, in the nights, the ones Arnie goes to with him?"

"Y-yes…"

"Well, Daddy goes to those meetings because they help him stay well. I help him stay well and Arnie helps him stay well, and so do Steve and Charlie. And Grammie and Grampie do too. We all love Daddy so we all watch out for him."

"But Momma…" The little blue eyes pleaded with her mother to listen, to understand, to put her fears to rest. "What if Daddy gets messy again while you are away?"

Unable to resist a tiny smile at the term 'messy,' Jessie brushed back wet strands of hair from her daughter's cheeks. She used her thumbs to wipe away the tears, and then reached in the small beaded pink bag her daughter had worn over one shoulder to the restaurant. Pulling out an iPhone, she held it up to her daughter.

"If you are ever worried about Daddy again, ever, sweetheart, you call me if you can, or call Grammie or Grampie or Steve or Arnie or Matt or Charlie or Dan and Susanne. Or FaceTime any of us. You see, sweetheart? You are not alone. If I am away, there are so many people who love you who you can call. Jacob and Talia, too."

Wrinkling her nose, she scrolled through the contacts. "Let me take your phone now, and I'll make sure you're up to date with everybody's numbers, okay honey? But also," she leaned nose to nose to her daughter, "you need to know that us Sawyers never listen to random crazy people at restaurants. And why don't we listen to them?"

"Because yours and Daddy's works make people curious and sometimes they have no idea what they are talking about."

"That's right. So, for tonight, you need to have a bath, and your brothers need to come off their sugar high and have baths, and you need to call Jacob and tell him thank you for dinner, and tell him you love him and will see him soon. And then you need to give your daddy a great big hug and tell him you love him. He needs that, honey, from you. Tonight. And you and me need to trust that Daddy is doing just fine staying well, and that he will stay well."

"No more messed up."

"No more messed up." *Please God,* begged Jessie. *Please.*

Once the kids were finally sorted and in their beds, even Emily-Grace snoring peacefully, Jessie tiptoed into hers and Josh's room. Prepared to settle into a quiet discussion about their daughter and what set her off that night, she stopped suddenly at the doorframe. Then, moving quickly into the room, her heart racing, she grabbed Josh's wrist.

"What are you doing?" she asked him. "Why are you packing?" Fear criss-crossed her suddenly pale face. *You can't leave.*

"I'm going with you," he said. "In the morning." A set of tidy gym socks was tossed into the open duffel on the bed.

Slightly relieved, Jessie countered. *Thank God.* "Oh no you're not." Hastily, she grabbed the socks and a handful of T-shirts and threw them on the bed.

"Yes, Jessie, I am," Josh insisted. "Emily-Grace needs a few days without her daddy to cool off. I've already texted Charlie about the meeting tomor-row and set things up with Carlotta to watch the kids, Dylan during the day and David and Emily-Grace when they're not in school. I talked to Ulysses about security. I'm going with you."

He grabbed the socks and T-shirts and threw them back into the bag.

Gripping his left forearm, Jessie whipped her husband around to face her.

At the fear in her eyes, Josh respected that she had something to say, and he cocked his head to listen, his shaving kit dangling at the end of his right hand. But he was wary. His eyes were dark and the nerve on his cheek was pulsing.

"No. No," she told him, almost dancing with nervous energy. Placing a palm against his cheek, her eyes welled up. "If something hap…if something happens, Josh…" The rest of the thought remained unspoken.

"Jesus Christ, Jessie." But Josh knew what she was telling him. The kids. They would need one parent. Drifting backwards, Josh dropped onto the bed and stared at the leather bag containing his shaving essentials. "She doesn't even want me."

"She wants you. She just keeps getting mixed messages from the nosy and ill-informed public." Taking the shaving kit from Josh's hands, Jessie laid it next to her stuffed tiger, which was courageously guarding the pillows. Sitting next to her husband, she wrapped her fingers around his. "I'm just going for a few days. This might be good for you and Emily-Grace, since my visit was cut short in the first place. She needs to see her daddy the way he really is, instead of the way people tell her you are."

"Do you know what they're saying on the news, Jessie? They're saying two planes on their way to Paris were diverted to Halifax today because of bomb threats. I don't want you going at all. But since you seem to be your usual stubborn self, I really want to go with you. I want to be there by your side."

"I'll be okay, Josh. No lie, it's going to suck. But I'll be okay, I swear. And you'll be fine without me."

"I am never fine without you, little one. You know that."

"I do. I know it." A sweet smile lit up her cheeks then, accompanied by a pretty pink blush. "Look what you do to me," Jessie murmured. "I'm all mush now."

"I couldn't stand it…if I lost you. For good."

"Same. Babe…" The piece of hair Jessie loved to tuck behind his ear fell forward as Josh bent his forehead towards her. Jessie lifted her left hand and grasped it between her fingers. She tucked it solidly in place as Josh's eyes slowly opened. "I love you so much. I'll be back, okay? I'm not planning to shuffle off this mortal coil just yet."

"Is anyone ever planning it?"

Leaning into him, Jessie brushed her lips over her husband's. "Don't let Emily-Grace get to you. Just love her, okay Josh? The more she fights you, the more you just love her. Unconditionally. Remember who the parent is here, and who the child is. Remember what she's been through, and how confusing the world of celebrity is for all of us, never mind for the kids of celebrities. So don't try to fight her, and don't let her hurt you. Just love her. She'll come around. I know she will."

"Jess? How did you get so wise?"

"Easy," she laughed quietly. "I have a lot of love around me. It makes it easy to see the world that way, infused with love, you know?" Taking his hand and planting her lips against Josh's knuckles, Jessie had one last thing to say. "There's enough hate in the world, Josh. There's enough violence, there's enough hurt, and there's enough pain. We need to change our own little corners with love."

"You do more than change your own corner, little one. Your songs change the world."

"And that, beautiful man of mine, is why I am going to Paris."

"Ah. I see."

"But before I go…" Standing, Jessie stood and pulled her sweater over her head. Grinning seductively, she crooked a finger and urged him forward. Chuckling, Josh stood and stepped towards her.

"You are insatiable, sweet girl," he told her. "Steve and Charlie totally didn't believe me when I told them you never turn me down for sex."

"You told them that? Eewww! Like our sex life is any of their business. And it's not true. We have three small children, remember? Those little people that run around and exhaust us all day long, and often end up in our bed by morning?"

"I take it Charlie got turned down a few times." Planting soft kisses on her cheek and neck, Josh could feel Jessie almost purring. A slow Thomas Rhett country ballad was playing on low volume in the background, a perfect backdrop to the lilting waltz steps Jessie initiated, while her husband's arms snaked sensuously around her neck.

"No, actually, there were no little people around then." Giggling, Jessie tilted her head back and let Josh's lips make their way to the base of her neck. At that comment, he stopped, though, and she could feel his gentle laughter tickle the top of her chest. "Charlie didn't have any complaints. But, Josh," Jessie pushed him gently away from her so she could meet his eyes, "he only got half of me. You've got my soul."

He melted. "Always and forever," he breathed. "Come home from Paris safe and sound, little one. Please."

The buoyant moments were now once again encased in a serious light. A lump settled in Jessie's throat and so she simply nodded until she felt she could speak. "You take care of our babies. I'll be home, you'll see."

The unspoken reminder of a past that had almost sunk them engendered a new level of need into their lovemaking. It lasted just long enough for Josh and Jessie to soak briefly in the afterglow before there were young feet at the door, a small body in bed, and lunches for tomorrow to be made. As usual with a young family, reality made its way back into the Sawyer household fairly quickly. Outside, as the moon rose higher in the sky, a light snow tickled the back deck and rested on the long-covered pool.

"Three times today," Jessie teased, as her fingers eased out of Josh's when she left the bedroom to start the lunches. "Must be some kind of new record for couples with young kids."

"If you count the orgasms, you're easily at six or seven."

"I thought it was closer to ten or eleven."

She kissed the knuckles one last time, but didn't leave immediately. The small body that had wandered into their room was their daughter's and, as Jessie closed the door gently behind her, the image she was left with took her breath away.

Josh, lifting the little girl up so he could push back the covers and place her carefully underneath, then touching her cheek and whispering that he loved her...

Emily-Grace, singer-dolly tucked under one arm, slightly guarded, sleepily watching him as he tucked the covers up underneath her chin...

Then a sad smile and fingers grasping her father's hand, pulling it close, so she could hug it.

"I love you back, Daddy."

Jessie wasn't surprised that it took Josh some time to gather his wits and join her downstairs after he left Emily-Grace to doze off in a room where she felt safe.

"I'm glad," she murmured to him when he appeared at the kitchen island. "I'm so glad."

His happy glow stayed with her all evening, infusing the night's usual activities with sunshine and roses.

"I must be the luckiest woman alive," she caught herself thinking when Emily-Grace was removed back to her own bed, and Jessie drifted off to sleep. The many lonely nights of the past faded off into oblivion as, with one set of fingers tucked under Josh's T-shirt sleeve, Jessie slept, her slumber filled with peace and wonder.

Chapter Sixteen

"Okay, we're starting today in push-up, or plank position, arms straight, legs about a yoga mat wide," instructed Kayla, scratching an itch on her chin before straightening a baggy graffitied tank she had pulled over a black sports bra that morning. Bounding easily down to the floor, she demonstrated the pose for the twenty dancers and musicians gathered in the Deacon space which, dimly lit as usual, was now emitting a festive green and red aura from lights strung around the perimeter of the walls and stage.

Resting on one arm, almost in a side plank so she could talk to the dancers, Kayla caught Casey's eye. She spoke directly to her. "You missed a lot, Casey, but this stuff's a breeze. Pay attention. One, right leg comes under and stretches out to the left side like so," she demonstrated, "then two, left leg bends and comes towards the right knee, tucking into the crook of it like this." A quick move, and Kayla was leaning a little to her right, on her right arm, both legs in place to the left.

Female laughter alerted her to a spot just behind Casey, who stood watching five feet to Kayla's left with both arms crossed and sneakered feet planted widely apart.

"Mandy," mouthed Kayla under her breath as she reset and demonstrated the move a few more times. "I really gotta talk to her about distracting the class."

Just beyond the group of dancers, Mandy moved slightly towards the front window of the space, her high black leather boots smacking the wooden floor like firecrackers as she moved. Jack's assistant was on the phone, as Kayla often found her of late. With no music playing during this demonstration part of the workshop session, it was easy to tell that the gorgeous woman was enjoying a flirtatious conversation with someone. *Jack?* thought Kayla suspiciously. *Sure as hell hope not. Likely some exotic, rich boyfriend.* Immediately she chided herself for her nosy thoughts, pulled at her blue-tinged blonde ponytail, and refocused.

"Next step," she spoke to the group, "right leg to right hand, so kind of backwards like you are doing the crab. Don't keep your heel on the ground, when doing footwork you want the ball of the foot on the floor instead. Now, left leg shoots out to the front, parallel to the floor, then shift your balance to cross it in front of your right ankle, weight shared between your feet and arms straight to the floor on your left, like this…" A quick movement, and Kayla was in place. "The last moves in this bit go like this. Right leg back, left leg back, almost like that plank we started with. So, all together it looks like this."

Counting, Kayla moved at a slow pace to demonstrate the overall sequence, then repeated the moves quicker and quicker each time so the youth could easily break it down.

"On your own now, go," she ordered, standing and once again rearranging her tank top over her hips and leggings. As she did so, the door opened and Jacob wandered in, casually slouching as always, minus Talia and the usual dozen uniformed security.

"Sharlyne, Cheyenne, supervise please." Kayla detoured to the Plexiglas enclosed sound booth at the back, selected some tunes, and slid up the volume with a smirk on her face as Mandy sent her a withering look, stuck a finger in an ear, and locked herself in her office to continue her iPhone flirting.

"Hey," Jacob said in greeting, watching the door slam behind Mandy before redirecting his gaze to a deliciously smug Kayla in the sound booth. "Someone didn't get their morning coffee today?"

"Hey, Jacob. I could give a shit whether Mandy's had her coffee or not, but I sure as hell wish she'd leave the phone sex to her home love nest. She's driving me crazy, pulling focus from my dancers. It's hard enough to keep this group on task."

"Gotcha. Now that I know what pulling focus means."

"You blow my mind, Jacob Ryan," Kayla blushed. "You've been on stage for years now, you did how many seasons of *Mystic Nights*, and I dunno how many films? And yesterday during the 'how to command the stage shit' you didn't know what pulling focus meant."

"I knew it, I just didn't know it had a name."

"And that's why you get the big bucks." She beamed adorably and pulled again at her ponytail, this time yanking out the elastic and roughly repositioning it. "Speaking of the big bucks…no entourage today?"

"Nope. Talia took 'em with her. Vamoose. Gonzo."

"Back to Nashville?"

"Sure as hell not to Paris." Toeing the floor with his boot, Jacob leaned against the door and let his gaze drift back up to Kayla. "Jessie get away this morning?"

"Yeah, yeah, she left at six, Josh said." Leaning on the back of a nearby chair, Kayla regarded him closely. "Do I detect disappointment in those soulful baby blues of yours?"

A shrug was his response. Shifting his weight to the other foot and inhaling deeply before looking back at Kayla, Jacob puffed up his cheeks, and then slowly let the air escape his lungs.

"She'll be okay, Jacob."

"I know," he said too quickly. "She always comes out okay."

"Jessie's a survivor, all right. She's got Matt with her. And Arnie. Those guys would die before they let anything happen to her."

Contemplating the stark truth of that—of how Matt had already proven his commitment to Jessie—Jacob sucked in a little air and tried to breathe.

When the blue eyes flickered back up to Kayla, she had to grasp the top of the chair to keep from melting. This guy's aura was strong enough at the best of times; put him on stage with a guitar or laden him with worry over a woman he cared deeply for, and his 'just love me' energy made him irresistible.

Kayla swept the three feet over to Jacob and briskly offered an embrace that she hoped wouldn't come off as too intimate. The green apple scent encircling him struck her funny. It gave Jacob a down-to-earth homey air that made him positively huggable. "Come with me," she commanded with a happy smile. Backing off and exerting a little pressure on one hand before brushing by him, her face embarrassingly flushed, Kayla let her hand slip up to his elbow. "When in doubt, dance it out," she challenged.

"I am not a dancer, Kayla. Look at me." Following her at first, then gesturing to his tight black jeans and expensive stiff boots, Jacob stopped mid-step.

Kayla turned around and let her gaze wander appraisingly up his body, from the sexy toes right on up, halting for a second at the shiny belt buckle before eyeing his tight navy T-shirt and usual denim jacket.

"Oh, I'm lookin' at you," she teased, placing her hands on her hips and stepping back, putting most of her weight on one foot. "God, what the hell was Jessie thinking? My doofus brother over…this?"

A crestfallen look washed over Jacob's face.

"Oops. Oh shit, Jacob, I'm sorry. Once again Kayla sticks her stupid foot in it." Moving towards him again, she grasped the bottom of his jacket. Giving it a moderate tug, she tried more emphatically to convince him to dance his worries away. "Come on, Jacob. I mean it. It's going to be a tough enough day on all of us, worrying about Jessie's brazen stupidity. The girls and guys here are learning a new B boyz footwork sequence. It's super simple. Come have some fun."

An outstretched free hand encouraged him. Accepting it, Jacob let Kayla lead him to the group of dancers laughing and carrying on nearby. The only one who seemed to be seriously working, who had the steps doggedly nailed, was Casey. The teen peeked up from behind cascading hair to let her focus land on Jacob.

Acknowledging her with a nervous smile, Jacob allowed Kayla's good-natured ribbing to relax him as the group's cheers and jeers welcomed him.

From her office, Mandy saw the interaction. She spoke into her phone with more than a little gossipy verve, then disconnected and selected her photo App. A few quick steps and she was at the door, which she flung open and shoved out of her way so she could zoom in on Jacob and Kayla's entwined fingers.

"Thanks, Kayla," she huffed. "Call us square." Closing the App, Mandy *harrumphed* in a decidedly unfeminine way and stole back behind closed doors.

On the workshop floor, Casey quickly became the focus of attention when a thump near Kayla's feet attracted her firm gaze.

"What the hell?" asked Kayla, grabbing the girl's phone from where it landed on the floor. Holding it up, she faced her. "You know the rules, Casey. No phones while Jacob's here. You're supposed to put this in the basket in my office the second you arrive."

Embarrassed eyes flicked over to Jacob, but Casey enlisted her defenses immediately. Puffing up her chest, she glared at Kayla. "I know he's leavin' today. I just want one picture."

Jacob started to speak but Kayla stuck a hand out to the side and grimly air-palmed him. "If you had been here at the top of day one with Jacob you would know that he agreed to let us take pics at the end of today. Nothing can hit the Internet before he is safely out of here. You know this because you signed a non-disclosure confidentiality agreement when you signed up for this program. We won't get any work done if throngs of women invade our space."

Embarrassed, Casey shuffled her feet and avoided Jacob's searching eyes.

"Look, I don't mean to be a bitch about this, Casey," Kayla softened, as snickers behind her rankled up her spine. "But we have rules that need to be followed. They've been set for a reason. In this case I think you would agree that Jacob's safety is important."

"He don't have no security with him. I don't think he gives a shit about his safety today."

Jacob stepped in. Kayla didn't notice his approach until his warm fingers sizzled against hers as he released her grip on Casey's phone.

Good Lord, she caught herself thinking, as she looked over at him and got lost in his gentle gaze. *Thank God he's going home tonight.* Sheer electricity shot from his fingers to hers, up her arm and down the entire left side of her body. Unable to look away, Kayla swallowed, and wondered if Jacob was feeling the same damn crackling that was completely disarming her. She grabbed at her frizzy, loose, blue-tipped blonde ponytail and nervously yanked at it as Jacob lightly touched her back and faced Casey.

"You're right, Casey. Sometimes I just duck my head and move around below the radar. It's easy when Talia's not around. She's the one who attracts the most attention. And today I have to admit I'm a helluva lot more worried about someone else's safety than either Talia's or mine. So maybe I was a bit careless coming here without security today. But the thing is…" He tapped her phone against his thigh, as both she and Kayla melted, "I trust you guys.

All of you. And I am more than happy to stick around for photos at the end of the day. We're getting pizza, right?" Twisting his head back around, he directed his steady gaze towards Kayla, who was staring at a black scuff-mark on the floor. "Kayla?"

"Huh? What?" *Jesus, those eyes.*

His voice was dusky. "We're getting pizza later?" Jacob watched her for an extra moment before he chuckled lightly and turned away, which only elicited a slightly strangled grunt of embarrassment and dismay from Kayla.

"Yeah," she managed. "Pizza. Tons of it. Vegetarian, Mediterranean, and otherwise." Grimacing, she pivoted around on one heel and gestured to her workshop participants. "Come on. We've got work to do. Let's beat those Christmas calories before we eat 'em."

As they got back to work, Jacob let the phone slip back into Casey's outstretched hand. "I'll make sure you get the first picture," he smiled warmly. "Okay?"

A slow grin spread across the young girl's high cheekbones and elegant nose. "Okay." Drumming her fingers nervously against the phone, she slid past Jacob and made her way to Kayla's office. Dropping the phone in the basket, Casey sent herself an inward rainbow of hope. Having someone like Jacob Ryan on her side was really something. She prayed she would have a chance to play the drums for him later in the day before he slipped out of Vancouver—and out of her life—forever.

⌒～⌒

That evening, full of pizza and a confused sorrow at Jacob's parting in late afternoon, Kayla climbed into Paul's jeep so they could head up to nearby Cypress Mountain for an evening ski. With Jessie off on her nerve-wracking adventure, and a giddy sensation clouding Kayla's brain and floating over her soul, Kayla, despite the exhausting physical dancing and overall workshop mental fatigue, needed an outlet to expend a growing anxiety and... sense of loss.

Get it together, Sawyer, she chided herself as she slid into the jeep. *Even if he wasn't happily engaged, Jacob is Jessie's ex and a thorn in my brother's side. And then there's Paul...*

Glancing to her left as Paul eased the vehicle over the Lion's Gate Bridge while he hummed along to a Tim McGraw tune on the radio, she couldn't help but laugh. "You're such a conundrum," she said, waving an arm towards the dashboard. "You're a hipster lawyer who has learned a lot of street dance B boyz moves over the past few months, yet you're listening to country music. Talia must have left quite the impression."

"She's got some great tunes, Kayla."

"Some great moves on stage, you mean," joked Kayla. "Anchored by hot cowboy boots."

"Gazillions of people seem to agree."

"She's a flash in the pan. Jessie'll nip her star dusted little blonde head in the bud real quick the second Charles releases her next Grammy worthy single. Speaking of which, the last tune Jessie and Jacob released from their old album is still this year's biggest hit."

Raised eyebrows aimed themselves at Kayla. "Someone not too impressed with Jacob's main squeeze?"

"Nah. I mean no, I…Ah, forget it. Just drive." Settling back against the seat, Kayla crossed an ankle over a knee and pushed thoughts of Jacob away. Brightly lit shops greeted them as they passed, slower than they would have preferred, since the jeep was stuck in dinnertime traffic.

"Rough day?" Paul leaned an elbow on the window and nudged his usual fedora down over his locks as he grunted in frustration at the gridlock in front of them.

"It was fine," Kayla huffed.

"I can tell," Paul intuited. But the thick traffic wasn't helping him relax either. He bent forward, leaned over the wheel, and fixed his gaze on the top of Cypress Mountain. "They've got more base now than they had all season last year," he told her.

Kayla looked up at the sparkly snow-capped mountain and wished they could just bypass all this traffic and morph up there. Her eyes dropped to her boyfriend's hands, which were fidgety as they white-knuckled the steering wheel. *What the hell,* she thought, a tiny alarm bell ringing in her body. "Did you have a rough day?"

"Me? No," answered Paul rather quickly, studiously avoiding her stare as he did so. "Sorry I couldn't be there with you today."

"Yeah, no worries." Kayla's words were careful, deliberate. "I'm not surprised that the workshops started to bore you."

"No, it's not that, Kay, I just…Things were piling up at work, that's all. I had to play catch-up."

"Did you."

The tone was clear. There was a nasty undercurrent to Kayla's words.

Paul took the high road. He knew that if he didn't, their fantastical evening of slick, smooth coasting down Cypress, still a new adventure this early in the season, would be more like a descent into hard-edged jags and cracks.

"All right," he said amiably as the fuzzy line of red lights finally started edging forward. "We're moving now. Have you checked on Jessie? What are her plans for Paris tomorrow?"

Jessie. Jacob. Sighing, Kayla sat up straighter in the jeep and tried to focus. "She's fine, I guess. I haven't heard that she isn't—she's not, like, trending on Twitter or anything. It's the middle of the night there, so I'm sure her highness is all snuggled into some hotel watching porn."

"That time of the month already, is it?" So much for trying to salvage their evening. Paul gritted his teeth. "Need me to drop out of this interminably never-ending line-up to grab you some chocolate?"

"Take a chill pill, Paul." Kayla picked at a hole in her leggings, cursing it as she stuck a finger right through to her thigh. "Damn." To Paul she said, "I'm sorry. I'm just wound up today. I need to hit that hill." She added that last bit almost as an afterthought, as if the cozy nighttime lights of the Cypress ski area had the power to eradicate the weird ache in her soul at Jacob's departure that day.

Her man switched tactics. "Did he invite us to the wedding?"

Her head snapping suddenly around to scrutinize Paul, Kayla reached for words. "What? Who?"

"Jacob." Paul's eyes narrowed. "Who the hell else?"

"No! No, of course not. It's a private affair."

Thankfully, Kayla didn't notice the sweat break out on her man's brow at that remark. But the remainder of the trip up Cypress was a silent one. In the parking lot, Kayla pulled out her phone to see if there were any messages.

Her heart leapt when she spotted a note from Jacob. She turned away from Paul to read it.

Thanks for everything. I had a great day. But I'm never doing B boyz moves again. Ouch.

Kayla shoved the phone back in her pocket without answering, then moved to assist Paul with their skis, hoping he wouldn't notice the red blush that lit up her cheeks like a Christmas tree.

Later, at home, rosy-cheeked after tons of perfect snow slicked rides down some decent black diamond runs, Kayla locked herself in the bathroom and sent back a few carefully edited words.

Thanks for hanging out with us, it was a blast. Re: B boyz wear baggy jeans next time, I recall u used to wear those a lot in the old days

Cringing after she sent it, because Kayla had erased and rewritten the text a number of times, she sat on the toilet fully dressed and buried her head in her hands. *All right, this is just a celebrity crush. Leave me be, Jacob Ryan. Everybody gets crushes. No biggie.*

Resolving to do better by Paul, Kayla brushed her teeth and dragged her 'fresh-air weary' body to the bed. His back to her on the opposite side, Paul was sitting, waiting for her. Wordlessly, he twisted around and showed her his phone.

"What?" Kayla asked, taking it from him as she slid under the covers. Curious, her heart rate picked up as she fluffed the pillows up behind her back and bent over the phone. *Is it Jessie? Did something happen in Paris?*

But the picture on the screen, which Paul had scrolled to by virtue of Twitter, was of Kayla and Jacob at the workshops. Granted, the picture was a little fuzzy, but it was clearly the two of them. Fingers wrapped up in each other, they were radiant.

After a moment to rationalize what she was seeing, Kayla tossed her hair and threw the phone onto Paul's side of the bed. "Mandy," she seethed. "What a bitch she's turned out to be. Surprise, surprise."

Paul was still sitting with his back to her. He recoiled when Kayla touched him.

"What? Paul, I led Jacob over to the dancers because he was unsure about doing the B boyz stuff. He needed a little encouragement, that's all that is.

It's nothing. I mean, I wish! He's a rock star and I'm bad boy Josh Sawyer's baby sister. As if."

Finally, Paul stood and faced Kayla. "I guess I should have been there today after all, huh?"

"We worked our asses off, Paul. The only one flirting, besides my love struck troupe of the downtrodden but hopeful, was Mandy, who barely put her phone down all day. She took that picture because she was pissed at me for amping the sound up while she was having phone sex. Now if you don't mind, I'm tired. I need sleep."

Kayla grabbed the pillow sham behind her head, heaved it onto the floor, rolled over onto her left side, and flicked off the small pink Ikea lamp on her nightstand. It was a full five minutes before Paul joined her. They tossed and turned in uncomfortable silence until the sandman took over and urged them both into a confused, almost sleepless night.

Chapter Seventeen

*S*tartled out of a vivid dream, Josh woke suddenly at five thirty to a dim darkness and a jumble of small arms and legs. As his vision adjusted, his sleepy eyes at first took in the abstract corners of the room while his mind was still on the dream, which made the objects bats and bugs and snakes instead of comfy jeans and hoodies.

Shuddering as he moved a small arm aside, Josh slid off the bed.

A sudden noise had awoken him, but it wasn't the usual childish snuffling or fervent 'Daddy, I have to pee' voice. Instead, it was an incoming Facebook Messenger chime.

"Jessie," thought Josh, more fully awake now as he grabbed the phone. He stopped in his tracks at the sight of all three children cuddled up on the bed, cheeks a healthy pink and hair tangly and perfect.

Unable to suppress a grin at the sweet sight, sighing at the perfect bliss of his three sleeping babies safe in his and Jessie's bed, Josh finally turned to the small screen. The message wasn't from Jessie, though, it was from Charlie. It read *get ur ass to the hospital a new son is born, bring the kids.* A second chime came in as a wide smile lit up Josh's sleepy liquid chocolate eyes. It was a Twitter link sent to him also courtesy of Charlie. *Guess who is healing the world again. God, I love our girl.*

His heart in his throat, Josh sucked in a breath before clicking on the link. #JessieWheeler was trending at number one on Twitter. #Imagine was second, #HealParis was third.

Josh's gruff voice broke the early morning silence. "What have you done now, little one?" A video started to play. It was Jessie, all right, finger picking on the replacement Gibson guitar Jacob had bought her in a vintage New York music shop. She was standing outside the Olympia, Josh asserted, based on the assembled weepy folks captured in the video and on the glaring title of the Twitter link. And she was playing John Lennon's *Imagine*.

Josh let the video play as warm tears filled his eyes and trickled down his stubbly cheeks. The volume was on low so as not to wake the children, but Josh didn't need to hear the lyrics anyway. He'd heard them a thousand times at Jessie's shows. Since the abduction of her and the two older children a few years ago, this song was a staple at most of her concerts. So instead of listening outright, Josh absorbed Jessie's essence—her voice, her sad eyes, the way she stood with her feet slightly parted, one old dusty brown boot marking time. There was a beatific peace about her as she sang in the place where people died less than a week earlier. It glowed around her like snow around the sun, vague and diaphanous but oh so real all the same.

As she strummed the last few chords, Jessie did what she always did after playing a song straight from her soul. She peeked up at the silently weeping crowd around her, some of them a mere unobstructed three feet away, and nodded a quiet *Thank you*. Josh noticed one thing different about his wife this time, though. There was a wetness on her cheeks and a drained, seriously fatigued crumple to her shoulders. But there was hope in Jessie's tired eyes, and there was light.

The video continued for another few seconds until Jessie lifted her guitar off her body and handed it to Matt, who was on hyper-alert nearby. Josh saw Matt pass the Gibson off to Charles, and he was grateful for that small move, because Matt moved forward with Jessie then and sheltered her with his body—with Arnie flanking her on the opposite side—while she accepted grateful hugs and tears from a crowd whose spoken language she could barely understand, and certainly couldn't speak, but for whom the universal language of music spoke loud and clear.

The video was shot hours earlier. Josh took a chance and punched in Jessie's number. When she picked up, Josh padded softly out of the bedroom in bare feet and boxers topped by a white T-shirt, pulled the door almost closed behind him, and sat on the stairs.

"Hey, little one," he said, still feeling the powerful, buoyant glow from the healing light given off by his often troubled wife.

"Josh. Hey, you're up early, babe."

"Charlie and Jane had their baby. Charlie just messaged me."

"Oh, that's really great! How wonderful! A boy, right? So they'll be calling him Lucas, Jane said?"

"Yep, a new cowboy for good old Jack to spoil."

"Just what we need. Another spoiled Deacon male. He's good? Healthy and all that?"

"I haven't talked to Charlie yet, but the message sounded fine. He asked me to bring the kids over to meet the little guy."

A quiet hum of background traffic noise filled the empty space. Then, from Jessie, "Are you okay, babe? You must be tired. You sound beat."

"I'm good," Josh answered, with a bleary rub to the eyes courtesy of a thumb and forefinger. "I saw a video of you outside the Olympia."

"Umm. *Imagine*. That song does me in every time."

"Yeah. Me too." A heavy sigh made its way to Jessie. "Jessie, I'm so sorry. I owe you an apology. I was selfish."

"And scared, Josh. It's okay, I get it."

"You realize what you've done today?"

"Yep. According to some bloggers and news type folks I just did a massive publicity stunt. But I don't care what anyone thinks. Josh, the people here…there were so many tears. But there was also healing."

For you too, I hope, Josh thought. He added, "I expect there are a lot of folks who see it that way, Jess."

"I just did what I had to do, Josh. You know me. I had to follow my heart here, y'know?"

"I know, baby girl. But…"

"But what?"

"But now will you come home?"

Her laugh warmed his heart. "Of course. One more night. I have another hospital to visit and then we're meeting one of Charles and Dee's good friends for dinner. But I'm okay, Josh. It's better now, you know? The ache?"

"I know," Josh murmured as David climbed onto his lap and snuggled in. "One of your babies is awake," he told her. "Or should I say half awake."

"David, huh?"

"You know your babies."

"He's our earliest morning boy. Tell him Momma loves him."

"You tell him," Josh smiled, and put the phone against David's ear.

A slight upturn to the pinched little lips was his reward. "Momma," was all the tired little boy could manage, though.

"You know he always takes a while to wake up, Josh." Josh could hear the smile in the faraway voice. "Carry him around with you for a bit and then he'll be good to go."

"Are you in the hotel now?" Josh asked carefully so as not to sound over protective.

"No, um, the car actually. Everyone's here and they all say hi. We're pulling into the hospital. Can I call you in a bit?"

"Yeah, sure. Emily-Grace will want to talk to you when she wakes up. I think I'll just run the kids back through IHOP for breakfast. Two meals in a week from there won't hurt them, will it?"

"Don't you dare! There's lots of fruit and yogurt—Oh, you dork, you're joking. Okay. All right. I'm on to you. Dork."

"No sugary pancakes for Jessie Wheeler-Sawyer's babies."

"And not too much coffee for their daddy today, or your belly will protest. Drink tea."

"I like the hard stuff, Jess. Sorry."

"Arnie's giving me the evil eye. I think he overheard that. So before I tell him about our conversation I will assume you mean drip coffee."

Josh's hearty laughter filled Jessie with joy. Memories of the bad days swooped off with the Paris breeze.

They signed off with promises for a call later in the day, and Josh set down the phone and pulled his longish-haired middle child close.

Not too far away, in the leafy Dunbar neighborhood, Kayla, too, woke early. She did what she always did first thing in the morning, and checked Facebook, email and Twitter. She found herself sitting on the closed toilet lid for the second time in less than six hours, overwhelmed and in tears, when she got up the guts to click on Jessie's name in Twitter, and watched the video.

"Thank you, Jessie," she breathed. "Thank you."

Farther away, in Nashville, Jacob and Talia slept until a quarter to ten. In their grand four-poster bed, Jacob tucked Talia under his arm and flicked on the remote. He caught an American lifestyle newscast and turned up the volume. After ten minutes, the top of the hour news came on. All of a sudden he was faced with a clip of Jessie outside the Olympia, playing John Lennon's lyrical wish for world peace.

"Leave it to Jessie," he chuckled lightly as Talia snuggled in tighter. "Sometimes I think I know her. And sometimes I don't know her at all."

Incredulous, Talia added, "She has guts. I give her that."

"Listen, Tal. Catch this."

Jacob pointed the remote at the big screen and cranked up the sound. The announcer wrapped up the piece about Jessie by saying, "Although some are calling this a publicity stunt, there are many others who are quick to say the other artists scheduled to play the night of the Olympia attacks are safe at home. It took bravery and courage for Jessie Wheeler to do what she did, and for that, we are proud to call her ours."

"Goofballs. She's Canadian," grinned Jacob.

"She's amazing," replied Talia.

"She's crazy." After a thoughtful moment, Jacob flicked off the TV. "Hungry?"

"Always, big boy."

Hearty giggles floated out from under the burgundy and gold-threaded duvet covering the large bed. Needless to say, Jacob and Talia were late for a noon meeting with the wedding planner.

Two days later, Josh held Dylan close to his heart while David and Emily-Grace ran jubilantly across the tarmac into their mother's arms as Jessie descended safely from the Keating jet. That night, as the world healed around them, and as folks prepared for the peaceful Christmas season, stars lit up the Pacific sky, and it seemed the clouds were far behind the little Sawyer family once again.

Chapter Eighteen

"We have a rule," Jessie was saying to Talia as the women sipped Baileys and coffee at La Casa after Deirdre's Boxing Day extravaganza dinner, which was growing larger each year as families expanded. Watching Josh and Jacob horse around with the kids, Jessie and Talia were seated on a full sized couch Charles had purchased for the playroom. Charlie, Steve, and their families were there too, but Charlie was wandering in and out of the room, scratching his whiskers and trying to stay awake, since his new son was only a few weeks old. Jane had Lucas upstairs at the moment, where she was breastfeeding and changing him. He was the darling of La Casa this year, and Charlie and Jane's firstborn, Stella, along with Emily-Grace, were beside themselves, following his little carry-bed wherever it landed and trying to get him to wrap his little fingers around theirs.

A lovely hum echoed through the cozy Spanish style villa. It was the sound of happiness and contentment. Even Jacob seemed at peace, and why not? His wedding to Talia was less than a week away. The pain in his belly was less acute than usual while in the presence of the 'perfect' Sawyer family. Josh was more than happy to let Jacob bond with their shared son, and Jacob felt like life was starting anew. Soon he and Talia would have more children to bring to this annual get together, to this gathering of people who, together, were one big family.

Jessie took a sip of her warm, soothing drink and continued voicing her earlier thought to Talia, who was quickly becoming a kind and trusted friend. "The rule is that in the interest of not spoiling our children more than they are already spoiled," she raised an eyebrow and pointed her mug towards

Charles, who had just wandered in with a Christmas tin full of Carlotta's sugar cookies for the kids, which the older children had helped decorate earlier in the week, "we stick to a few main gifts each. A toy they asked for, a surprise toy we choose, an outfit or two each, a book or two, and a type of candy they like. They get lots of other gifts too from family and stuff, so believe me they are well spoiled anyway."

She smiled as David dropped a plastic teacup in her lap, and continued.

"We also help each of the kids choose a charity, and they spend time learning about the charity and how they can help. Josh and I make donations to those charities on behalf of the kids. I got a huge kick out of Emily-Grace this year. Her choice was to help Kayla with her workshops. Anything dance oriented, she loves! To Emily-Grace, Kayla's a goddess. But myself and Jack—Charlie's dad—have funded the workshops in entirety and the spring tour is also taken care of, so Emily-Grace and I talked it over and decided to go shopping. We bought stuff for the participants. Dance clothes, workout clothes, casual stuff like jeans and sweaters, winter boots and coats, and a nice outfit they can wear to a Christmas party or to church. We also gave them each $200 gift cards for groceries. The best part was that Emily-Grace and I did the work ourselves. So she helped pick out the clothes and she and I, and Dee, Carlotta and Susanne, oh and Matt's Julie too, had a wrapping party last week. We took everything down to Kayla and Mandy, who distributed the whole kit 'n caboodle to the gang."

"It's a little bit ridiculous, isn't it? The money?" Talia was shy but curious as to how Jessie dealt with her extreme wealth. "It's a lot. I know you give a lot away. And I was surprised, I admit, to see where you and Josh live. You're just like anybody else."

"Well, we are and we're not, I guess. I mean, we love the house but as the kids get older we might consider moving. Maybe over here closer to Charles and Dee, I don't know. I suppose that might depend on schools. And we'd have a hard time giving up our fave coffee shop, ROAM, which is close by. But what do we really need, Talia? Any of us? Money just messes people up."

She shifted in her seat so that she sat taller. "There's this one girl at the workshops. Casey. Remember her? The prodigy drummer? She was without a home for a while but now she's working towards getting her shit together, like the others. She has a room downtown and she's finally attending the workshops regularly. But she has this huge chip on her shoulder. I don't know if it's the aboriginal card or what, and if it is, fine, she's absolutely beautiful when she lets herself be seen from underneath all her layers of fear and anger and shame or whatever, and I totally get why some First Nations women, at least the ones who end up on the streets, feel they have to try harder to belong, to fit in. I don't mean to be stereotypical, but let's be honest. Many of the girls on Vancouver's Downtown Eastside have had tough upbringings. But this girl, Casey, somehow she found her way into music, and she's incredibly talented. As you know, she's got rhythm, but she's also got a single-minded focus and work ethic that has put her at the top of the class despite missing the whole first month. So anyways, Kayla told me yesterday that Casey wouldn't accept our Christmas gifts. Reason being? She hates my guts. Why does she hate my guts? Because I have what she maybe wants, I guess. Money and a life she thinks is glamorous. And because of Jacob, I think. Because I went back to Josh."

"I'm glad you did. But that's just me." Talia's green eyes danced a little beneath the serious tone of the conversation.

"Thanks, Talia. Really." Jessie laughed lightly, and tilted her head to study Talia for a moment. The country artist's blonde hair had just been trimmed and styled for the round of Christmas parties, and the woman was alight with the joy of her upcoming nuptials. "You're glowing," Jessie smiled. "I wish Casey could see you now. You and Jacob both. Maybe she would cut me some slack. You're so good for him, Talia. I mean that. He's crazy in love with you."

"It's a little weird talking to you about him." A slow, bashful smile pinked up the dimpled rosebud cheeks. "Since you and he…you know."

"Ah. Yes. The man is everything his fans think he is, isn't he, Talia? He can work the bedroom."

Talia buried her face behind her mug. "I'm so not having this conversation." Looking up, she grinned. "But how about that Celtic cross inked across his back, huh?"

"Uh, yeah, about that. All right, we need to talk about something else." Quickly feeling her face grow hot, Jessie laughed outright.

Dylan chose that moment to climb onto his momma's lap and lean his dark curls against her chest. Jessie frowned and touched the back of her hand to his forehead. "You okay, big fella? Are you just tired? Ready for bed after this crazy day?" Glancing down the room, she wasn't surprised to see both Josh and Jacob watching her.

Hands on his hips, Jacob cocked his head and peeked from underneath his long lashes at Josh in order to get a reading on how he should respond.

Catching the vibe, Josh gestured to him. "Go ahead, Jacob, if you want. Dee's got a room upstairs pimped out for the kids. Dylan likes to be rocked. His favorite pajamas are in his bag. His is the one with—"

"Winnie-the-Pooh. I know." Hesitating, Jacob eyed Talia nervously before he let his gaze drift sideways to Jessie, who had set down her coffee cup and was cuddling her youngest against her. "I don't know if he'll come with me if you guys are here," he finally said, which sliced Jessie's heart in two.

Biting her lip, Jessie caught Josh's eye and then, seeing the love and support she knew she would find in those solemn chocolate eyes, she looked over at Talia. "Do you want to try?" she asked her, a solemnity and respect in the query that both Talia and Jacob were grateful for.

But Talia was wise as well as sweet. "I think he wants his momma right now," she smiled, and lightly touched Dylan's back.

Slightly relieved, because she sensed that Dylan was finding the noise and gaiety a tad overwhelming, according to his clinginess and the half-crying whines he was currently emitting against her chest, Jessie agreed. "Okay." Standing, she faced the boys and fixed her gaze on Jacob. "C'mon. This little guy likes to be sung to as he falls asleep."

Moving towards the hallway, Jessie let her hand fall to her husband's stomach as she passed. Slightly apprehensive, she looked up at him, anxious to read the cues in the steady gaze she loved, but willing herself to understand if this was awkward for Josh. It was apparent Jacob felt the same way, a mite confused, because he remained still for the moment.

Josh did have to blink away the spark of jealousy that streaked across his eyes, but Jessie was the only one to see it, and he swallowed and reached inside for the strength she sent across their invisible wire into his soul. Laying a hand over hers on his stomach, and then touching Dylan's limp curls with the other hand, he leaned forward and kissed his son goodnight. "Sleep well, little buddy," he said, before moving his hand to the back of his wife's head and brushing his lips firmly against her forehead as well.

Stepping out of the way, Josh watched as Jacob left the room with Jessie and Dylan. Charles walked them out, munching on an angel cookie as he left, and the playroom melted into a peaceful silence as a few of the other children, also just about ready for sleep, played quietly.

Talia shifted on the couch, and set her empty mug down next to Jessie's. Josh wandered over.

"Okay, I'll say it," he said as he dropped down next to her. "It's a little awkward."

"You and Jessie are wonderful parents." A wistful aura surrounded Talia. "I hope Jacob and I can manage to keep your children in our lives. Our schedule over the last two years has been exhausting."

"I don't see you slowing down anytime soon, Talia," Josh said honestly. "But we'll do what we can to accommodate the two of you. Dylan needs to know Jacob."

"Jacob needs to know Dylan."

"Do you and Jessie have the travel plans sorted out for the wedding?" Josh asked.

"Yes, we're good. Matt and Susanne are bringing Emily-Grace and Dylan. Julie and Katy are coming along too. And of course Charles and Deirdre will be there, but they're travelling earlier. You know those two—managing Jacob's career isn't going to grind to a halt for his wedding."

Conspiratorially leaning forward, Talia added in a low murmur, "I can't wait to see my mother and Deirdre together for the first time. They're both society socialites. They'll either kill each other or be best friends by the end of the reception. Of course I'm hoping for the latter, but the first option would no doubt be the most entertaining."

"You seem way too relaxed considering it's only a few days before one of Nashville's biggest weddings, Talia."

"I think one of the country's, actually, although my mother gets the credit." She winked, then sobered. "I really wish Jacob would give in and let you and Jessie come."

"It's all good, Talia. We'll spoil David rotten and enjoy some quiet time before Jessie has to fly to Belgium for her shoot. Although you know we'll be there in spirit, right?"

"Still. He's a stubborn old coot sometimes."

"Nah. He's just human. Although the stubborn part really makes me wonder how he and my obstinate wife managed to stay together for as long as they did."

Leaning forward, Josh rested his elbows on his knees to study a book David brought him. After a moment, he picked his older son up and settled him on his knee so David could show him a colorful array of teddy bears parading across the pages.

"They'll always love each other, won't they?" Talia asked softly.

"It's better than hating each other," Josh replied with a smile.

"I wonder how things are going upstairs…"

Flipping the page of David's book, Josh considered what to say. He went with, "Don't overthink it. Overthinking those two will drive you crazy. Trust me."

"Been there, huh?"

"You don't want to know. Although I suppose maybe you already do."

"Some, but not all. Apart from a few good chats, I've had to come to terms with the fact that Jacob's not really into sharing that part of his life with me. Although I think I've gotten pretty good at reading between the lines."

Hand in hand, Emily-Grace and Stella wandered into the playroom. The little girls stepped over and around toys to get to Josh and Talia.

"Daddy," Emily-Grace started, leaning on Josh's knees and annoying David enough for Josh to shift him to his other knee, "me and Stella wrote a song. Can we sing it for you?"

"I think my heart is full," Josh murmured to Talia after he said an emotional *yes* to the daughter that, these days, was learning the hard way about the cruelties of the world outside their door. Discovering things about his turbulent past, in fact, that Josh knew she was struggling to reconcile with the father she was trying to love. To Emily-Grace he said, "You're a mini-momma. You know that?"

"I'm not gonna sing for work, Daddy. This is just for fun." Stella was already gathering up what they would need to sing their song—a plastic pink microphone and stand, and a small plastic guitar. "I'm gonna dance when I'm big," Emily-Grace added. "Like Auntie Kayla."

But Josh doubted she could put the music aside as she grew and became immersed deeper into the harsh realities of the world. For music, as far as Jessie taught him, was a great place to hide, a healer for the truly devout. Besides, in between the girls' giggles, the song they sang for Josh and Talia was good...for a couple of youngsters. *I wonder what Jessie's first song was,* Josh thought. *I wonder how old she was when she wrote it.*

He closed his eyes for a moment and let the voices of the two silly girls in front of him carry him away. All those days alone...drinking, hiding... Nadia...There was no way Josh would ever go down that dark path again. The biggest struggles these days were, thankfully, simply managing his and Jessie's busy lifestyle, keeping his family safe, and somehow being the man Josh's wife and children, especially Emily-Grace, needed him to be.

Upstairs, in the room to the right at the top of the stairs, Jessie was handing Dylan to Jacob. She pointed towards the adjoining washroom. "The kids all have their own toothbrushes here. You'll recognize Dylan's."

"Silly old bear," teased Jacob, as he carried the little boy into the washroom. "What is it about Winnie-the-Pooh that you like, huh Dylan?"

"Siwwy owd beaw," yawned Dylan. "Jacob sing."

"Okay. What do you want me to sing?"

Settling into the rocking chair later with his biological father, damp hair combed back, teeth brushed, and warm, snuggly blue pajamas covering him from his toes to his neck, Dylan fought to stay awake, but the day's post-Christmas exertions and Jacob's warm tones had him asleep in minutes.

But Jacob shook his head at Jessie when she reached for the little guy so she could lift him and position him in his toddler bed.

"Just another minute," he begged.

"I'll go," she said. "Just put him down when you're ready, Jacob." Turning to leave, though, Jessie was surprised to find Jacob's hand grabbing hers and urging her back towards him. Retrieving a small leather ottoman, Jessie eased down onto it. She faced Jacob and their sleeping child.

"Can I just pretend?" he whispered. "Just for a minute." The heartache in his eyes humbled Jessie. The deep cobalt she still loved was flickering as if a lantern was pulsing somewhere inside Jacob, sending light and taking it away, owning it and controlling it. The uncertain light gave off the impression that Jacob had no idea how he should feel here, tonight.

"Jacob…"

"No," he insisted. "Don't say it. Just let me have this, Jessie. It's just a few goddamned minutes, that's all. I'm not asking you for forever. Not anymore." He almost choked on the words. This, tonight…their sleeping child in his arms, a soft light sculpting Jessie's face into enchanted edges that begged to be touched, and a fairytale-like Eva Cassidy ballad playing beneath the stillness…was too much.

"You take my breath away," he murmured, lifting their hands to brush her cheek with the backs of his fingers. He brought her hand to his lips then, and kissed her long fingers with a tenderness borne of a deep, abiding love. "Always, Jessie."

Closing her eyes, Jessie swallowed and let her chin drop so, when she was ready to open them again, she wouldn't see desperation in the love radiating from Jacob's soul.

"Babe," she managed, "don't do this." But she didn't force her hand from his.

Slowly, Jacob rocked back and forth, holding Jessie's hand and aching for these few precious moments to last. He, too, closed his eyes, and a deep sigh that filled his body with yearning escaped his lips and landed in the shadowy corners of the room, depositing a pain earned from years of something worse than unrequited love. It was born of a love felt deeply by both that was in fact returned, but with a hard barrier and what felt like a soulless, inflexible rigidity.

Downstairs, as above them the rocker marked Jacob's limited dreamtime with its creak, creak creaking, Kayla was pausing at the entrance to the playroom. With a light heart and a happy smile, arms and ankles crossed as she leaned against the doorframe, she was listening to her niece and Stella sing for Josh and Talia. When the kids finished, their curtseying accented with more little girl giggles, Kayla clapped enthusiastically.

Emily-Grace floated over the room towards her and catapulted her lithe body into Kayla's welcoming arms. "Where's Momma? I want to sing it for Momma."

A voice came from behind her. "Momma took Dylan up to bed, sweetheart. She'll be down in a few minutes, okay?" Josh was starting to hope Jessie and Jacob would hurry. By the looks of the little guy on his lap, it would soon be time to deposit him in bed too, but Josh didn't want to wake Dylan or interrupt Jessie's time with Jacob. He knew this time, when they were all together, would be sacred for her. And he knew that the Christmas season, with its ability to discard pain and hostility and old hurts, and instead wrap a big peaceful bow around family time, was an opportunity for healing.

But Emily-Grace was insistent. "Come on, Kayla," she demanded. "And Stella. Momma sings for Dylan. Tonight we can sing him our song for bedtime." She was so hopeful that Josh just laughed and shrugged when Kayla sent him a questioning look.

"We'll be quiet," she said, partly for his benefit and partly in lecture mode for her niece. "We'll tiptoe in case Dylan is just drifting off. We don't want to wake the little monster, I mean, er, the little guy."

"I'm gonna tell Momma you called him a monster," was the seven-year-old response, accompanied by a pouty lip.

"Don't you dare," laughed Kayla. "She'll never let me babysit you kids anymore."

"I'm gonna tell her right now!" Emily-Grace started down the hall towards the stairs, but Kayla, followed by the bouncy Stella, caught up to her quickly.

Putting a finger to her lips, Kayla whispered, "Shhh," and the threesome tiptoed upstairs, still giggly, but quietly so.

Kayla peeked in the dimly lit bedroom just ahead of Emily-Grace. Unaware that they were being somewhat spied upon, Jessie and Jacob didn't move. They presented a sweet, serene tableau to their watchers, who all seemed to inherently understand the intensity of the feelings laid bare before them—regret, ache, and love. But what the watchers didn't understand was that the two adults in the room had long ago acknowledged their loss of each other—they were aware that things were supposed to remain the way they were.

Jacob's foot continued to propel the rocking chair slowly back and forth. His hand squeezed Jessie's tight and pulled it back to his lips again.

But then, it was too much. The emotion—filled with loss and heartache and impossible truths—was too much.

"You take my breath away too, Jacob," Kayla and the girls heard Jessie say as she stood. "I'll see you downstairs, okay?" The words had come out choked and raw. It was so hard to let this man go…again and again, it seemed. Easing her fingers out of Jacob's grasp, Jessie bent forward and kissed him fully on the lips, on those soft, cherished lips whose taste she once loved and craved the way the ocean needs salt. "Good night."

His eyes were closed as she kissed him in a long and lingering way, as she tasted the sweet essence she missed and lightly let her tongue touch his, but they darted open quickly when Jessie turned, because she gasped.

A small hand resting on the doorframe, Emily-Grace was standing in bewildered stillness at the entrance to the bedroom. Kayla and Stella were moving into the room, and it appeared, by the way Kayla's eyes were wide and laced with confusion, that what was heard and seen was hugely misinterpreted. The rocking ceased, and the Eva Cassidy ballad ended.

Stella seemed to be oblivious. She bounded over to Jessie and grabbed her hand. "Me and Emily-Grace wrote a song and we want to sing it for Dylan."

At that, Jessie's eyes dropped back to her daughter, who was clearly as puzzled as Kayla. The little girl's mouth worked as she tried to reconcile what she had just seen with what her mother kept telling her, which was that Momma was with Daddy now, and that she and Jacob didn't love each other that way anymore.

"I don't want to sing anymore," she managed to say, her little girl voice a soft whisper. "Dylan's already asleep."

Thoughts were racing a mile a minute in Jessie's head, bouncing around like high-speed bingo balls. *What exactly did she see? How am I supposed to explain this?* Jessie reached for her. "Come here, darling. We'll go down the hall to the room Momma used to use when I lived here. You can sing for me there."

A crisscrossed uncertainty swayed through Emily-Grace's body. She didn't voice her thoughts because she was utterly incapable of making sense of anything, it seemed, these days, which had anything at all to do with Jacob and her mother. All she knew was how she felt when she saw tenderness pass between them tonight, and when she spied the pain deep in Jacob's eyes as her mother let him go. And this new clarity seesawed through the child like lightning, strangling her with its intensity, yet alighting her with hope. It was a heady cocktail of emotions for a seven-year-old child to even begin to process.

Still, somewhat dazed, Emily-Grace let her mother lead her out of the room and down the hall. Like an overexcited puppy, Stella bounced along behind them.

The girls' voices were soon soft whispers fading down the hall into La Casa's homey wilderness. Jacob groaned and stood, moved Dylan full against his chest, and then laid him on his back in the toddler bed. Jacob had his back to Kayla now, but he sensed that she hadn't moved—or breathed, even—but he took his time turning around to face her.

When he did, he confronted the unspoken demons in the room head on. "You don't need to look so scared, Kayla. Or judgmental, for that matter. We shared a moment with our son, that's all."

"I'm not your judge, Jacob." Still, she didn't move. Kayla was blocking the doorway, so Jacob stayed put. *I'm frozen,* she was thinking. *I'm seriously crushing on this man, but right now I hate his guts.*

He waited, still fighting the powerful feelings that had swept over him, and over Jessie too, Jacob knew, because he felt her respond to him when they were rocking their child to sleep. And that kiss…her tongue touching his, probing, searching…the immediate physical reaction in his groin that, even now, was still uncomfortable. Breathing her in again weakened, yet set on fire, his entire body.

Words were not readily available. Coherent thought was barely available.

Kayla broke the silence. "You're getting married in a few days."

He blinked, and then nodded. To both of them, it seemed as if he had forgotten.

She had more to say. "But you're still in love with Jessie."

Finally Jacob's thoughts found a voice, even though it came out rough and ratchety. "What you need to understand, Kayla," he drawled, "is that it doesn't matter. Talia is well aware of how I feel about Jessie. And after today, I won't have to see Jessie again for a long time. So it won't keep hurting this much anymore." He pounded his chest lightly as he said that, burying both hands in his jeans pockets immediately afterwards as if to steel himself for the onslaught he knew was coming.

"Why would you marry someone when you're in love with someone else?" She was incredulous.

"I love Talia, and she knows it." Stepping towards her so he wouldn't have to speak louder than he dared, in case more ears happened to steal quietly up the staircase and into the room, Jacob continued. He was close enough to Kayla now that she could breathe in the heady muskiness that circled his body like a halo.

She pocketed her hands too.

"Kayla, I have no intention of trying to steal Jessie away from your brother again. I was there for her when she needed me, when they both needed me, the kids too for that matter. That time has come and gone. I've moved on with my life. I have an amazing woman who sings circles around Jessie—"

A loud guffaw telegraphed Kayla's loyalty, but she said, "Continue."

"And I intend to keep her. We're already trying for a baby of our own."

"So why…"

"What, tonight? Jesus, Kayla." Jacob unpocketed a hand and ran guitar-callused fingers through his curly locks. "Look, I try and I try and I try to tell everyone I can't do this. Spending time with the kids, seeing the whole cozy glued-back-together Sawyer family all snuggled up and lovey-dovey all the time again…I keep trying to tell people, but they don't listen. It hurts, you know?"

Omigod, is he…is he crying? A moist sheen was clearly evident in Jacob's eyes but he swallowed and forced his emotions back down to the black abyss from where they assaulted him. Kayla relaxed.

"So," he finally continued, "I get here, to this magical Spanish castle, and I find myself for the most part safely surrounded by people. And it makes it easier. But what the hell do you expect me to do when what I've dreamed about forever is handed to me? Even just for a blink of an eye? My family… the way it should have been."

"I'm sorry," Kayla managed. "I'm sorry she hurt you so much."

Down the hall, the little girls stopped singing. Stella grabbed Emily-Grace's hand and skipped down the hallway and back down the stairs, dragging her rather subdued companion along behind her. Jessie, slightly hunched over, an arm around her belly as if she was trying to keep her insides in, made her way to the doorway where Jacob and Kayla stood frozen, each lost in a silent attempt to understand.

When she saw Jacob's eyes flick back to Jessie, Kayla twisted around and stared. Then she brushed hard by her, almost knocking her into the wall.

"Kayla, wait—"

Before she started down the stairs, Kayla whipped back around and faced her sister-in-law. "I no longer support Jacob taking your kids, Jessie. Just so you know. He doesn't want to, and you know that. So stop fucking making him. Walk away from each other. Just walk away, before…before what myself and the girls saw tonight escalates into something that's only going to tear everyone apart again. Please."

Jessie's eyes flicked past Kayla to the floor below. Somewhere in her brain she was aware that the sound in the big house had changed, that it was different somehow. As her eyes focused on the people below, she understood why. Deirdre was there, with Charles. They were saying goodbye to Charlie and Jane who, as the parents of a new baby, were tired and heading home. Jane was trying to shrug Stella into her coat, and Emily-Grace was a pensive nearby statue. And, behind her, was Josh.

Jessie caught her breath. The way he was looking at her…it shook her to the core. Fear has an energy, an electric sizzle that far outweighs sense and reason. And now, fueled by a history of loss and abuse, brought to the surface on her husband's face, it had the power to sink Jessie to her knees.

Grabbing the mahogany railing, her knuckles went white. A quick flash, and Jessie's eyes were back on Kayla. A voice Jessie didn't recognize escaped her lips. Its power was fury.

"Jacob and me do not concern you, Kayla. We are nobody else's business. What we had, and what we have, is ours, and ours alone. I never want to hear you speak of him or us or our children again the way I just heard you talk now. Because you do not understand—you, none of you—have the capacity to understand what we will always mean to each other. Josh and Talia are the only ones who have a sweet clue how much we lost. How much we chose to lose. And how much we continue to lose."

"I beg to differ." Kayla's angry rebuttal was accompanied by a gesture towards the first floor. Towards Emily-Grace, who stood alone now, for the most part unnoticed, eyes squeezed shut, fingers stuffed in her ears, and tears freely streaming down both downy cheeks.

A quiet voice came from behind Jessie's back, but it was loud enough in the shocked silence for everyone present to hear. It came from Jacob, in a flat monotone from a soul with nothing left to give the hard day.

"I beg to differ too, Jessie. About the 'how much we chose to lose' part." Moving out of the bedroom, he faced her. "I didn't choose to lose anything. You did. You did all the choosing, like I think you always still do, with him. Have I forgiven you? No. Never. But," he said to Kayla, and by transference to the shocked audience below, "I have given up. I am marrying Talia on Friday, and Jessie is not welcome at our wedding. But that doesn't mean I won't be wishing she was there."

In the congregation or standing next to you? Kayla wondered.

Without hesitation, and in front of everyone, Jacob placed his right arm around and behind Jessie's neck. Pulling her close, wrapping his left arm low around the familiar waist so he could press her body to him, he kissed her, and let her go.

"Merry Christmas," he whispered. Brushing a tender thumb over her lip, he jogged past Kayla and then down the stairs, grabbed his leather jacket from a vintage hallstand, and passed off into the night.

"Jesus," Josh cursed, turning to his daughter, who continued to sob in choking gasps, but who screamed when he tried to touch her. "He's the one who should have an Oscar."

His attempt at a false bravado landed flat. Charlie laid a comforting hand on his shoulder as he gathered his family to leave, and Deirdre took Emily-Grace's hand. Kayla called for Paul and they, too, left the home.

Jessie plopped down on the top step and met her husband's eyes, until a new noise from the lower hallway caught both hers and Josh's attention. It was Talia, tiptoeing on her impossibly high heels, trying not to garner the stares of anyone else tucked into the kitchen or media room or formal front room as she passed. But she had no choice but to go by Josh, who studied her for signs of anguish. Had she overheard? Had she seen?

Talia touched his arm as she passed, and twisted her head around to look up the stairs at Jessie, who parted her lips, unsure, as she straightened.

Reaching for her coat, Talia moved to put it on, but Josh took it from her and, always the gentleman, helped her into it.

"I hope he waited for me," Talia managed, with a tiny forced spark in her eyes. "Otherwise I may be needing a ride home. I'd say maybe even a couch, but..." She sighed and looked back up at Jessie, who shrank back into herself and rested her chin on her hands. "Well, you know."

Josh pushed the large curved mahogany door open, and Talia exited under his arm out into the wintry Vancouver chill.

Under a soft blue-white light twenty feet away, leaning against Matt's Audi, was Jacob, ankles crossed, a thin wisp of smoke trailing from some weed he had tucked into his jacket pocket earlier for strength, should he need it. Matt was next to him, a silent, trusted companion.

"I did good until the last bit," Jacob told his new audience as Talia and Josh approached, Talia with an arm delicately hooked into Josh's bent elbow so she could more safely navigate the flagstones and then the asphalt on her Manolo Blahniks.

Jacob's eyes darted to the arched doorway. The door was opening again. Shivering in the cold, Jessie stood silhouetted against La Casa's buttery golden light, arms crossed.

"Talia," Josh started when they stopped a few feet in front of Jacob. "This is what you need to know." He wheeled slightly around so he could face her, catching her off guard so that the mask she wore, the always 'up' one that belied her true feelings at any given time, was not in place. Josh hesitated for a second, until she was able to wipe away a stray tear and focus her hurt gaze away from Jacob and onto Josh.

Josh continued. What he had to say humbled Jacob somewhat, but it didn't surprise Matt. If anything, it raised Jessie's husband in his esteem even more.

"I can't begin to guess how you're feeling right now," he told Talia. "Or what, if anything, you intend to do about what you saw and heard tonight. But what I can tell you is that this man is a good man. He took care of my family when I couldn't. And I know he loves you. But more than that...he needs you. Talia, I'm not worried about Jessie going back to Jacob. It's a non-issue. Jacob knows this too. Please, the two of you…drive away from here and go live a happy life."

Stealing up his nerves, Josh turned to Jacob next. "You're the biggest fucking quandary of my life, Jacob. I'm indebted to you for so many damn reasons, and I can't help but like you. But my wife loves you to pieces and my daughter keeps hoping she can trade me in for you. You just hurt this beautiful woman in a way no woman should ever be hurt, especially a few days before her wedding. Go, please, soon. Because I might put a fist through your face if you hang around here much longer. And I mean that in the nicest way possible."

"You remember the night Deuce McCall tried to kill you, Josh?" Jacob spoke matter-of-factly, but the sinister reminder shocked the listeners. Somber, Matt angled his head to hear better, and Josh froze, with the exception of the fists that suddenly curled up at his sides.

A long, slow toke was pinched between a thumb and forefinger, and inhaled before Jacob continued. "I could have killed you, too. But that's old news. I can't tell you how many times I revisit that night in my head and wonder, if I had pulled the trigger when it crossed my mind, and later told the police I just wasn't a good shot, you know," he laughed weirdly, "if I could have had her then. Would she and I be the ones here with three kids, fitting right in there with Charles and Dee the way you never will. Jessie and the kids wouldn't have had to go through all that shit when you were drunk and with Nadia because I would have insisted she had security and she would *never-have-been-abducted.*"

Spitting out the last words, Jacob dropped the remainder of his toke onto the asphalt, and ground it in with the narrow square toe of his boot. He planted his feet wide and nodded at Josh who, like the others, was standing in stunned silence.

"But you know what I think about more when I wake up sweating at three a.m.?" Pointing a finger at Josh, Jacob shoved it hard against his chest and pushed. Josh lost his balance for a second, but quickly recovered, and grabbed Jacob's finger and shoved it downwards.

Eyes flashing, Jacob went on. "I think about McCall. I think about what he said to Jessie that night, and what kind of fucked up person he was. Only what I've come to realize is that he wasn't as far gone as I thought he was. He was just a man in love with a woman he finally realized he could never have. And that's the worst kind of fucking pain there is."

"Yeah, Jacob, been there done that, remember? A few times. Because of you."

Slowly, Jacob shook his head. "Nnnoooo," he finally said, in an almost singsong-like pitch. "You've never been where McCall was. And you've never been where I am. You know why? Because you...always had a chance to get her back."

"For a while I thought I didn't, Jacob." Curling and uncurling his fists, Josh tensed, ready to lash out.

He heard Steve's voice behind him, saying, "Go back inside." A small voice of protest, then a louder, "Damn it, Jessie. Go. Now. You're freezing." Steve's footsteps sauntered up behind the odd tableau. "Break it up, boys and girls. Get the hell out of here, Jacob. Matt, are you driving this asshole tonight?"

Nobody moved. Steve rubbed his hands together and exhaled. A short, moist breath escaped into the cool Pacific air. "Why do I always miss the good stuff?"

Josh and Jacob's stony eyes were locked onto each other like missiles to targets. Neither moved.

Finally, Talia reached for Jacob's arm. "Come on, Jacob," she demanded. "You've been drinking and now you're high. And I admit I'm as guilty as anyone about pushing you to be in situations you readily admit you don't want. I guess I was hoping your feelings for Jessie had cooled. The old 'time heals all wounds,' you know? I was wrong to insist we come back to Vancouver, and maybe I've been wrong all along about you getting to know your son."

Matt, Steve and Josh all cringed. But Jacob remained impassive, his death ray stare not diminishing, his eyes unblinking. The only thing that gave away his pain and softened Josh towards him was the wetness in his eyes.

Matt, too, reached for Jacob then, but Jacob, his body rigid and poised for a fight, reacted instantly, throwing Matt's arm off. Talia, suddenly unbalanced, stepped backwards, tripped, and was caught by Steve. Still, Jacob didn't so much as look at her.

Cursing, Talia tossed off Steve's arm and moved towards the back seat of the Audi. Matt opened the door and helped her slide in, then gently closed the door behind her. He shot Steve a wary, cautious look, stepped quietly around the back of the car to the driver's seat, slipped in, and started the ignition so he could throw some heat on for Talia who, like Jessie, was now shivering.

The light shifted at La Casa's arched doorway. The door was opening again. It was Jessie, moving to go indoors finally, but she stopped when she saw Jacob's gaze flick from Josh to her.

Guarded, Josh watched him dissolve, watched the tension leave his body. At the same time, he saw an ache, a sadness, a simple lust cross over his face, and it struck Josh in the gut to realize that what Jacob had said about Deuce McCall was horrifyingly true.

Josh's words forced Jacob's attention back to him. As he spoke, in his peripheral vision Josh saw the quiet, watchful Matt walk back around the car and stop a few feet away.

"So what, Jacob?" Josh asked. "You want to die too? Or are you still plotting and planning to kill me someday?" Taking a step forward, he stopped barely a foot away from Jacob. "You really think that'd bring Jessie back to you?"

"Nah," Jacob sneered. "I'm Deuce now, remember? I know I'll never get her back."

"Don't you ever fucking compare yourself to Deuce McCall."

A loud guffaw escaped Jacob's lips. He almost danced in delight—a very McCall kind of move, Josh thought. *Eerie.*

"You trying to warn me, Sawyer?"

"I'm trying to help you, asshole! Jesus, just go marry this gorgeous, talented girl and leave us the hell alone! Okay?"

"You want me to leave Dylan alone too, huh? So now you're cool with me walking away from him."

Steve interjected. "That's not what he means, Jacob."

"Oh yes it is," Josh growled. "That's what I fucking mean."

"Ha. You scared of me now, Sawyer?"

At his side, Matt bristled. They'd had way too much experience with twisted men around Jessie. Jacob was a good guy. But suddenly he had just put himself on a list Matt feared, when it came to Jessie's safety.

"Leave my family alone, Jacob." The warning was soaked in dread, and delivered in dismay. "Please." The last word was tiny, it sounded like he was begging, and later Josh wished he had never said it. But he did, indeed, remember that terrifying night at the base of the mountain with Deuce McCall's jagged dagger at his neck, although the memories were foggy, since he'd been drugged and beaten so the earth seemed crooked and off its axis. So the tiny *please* was Josh's admission that unrequited love made men and women do things they wouldn't, as good human beings, ever do.

Nadia, he thought, an increasing gagging feeling in his throat as fear came rushing back.

Jacob saw the look and recognized Josh's fear. He laughed oddly. "You need to get a grip, Josh," he said with an arrogance that pissed Josh off even more. With a final heated glare, Jacob pivoted around and slid into the back seat of the Audi next to Talia. Matt closed the door behind him, sent Josh a warning look, sauntered back around the car, and eased behind the wheel.

As the sedan pulled out of La Casa's elegant driveway, lit tonight for the festive season with white, green and red bulbs and live evergreen wreaths bedecked in wide wine ribbons and spritely red holly berries, Josh and Steve stood rooted, and watched the Audi glide off into the darkness of the street below.

Steve spoke first. "He's just hurt, Josh. He had too much time watching your perfect family love each other tonight, that's all."

"The perfect family, is it?" Josh said quietly. "What everybody wants, we have?" Emily-Grace's earlier screaming when he tried to touch her slithered across his brain. "I had enough of that with Nadia. I thought Jacob had moved on."

Encouraging Josh to move back towards the house, Steve put a hand on his friend's back. "I think he was trying to, Josh. But it seemed nobody else would let him."

"I wonder if they'll still tie the knot."

"He'll hate himself in the morning. But I'm sure once Talia gets Jacob back home they'll be fine. Liquor and pain are a reckless combination, Josh. Eh?"

"That Deuce McCall shit scared the crap out of me."

"Oh, is that why you're shivering? I thought it was from the cold." Ruefully,

Steve grinned, but his eyes landed on Jessie as they turned to head back inside. He frowned. "Speaking of cold…"

Jessie held the door open for the guys, but Steve shoved her inside first. She was shivering so hard her teeth were chattering. Wrapping his arms around her, Steve breathed warm air into her neck.

"Thanks, Steve," she mumbled, staring at Josh over Steve's shoulder and praying he wasn't as upset as Talia appeared to be.

Steve brushed his lips against her cheek and let her go.

Jessie watched him disappear into the distant playroom before she trained her gaze back on her husband. "What'd he say to you?"

Josh didn't answer. Instead, he stared at his wife with a hard intensity that frightened her.

"Tell me what he said."

Josh chose to ignore Jacob's Deuce McCall references. It wouldn't serve any of them any good to relive that old nightmare. He chose the wedding instead.

"I don't know if we will be sending our kids to Nashville in a few days."

She swallowed. "Sure we will. He'll sober up and tell Talia what an idiot he was and she'll forgive him and everything will be fine."

"Was he?"

"Was he what?"

"An idiot. Upstairs."

Jessie's silence unnerved Josh. Her eventual response was hurtful and honest in its ambiguity. "No. He wasn't. What happened upstairs was nothing, Josh. It was nothing and yet…it was everything."

"Okay," he said quietly.

"I'm sorry."

"Me too."

"You heard him. You know our story as well as Jacob and I do. There's nothing to be afraid of."

"I know," Josh managed. He pulled her close under the mistletoe, under the chandelier's flickering and constant beauty, and held her until it was time to part.

Chapter Nineteen

$\mathcal{J}$acob and Talia lived in the silent flux of an automaton-like prep and ill will until three days before the wedding, when something finally had to give.

They were in her car, a white Mercedes sedan she was navigating through the outskirts of Nashville when Jacob started the difficult conversation with what seemed an easy intro.

"That was cool. Your manager's suggestion for your tour openers, I mean."

She seemed willing to talk, but kept her eyes carefully trained on the road ahead. "I like The Band Perry. It won't be long before they're headlining their own tour."

"Then I guess you should take advantage of them while you can."

Humph, was her 'I'm still pissed at you' response.

"Quite the spread old Dick has there."

"He's managed a lot of talent over the years." Talia brushed back the long locks of her wild blonde bob. "He deserves to reap a few benefits, don't you think?"

"Yeah, but it's like acres and acres of waterfront property. And isn't he on, like, his fourth gay marriage? I'm surprised he has anything left."

"Fourth marriage, huh?" Gripping the steering wheel, Talia sighed and sank a little into the soft tan leather seats.

"Uh, yeah, well that's him, not us, Tal." Jacob leveraged his body with his palms and sat up straighter. He dove in. "You're still doing wedding shit. So am I to assume you've forgiven me for my Boxing Day stupidity?"

"You know, I could let the Boxing Day stupidity go if it was just that. But it isn't, is it Jacob?"

Nausea gutted Jacob. Inadvertently, he grabbed his stomach. "I've never lied to you, Talia. Don't be stupid."

"Stupid, my ass. I'm the most stupid person on the goddamned planet, apparently."

Leaning on the horn, she hollered at the driver of a blue minivan who slowed down after passing them. "Speed limit's 60 here, you asshole!"

"Easy, girl. You're, like, the worst tailgater ever."

With great reluctance, Talia eased off the accelerator. "This from a man who has only had his license for six months. You never used to care about my tailgating. Suddenly it's an issue."

"Talia, I don't want to fight, okay? Tomorrow you're going back to Seattle until the wedding. We need to air this crap before we stand before the altar on Friday."

"There wouldn't have been any crap to air if one of us hadn't kissed the ex he apparently still loves in front of some of the people who will be at our wedding!" A quick swipe of the back of her hand erased a tear before Jacob had the chance to see it. "And by the way, you creeped the hell out of me with all that Deuce McCall bullshit. How do I know I'm not marrying a psychopath stalker?"

"Oh Jesus, Talia!" Rolling his eyes, Jacob sucked in a breath. "I was embarrassed and high. Josh and his fucking almighty 'I won' arrogance just pissed me off. I was trying to get a rise out of him, that's all."

"Well, you should know that it worked." She darted a glance to the passenger side. "I heard from my own security that Matt called a meeting with Ulysses and Charles to talk about what you said to Josh. He doesn't want you near Josh or Jessie without supervision."

"You've got to be fucking kidding me." Astounded, Jacob squeezed his eyes shut, leaned back, and exhaled slowly. "I was just being stupid."

"Fine, if that's the case," Talia spat at him, "and I don't care about that anyway. Nor should you, if you were telling the truth the other night and you really want to just stay away from her and the kids. If that's the case it's a non-issue unless you and Jessie get booked in to play somewhere together. What we really need to talk about are your feelings for her. How am I supposed to marry a man who's in love with someone else?"

"You always knew that was the deal with me, Talia. It's nothing new. You said you were cool with it. You fucking acted all cool with it, in front of Jessie, as I recall. What was that, some kind of 'oh, look at me, I'm Mizz cool, nothing phases me' game? It's apples and oranges. I will never stop loving her. Ever. But it's different now. It's changed, it's—"

"Hopeless, apparently. So Jacob settles for second prize. You said it yourself. You said you were giving up and marrying me."

"No. No! Talia, what you and I have is spectacular. It's good and real and perfect. But you have to understand that Jessie and I first met and connected over music, at a time when both of us were desperate for something, anything, to hold on to. But it was never complete for us. Josh was always there, in the middle, lurking and stalking and waiting."

"But then there was a time when you thought you had her."

"No. I always knew I never had her, Tal. Not really. Not really ever." He took her hand off the wheel and ran his thumb over her fingers. "And when she got pregnant, by the time she told me she was already back with Josh. It was like a gunshot to the gut, knowing that I lost not only Jessie, but our son too, and the life I told myself I could accept, which meant being with her even though she loved someone else more. I was ready to take that on, to be number two if that's the way it had to be."

"Is that what you're asking from me, Jacob? To accept being your number two? To live with that?" Salty streaks now made their way with a regular rhythm down Talia's pale-pink cheeks. "I can't fucking see!" she wailed, slamming a palm on the wheel and turning the wheel sharply to the right. The car skidded crookedly to a halt, barely on the shoulder of the busy road.

"Jesus, Talia!" cried Jacob as two trucks zipped past, their horns blaring their disapproval at Talia's hasty decision to pull over. "Are you trying to get us killed?"

"No!" she shouted. "I'm trying to figure out if I'm still getting married on Friday, and if I go through with it, what kind of life I'm going to have! Every time I look at you, Jacob, I'm only going to see *her* reflected in your eyes! Aren't I? Aren't I!"

Slowly, Talia pulled her hand out from under his.

Jacob tried to speak, but he couldn't. This woman beside him was the real deal. Jessie was a lost fantasy. He tried to tell Talia that, but the emotion was too heady, too strong, the old pain too suffocating and debilitating, to put into words. "Tal," he managed, moving his palm to her cheek. He wanted to say, "I love you," but could only sob instead.

She didn't take his emotion for what he meant it to be. Talia took the aching sobs for acquiescence that what she'd voiced was true. That Jessie was, and always would be, Jacob's truest love. The hard part was that, on some level, Talia knew Jessie loved him too. She tried to understand. She tried to reconcile the truth with reality. Yes, Jacob and Jessie had a connection that would bind them together forever. Still, they had moved on. They had geared up their courage and moved forward in the best way they knew how. Jacob and Talia could avoid the Sawyers as much as possible. They could manage, without Dylan, without Jessie, without pain, and continue to build a life together from the ground up the same way they had been doing for the last two years.

But it would be like putting on a false bravado. Dylan and Jessie existed. They were real people. Jessie and Jacob would often be playing the same shows or showing up at the same awards events and concerts. It would be impossible to keep Jacob away from her entirely. And if he chose to shut Dylan out of his life? A part of him would always be missing, as it had been from the day Jessie told Jacob she was pregnant in the first place.

With a soft shush of her sleeve against her body, Talia reached for the door beside her. "What am I supposed to do?" she wept to Jacob as he tried to loosen the knots in his throat so he could speak, so he could beg her not to give up on him, on them. "I'm sorry Jacob but I...I don't want to be you. I thought I could deal until I saw you kiss her...it's so fucking real now... I can't accept being someone else's second love. I'm sorry."

A quick turn of her head and Talia was opening the door. Jacob moaned in protest and moved to open his own door and jump out, to head her off at the pass, as it were.

But fate had other plans. The last thing Jacob remembered was hearing the godforsaken splintering of twisted metal, and the otherworldly explosion of smashing glass. He didn't hear a scream, because Talia never had a chance. She was gone the instant a speeding car rammed into them, before Jacob had the chance to beg her to stay.

Chapter Twenty

*J*osh had the kids at Jack and Lydia's when he got the news. He was holding Dylan to keep him from climbing into Blue's paddock, but it wasn't going well. It was as if the little boy sensed the earth move from beneath his feet that day, because he was in a foul mood, refusing to settle or sleep or listen or stop an incessant whining. Ready to toss him over his shoulder and order his other two kids back to the main house and into his King Ranch, Josh halted when he saw Jack leave the home in his slippers, his phone in his hand, no coat, and a panicked gait that landed somewhere between a walk, a skip, and a run.

Steve and Charlie were there too, and both started towards Jack as he called out to Josh.

Jack had Dylan out of Josh's arms and into Charlie's before anyone could ask what the hell had upset him. "Take him," Jack demanded sharply to his son, and Charlie knew to do just that without complaint or question, because this was a version of his handsome father he rarely saw.

"What is it?" Josh begged. "Just tell me, Jack. Is it Jessie?"

"Where is she?" Jack demanded, grabbing Josh by the collar of his plaid fleece lined denim jacket and dragging him up the hill towards the pool. Jack hollered back over his shoulder at Charlie. "Keep the kids, Charlie." He nodded grimly in Steve's direction. "You might want to come along."

A little freaked out now, Josh whipped around and walked backwards. "Charlie, don't let the kids in the corral with Blue. Don't let Dylan in any corral, for that matter."

"Listen to me," Jack said urgently, garnering Josh's attention again just as Steve caught up to them. "Josh, where's Jessie now?"

"She's down on Robson, in her office. She's doing research on bluegrass music for the Belgium film, I...I told her I'd take the kids for a few hours so she could get some work done." He threw off Jack's arm and stopped walking. "Jesus, Jack, you're scaring the shit out of me! What the hell!"

Jack glanced at Steve before he fixed a worried eye back on Josh. "I just got a call from a friend in Nashville. From a friend who knows Talia's manager, Richard Newton. I need to reach Charles, Josh, and someone likely ought to tell Jessie before this hits the Internet."

"What? Is it Jacob?" A lead weight crushed Josh's chest. It threatened to strangle the breath right out of him. He could feel Steve's steady grip on his arm. If this was about Jacob...if something happened...if the crazy guy had gone over the edge and done something...

Jack's voice seemed very far away when he finally said it. "Jacob and Talia had a car accident on their way home from a meeting with Richard. Talia was killed, Josh."

"What? Talia?" *Oh Jesus.* "Jacob. What about Jacob?"

"Jacob will recover. He's in the hospital but he'll be okay."

Oh no, he won't. He won't be okay.

The voices around Josh disappeared as he stared at Jack. The man's mouth was moving but Josh didn't hear a word. Propelled forward by Jack's death grip on his arm, Josh managed to climb into his truck—in the passenger seat—as Steve took the wheel.

By the time Steve lurched onto Robson, Josh's thoughts were melding into panic mode. He had considered texting Jessie to tell her he was on the way but he knew that would only serve to worry her, since they had parted barely more than an hour and a half earlier.

"Steve," he begged his friend, "tell me Jessie's not going to go running to Jacob the way he came to her aid in New York. I need to hear this from you."

"You want me to lie? You know she'll go."

"Charles and Matt are concerned. After Boxing Day—"

"Jacob was an ass on Boxing Day but with the exception of his friends from Scotland, the guy's a loner. No way is Jessie not going to try to help him through this, Josh. We're talking about the girl who pretty much threw herself under the bus by going back to Paris after the shooting! She goes where she feels she's needed. We know our girl. I'm sorry, Josh, but we know her. And as her husband, you have to trust her."

"I trust her, I think, I...I just don't trust Jacob."

A long silence followed as Steve did a loop around and pulled up directly in front of the Keating Building. As Josh moved to open his door, though, Steve grasped his shoulder and spoke. His voice was gruff. "I don't trust him either, Josh. He'll be out of his mind."

"I feel like shit, Steve. Talia's dead and we don't have a clue what kind of shape Jacob's in. And here I am worrying about Jessie taking up with him again."

"Hey. As long as you're okay, she's okay. She won't hook up with him again. And for now, Josh, you have a more immediate problem. Go tell her before she finds out on the Twitterverse."

"All right. I'm going. Jesus, this sucks."

"I'll park this beast and meet you on the 31st floor. We'll sort out what needs to be done and figure out how to protect Jessie later. She needs you, buddy."

"I know." Josh slid out of the truck and leaned against the door before letting it go. He looked back at his friend. "I feel like I'm going to puke."

"Hold it together, Josh. I'll see you in a bit."

Upstairs, on trembling legs Josh pushed open the heavy glass door to Magda's reception space. "Is Jessie in her office?" he croaked.

"Yes, she's..." Magda stood. Josh was trembling. "Josh, is everything okay?"

"No," he told her. "Nothing's okay. And Jessie's going to need some privacy, okay Magda?"

"Yes, of course. Is there anything I can do?"

"Is Charles here? Can you find Charles?"

Josh kept moving as he talked. Now, he ducked into the dimly lit hallway and paused a few feet from Jessie's office door to the right. Peeking around the corner, he spied her buried in her big comfy black leather chair, feet up on the desk, crossed at the ankles. The old brown boots she loved to wear spoke legions of comfort to Josh, and so did the long, layered loose curl that fell over her cheek as she read from a printed document on her lap.

As always, she sensed his presence and wrinkled her brow. The feet came down off the desk as Josh entered.

"Hey, Josh, what…" Shoving back her chair, she stood and stared. Her husband's face was a swampy shade of green. Jessie bolted to him. "The kids," she gasped. "Where are the kids?"

Grabbing her biceps, Josh forced Jessie to remain still. "It's not the kids," he told her, his voice thick with emotion. "It's not the kids. They're fine, they're with Charlie and Jack."

"Who? What? Is it my mother? Sara?"

"No, Jess. No." It pained Josh to look in the eyes he loved and have to tell his wife something that was going to change allegiances for Jessie once again, at least for a while. It hurt her more, he knew, when Jacob was hurting, when she was powerless to release his agony. By virtue of choosing Josh, Jessie would not be accessible to Jacob in the way she would want to be on this terrible day. She would lose it, knowing he was alone. So this was gonna suck.

"Oh fuck, Josh. What? Just fucking tell me."

Charles careened around the corner. Josh knew it was him by the sharp sound of his dress shoes, and by the strong aftershave he wore like a mantle. Jessie's eyes darted up to him. Charles was already crying, and Jessie could feel herself shaking, but as yet she had no idea why.

Then it hit her. Like a wave, it crashed over her, burying her in a sea-salt spray of coarse sand and seaweed. "It's Jacob, isn't it? Oh God, Josh, please tell me it isn't Jacob."

"Talia." Josh held himself together long enough to get it out. Gripping Jessie's biceps tight enough that his fingers left bruises, so she wouldn't—couldn't—run, he caved her world in enough to set them on a new path of fear and grief. "Talia's dead."

Confusion laced Jessie's brow together. "No," she breathed. "Tell me you're joking."

"I wouldn't joke about something like this, Jessie. They had an accident. A car accident."

"Th-they?"

"He'll be okay, Jess. He'll be okay."

The other night careened through Jessie's mind. Jacob holding Dylan, singing to him, the three of them together in the nursery. After Jacob's song ended, Eva Cassidy's haunting voice playing over the iPhone dock. The perfect lingering memory of those moments before Jacob fell victim to his feelings. The moments when he was still supposed to marry Talia, a woman Jessie knew he loved, who was likely the only person in the world who had the power to hold onto him, who was willing to hold onto him as far as she knew, despite the connection he shared and longed for with Jessie.

"Jacob!" she keened in agony to Josh, who she knew could take it. Who she knew was here for her now because he loved her enough to set aside his own old jealousies to help Jessie grieve for a man in unbearable pain whom she loved dearly. "Jacob!" she wailed again, and crumpled, in her husband's trusted loving arms, to the floor.

Chapter Twenty-one

$\mathcal{S}$teve, who eventually returned to Southlands with Josh's truck and the kids' car seats, planned to enlist Charlie to help transfer the children to La Casa for the evening. First though, Emily-Grace, David and Dylan would stay for an afternoon of playtime at the Deacon mansion in the upscale Southlands neighborhood of Vancouver. Emily-Grace was astute enough to know something was up, but the two younger boys relished the big playground that was, in fact, an expansive ranch. For the better part of two hours the littlest Sawyers mucked about the stalls and paddocks with Jack who, if he hadn't been so concerned for Jessie, would have been over the moon to have the little folks around.

"You like those rubber boots, don't you, Dylan?" Charlie said at one point to the smallest Sawyer guy, who was jumping repeatedly up and down in a puddle and was, in fact, apparently ecstatic. "Josh has a couple of cowboys on his hands, methinks."

Late in the day, Jack saddled a gentle paint pony he'd bought for Stella, his first grandchild, and led the children around and around until his tired bones gave up and he handed the lead to Steve. Emily-Grace, by then, was aching to know why her father tore off earlier, and why Jacob's name had come up at the time. She refused her turn to ride and, in fact, sank deep into herself in a way that alarmed the men, given the fact that she really only recently seemed to be doing so much better.

Stella got annoyed with her and ran off to play with David.

Watching his dark-haired daughter go, Charlie sauntered down to where Emily-Grace was sitting on a bale of fresh straw where she'd taken up residence.

He wondered how much he could, or should, say.

"Emily-Grace, don't you want to ride Flicker?" was what he started with, since it seemed like neutral ground, of sorts. "You always want to ride Flicker when you come out here. She'll be missing you."

"I really just want to go home," was the almost haughty response, spoken without looking at Charlie. Emily-Grace picked at a strand of straw instead.

"I think the plan is to take you kids to La Casa for a bit. Would that be okay? Once the boys are done exercising Jack and Steve and Flicker?"

"I want to see Momma."

"Baby girl," Charlie said softly. "You know something's wrong, don't you?"

Twisting the straw around and around in her dainty fingers, Emily-Grace nodded.

Charlie hesitated, and looked up to see Steve's alert eyes narrowed at him as he drew the pony, now with both boys on its swaying back, closer. The look was clearly a warning. They all knew this sensitive child would need to hear only the right words, ones that wouldn't send her deeper into herself or into a panic.

"Okay, Emily-Grace," Charlie said, somewhat awed for being granted this moment alone with Jessie's daughter, and overcome by the great responsibility it suddenly carried. He couldn't help wondering what their life would have been like if he and Jessie had stayed together. Would they have a daughter? He shook the thought away and dove in. "Scooch over," he demanded in a soft murmur.

Dropping down next to her on the rectangular bale of straw, Charlie could see that Emily-Grace was expectant, waiting. Her jaw was set and he was fairly certain there were tears floating just under the surface of her mini-Jessie baby blues. Was she holding her breath?

"Sweetheart," he tried, speaking slowly. "The thing is…your pretty momma's going to be a little sad when you see her."

The shoulders sank. It was no secret that Emily-Grace had vivid memories of a very sad momma. Suddenly the world was too big again. "Why?" came the small voice.

With a heavy sigh, Charlie pulled his seatmate onto his lap and wrapped an arm protectively around the diminutive shoulders. Emily-Grace knew him well. Charlie was like a second father to the Sawyer children. She listened closely.

"Sometimes things happen that we have no control over. And now we've all lost someone we were just getting to know. Someone who we were starting to care about very much."

"Someone died."

"Talia died, honey. You know Talia."

"Oh. Yes." She set her serious, pale eyes upon him.

Charlie was immediately taken aback at the age-old wisdom he saw there. "You're an old soul, aren't you, Emily-Grace?" A shrug and a sad face caused him to smile a little. "You know what this means. About Talia."

"I'm their flower girl."

"That's right, Emily-Grace. You were supposed to be. So there won't be a wedding now."

"And Jacob will be alone again."

"And your mother…"

"Loves Jacob."

After a hefty pause in which to recover from Emily-Grace's quick and spontaneous response, Charlie found a few more thoughts to share, but he felt like he was reaching. Like he was out of his depth with this solemn little girl.

"See?" he finally said, lightly tweaking her cheek with a finger. "An old soul. A wise old soul, you are." Inside, he was recoiling. The two words, *loves Jacob,* sent a current of fear up his spine. Yes, Jessie loves Jacob. They all knew that. This was gonna hurt.

Charlie took a chance. By virtue of this almost-alone time with Josh and Jessie's daughter, he had the opportunity to check out her feelings on a few things he knew both were concerned about. "Do you remember much about when you and David and your momma lived with Jacob?"

Instantly, she lit up. The shoulders straightened and a vibrancy fluttered up and down her body. "Yes!"

"Were you happy then? Happier than you are now? Because sometimes you seem sad to me. Like today because you don't want to ride Flicker."

"I was happy sometimes. I miss Jacob."

"Was she happy then? Your mother? Do you think?"

The child curled up in Charlie's arms and thought for a moment. "Not all of the time," she answered honestly.

"Do you know why she wasn't happy all of the time?"

"Because she missed Daddy."

"Is she mostly happy now?"

Steve was close by, taking the boys off Flicker's back. He handed the reins to the Deacon family's groom and shot Charlie a second warning, more harsh than the last. Charlie ignored him.

A heavy sigh burdened Emily-Grace and she sank deeper into Charlie's chest. "Yes. She loves Daddy a lot."

"And you love your daddy too."

No answer.

"You know it's okay to love them both, right Emily-Grace? Your daddy and Jacob? You don't have to choose, baby girl." His voice was barely distinguishable.

But Emily-Grace heard Charlie loud and clear. "Then why did Momma have to choose? Why did she have to leave Jacob?"

"It's hard sometimes when you're a grown-up."

"Then I don't ever want to be a grown-up."

"Don't say that, honey. Grownups get to do lots of cool things."

"Can we go now? I really need to see Momma."

"She's with your dad, kiddo. He's taking good care of her." Saddened to see a tear slip down the child's cheek, Charlie shifted her off his lap and took her hand. "But let's gather up those two ruffian brothers of yours and take you to La Casa. I'm sure your mother will want a pretty big hug when she sees you."

"Charlie?"

Emily-Grace's pink rubber boots made a squishy sound as they followed the others outside the spacious and cozy red and white barn and headed towards the house. Charlie wanted to smile because he remembered the sound and feel of his boots as a child, and memories of a long gone innocence that sustained him now. The smile came out a frown, though, because it seemed any pure living this child ever did had already long disappeared, gone the way of simple mysticisms like unicorns and fairies. Not for a long time had her world been incorruptible.

"Yes, Emily-Grace?"

"I think Jacob is going to need a pretty big hug too."

"I think you're right, sweet girl. I think you're right."

They made an odd couple in the diminishing light, Charlie and this young daughter of Jessie's, as they made their way to the warm, golden light beckoning them from Jack and Lydia's home, where chocolate chip cookies and mugs of hot chocolate would further stall and frustrate Emily-Grace in her desire to hold her mother. Now though, somber, lost in thought, she and Charlie passed by the corrals. Soon they would circle around the pool.

The pen containing the abused horse, Blue, was en route to the house. Both Charlie and Emily-Grace instinctively slowed and held a silent communion with her as they passed.

Blue, the horse with the wounded eyes, seemed to somehow understand that a new-old pain had entered the child's world today. With a raised head and a shake of her wild mane, she saluted Emily-Grace, and sent her strength.

~ ~

La Casa was yet to be brightly lit when the kids were delivered to their parents. It was late afternoon and a tired Vancouver sun was just starting its descent, leaching into the ocean wispy trails of wintry pinks and oranges that bled into English Bay and into the Burrard Inlet, where frisky seaplanes buzzed and floated and drifted and played.

Carlotta had made steady pots of tea all afternoon, and coffee for Jessie, each steamy cup delivered to her with a faint scent of Baileys to steady her shaking nerves despite the coffee's efforts to do the exact opposite.

Tapping the 'end' icon on her iPhone, Jessie stood at the entrance to the home's formal front room and told those gathered there—Matt, Charles, Deirdre and Josh—that JP, Charlene and Katrine now knew they would be attending a funeral instead of a wedding.

"Can we still send the jet for them, Charles?" she asked, numbly sliding into a seat on the Louis XIV sofa next to Josh, who entwined his fingers in hers. "And drop me off on the way?"

The room fell silent. It was disconcerting. The last time Jessie recalled it being this quiet was the night she and Charlie were telling Jack and Lydia that their engagement could not be reinstated. Only the clicks and clacks of the refrigerator in the nearby kitchen could be heard now, as then, uncannily marking perfect time with the ticking mantel clock below the fire-glowed warmth of Deirdre's Paul Peel painting.

"What?" Jessie asked, a hint of urgency in her voice. "What aren't you telling me?"

Dee was the first to detract Jessie's frayed nerves from focusing on the ticks and clicks. Crossing the room, an elegant lilt to her movements, she glided gracefully onto a plush white ottoman in the palatial, distinguished front room, faced Jessie, and lifted her pseudo-daughter's hand away from Josh.

"Honey," she started, and Jessie, guarded, puffed up both cheeks and exhaled slowly at the way Deirdre's face had settled into her apologetic 'this is going to suck but we're going to make it business' look. "Charles spoke with Talia's manager, Richard. He's at the hospital with Jacob now. It would appear…I'm really sorry to have to tell you this…that Jacob doesn't want to see you."

Shock shattered Jessie's attempt at civility. "Like hell he doesn't. I can't imagine he knows what he wants right now."

"He needs some time, honey. Just give him a few days."

"No." Throwing off Deirdre's soft white hands, Jessie stood.

Josh grunted in warning to Dee, who was opening her mouth to speak again, but they both knew their girl would get her feelings out regardless of where she knew they might land. They waited.

"You all know this is bullshit. Jacob has no close friends in Nashville. Even if you send the jet, our friends will be a while arriving from Scotland and anyways none of them know him like I do. Guys, he was always there for me when I needed him, and you heard him on Boxing Day. He and I will always mean something to each other, even if it's never going to mean we're together again the way we were before."

Recognizing that this must suck for Josh, Jessie sighed and addressed him. "Babe, you understand, right? I'd ask you to come with me but I don't see Jacob responding well if you're there. And someone has to stay with the kids."

Matt and Charles avoided each other's eyes.

Deirdre touched Josh's knee and stood. "Jessie, Richard was very clear. You are not to go to Nashville."

"What? Dee, I find it hard to believe that this is Jacob's doing. Maybe it was Talia's parents who asked for me not to be there. Or…it's not you guys, is it? I wouldn't put it past you all!" A quick scan of the room gave Jessie her answer. "Oh, hell," she breathed, and landed hard on the sofa next to Josh again. "Seriously?"

"Call it a community decision if you want to, Jessie," Charles explained, a severe yank to his tie accenting his words. "The initial directive came from Jacob, yes. But we agreed. The jet is fueled and will fly to Scotland imminently for your friends. It will travel direct and you will not be on it. I'm sorry."

Matt was less harsh. "Jessie, give Jacob the time he needs. Let him mourn Talia without being confused about his feelings for you."

Brushing a palm over and over his rough cheek, Josh peered up at Matt. Confused and uncertain just how he should feel, and how he should support his wife on this difficult day, he almost felt as if he was invisible or, at the very least, that he should be. The conversation taking place around him was awkward and unreal, in his opinion. He could feel Jessie's eyes on him, and the illusory weirdness of the day was about to take on a new energy. At that moment, Steve and Charlie were arriving in two vehicles with the kids in tow, Stella and Caleb included, and the house was about to become busy and noisy.

An earnest plea was Josh's reminder to the room that Jacob still had the power to threaten him. To hurt him.

"Jessie," he begged, "please listen. This kind of thing…this kind of pain… it makes people crazy. I hear you, that Jacob needs you. But he very likely needs you in a way that I'm not willing to give."

"Josh, come on. You know I'm not going to do anything stupid with Jacob. You and I agreed, hell, when I let him go we both knew we'd been together for the last time, you know, like," she waved her arms in the air in frustration, "sexually speaking! Or like…partner speaking, for that matter. He and I are done that way."

Josh tried again. The tone he used had everyone in the room holding their collective breaths. It was a combination of forced calm and sheer terror, and it came out sounding uneven and scratchy.

"Done like…the way you were done here, right up those steps, the day after Christmas? Done like that? You in his arms after, may I add, Kayla and our daughter saw you kiss him in the nursery? Done like that?"

Crumbling, Jessie fought for control before she grabbed her husband's hand. Fruitlessly, with her other hand she swiped at new tears before they threatened to overwhelm her again. "Josh, you know where we stand," she pleaded. "You know where things are with me and Jacob, and where they will remain with you. Do you seriously think I'd take a chance at messing us up again? No! No fucking way."

The liquid chocolate eyes were serious now, more serious than Jessie had seen them for, thankfully, a very long time. Everyone else in the room was a statue, as still and quiet as Charles' soapstone bust of Beethoven in the southwest corner. "I know that, Jessie. But I stand by my claim that things can get out of control super fast when people are hurting the way Jacob is hurting right now. And you know what I think is really cool?" He reached out a finger and gently cupped his palm around her cheek. "I think it's really cool that Jacob apparently knows that as well. He doesn't want to see you, Jess. And I, for one, am really fucking glad of that."

The curved mahogany door opened, then, and Charlie and Steve's voices could be heard hushing the kids and coaxing off their outerwear.

Emily-Grace's light footsteps, still in her messy pink farmyard boots according to the loudly whispered shouts of, "Emily-Grace! Your boots!" from Charlie, trod softly down the hall. The seven year old parked herself in the large open arch where Jessie remembered Charlie leaning, lost and alone, all those years ago. But Emily-Grace didn't appear lost and alone. Instead, she carried an air of utter determination, and wisdom far beyond her young years.

"Momma," she said directly to Jessie, as if there was no other living soul in the room, "I'm here." The small shoulders were strong, far stronger than they should have been for a child that young, but this was a child who knew she was needed.

As her daughter carefully wiped a loose strand of hair from one eye, Jessie fixed her gaze on her. At the same time, she let go of Josh's right hand, which she'd covered with her own hand a moment before.

She stood and faced Emily-Grace, but her words were meant for Josh.

"Well," she stated with authority. "Jacob may not want to see *me* at the moment, but he needs somebody he loves and trusts to be with him right now. And I know who that somebody needs to be."

Deirdre gasped and turned to Charles, who met her eyes, swallowed, and fingered his tie. Matt shifted his gaze from Emily-Grace to Josh, and wished he hadn't. With complete dismay, Josh was watching Jessie tiptoe across the floor and stoop before their daughter.

"Emily-Grace," Jessie whispered when she was at the child's eye level. "You and me need to take a little trip."

"To Nashville. We need to help Jacob."

"Yes, baby," Jessie replied, struggling to contain a new surfeit of emotion. "To Nashville. To help Jacob."

Behind her, Jessie could feel a new hot glare sizzle in a quickly escalating anger up and down her back. She shivered, picked up her child, and turned to face its source.

Josh stood too, his useless attempt to stay calm utterly defeated. Gone, too, was any pretense at pretending that he had control over this situation; that he could still choose to order Jessie to stay. They faced off against each other in a room where Jessie had fought for him years ago, long before either had ever heard a single rumble about some sad guy named Jacob Ryan who roamed the world with his guitar in one hand and his heart in the other.

There was more at stake here now, though, besides Jessie's need to be with Jacob during this terrible time. There was Josh's pride, and everyone in the house knew it. He was faced with Jessie's need to go and, too, he was faced—almost on a daily basis—with a daughter whose allegiances seemed to always lie with Jacob.

Emily-Grace was utterly calm now, in her mother's arms. Jessie was quiet now too, a determined fury underlying her usually pacific features. They were challenging him, Josh knew. Mother and daughter were united, and they were defiant. He could hear the words as clearly as if they were being spoken.

We dare you to stop us. We dare you to stand in our way.

And Josh knew that he would lose no matter what he said. Averting the stares of Charlie and Steve who, now, had appeared behind Jessie, and the stares of Dee, Charles and Matt, Josh kept his gaze trained solidly on his wife.

One at a time he positioned his hands on his hips. When he spoke, bitterness rang in his ears, and he tasted blood from biting hard on his bottom lip just before the words tumbled out, not all loving and kind and understanding the way they should have been, but instead tainted and raw and infused with a horrific past.

Over the ringing in his brain, he whispered them, hoping only Jessie and their daughter would hear.

Emily-Grace snapped her head around to her father when the words were spoken, and her tiny pink lips parted.

"Come back to me," she heard her father beg, his dignity and his pride at his feet in the grand room where Jessie, stuck entertaining the Deacons at the time, had ached to be with him years before.

Jessie straightened in alarm. But she, more than anyone, knew how close she and Josh had been to being lost to each other forever, only a few years earlier. And so she, more than anyone, could read his unmitigated, raw fear the way a hunter sniffs for grimy, musky bear.

She spoke for both her and Emily-Grace. "Of course we will," she murmured, the sea-pearl eyes luminescent and pale in the dimming light.

Small eyes that held the same mysteries of the soul were locked on Josh. After a moment where he tried to gain back his ragged breath and some semblance of a regular heartbeat, Josh let himself risk a peek at the unwavering truths they emitted forth from his daughter. She was speaking to him now too, by virtue of the way she openly watched him struggle, there in front of everyone who knew very well his weaknesses and how Josh was sometimes preyed upon.

Emily-Grace was in the safe tranquil curve of her mother's arms, too big to be there, but there nonetheless. Her small mouth closed into a firm straight line, the pallid eyes darkened, and she rotated her face away from her father, and into the familiar hollow of her mother's neck and shoulder.

And that, Josh knew, was his seven year old quite clearly telling him to leave them alone, that going to Jacob's aid was no business of his. This was his child clearly telling him, for the first time ever, to fuck right off.

Chapter Twenty-Two

When the Keating jet disappeared into the fluffy clouds over Vancouver, besides the small crew, only Jessie, Emily-Grace, and Matt were belted into the wide leather seats. Jessie was insistent about who travelled with her, and the obstinate mood she was in was familiar enough to those closest to her that they had no choice but to let her go with whomever she chose. Matt was the most trusted security, friend, family (of sorts) and advisor in her inner circle. It was a given that he would go.

There was one problem. Talia's manager, Richard, had informed Charles that Jacob had flown the coop. It took some digging, but an email from Jacob's dad, Tom Ryan, came through in the end, alerting them to his whereabouts.

I have a place in Florida, a small camp I used to go to with my parents when I was a boy, which the sentimental part of me can't let go. Jacob's there. But he wants to be alone.

The funeral would be in Nashville, with a post-service reception at Richard's large estate. In the meantime, Jessie couldn't stand the thought of Jacob cordoning himself off from everyone. Against his better judgment, Charles ordered the jet to file a flight plan to 'redneck,' Florida, and off it went. It would then travel to Scotland to pick up Jacob and Jessie's good friends, deposit them in Nashville, and head back to Vancouver for Josh and the kids, Charles and Dee, Carlotta, and Steve and Sophie and their two boys, Caleb and Cole. Charlie and Jane, their children, and Jack and Lydia would travel on their own chartered jet. Jessie, Matt and Emily-Grace would charter another jet to take them to Nashville from Florida. Whether Jacob would be on it was anybody's guess. Charles and Richard would decide how to get him back to Nashville after Jessie reported in on his wishes.

Talia's funeral would be a large private event with a live Internet stream for her and Jacob's overwrought fans. Celebrities in attendance would be numerous; security would be a brick wall.

On the jet, as Emily-Grace drew fashion pictures next to Jessie, and Matt sat opposite sipping lemon zinger tea prepared by Victoria, the long-time flight attendant always encircled by lovely scents (*jasmine today*, Jessie thought), Jessie tortured herself by picturing her husband's concerned eyes when she hugged him before leaving their driveway.

Josh had pretty much bit his lip and fought back the urge to tie up his wife or lock her in the bathroom, because he knew how useless any attempt to quell her stubborn decision would be. What Jessie wanted, she usually got, and it pissed him off to no end, especially where Jacob Ryan was concerned. So Josh helped her pack Emily-Grace's bag, and he carried both the small princess bag and the larger suitcase belonging to Jessie out to Matt's Audi, and waited until his wife was gone before he had a complete meltdown.

"Josh," Jessie had told him, remembering now while the jet coasted south, "I'm a big girl. I can take of myself."

He had answered with a fixed stare and a twitchy facial nerve.

"Babe, please," she insisted. "Don't say goodbye this way." The imperative was issued with an accompanying foot stomp.

"You stomped your foot," he told her, crossing his arms, upon which Jessie groaned and grabbed his wrists.

"Say goodbye to your daughter. Then kiss me and hold me tight. We'll see you in a few days."

He did as he was told and, to her credit, Emily-Grace hugged her daddy back, but it was a quick movement with a happy, "Goodbye, Daddy," because, well, on the other end of this journey was Emily-Grace's beloved Jacob.

Her brusque action only increased the intensity of the worry and sorrow in Josh's eyes.

"Our family says way too many goodbyes," he murmured, pulling Jessie to him.

"I know," she whispered into his neck, soaking up her husband's energy and fueling herself for the difficult job ahead. "But at least on the other end are a lot of hellos."

"Always the rainbow for you, isn't it, Jess?" Josh asked, using his strong right hand to lever her head back a little so he could lose himself in the pearlescent eyes he loved.

"Is there any other option?" she replied, a tiny forced smirk quite succinctly in place on the rather smug pink lips.

"I love you so much," Josh stated in a solemn tone, not rising to the bait. This occasion was far too frightening, from Josh's perspective, to settle into humor, even light humor, at this point.

"Don't look so scared, Josh. I promised you that I would not go there with Jacob. I'm never going down that road again with him."

"Then you should not be going to see him when he's in this state, Jessie. Period."

"He needs a friend."

"You're not his friend. You are his ex-lover. There's a difference, little one."

"He has no one, Josh. Nobody knows him like I do."

"I can't handle sharing you with him, Jessie. Not like this."

A frustrated *ahhhhh* sound escaped Jessie's lips and she stomped the other foot. "For God's sake. Is that some kind of ultimatum?"

"Jesus, Jessie, calm down, will you? I'm just telling you how I feel. I'm fucking scared. And don't tell me you aren't as well. I know you, and I know Jacob."

Her silence catapulted Josh's fear to a whole new level. This was a woman for whom sex was business, at one point in her life. This was a woman who endured forced sex for far too long; this was a woman for whom sex was a way to express love to those close to her when they needed it. Of course she was scared too.

"Matt will be with me," she choked.

"Yeah, so that fucking helps. Jesus Christ, Jessie! Just fucking go, will you?"

There it was, the temper Emily-Grace feared, the hot flare of emotion that frightened her and David and Dylan, that they rarely saw in the Sawyer household these days, but which she clearly recalled from 'the old days.' In the car now, she cringed, closed her eyes, and plugged her ears.

Matt, who was watching Dylan and David to be sure they didn't push their kid-sized plastic snow shovels onto the street, saw her reaction, and he sighed helplessly. With one hand gripping each of the young Sawyer sons and handing them over to their father, Matt intervened in what was now a tense, teary standoff. His curt words were to be listened to. This was a tone that, when Matt utilized it, demanded action.

"In the car, Jessie," he commanded, and neither Jessie nor Josh was certain which of the two of them he was more upset with.

Pouting, her lips set in a grim line and her eyes moist, "I love you back," Jessie finally sulked to Josh, by way of capitulation. "I love you the mostest. Always and forever, remember?"

Leaning forward, she tucked the favorite piece of rogue hair back behind Josh's ear. He let her and, as she turned to go, Josh grabbed her roughly and pressed her to him. She eased away, kissed him one last time, gave each of her boys a hard squeeze, and slipped into the car.

And that was that.

Now, on the jet, Jessie felt a small tug at her sleeve.

"Momma, how about you get this dress for the Grammys?"

Emily-Grace had drawn a sleeveless gown and carefully colored it blue. On Jessie's head was a golden tiara. On paper next to her was a man in a suit, his fingers entwined in hers.

"Ah. You made Momma a princess, I see. And look at Daddy. Isn't he handsome?"

"That's not Daddy, Momma. It's Jacob, look." Emily-Grace dug for a brown pencil crayon and drew a guitar in the man's other hand. "It's Jacob."

"Oh, hell," Jessie breathed, for the first time seeing what everyone else saw at La Casa the day before. "I'm a fucking moron."

Twisting slightly in her seat, she glanced over at Matt. He was staring at Emily-Grace's picture, and the happy smile lighting up the usually somber child's rosy cheeks. The little girl was singing.

Matt's gaze darted up to meet Jessie's chagrined eyes. Growling, a rare move for the usually composed Matt, he shook the pages of the newspaper he was reading, and cursed under his breath.

Chapter Twenty-Three

*R*edneck, Florida, as Tom Ryan had called his childhood holiday town, was practically a ghost town. There were remnants of life here and there, depicting what must have been a bustling little place decades ago, but all that remained now were decaying buildings with faded, painted signs. *Coca-Cola,* read one. *Mountain Dew,* read another.

"Welcome to Hicksville, U.S.A.," Jessie muttered, ogling first one rickety building and then another. "Home of the…" Turning to Matt, she asked, "Does anyone actually live here?"

Consulting his GPS, Matt ground the vehicle to a dusty stop. They'd landed the jet in Orlando, and driven two-and-a-half hours already. It would be dark soon, and he was getting anxious to settle his celebrity charges, who he planned to scuttle into their motel room unnoticed and unseen. "The motel is about six miles from here. I'll make the assumption there are actual humans in that general vicinity."

Crossing over a small worn wooden bridge, he drove slowly, impatiently looking left and right, scanning the woods for signs of wildlife or, Jessie mused to herself in a nervous kind of way, duck hunters in green military camouflage, with automatic rifles poised and ready. It seemed they were in that kind of neighborhood.

"Way to go, Jacob," she breathed to the window. "You got yourself a right good hidin' place."

Already Emily-Grace was yawning from her booster seat in the back of the rental vehicle, a nondescript Dodge Caravan that Jessie teased Matt over choosing for his hope that they would meld into the local population. "You shoulda got a pickup truck," she told him now. "Like, an old faded red Ford like Michael used to own. Something to, you know, tie your croc to after you wrangle it into submission. Across the hood, maybe."

"Jessie, do you mind…"

"Fine, I'll shut up," she chuckled. She winked at Emily-Grace via the rearview mirror. "But I don't see any other mommy cars around here. Or mommies, for that matter."

A string of curses erupted from Matt's otherwise potty-free mouth. Thankfully, they were low enough in tone that Emily-Grace only got the gist of his mood, and wasn't subject to the actual words. Still, Emily-Grace giggled at her mother's good-natured teasing. The tinkly laugh did its job. Matt couldn't help but let his lips curve up just a little as he pulled into their motel's parking lot.

Disappearing into the office of the one-story one-horse-town motel, he reappeared five minutes later with a larger frown than he'd sported upon sighting the place, which was populated by one less than two dozen vehicles (pickup trucks mostly, but Jessie just grinned to herself and held her tongue), and which seemed tidy enough on the outside. It was very plain overall, and closer inspection as they settled in revealed the occasional paint chip or 70's era décor, but what the heck, they soon discovered that the television, at least, was a flat screen.

The problem was that there were only twenty-four units in the place. "Did Dee not book this for us before we left La Casa last night?" Matt asked as he slid back into the driver's seat with their registration.

"I thought she did," answered Jessie, wrinkling her eyebrows in confusion. "Is it full?" She pictured them knocking on Jacob's door unannounced, saying, *Oops, can we crash with you?* They would be doing that tomorrow, regardless, well not the crashing part, but tonight she and Matt had a child to care for. Since Emily-Grace was Jessie's excuse for coming here, she couldn't very well just take off and leave her with Matt right now, no matter how desperately she ached to eyeball Jacob to make sure he was holding up okay.

Matt grunted before replying. Chewing on a fingernail, he sat quietly for a moment and stared out the driver's side window at a pink uniformed

Cuban cleaning woman making the rounds with a stack of clean white towels. "There's only one room, Jessie." He turned to look at her.

"That's fine," she said, although she was clearly startled. "Usually these places have two beds, don't they?"

His grimace telegraphed his thoughts. *And you know this how?*

"Spike," she chided him, "I haven't always been treated to the best hotels in town, you know. There was a time when I slept on the streets, remember?"

A shake of his head, and Matt restarted the engine. Pulling up to their assigned room, which was smack dab in the center of the single-story motel, he parked cleanly between painted lines and grabbed a baseball hat from the console before Jessie had a chance to gather her things and exit. Slamming it onto her head and over her eyes, he smiled affectionately when she tilted her head back and peered up at him from beneath the brim, a frown on the pretty face Matt adored.

"Seriously, Matt?" was all she said.

"You called it," he told her, tapping on the brim with the unit's key, which dangled from a small white plastic card with the room number stamped on it in bold black numbers. "We're in Redneckville. Get inside. I'll retrieve your daughter."

"Grrrrr," Jessie said, in an attempt to lighten him up further. But she grinned at her daughter and said, "Wait for Matt, honey. He wants to be sure we can make it the six feet from here to the room."

"We don't want to be stolen by gypsies again, Momma," was the child's wise but fear-inducing response. To this day, she was not aware that Morgan and Nadia were responsible for what happened that long ago day when they were supposed to meet Josh at ROAM. Now, the fact that she brought that up rocked Jessie to the core.

Staring at Emily-Grace as Matt went around the vehicle, Jessie just nodded slowly. "Yeah. Something like that." An icy chill up and down her legs caused an inadvertent shiver. *I'm an idiot,* she chastised herself for the thousandth time that day.

Safely inside, she took a leaflet from Matt and selected a pizza from a nearby shop that the motel owner, a kindly grey-haired man apparently, told Matt was only a few miles away. "Good thing," Jessie said when she saw the flyer. "Jacob won't be starving, at least." To Emily-Grace she said, "Jammies, sweetheart. Then you can watch some TV while we wait for the pizza."

Matt deposited their bags on the beds—his on the one near the door, and Emily-Grace's and Jessie's on the second big double.

Sitting on the end of the second bed, Jessie smirked and opened her mouth to speak.

Cutting her off before the words were uttered, Matt pointed a finger sharply and said, "Don't say it. Not a word from you."

"Are you nervous, Matt?" In feigned surprise, she threw up her hands. "I no touch. I swear." At that, she yanked her iPhone from her pocket and chuckled while she speed dialed Josh.

Later, Jessie snuggled with Emily-Grace and fought her own case of nerves. By the time the child was sleeping, Matt was snoring too, stretched out on his bed on top of the covers, fully clothed. After a bit, Jessie tiptoed into the washroom with her pajamas, which she'd teased Matt earlier about remembering to bring (*Thank God*, he'd thought), and she unfastened her jeans. When she was dressed for bed in light cotton pink pj pants and a lacey tank top, she went through her usual nighttime rituals, and finally let her mind wander to Jacob. Staring at herself in the mirror as she brushed her teeth, Jessie wondered what to expect the next morning. Surely Jacob would welcome her presence.

I just need to see you, she said inwardly. *I just need to know you are okay. Then I'll go. I swear.*

Even through the phone earlier, Josh's worry was transparent. Matt's tension was such that he only seemed to relax when Emily-Grace crawled under his arm to share pizza and watch *Phineas and Ferb*. Otherwise, his shoulders were taut and his eyes snapping.

"Okay," Jessie declared to her reflection as she spit. "We've got one more hurdle and then we're home free. Not counting Jacob's mood. That stands on its own."

She crawled into bed next to her daughter, yawned, and watched a Food Network special about a worldwide quest for the perfect lentils, wishing that was the world's biggest issue, ever. When the credits rolled at the end of the show, she poked the power button and the room went dark, with the exception of a red neon sign that pulsed regularly outside their window like a heartbeat. With it as her night vision aid, Jessie climbed back out of her covers and retrieved a wool blanket from over the small coat rack at the room's entrance. Unfolding it, she laid it over Matt, who stirred, momentarily confused at the pretty face smiling down at him, and the long layered curls framing it.

As Matt blinked up at her, Jessie tucked the blanket over his chest. "I know you are responsible for the safety of me and my daughter, Matt," she said, "but you are still allowed to wear pajamas to bed. If you so choose." A small giggle escaped her lips and she bent over and brushed her lips against his forehead. "Sleep well, my good friend."

Curling her body back in bed against her daughter's small frame, Jessie forced herself to relax by starting at the toes first and concentrating on each body part until she felt duly ready for sleep. At her feet, Matt padded softly by, a toothbrush in his hand.

"You're going to hate me in the morning," she whispered to his shadowy form.

Then she closed her eyes, and slept.

⌒⌒

"Hicksville, U.S.A. ain't so bad," Jessie commented aptly as she forked scrambled eggs between her lips. "Here, Emily-Grace," she said, reaching out to help her daughter navigate a package of pancake syrup, "the top comes up at the corner. Like this." Setting down her fork on the round table where she and her child were having breakfast, Jessie reached over to help.

Seated on the edge of his bed, using the table for his coffee and orange juice, Matt was facing them. He shoved a thumb and forefinger into his forehead and closed his eyes with a sigh.

Squinting at him as she picked her fork back up, Jessie asked, "Do you have a headache, Spike?"

"I'm fine," he grumbled, but his bloodshot eyes said otherwise. "Eat so we can get this over with."

Jessie froze, and poised her fork by her breakfast plate. "That was uncalled for, Matt." She frowned. "Wouldn't you say?"

"Jessie, I appreciate your concern for Jacob. But we're out here in God-knows-what-land and…" He caught Emily-Grace's frightened eye. "Go watch television," he told her. "Take your plate. I need a minute to plan our day with your mother."

Obediently, Emily-Grace did as she was told.

Leaning back, Matt grabbed the remote from the bed and turned the volume up high enough so that she wouldn't overhear his chat with her mother.

To Jessie he said, "Even after all these years, you still fail to realize what I'm up against when you pull your boss card on me and drag me into situations like this. I will simply feel better when we are no longer in this town."

"And what about Jacob? He's out here on his own."

"As you are well aware, Jessie, Jacob has been for the most part under Talia's security team for the last few years. By choice, as he continues to distance himself from you."

"Ouch."

"Sucks, I'm sorry, but it's true."

"So you just don't give a shit about him anymore? Does anyone?" Suddenly the eggs tasted like cardboard. A quick spike in blood pressure, and Jessie grabbed the plate and tossed its contents into a nearby garbage receptacle.

"Was that really necessary, princess?" Matt asked her, an edgy verve to his usually calm voice.

"Don't call me that. Ever, Matt. Ever ever ever, in fact."

"I care about Jacob. But my job today is you. You and Emily-Grace."

"You and your fucking job, Matt. Well, for today you can take your fucking job and shove it." *This is exactly the 'out' I need. Thank you for playing right into this for me, Spike,* Jessie told herself with a certain smug sense of satisfaction. She peered down at him from her haughty raised head. "Emily-Grace, hurry up, sweetheart. Finish up, and brush your teeth. We're on the move."

"Oh, so this is what's happening, is it Jessie? Planned all along, I suppose." Matt stood and placed his body in front of Jessie's as she tried to make her way along the narrow space between the beds and the wall unit to go into the washroom. "'She-who-must-be-obeyed,' I've heard Josh call you."

"I don't need you there, Matt, watching over every little thing Jacob and I say to each other so you can report back to Charles and Josh. I don't need you there, and I don't want you there."

"You will not go without me. Period."

"Oh, yes I will. Watch me."

Shoving him back, hard enough that he lost his balance and almost tripped over Emily-Grace's small knees, which still dangled from the end of the bed, Jessie stormed past. At the entrance to the bathroom, she shouted back at him. "I choose when and where I have security, Matt. I always have and I always will. Yes, it gets me into trouble sometimes, but this time I will be in more trouble if you go ratting me back to Josh. Am I planning to do something stupid? No. Not in my eyes. But maybe in yours. So do what you're told, and stay here today. Go," she waved an arm in the air, "wrestle yourself an alligator."

"Crocodile, Momma," Emily-Grace corrected her. "You said croc yesterday."

Jessie softened. "Two more bites," she told her. "Then we go."

Matt slammed a fist hard enough into the wall that he left a hole in the gyprock. Emily-Grace jumped and Jessie re-emerged from the bathroom, toothbrush in hand. He knew he was sunk, that he had no choice. Nor did he have a vehicle with which to follow her, although Matt seriously considered borrowing one.

"You go," he told her, his fingers trembling as he pointed them at her, "but you will call Charles first. I won't concern myself with Josh, because this is between you and him to sort out. If you want those kinds of secrets in your marriage, far be it from me to stand in your way. But Charles is my boss, technically, not you. He hired me to protect you. So if you want me to stand down and let you do this, then I will hear it from him."

"Semantics," she shrugged arrogantly, although Jessie's heart was pounding in her ears the way the red sign pulsed last night. "It's just words, Matt."

Ten minutes later they were on their way. Matt stood framed in the doorway of the small motel and watched them go, the Dodge Caravan's taillights disappearing around a leafy bend just before eleven, Florida time. Once they were out of sight, he put a second hole in the wall of the small room, and cursed til the air was blue.

Jessie figured she owed her daughter an explanation. "Your mother can be a stubborn old girl," she told her, depressing the gas pedal and eyeing her rearview mirror to be sure Matt wasn't careening around behind her in some 'borrowed' vehicle. "But Emily-Grace, there are some things that just plain need doin' alone."

Part of her deal with the very angry Charles, who Jessie spoke with mostly in order to heal her rift with Matt, was that she text Matt regularly. When they arrived at the densely forested 1960's era camp where Tom Ryan told them Jacob was holed up, she pulled slowly into the desolate yard and sent her first note.

We're here. I'll text once I see Jacob.

"Okay, my darling girl. We're on," Jessie muttered, sliding her seatbelt off her body and opening her door. "Do you remember everything we talked about, Emily-Grace?"

Emily-Grace was lithe and quick, and overtly anxious to see Jacob. Clutching her singer-dolly against her chest as she jumped out of the van, she peeked out from behind a curtain of blonde ringlets and spoke with an effusiveness Jessie had not heard from the child in a very long time. "I know, Momma. I'm just supposed to hug him back, that's all. He'll be sad."

"Let Momma go in first," Jessie ordered, with a hasty nervous exhale to blow a strand of hair off her cheek. With one hand she reached for her daughter, with the other she twisted a ringlet in her hair. "Remember, I told you he might be sick. I need to be sure he's okay before you go in. Okay, honey? Here. You sit on the step and just give me a minute."

"Okay, Momma." Emily-Grace did as she was told, although she hoped her mother would hurry. It was more than a little scary out here in the yard, what with the wind blowing through the tops of the trees and all this talk about alligators and crocodiles. "I wish Matt was here," she sighed to singer-dolly, and coiled her small body up into itself.

Behind her, Jessie stepped lightly into the wood-framed cabin. It was a remote dwelling, to be sure, but Jessie knew there was a lake nearby, and other cottages nestled into secret hiding places in the woods. She knew, because she'd seen some on the drive in. They were all at the end of long gravel laneways, some of which were untended and unruly, covered in an assortment of wildflowers and weeds Jessie couldn't even begin to identify. The shelters themselves were in varying degrees of repair and disrepair, judging by the faded paint peeking through the trees as they navigated the empty two-lane country road.

This camp was dusty and old, but at some point in time Tom Ryan had obviously furnished it and had someone, if not himself, hammer a few good boards here and there to replace rotten ones. There was a swing at one end of the open verandah, a white one, wooden, with a striped blue and cream cushion on it although, as Jessie squinted closely, it had faint black mold spots scattered throughout. Inside, a black wood stove radiated warmth to dispel the grey day. Many white-framed windows surrounded the first room, which was a small kitchen complete with open cupboards and a cozy low black Windsor rocking chair in one corner. There was no sign of Jacob, initially, and Jessie's heart raced as she trailed a finger alongside the cupboard, but the stove was on and there was a rented vehicle in the yard, so...

Slow booted footsteps emerged from the back, from either a bedroom or living room of sorts, Jessie surmised. She pivoted counter-clockwise, absently shoving up her red plaid shirtsleeves as she did so.

He stood there, face pale and beard three days old, his 'Jacob special,' Jessie used to call it, and stared at her. Jacob's eyes were the darkest shade of blue Jessie had ever seen; his eyes always seemed to morph with his feelings, and these orbs were absent of light here, today. She shivered, rubbed her arm, and granted herself the sweet pleasure of looking him over more closely.

The boots were her favorite—his old dusty black ones, with pointed toes. It seemed he had not yet capitulated completely to the country music trends with Talia, at least. Jacob was not wearing new, or elaborately stitched boots. The hems of his usual black jeans were as frayed as always, dragging over the wide pine floor. His belt, too, was black, and had a wide elaborately engraved silver buckle that, to her chagrin, brought Josh to mind, since he was the real cowboy in her life, and Jacob was really just an imitation who likely got the buckle from his country singer girlfriend at one time—a birthday, or for Christmas, maybe.

Jessie licked her lips and planted her feet widely apart. She, too, had floated into the room in faded jeans, although hers were denim and multi-holed, as seemed to be the trend every few years. Her boots, of course, were her favorite brown ones, the dustier the better. Jacob had pulled a V-necked T-shirt over his head, also black; Jessie was wearing her plaid shirt over a white tank top with thin shoulder straps.

Hooking her thumbs over both front jeans pockets, she shrugged. Her words emerged cracked and blistered. *Fear.* "I know you don't want to see me," she started, "but I needed to see you."

Half expecting him to break down, Jessie was surprised when she saw anger flicker over Jacob's face. He moved to the wood stove, opened the door, and shoved in another piece of split wood. Standing with his back to her as the wood caught, he told her to get out.

"I'm not going, Jacob," she said softly, so softly he had to twist around and face her to ensure she had indeed spoken. Jessie's eyes were pleading, insistent. "Let me be with you for a bit. Just today babe, okay?"

The old tenderness was there, as Jessie knew it would be, and the old endearment just snuck out. It pissed her off, because she called Josh babe a lot these days, but she had no idea how much it derailed Jacob to hear it. He had heard her call Josh babe more than once during the Boxing Day gathering at La Casa.

He was a time bomb, and he was ticking.

"Jacob..." Jessie stepped forward and, immediately, Jacob stepped back.

"Don't," he demanded, and raised a hand to air-palm her. "Don't you touch me."

"All right then," she whispered. *He's like a caged animal,* she thought. *Such anger...why?* "I know you're hurting, Jacob. I know how bad this is for you. I need to be here for you. Please. Just let me be here for you, the way you were there for me...in New York..."

"You used me," he accused, icicles dripping from the simple words. "You used me, you took my child, and you threw me away."

"I needed you. We all did."

"And look where that got me."

"Nobody could have predicted that Talia...that she..."

There was a cut above Jacob's left eye. It had been stitched and bandaged, but all that remained was a jagged gash. The bandage had long been discarded. It was Jessie's reminder that Jacob had been in the accident too.

"I was so scared," she moaned. "I thought it was you...when Josh came to tell me."

"And how is your cowboy, Jessie? Are you getting bored of him yet? Is that why you're here? You need some real action?"

"No, look, I, I came because I—"

"I don't need you here. And I don't want you, Jessie. I've hardly seen you in the last few years, and what happens when we're alone, huh? I just end up back in the same puddle on the floor, that's what. Or worse."

A sadistic guffaw escaped his throat then. It gave Jessie the chills. She sucked in a breath and steeled up her resolve. *I didn't expect this,* she told herself. *But okay. I came, I saw, I lost.*

It was time for tactic number two, which was, in all reality, Jessie's excuse for coming.

She moved to the door. "Honey," she started, and Jacob froze.

In walked Emily-Grace, all sweetness and lost innocence and childlike concern for someone she loved dearly. Concern for, she remembered, the guy who baked cookies with her when her momma was 'sick' and her daddy was too busy with Nadia to even care. The pale blue eyes were firm, strong and steady. She was an odd picture. She, too, was wearing jeans today, over small cowboy boots Jessie knew Jacob would love, because Talia had picked them out for Emily-Grace for Christmas. The child had on a pretty white cotton frock top in the empire-style. Over that was a soft cashmere sweater, lavender in color, the perfect type to hold and snuggle against a body when a person is sad.

It worked. Something flickered in Jacob's eyes when he saw Emily-Grace, as his anguished eyes scanned the child from the boots on up. He bent one leg and rested his weight on the other, struggling with what to say or how to say it.

Emily-Grace saw this in him. She, like her mother, had an endless capacity to feel other peoples' pain. She was in Jacob's arms in two seconds flat and he, despite all wishes to remain caged and alone, gave in to her.

His bare arms wrapped around her waist and lifted her and, as Josh and Jessie's daughter buried her face in his neck, and wrapped her legs around his waist, he wheeled around and carried her into the dimly lit room beyond.

Jessie moved forward so she could see where he took her daughter. Resting a trembling hand on the doorframe, she bit her bottom lip and watched Jacob drop his butt onto the edge of a double bed, hold her daughter tight, and pour out his grief.

Rocking back and forth, Jacob held Emily-Grace while she, too, sobbed for love of him and for the great pain that consumed him. He called out her name and then it changed to Talia's name, a refrain of constant burden that hurt Jessie deeply to hear.

She ached to go inside, to join the two, but this was a silent solitary grief that these two hearts, united in a different time and place with its own sweet sorrow, needed to let loose together. Instead, Jessie sank to the ground, her back to the doorframe, stuck her knuckles in her mouth, and cried alone.

Chapter Twenty-four

$\mathcal{L}$ater, as the sun was at its highest, Jessie nosed around the kitchen. She was surprised to find it almost fully stocked, including veggies and a cooked supermarket rotisserie chicken. Tom, or maybe Richard, had obviously ascertained that Jacob would want to hole up here alone and not venture into the small village nearby. Not that it seemed Jacob had eaten much, if anything, judging by unopened packages and a lack of empty pizza boxes.

"Biscuits and soup," she determined, her own cathartic cry having emptied her of the lingering anger and annoyance at what she felt was Matt's impudence that morning, but leaving her bent over and spent from the effort such a huge cry demanded. "Emily and David Wheeler's remedy for 'what-ails-ya.'"

Removing baking soda, flour, and the other ingredients from the cupboards, Jessie glanced down at her iPhone, which she'd set on the counter before she started rooting around for food.

A message glared up at her.

How is Jacob?

"Spike," Jessie murmured. "Terse and to the point. Just can't wait to go home to him tonight. Grrrr."

Picking up the phone, she typed *Gloat all you want. He hates my guts. He and Emily-Grace are lying on the bed telling stories.*

It was a bit of a stretch since Emily-Grace was doing all the talking, well, whispering mostly, but judging by the occasional chuckle from Jacob she was at least having some luck distracting him from the hard loss Jessie knew had completely debilitated him just a few days earlier.

Jessie added another line. *I'm making food. We'll be a few more hours. Go for a run.*

The phone bleeped almost immediately. *Text when you are ready to leave.*

Fine. Bringing soup and biscuits.

The bleeping stopped.

After a bit, Emily-Grace's giggling increased. Deciding to take advantage of what she hoped was the child's ability to soften Jacob's anger, Jessie stepped to the doorway.

"Want to share your jokes with Momma, Emily-Grace?" she asked her.

"No. Maybe. Can I tell Momma, Jacob?"

Jacob rolled over onto his back and eased himself up a little higher on the bed. Emily-Grace scooted up next to him. Singer-dolly was in Jacob's hands.

"Ah," Jessie sighed. "Jacob's got singer-dolly in his hands. That can only mean one thing."

"He's making fun of you again. Like he used to. Show Momma, Jacob."

Inside, Jessie could feel her heart screaming *please. Please please please. I need you to let me in.*

But Jacob tossed the doll on the bed and fixed Jessie with an implacable stare. Interlacing his fingers across his tight black T-shirt at his chest, he crossed his boots at the ankles.

Emily-Grace was non-plussed. She imitated Jacob's movements herself. Her laughter would have been balm for Jessie's soul, if the child ever laughed around her own father the same way.

Moving to exit the room and add carrots to the chicken soup, Jessie stopped when she heard a voice behind her. She turned back around.

"What?" It was a quiet question. This day was harder now than Jessie imagined it would be. She couldn't help herself. She wanted to be lying next to Jacob on the bed, soothing his hurts and holding him. Not sex, no, she didn't want that and nor would she ever, she told herself, with this man again, both as self-preservation and for the preservation of the two men she dearly loved.

"Who's with you?" Jacob was asking.

"Just Matt," Jessie whispered, and Jacob paused before nodding.

"In the car?"

"No. At the motel in the village."

"Why didn't you bring Dylan?"

"He's coming…" She swallowed and omitted *to the funeral.* "He'll be in Nashville. I thought for now…just Emily-Grace."

That seemed to be all, and Emily-Grace was dancing her doll over Jacob's belly again, which elicited a small smile from the wan face, so Jessie went back into the kitchen and finished making them an early dinner.

They ate in relative silence, with the exception of a few oohs and ahhs from the seven year old in the group when a rabbit hopped into the matted clearing beyond. It seemed to salute them, either that or it was hungry and smelled the soup, Jessie figured. She spooned some soup into her mouth and watched Jacob to be sure he was doing the same.

He was, he was eating, but to him, the soup and biscuits were another slap in the face. They were memories, the wrong kind. Good ones, but good ones in a relationship gone sour always became bad ones. The sensations on Jacob's taste buds were heaven, but in his heart were hell.

He shoved the feelings deep down inside, but Jessie saw unease dance across his face during the meal. Thinking it was related to Talia and an emptiness she prayed she would never have to experience for its permanence, she inhaled to a count of six and slowly moved her hand across the table to cover Jacob's. Emily-Grace was watching the bunny, and anyway, this was something friends could do.

Jacob felt the familiar hand cover his. The warmth it gave off was sweet; the fingers twining his were desired. His breath caught. The dullness in his soul waned, and became something hot and alive again under a remembered touch he coveted even when Talia was by his side.

Jacob let Jessie play with his fingers a little; let her hold him in that small way for a moment, because he needed it. He needed to feel her climb back inside his soul. A gentle squeeze was his reward for letting her touch him.

But no. It couldn't last. Jessie was his friend at one time, his lover a few times. Was this what she came here for? His touch? To feel his skin on hers again? Did what Jessie wanted even matter?

No. Talia was who mattered. And now Talia was gone. Because of Jessie.

Shoving back his chair, which screeched across the floor and startled Jessie, Emily-Grace, and the bunny in the clearing, Jacob grabbed his dishes and literally threw them in the sink. The bowl split in two. Gripping the sink with both hands, leaning on them, Jacob felt his blood start to boil. It raced up his chest and into his head, and stayed there, pounding, pounding, pounding. There was a voice there, too, and it was Talia's, telling him again and again and again why she couldn't marry him. After that was a scream, which Jacob, in all honesty, wasn't entirely certain he'd even heard on that fateful day. But he heard it now, all the time he heard it, louder and louder and louder so that it seemed it might break free and split his brain—or at least his heart—completely in two.

Glancing at Emily-Grace, who sat with her spoon poised over her bowl, Jessie touched her thin wrist. "Go outside, sweetheart. See if you can find where that bunny went."

Jessie plopped a warm biscuit into her daughter's hand as Emily-Grace slid by. The child moved towards Jacob first but Jessie grabbed her and shook her head no. "Outside, baby girl," she ordered. "He just needs a moment."

From the well-windowed interior of the rustic camp, for a minute Jessie watched Emily-Grace tiptoe around the area where the bunny was hopping around earlier. Nudging herself back around to face Jacob's hunched shoulders, she was heartbroken to see that they were shaking.

"You need to stop pushing me away, Jacob." Rising, Jessie moved towards him. "You need to let me help you." A hand floated aimlessly in the air as she reached in vain for him.

"You can't!" he cried, his voice high-pitched and weary with effort. He whipped around. "You can't help me. You said it yourself, Jessie. All you do is hurt people. That's who you are. That's what you do."

His boots over the pine floor as he stormed away left small indents. Jessie crouched down to touch them. One at a time she ran her fingers through the soft wood. And one at a time her tears splashed down alongside.

At what point do I have to let you go forever? she asked herself. The answer came quickly, and with a fury and intensity she hadn't counted on. *Never!* she screamed inwardly. *Fucking never!*

Jacob was gone for twenty minutes. In that time, Jessie cleaned up the dishes and set some soup and biscuits aside to take to Matt. The sun was lowering itself into the woods by then, its rays creating tendrils of airy glowings that were dispersed throughout the treetops like beams of hope.

He'll be okay, Jessie whispered as she sat on the top step scanning the trees for Jacob's return, and bending an ear in search of his footsteps.

Emily-Grace, who was practicing her ballet in the clearing with singerdolly suspended outwardly as her partner, saw him first. She was yawning.

Jacob picked her up and held her close before wandering over to face Jessie, whose desolation was apparent by the way she was leaning her cheek into one elbow of the arms she'd folded across her lap.

"Vancouver's three hours behind us," he lectured. "She was likely up super early compared to what she's used to. She's tired."

"Okay. I guess we'll go, then."

"All right," Jacob said. "Go." He waited a moment, then wheeled around and carried Emily-Grace to the van.

Jessie stayed put and watched him with her. Jacob was so sweet, so gentle, despite the soul-crushing hurts she knew disabled him today. Emily-Grace clung to him in tears. It took him a bit to coerce her into her booster seat. In the end, it was the weird promise to see her in Nashville in a few days that convinced her she would see her beloved Jacob again.

"I'll be there in a minute," Jessie called quietly to her through the open doorway of the van. "I need to get the biscuits and soup for Matt."

Jacob slid the van door shut. "She'll be asleep before you're up the stairs," he told her.

Inside, Jacob took up his position leaning against the sink again, and watched Jessie remove the soup from the fridge.

"Hope you don't need this back," she said, holding out the Tupperware container into which she'd scooped the soup.

"Not hardly likely," was Jacob's curt response, as he folded his arms and, inside, fought a war with his soul. Jessie…Talia…Jessie…it seemed no matter what or who he thought about, it all wrenched him apart. Everything hurt.

Jessie herself delivered the coup-de-grace. The thought was intended to heal, to give Jacob something to hang onto, because she felt he would need it today, tonight, overnight, in the difficult days to come. But he took it the same way he took the soup and biscuits. Victims of war. Good times gone very, very bad.

"You're so good with her," Jessie said. "Josh hasn't had a hope with Emily-Grace since you were in her life."

"Are you fucking crazy?"

"What?" Jessie looked up from putting the food into a plastic grocery bag to spy Jacob leering at her, standing now with his feet planted wide apart. "What do you mean, Jacob, I…" She stopped. The man before her now was not the Jacob she knew. He was partly there, the old soul Jessie loved and cherished but, like Josh so long ago, he was a man stripped of what mattered to him, of who he could love and cherish back. It scared her, the way he was staring at her now, with an odd mixture of hate and disgust in those once tender eyes.

"I said, are you fucking crazy? Why the hell would you tell me that? That I am better with your daughter than her own father?"

"Because I…I…" Jessie started to back away, Matt's food in her hands held out like an offering.

"Your cowboy is raising *my* kid, Jessie."

Jessie stopped moving. She found a nugget of fight. "Yeah, and you've seen yourself how good he is with Dylan. But he can't get through to Emily-Grace, he tries but he just can't."

"And why do you think that is, Jess? Huh?"

It hit Jessie like thunder. After it was crushed, her chest heaved with the effort to speak. She winced. "Because she can't get over you, that's why."

"Ah. I see."

The big shoulders started to shake again. This time, after Jessie set Matt's food on the counter and moved to him, Jacob let her stay near, although he tried in a half-hearted sort of way to push her away. In the end, though, the battle in his heart needed the physical person to hold, so he let Jessie hold him and he held her back. Melting onto the floor, Jacob let Jessie rock him until he had nothing left, and through it all he breathed in the familiar lavender scent of her, and let the images from their time in Scotland, Vancouver, even Miami, and then New York, dispel in his mind like confetti, scattering to different parts of his brain and staying there.

230

"It hurts," he gasped as he tried to catch his breath. Jacob unleashed his pain onto her the way she once did with him, and Jessie soothed him with soft, "I knows," and gentle caresses, smoothing his long curls back from his cheeks and holding him together the only way she knew how.

It took a few minutes for Jacob to calm himself enough to gather his wits and, when he did, he begged her to stay just for a little while. "Emily-Grace is asleep." Shifting his position on the floor, he let a hand linger on Jessie's thigh. "She's asleep or she would have come back in."

"I can't stay, Jacob." Jessie was insistent. "You know I can't, babe. It wouldn't be right for me to stay. It would be too easy. You know that. And Matt, he's waiting. He's waiting for his food."

"Okay, okay," Jacob agreed. "Fine, then. I get it. Just one kiss, Jessie, one kiss and then you can go."

There was a suspended breath in the moment between his begging and when she touched his lips. Her finger was trembling, and she wanted to kiss him—how bad she wanted to erase his pain by placing her lips on his—but Jessie let the finger hover there in front of him first.

To Jacob, it was just another tease. He closed his eyes, kept them closed when the finger finally touched him. Jessie was crouched in front of him now, on her knees. The finger was soft on the lips, barely there. It traced the bottom lip first, and then the top.

Jacob reached up and grasped her finger in his hand. He parted his lips, and gently placed her finger inside his mouth.

"Jesus," she moaned, following it with a, "no, Jacob. This can't happen."

His eyes were still closed, but he could hear her breathing quicken. Jacob took a chance. He paused for a second, first, but then he closed his lips over her finger, clutched hard at her wrist so she couldn't remove her hand, and he started to suck.

Another moan. Jessie leaned towards him, and laid her cheek against his. She moved a little, rhythmically, against him, the little mewls he remembered from *before* igniting a fire in Jacob he was powerless to resist. The fire was anger more than love, but it was both, just one more than the other today, a few days after Talia's death.

Grabbing Jessie's other wrist, Jacob removed her fingers from his hair where she was caressing him, and shoved her hand onto his crotch. Pushing her hard against him, he gasped and kept sucking on her finger until he felt her lips against his eye, his cheek, on the corner of his lip. Hungry to taste her now, he let go of the wrist he held against his mouth, and sought out her lips instead.

Jessie climbed onto his lap facing him—Jacob was sitting against the lower cupboard—and she straddled him, and rocked herself hard against him, and held him and loved him in a way that felt familiar to her, that she understood was love, that she needed. Their kissing was passionate and desperate, but when Jacob ripped open her shirt and grasped her breast, Jessie froze.

She started to pull away. "I can't…Jacob, I can't…"

"Yes, you fucking can," he growled. "And you will. You owe me, Jessie."

"I know I hurt you, Jacob, but that doesn't mean I owe you." Panic started to set in. This hard voice, the angry man in front of her, was not Jessie's beloved Jacob. Again he seemed a man divided. Confused, Jessie tried to skitter away. She crab-walked backwards on her hands and knees, her body still aching for him but her mind screaming a very definitive *No*.

Josh flashed across her mind. Josh, loving and sweet; he'd been badly hurt when Jessie took up with Jacob in New York.

"I need to get a grip," Jessie chastised herself.

Sex was far too easy for her. Her body craved the carnal pleasures she knew this man could grant with his tongue, his hands, his lips. Just looking at Jacob in his tight black jeans and the sexy boots she remembered from the New York days undid Jessie entirely. A vision of Jacob bathed in stage lights as he urged sweet and perfect notes from his guitar drifted through her mind; Jacob, singing and moving his hips, pressing the guitar against a thigh above a bent knee so he could exact, from white-taped blistered fingers, the right tone and texture from his instrument; Jacob, loving her through a ballad they wrote together to help Jessie heal from the loss of her husband after Nadia came into Josh's life and seduced him with her curvy body and sensuous lips.

Jacob was quick. He, too, was on his knees in a second. Shoving Jessie backwards so that her head hit the floor, hard, sending a hot lightning strike through her brain, he bent over her, knees on both sides. A quick flash and he had both of her wrists gripped tightly above her head.

Tightening her abs, Jessie cried out and mobilized her strong dancer's body to try to get out from underneath him.

Everything in Jacob's brain was wild now. There was an excruciating ache, a hollow white emptiness, and a flashing swirl of color, all of it rebounding and echoing and screaming and hurting. It was madness, the worst combo of emotions he'd ever felt; every bit of the spectrum was there— anger, hurt, loss, frustration…fury. Rage. And this woman underneath him was the cause.

His hand reached up, high, and came down on a sweeping arc that caught Jessie on the side of her cheek and split open her lip. "I don't fucking care," she heard him cry. "I don't fucking care if I kill you! That's about what you deserve, Jessie! You took Talia from me so I should take you from Josh! You hear me?"

She couldn't respond. Jessie was numb from the pain of him striking her, and numb from the agony she saw in Jacob's crazed eyes. Swallowing, she tasted blood, and so did he when he bent forward and sucked hard on her lips. Jessie remembered well this impossible feeling, this unbelievable feeling of being wanted in a violent way that had nothing really to do with sex, and everything to do with anger and power.

Jacob shoved up her tank top and bra. He sucked hard on a nipple and, as Jessie moaned with grief and turned her head away, he tore off her boots and ripped open her jeans, yanking them down as she started to cry.

"I said no, Jacob," she was sobbing. "I said no!"

But he restrained her arms above her head again and forced himself inside her, and as she kicked and struggled, gasping at his urgency and the hard thrusts that hurt, she cried. Jessie could hear him screaming as he took what he wanted from her. She prayed Emily-Grace was indeed asleep in the van because this version of Jacob would destroy her.

Tuning back into him, Jessie tried to understand what this shell of a man she loved was screaming. Her brain was muzzy but still she heard, "Do you want to know what we fought about in the car the day Talia died? Why she pulled over? Do you want to know, Jessie? Just before she called off our wedding? I'll fucking tell you! I'll fucking tell you! We were goddamned fighting…about you!"

Two more brutally hard thrusts and he was done. By then, Jessie had no fight left. She wanted to die. Once again she was reduced to everything she always thought she was. A whore. Someone who hurt people. Who hurt them badly.

Jacob stayed there, moaning, for two full minutes before he backed off and left Jessie on the floor. She could feel him pulsating inside of her while he lay on top, panting and trying to regain some sense of equilibrium, she supposed. When he shoved her aside and stumbled away, into the bathroom, she heard him retching.

Curling up into a little ball, Jessie shoved the heels of her hands over her ears and squeezed her eyes tightly shut. Inside, she was wailing. Outside, she was bruised and bleeding.

Great sobs overcame her but she pushed them away. Her jeans were on the floor. Grabbing them, she put them on, leaving her panties lying where Jacob threw them. The plaid shirt was ripped so she left it too. Her shaking hands managed to pull her bra down over her sore breasts, and the white tank top over the bra.

Jacob had thrown her boots into the far corners of the room. On all fours, she scrambled for them. Hopping over the pine floor, she yanked them on. Matt's food was on the counter where she'd left it. Somewhere in the far reaches of her whirling brain, Jessie knew she would need it to distract him. She grabbed the bag, and ran out of the door.

Emily-Grace was asleep, her cherubic face and the limp, tired ringlets completely devoid of suspicion or worry. She slept like an angel, while Jessie drove like a bat out of hell.

Nearer the motel, she realized she had forgotten to text Matt to tell him they were on their way. It was pitch black with the exception of occasional streetlights and the neon of the pizza joint just down the road.

Jessie swerved hard to the right and skidded to a stop on the deserted road. Throwing open the door, she ran around the front of the van and puked until she was dry. Leaning against the van on the shoulder side of the road, she swiped a palm across her mouth. It wasn't until she went to text Matt that she saw the blood on her hand.

"Jesus," she moaned in exasperation.

The text sent, she searched the car for napkins or Kleenex. There were none. She got down on all fours and grabbed big handfuls of grass, and did the best she could wiping away the stain of her sins.

She was a coward at the hotel. Matt swung open the aluminum door when she pulled up, then stepped aside to allow her to carry Emily-Grace inside. Jessie made sure her face was angled away from him, hidden by her daughter's curls.

"Your soup and biscuits are in the van," she said. "I need a shower."

Turning to watch her, Matt's heart started pounding. Jessie wouldn't even look at him, and she wasn't wearing the red plaid shirt she'd had on when she left the motel this morning. He was disgusted, and sorry for both Josh and Jacob. *Sometimes I wonder who you are*, he told himself as he watched Jessie lay her daughter on the bed before making her way into the washroom and quietly closing the door behind her.

But then he looked at Emily-Grace, who was sleepily snuggling herself up into a ball in the dim light. Matt stepped over to her so he could tuck her in. When he saw a dark patch in her hair, he reached out his hand. Thinking it was a reflection of the red neon motel sign, he pulled his hand away.

And held it up to the light.

His fingers were covered in blood.

Chapter Twenty-five

$\mathcal{M}$att grabbed Emily-Grace and hauled her up. Protesting his rough ministrations as he searched for damage on her half-awake body, she started to wail. When he was convinced she was okay, Matt set her on his lap and hugged her to him. A tremor started in his gut and worked its way outwards until the hair on his arms stood straight up.

Somebody was hurt. Somebody was bleeding. Thank God it wasn't this child. By Jessie's quick duck into the shower, and the way she held Emily-Grace on the way in, it didn't take a rocket scientist to ascertain that the blood was more than likely hers.

Emily-Grace hiccup-cried herself back to a world of dreams that, Matt hoped, were good ones and not some new nefarious nightmare world that her mother had, quite intentionally, put the child back into. Lifting the covers of the bed, he tucked her in, removing the pillow with the blood on it. For a moment Matt considered hurling open the door to the bathroom and giving Jessie the same damn inspection he had given her daughter, but sense and propriety won out and he sat on the edge of her bed instead, hugging the pillow to his chest and waiting, just waiting, for the faucet to be turned off and the woman dousing herself underneath it to reappear.

Underneath the rush of water a new sound emerged. Great, gasping sobs have a distinct, gulping cadence. Jessie was sobbing in the shower. The sound sickened Matt. What the hell happened today? Did Jacob and Jessie have a knock down fistfight?

Jessie, in the shower, did her best not to let Matt hear her cry but in the end her innate rage at Jacob's actions and the futility of her ability to thwart him threw her spinning into a new emotional meltdown. Furious with herself for enticing Jacob in the first place, for reacting to his overtures, for falling into the trap she feared but walked right into, Jessie fell against the wall and sank to her knees in the attached tub. What Jacob had screamed at her tore her in two. Worst of all—her daughter was nearby and, had she been awake, could have witnessed the violent attack.

It was a long while before Jessie's shoulders stopped heaving, before the tears finally subsided. Outside the washroom, Matt sat in the pulsating red light cast rhythmically by the motel sign, and tried to control his shaking hands and the hard truths he felt he might holler at this headstrong woman, which he knew from past experience could easily escalate them into a nasty fight.

One thought calmed him. *I know her now,* he told himself. *This is no longer a stranger trying to hide things from me. Jessie is family. She'll talk.*

And the most reassuring thoughts of all. *She is here. Her daughter is here. They are safe.*

It was a full half hour before Jessie finally emerged, eyes red and swollen from the exhausting cry. In her rush to get into the shower, she had neglected to grab her pajamas. She stood before Matt now in a white towel she clutched at the top, and she started to shiver.

He stood, and Jessie's eyes dropped to the bloodstained pillow in his hands. The fear in his step as he approached her was palpable. Matt dropped the pillow at his feet, and grasped Jessie's chin with his thumb and forefinger, raising her face and turning it towards the yellow light bleeding into the room from the bathroom.

"Ouch," she gasped.

"Jesus Christ," he cursed when he spied the red welt on her cheek and the raw blood still draining slowly from her lip. A quick scan of the rest of her body—neck, arms and legs, the tops of her breasts from over the towel—revealed more bruising, most notably, Matt noticed as he lifted her arms one at a time so she could hold the towel in place, at her wrists.

Dropping her left arm, Matt took a step back.

In front of him, Jessie started to sob again. She covered her face with her sore left wrist, and ordered Matt not to speak. "Don't say anything," she begged. "Not one word, Matt. I don't need your judgment hanging over my head right now."

He ignored her. "You, Jessie Wheeler-Sawyer," he dramatically over-enunciated the Sawyer, "are the most headstrong, spoiled, willful, obstinate child I know."

"I'm not a child."

"You sure act like one."

"You're crossing a line, Matt! You do that a lot, you know?"

"Why did he hit you, Jessie? Tell me why he hit you. Did Emily-Grace see him hurt you?"

"No, no, she…she didn't. I don't think."

He gasped and cursed again.

"She was in the van. I went back for your food and…and…" The tears started again. Jessie moved to the end of the bed and collapsed down onto it.

Matt scooped up the wool blanket he'd folded over the end of his bed earlier in the day, and placed it over her shoulders. There was a chair nearby, a heavy wooden one with a low rounded back and a hard cushion. Dragging it over the floor, he dropped into it and took her left hand.

"Tell me what happened, Jessie." A new fear started in the pit of Matt's stomach. This was worse than a fistfight, and he knew it before the words were even uttered.

Jessie swiped the back of a hand over her cheeks and winced when she touched the sore side.

Pushing back his chair, Matt strode into the bathroom and soaked a cloth in cool water. Bringing it to her, folded three times over, he held it against her lip.

"Thank you," she murmured quietly before looking up at Matt and fixing a sorry gaze on his handsome, worried face. The bruised shoulders sank noticeably. "Matt, he wouldn't talk to me all day. It wasn't until we were about to leave that he finally caved a little. Then…" She bit her lip, winced, and looked away. Sighed.

"Look, Jessie, you're a grownup. I know you have feelings for Jacob, I was there, remember? I know how hard it was to let him go. Everyone knows. Yes, obviously Josh included. None of us are idiots, especially Josh. You left me here today for a reason. If you thought being with Jacob would somehow help him, then so be it. I'm not your judge, even though it kills me to think how much this must be hurting your husband right now."

"I didn't intend…Matt, I never intended to sleep with Jacob. I just wanted to hold him, you know? The way he held me in New York. We didn't have sex that night. And not for a while afterwards. I thought we could be together and I could just hold him."

"So what happened, Jessie?" Matt's voice was oddly calm.

Too calm, Jessie thought, scrunching up her nose as she pondered what to say.

She chose to tell him the truth. "I got too close. I wanted him. I'm sorry, Matt, I did. He's…he's Jacob, you know? Being with Josh, choosing Josh, does not mean I will ever stop loving Jacob."

"Hence everybody's fear, Jessie. How could you not see that? Are you so accustomed to getting your own way, to being treated special that you thought you could hurt Josh again this way? And how about Jacob? I would assume that's where these lovely new bruises came from. You…comforted him. And then you tried to walk away. He lost it."

"Oh, he lost it all right, Matt. But not in the way you think. And not for the reasons you think." The tears increased in intensity again, falling onto the towel covering Jessie's thighs, soaking it with lost passion and love gone awry. "He told me they were fighting about me when Talia was killed. That's why she pulled the car over. He told me I was everything I once said I was. A whore, you know? And then he treated me like one."

Matt's blood went cold. "You said you wanted him. Did he force himself on you, Jessie?"

"I did want him, Matt. But I stopped. I swear to God I stopped. I knew it was wrong, I knew it would kill Josh if I had sex with Jacob. I told him no. I told him no, Matt. But he was wild by then. He said he should just kill me so Josh would suffer the way he is suffering."

The pulse in Matt's neck was beating fast now. He swallowed, and tried to digest what Jessie told him. When he stood, and kicked the chair back with his foot, it started to tip. He gave it a final hard shove and it went skittering sideways into the wall.

Jessie rose slowly, and held one palm out to face him. The wool blanket fell to the bed. "Matt, I've had all the violence today that I can handle. And my daughter doesn't need to see me like this. Please, if you need to be angry at someone, be angry at me."

"Oh, I'm angry with you, Jessie. I think you know I'm angry with you. But kid, no means no, no matter how aroused your partner happens to be. And there is never a good excuse for hitting a woman, making death threats, and calling her a whore. Ever. I'm going to go wrap my hands around Jacob's throat and let him know exactly what I think of him."

"No, you're not, Matt." Jessie skirted the bed and grabbed Matt's white linen button down shirt by the fistful, at the back, since he was making a bee-line for the door. He shook her off and whipped around to face her, while she continued. "You attacking Jacob is not going to put this thing to rights."

"He can't get away with this, Jessie! The police need to know what happened so they can charge his lily-white spoiled superstar ass!"

"And what's that going to solve? I don't need the whole world reading and hearing about this on the Internet two days after Jacob's fiancée was killed!"

"You don't need Josh knowing, is what you mean." The words were stark and painfully real.

"Damn straight I don't need Josh knowing. Or Charles and Dee."

"Don't ask me to keep a secret I might not be able to keep, Jessie."

"Look, I won't get pregnant, I'm taking measures against that possibility at the moment. And Matt, Jacob has a right to be pissed at me. If I had any idea they were fighting…about me…"

Matt had one hand on the door. Groaning, he let go and faced Jessie full on again. No way could he leave her here alone in this appalling state. And no way could they call the cops. Jessie was right. The whole thing would explode in Jessie's face. And Matt cared too much for this mixed-up woman to let that happen to her just when it seemed she and Josh were finally destined to live a long and happy wedded life together.

"Jacob can't get away with this," he said again. "If nothing else, Charles needs to cut him loose."

Jessie flung both hands out to her sides, but brought them in quickly again when it seemed the towel was about to fall away. She shrugged her shoulders and held her chin up high. "It's me you're talking to, Matt. Jessie Wheeler, remember? What's a little forced sex and a few plump bruises to me? I'm just a whore at heart, remember?"

"Aw, Jesus, Jessie. Don't even go there." He waited until it was apparent she could no longer find the words, any words, to show that she thought otherwise. Then Matt stepped forward, wrapped his arms around the icy shoulders of the woman in his care, and eased her pain as she cried.

Chapter Twenty-six

*I*t was late in the day when Matt finally rousted Jessie from the passenger seat in the van at the Orlando Executive Airport, and nudged Emily-Grace awake from a nap.

"Our jet is ready," he told them. "Let's roll."

Sickened at the ugly purple bruise on Jessie's cheek and the swelling in her lip, not to mention the continuously leaky, bloodshot eyes, Matt sighed and took her hand to help her slide out of the vehicle.

The night before, he had finally let go of her and sent her off to the washroom to put her pajamas on, then he tucked her under the covers next to her slumbering daughter, where she continued to shiver, mostly from shock, he had figured.

She had turned around to him and asked him to lie down with her. The request startled Matt at the time, but there were things about Jessie's past that segregated her from others, that made choices that seemed a little weird to some, normal to her. Having a body she trusted to hold her in order to help her settle was an ordinary request from a hurting girl.

Matt had walked around the bed, grabbed the wool blanket, gone back to Jessie's side, and laid down fully clothed on the outside of the covers, pulling the wool blanket over his body as he did so. He wrapped one arm around her waist, and allowed himself to snuggle in close enough to offer her some warmth from his body, some healing semblance of calm, perhaps. It worked. Jessie took his hand, pulled it up under her chin, and drifted off to sleep.

For his part, Matt had lain awake most of the night, the pulse pounding in his ears loud and hard enough that he feared it might actually wake Jessie.

How could he not let Charles, at least, know what Jacob had done? Sure, the boy was out of his mind with grief. But that was no excuse for hatred and violence. Lying next to Jessie, though, Matt was grateful. A few years earlier, she would have suffered alone. His heart swelled as he listened to her breathe while she slept, as he watched her chest rise and fall, as he let his fingers wrap tenderly around hers. As he inched closer and buried his face in her hair.

When dawn broke, three hours earlier in Florida than it would in Vancouver, it dissipated their red neon heartbeat companion into less angry, jagged thrusts than the crimson stabs that lit up the darkness all night long. A quiet pink took over.

As he heard Jessie stir, Matt had hoped blue sky and sunshine would help her recover some sense of peace today, but in all reality he knew it wasn't likely.

"Matt," she blinked at him when she awoke and rolled slowly onto her back. "Thank you."

As he lay crooked up on one elbow beside her, the way she looked up at him—still drunk with sleep, warm fingers once again reaching for his—Matt had to stifle the urge to bend over Jessie, to tent her in his arms and brush his lips across her forehead. Instead, he forced himself to wipe a strand of hair off the bruised cheek, but unspoken thoughts and deep feelings passed between them. They came from heartfelt trust and a new, shared secret. Sometimes, in Jessie's company, Matt couldn't separate the need to protect her from the love he had for her. Inwardly, he considered Talia's security minions, distant and untouchable. Maybe that was the best way…Lying on this bed with Jessie, peeking down at her, brushing his thumb over hers, was like building a campfire with damp wood and wondering why it was smoking.

Suddenly Jacob's actions, if not still reprehensible, at least followed a path that could be understood.

"Don't thank me yet," Matt had finally replied before easing his tired and fatigued mind and body off the bed, and stretching with a wide yawn. "I still don't know how this is going to end, Jessie. But it's not going to go down well for Jacob, I'll tell you that much."

Emily-Grace had stirred then, and Matt found himself watching Jessie dream up a story to explain her bruised face. "I fell in the shower last night," she told her. "Momma's not used to that slippery kind of tub."

Can't see Josh buying that one, Matt thought wryly.

Now, leaving the van and taking her daughter's hand for the walk to the steps of their hired jet, since the Keating jet would soon be en route to Nashville from Vancouver, Jessie was telling Matt one last time to leave Jacob alone for the time being, and to swear to keep their secret. Emily-Grace's ears perked up, but all Jessie said after that was, "Tomorrow he's burying the woman he was supposed to marry today, Matt. It's New Year's Eve. Let him be."

"You are far too forgiving," was Matt's jaded reply as they approached the steps to the plane. "This isn't over, Jessie."

The plane ride was eerily quiet. Like an iTunes song on perma-loop, Matt, who was sitting kitty corner across from Jessie, watched her replay the difficult day and Jacob's actions again and again. The thoughts swept across her face like dark, grey clouds, growing darker as the jet approached Nashville. Sinking into a futile worry in the uncomfortable silence, Matt leaned on fisted knuckles and wondered how much damage Jessie's inner condemnations were doing to her already beat-up sense of self-worth.

Jessie stared gloomily back at Matt as the shadowy thoughts accosted her. Did she hate Jacob for what he did to her? No. It was wrong on every level, but when Jessie conjured up images of what happened and the sequence in which it happened, all she felt was desire followed by a repulsion that sickened her. *I should be so angry with him,* she told herself. *Why am I not angrier? Because I did this. I caused this. All of it—Talia's death, Jacob's rough treatment of me, Matt's anger. I am to blame.*

Soon they were on the ground, quietly and surreptitiously ensconced in the Renaissance Nashville Hotel awaiting the arrival of their friends and family. After discussing it with Jessie, Matt had switched Jessie and Josh to a separate hotel from her Scots and Vancouver friends, most of who were staying at the five-star Hermitage. The Sawyers would need some low-key alone time without references about Jacob, or any chance of running into Jacob, from the Scotland gang. Jessie had a nasty bruise and a cut lip, and no way was Josh going to let those go down easy.

Matt left Jessie and Emily-Grace in their large suite at the contemporary hotel with security provided by Arnie, who flew in with the Deacons on an early flight. Arnie's raised eyebrows questioned the welt, but he knew Jessie, and her cue to him was to remain silent about it. She would talk when she was ready.

All Matt said to him was, "Tough day yesterday. Let her be. Jessie just wants some quiet time with her daughter. Make sure she eats something."

Jessie never left her security outside in the hall unless threats demanded it. Instead, the gang was always invited inside to find a place to relax in front of a television or a plate of good food. Today, she invited Arnie in as usual, but had trouble making eye contact with him, and sequestered herself and her daughter off to the suite's master bedroom to watch Treehouse TV. Arnie stayed by the door, munched on an apple and some grapes, and speculated about how Josh would react to his wife's swollen cheek. For that matter, what would Charles and Dee say?

Turned out Charles and Dee had some time to process what happened before they would have a chance to run to Jessie and lecture her for setting herself and her daughter up in a precarious situation in the first place. They were meeting Jack and Lydia, and Talia's manager Richard and his male partner Tobias, as well as Talia's parents, for dinner at the manager's large home. Nobody besides the Keatings would be present to represent Jacob who, Matt told Jessie before he left for the airport to meet the Keating jet, was flying in late that night. The Keating jet was being sent for him immediately after it landed. There would be no one else besides Victoria and her pilot husband, and his co-pilot, on board.

Jessie thought that was likely for the best, although the solitary image of her beloved Jacob—or his shell, it seemed—ripped her in two.

She lay on the bed after Matt left and idly stared at the television, an ice pack on her lip and cheek to try to reduce the swelling before Josh saw it. Long sleeves and a high-necked top covered the lighter purple swaths on her wrists and neck. Quiet time on the bed helped ease the general overall soreness that commanded her body like a disease.

Emily-Grace channel surfed. At one point, Jessie grabbed her hand and asked her to leave the TV on a certain station, MTV.

"Just for this song, honey," Jessie softly told her.

The song was a rousing upbeat dance tune that rocketed to number one and stayed there for weeks after Jacob and Jessie recorded it, which happened after the Seattle concert where Jacob met his son for the first time. Jessie and Jacob had played around with the song when they were together in New York, but hadn't finalized and recorded it until after they messed around by jamming it on stage in Seattle, long after they were supposed to leave the stage but gained permission to stay, giving the fans an extra huge treat. Now, Jessie watched a live version filmed at the Seattle show with a growing sadness that was settling deeper into her heart and soul. Talia was on stage with them that night, and so were Josh and Emily-Grace, who was only four at the time but who knew all the words and sang them with gusto, as she did now, a wide smile on her face as she watched.

When Emily-Grace turned her head at the sound of her mother weeping, fear escalated in her bones as well. A sad momma was no longer the norm. That woman disappeared when Jessie took the kids and returned to Vancouver to be with Emily-Grace and David's daddy.

"Momma?" asked the wise seven year old now. "It's sad about Talia, isn't it?"

"Y-yes," Jessie managed to tell her as she wept. "And you know something, Emily-Grace?"

"What, Momma?" The pale blue eyes were watchful, waiting. Emily-Grace was sitting cross-legged on the bed while her mother lay on the covers beside her, her right cheek on a crooked elbow on a goose down pillow, the ice pack on the hurt left side of her face.

"It's sad about Jacob too."

"Oh. Yes."

From a lime-green stool in the small kitchen area of the large modern suite, Arnie went on high alert when he heard Jessie crying. Without wanting to appear intrusive, he stole by the open French door to the bedroom and peeked in. He saw Emily-Grace consoling her mother, whose body was racked with sobs, and he backed off. Whatever was ailing Jessie today was very likely related to Talia's death, because Arnie recognized the popular song playing on the television, and he realized how much it must hurt to hear and see it played.

Not long after, hurried footsteps down the hall announced the arrival of the two smaller Sawyer children and their father. Dan and Susanne were both with the kids, as was Matt, their escort who, along with a local driver, had picked them up. Steve and his family had been dropped at the Hermitage, which confused all of them, given Matt's quiet announcement that Jessie had requested the change. Now, Matt took Josh's elbow and asked him to hang back for a moment while David and Dylan ran in to see their mother, with their 'friends' Dan and Susanne in tow.

"Josh," started Matt, as Josh stopped and faced him, "we need to talk."

A long face and a hushed, "Okay," followed a moment of silence. Turning one foot over on its side and placing his hands on his hips, Josh settled into a tense stance as he waited for Matt to speak.

"Jacob," Matt said simply.

"I don't want to know, Matt. And to be honest, I don't think I need to."

"You're her husband."

"No shit. Although usually where Jacob's concerned there's a lot of grey there." Josh's sarcastic tone was well earned, Matt knew, but underneath were layers of fear and distrust. Not great recipes for success in a marriage.

Matt kept part of his promise to Jessie. He did not reveal intimacies related to what Jacob told her or of the violent sexual activity that left her bruised and broken. That would be up to Jessie. But the bruise on her cheek was noticeable and severe, and would not go unnoticed. It required some semblance of explanation before Josh laid his eyes on his wife today.

"You knew there would be tension when she saw him. Given what happened at La Casa on Boxing Day."

The nerve on Josh's cheek started to twitch. "What'd he do to her?"

"She takes equal responsibility, Josh." Matt felt like a goddamned liar, which in some ways he was if you factored in what he was leaving out of the conversation.

Josh laughed weirdly, throwing back his head and letting out a, "What? My wife? Piss Jacob off enough to start a fistfight? Did he hit her, Matt? Because if he did, I'll drive him through a brick wall."

"Josh, Jessie and I already had this conversation. She doesn't need to go through it again. Yesterday was a very tough day for her, and tomorrow's not going to be any damn easier."

247

"You asking me to cool it, Matt? Are you telling me there was a physical altercation between Jessie and her pansy lover boy, and you're asking me to keep quiet about it?"

Matt had one hand on a hip too. The other he raised between them, rigid palm facing down, to further accent his point and try to calm Josh. At the same time, his command was quick and clipped. "I'm asking you not to overreact. I'm asking you to consider the fact that your wife is not in a good place today, and that someone she cares for is the cause of that. Period."

Josh was silent. When he spoke, his words were careful and clear. "What aren't you telling me, Matt?"

"You only need to consider what I am telling you. And the blunt side of that is that you have three children here who need you, and a wife that is barely coherent today. She is bruised and sore, and yes Jacob is the reason why. But you will not go after him, and you will not give your wife the third degree over what happened between them. Not today, Josh. Not today."

"Did you want to fucking kill the bastard, Matt?"

"You're damn right I did."

"And you didn't because Jessie asked you not to?"

"How well do you know your wife?"

"Very well, my friend." Josh placed his hand on Matt's back and steered him towards the door. "Too well, in fact. But the down side of this is that she knows me pretty well too. So just a word of warning. If you're serious about me not going after Jacob for hitting Jessie, then it's going to take you, Dan, Susanne and Arnie to keep me off him. Capiche?"

"And Jessie?"

"I won't ride her about it until she's ready to talk. But I have a feeling it'll take all of you to keep me from throwing her around for flying to Florida to see him in the first place."

"Not funny, Josh."

"Figuratively speaking, of course. Not for real, Matt." Josh pivoted slowly around and looked Matt in the eye. "You know that, right Matt? I would never lay a hand on her."

Matt tried to smile, but it came out lopsided. "Of course, Josh. I know you would never hurt her."

But what will you do to Jacob when you find out he raped your wife, Josh? Matt wondered. *Likely what I've been doing to the kid in my head since I found out,* he answered himself. *And it sure ain't pretty.*

Josh opened the door, and they marched in, silent and thoughtful, to a room full of excited children and a mother beyond happy to have them crawling all over her sore body.

Taking a deep breath, Josh nodded at Matt in silent thank you for the advance warning, and he wandered into the bedroom where all three of his children were snuggled up to Jessie, telling her stories.

She was sitting up now, propped up against luxe pillows stacked against the headboard. When the presence of Josh's body changed the light at the entrance to the master bedroom, she looked up and met his eye. After Jessie removed the ice pack, Josh let his gaze drift down to the bruise, and to the swollen lip below it, and he curled his fists at his sides. Jacob would pay for this, no doubt about that, Josh swore. But because Matt asked him to err on the side of caution today, Josh simply blinked at the damage the asshole's fist caused, swallowed, and further entered the room.

Easing down on the side of the King sized bed, he grabbed Dylan, moved him out of the way so he could better see his wife, and bent down to kiss her forehead.

"I've been missing you," he whispered.

Jessie was incapable of answering. She turned her body towards Josh, literally crawled into his arms, and curled into him.

He held her close, and murmured that he loved her. From him, that was all Jessie needed to hear for the time being. Tomorrow would be another day, the day after—another.

There would be time for a fight.

But for now, there were children, there was happiness, and there was love.

Chapter Twenty-seven

Jessie considered not attending the funeral. The thought of facing Jacob again, in such a public place, consumed her. And would she even be welcome? Would he want her there?

"I don't know what he wants," Jessie said quietly to her reflection in the mirror as she applied cover-up over the bruising on her face. "I can't even guess."

In the end, though, she knew she had to attend. Despite the violent end to the other day, Jacob was still Jacob. Granted, he was hurt and angry. And sad. What he did to her was unconscionable and simply wrong on every level. But Jessie being Jessie, she carried a large amount of the blame upon her own aching shoulders.

"I never should have tempted him in the first place," she mumbled to herself. "What happened was my own damn fault."

There would be a great deal of fans and media behind barriers outside the church. The public had been asked to let Talia's friends and family mourn in peace, but Talia was a country music sweetheart. Like Jessie's, her music spoke to people. Talia's fans felt like they knew her intimately. She was a rare performer who connected with fans through her music and from the stage. Loved by all, her light was dimmed far too soon, and fans needed to come say goodbye.

For the celebrities in attendance, especially Jacob, and Jessie by virtue of her association with Jacob, the spotlight would be bright regardless of wishes for privacy. Systems were in place to streamline escorts into the church with as little hassle as possible. The kids' car seats would slow the Sawyers down, but they would at least disembark efficiently from a parking place directly in front of the church.

Kayla and Paul had flown in the evening before, after the end to Paul's workday. Kayla popped in now to see Jessie, and zipped up her black dress for her.

Behind Kayla, Jessie could hear Josh enlisting Paul to help corral David, who was protesting having to wear a tie. She could hear Josh pleading with him.

"See? Uncle Paul's wearing one!"

"A bow tie," Kayla mouthed to Jessie, using her fingers to imitate where and what kind of tie Paul was wearing. "Striped. My hipster man, reincarnated from the thirties."

"Classy." Jessie tried to smile, but there was still a surfeit of tension between the two women, another casualty of the Boxing Day fiasco.

Kayla tried to put it to rest. "I'm sorry," she said. "It wasn't my business. At La Casa, I mean." She moved in closer to Jessie, and touched the swelling on her cheek. "The man lost it, huh? Unless…" She sucked in a breath.

"It wasn't Josh, if that's what you're thinking."

Exhaling, Kayla closed her eyes in relief.

"I think you'll see today, Kayla," Jessie sighed, using her fingers to try to rub more makeup over the bruise, which made her wince, "that my relationship with Jacob is everybody's business. And yup. He lost it, all right."

"I don't know want to say. I didn't think Jacob would go there." Pondering Jessie, Kayla leaned back against the sleek white countertop. Inhaling, trying to reconcile this version of Jacob with the sexy man she was seriously crushing on, Kayla switched back to the 'everybody's business' comment. "Long lenses, huh?"

"Yup. As usual, we'll be micro-analyzed for every look that passes between us. I sure as hell wish they couldn't see my face. Although I admit I'm curious as hell which direction the media'll take it. My guess is the headlines will read 'Josh Sawyer beats his wife for covert visit to soothe Jacob Ryan in his new love nest.'"

"Love the 'let's blame Josh for everything' part. He's never been able to shake those old demons you saddled him with."

"Thanks for that lovely reminder. Yeah, this day's already off to a great start."

"Cool it, Jess. Let's start again, okay? How about I go back out and walk back in again."

She moved to leave, but Jessie reached out a hand and stopped her in her tracks. "How about you just go?" she said with a grimness mined from great sorrow. "Period." She was speaking to Kayla via her reflection in the mirror, which somehow seemed easier since it was like a barrier between Jessie and the real Kayla.

Unmoving, Kayla locked herself in place and fixed a confused stare in her sister-in-law's direction. "What's your problem, Jessie? I said I was sorry."

Slowly, Jessie wheeled around to face her. In the brighter light, straight on, Kayla grimaced at the welt and the cut lip, which the cover-up was practically useless in hiding. "But you're not, though, are you? Sorry."

"What the hell's that supposed to mean?"

"Jacob. My relationship with him."

"You want to fight, today of all days?" Shifting her weight, with a petulant frown Kayla crossed her arms.

"I'm tired and my body feels like it's been through a meat grinder. I'm not up for putting on a happy face and pretending everything is hunky dory when it's far from that, Kayla."

"Fine. Let's be real, then. Jacob's not a pet, Jessie, who you can keep at the end of a leash and haul in whenever you're feeling sad or lonely, or when Josh and you have a fight. He's a man incapable of letting go of his feelings for you, and you use that for your own good. How'm I supposed to be forgiving of that, especially when my own brother is another pawn in your game?"

Angry tears flashed in Jessie's eyes. She pointed at the welt on her cheek. "Do you think I did this to myself, Kayla?"

"Ha. Yeah. On some level, damn straight I do! And knowing you, I bet you feel the same way. I'm just wondering how you got to that point with Jacob. My guess is you like it rough."

"You—bitch."

"You shouldn't have gone to see him in the first place! You should never have gone down to Florida. You deserved what you got!"

"Tell me you're joking, Kayla," Josh said quietly, stepping into the open doorway.

Whipping around to face him, Kayla let loose on her brother. "You're such a fucking doormat! You should have tied her up at home! Why the hell would you let your wife go to a man she has a sexual history with—"

"Easy, Kayla, you're going too far—"

"Just after the woman he was supposed to marry, like yesterday, gets killed? What the hell were you thinking? You think this is all he gave her? I fucking doubt it, Josh. Think this through. Use your head."

Gripping the side of the door, sorry that everyone in the other room appeared to have heard her tirade, security and kids included, Kayla turned back to Jessie and spoke in a hushed but still angry tone. "You just can't let go, can you, Jessie? You want to wipe away everyone's tears and save the world. But what you fail to consider is that not everyone wants to be saved…by you."

Strangely, Casey flashed across Jessie's mind. The drumming prodigy sure wanted nothing to do with her. Obviously Jacob didn't, either.

Kayla's heels clacked across the floor as she stamped away. "Give me that tie," she ordered Paul, who was still trying to wrestle David into wearing it. David sat still when his Aunt Kayla approached, and let her settle it around his neck. Even at his young age he knew not to incite further anger by a woman already incensed.

From the bathroom doorway, Jessie watched Kayla yank the knot up and straighten the small tie on David's neck before she allowed herself enough dignity to be able to meet Josh's solemn gaze.

"We will talk about this later, Jessie," he told her, his wounded eyes flickering. "But I get that it shouldn't happen today. All right with you?"

Swiping at a tear, Jessie nodded and moved backwards so she could lean against the counter. "I don't even want to see him today," she said, though, by way of sharing some little part of her fear with her husband, the man she trusted most. Even though she knew, in her heart, that she had already lost a little of that trust and likely would lose a lot more if Josh ever found out the truth about what happened in Florida. "I really just kind of want to go home."

"It was that bad, huh?" Gently letting his fingers graze the welt on her cheek, and running a thumb over her lip, Josh's tone was dangerously quiet. But he was also offering genuine concern.

Dan and Susanne were already helping the kids with their coats. It was time to go. But Jessie needed Josh on her side. Despite all, she knew he wouldn't let her down today. Wrapping both arms around her belly, she squeezed tightly and hunched over a little. "He blames me," she admitted sadly. "They were fighting about me. That's why Talia pulled the car over."

"Oh Jesus, Jessie. I'm sorry." Studying her for signs of imminent melt-down, Josh moved closer to his wife and gathered her in his arms. It took everything Jessie had in her not to cry outright, but there were only so many times she was up to redoing her makeup today, and already the bruise was peeking through.

Josh studied the glaring welt further before glancing up at his wife's eyes. "It wasn't your fault, Jessie. Talia knew how much you two care about each other long before this happened. What happened to her was just a terrible accident. She and Jacob were hit by a man who should not have been driving. Who had too much to drink."

Jessie hesitated. "I feel like our fingerprints are all over Talia's death, Josh."

"Our?" He cocked his head at her. "What, so like the guy who hit them is supposed to represent me and my boozing days? Stop overthinking this. It's a tragedy, and I don't know how Jacob will get past it. But it doesn't give him an excuse to hit you. And it doesn't give him the right to blame you."

"Sure it does, Josh," she answered with moist eyes. "I'm his soft place to land, right? He can do whatever he wants to me. He knows I can take it."

"Jesus, no. Look, I'll book you in to see Trudy when we get back to Vancouver. You need her perspective on this."

"No, I don't," Jessie replied, straightening. "I have a pretty clear perspective, Josh. The problem is, so does Jacob."

"C'mere." Josh wrapped both arms tightly around Jessie's shoulders and held on tight. "We have to go," he whispered. "But I'm right here alongside you, okay? You're not alone, Jessie. I'm not going anywhere."

A quiet nod was her response. As Josh moved away for a final chat with Matt and Arnie about protocols at the funeral, Jessie rotated back towards the mirror and sponged away the latest round of tears.

"I don't deserve you," she told her reflection, but thinking about Josh. Blinking, she looked away, and threw the crumpled, damp Kleenex at her bleary image. It landed in the glass-fused sink, where it lay ignored to soak up excess water drips until it was as damp and sodden as Jessie felt.

~ ～

Josh managed to get Kayla's ear once on the way to the car. He had David in his arms, but he leaned over to her anyway and growled, "Today, Kayla? Really? Today of all days you pick a fight with Jessie? Would you mind telling me what the hell that was all about?"

"You heard," she answered in a righteous tone. "Get your head out of the sand where you buried it. I have no tolerance for how she's hurting either of you."

"Why the hell do you all of a sudden give a shit about Jacob?"

They were walking quickly, leaving the luxury hotel by a back door in the hopes of avoiding fans or paparazzi. Kayla was clinging to Paul for support as her heels clicked on the asphalt.

Paul bristled, and both Kayla and Josh noticed the rigid change in posture.

"What?" she asked him.

He shook his head, but Josh tensed and made a mental note to ask Paul what that was about.

At the cars, the families were ushered into multiple vehicles to accommodate their security as well as Kayla and Paul. Josh paused to deposit the still fussy David in his car seat. While he was fastening the little boy in, Dan secured Dylan in the adjacent seat. Josh made a quick dash over to Jessie in the first vehicle. Bending forward for a kiss before she slid into the car, he touched Emily-Grace's head too, and wished them well on the drive downtown.

"Let's go, Josh," Matt ordered, as Susanne ushered Emily-Grace into the back and fastened her booster seat.

"We'll get through this," Josh told Jessie as Arnie gave her shoulders a gentle turn so she'd climb into the front passenger seat of the large black SUV.

"The funeral, or Jacob's reappearance in our lives?" Jessie muttered under her breath as she watched Josh head back to the second vehicle, tapping on the back window of the first car to force a smile in Emily-Grace's direction as he went by.

Kayla and Paul were in the third vehicle, piloted by Dan, with Susanne marching back to the front passenger seat. Arnie drove the second, with Josh and the two boys inside, and Matt was behind the wheel of the first, with Jessie and Emily-Grace as his passengers. When they pulled up to the church, stopping directly in front, Jessie shrank down in her seat.

"I hate this part, Matt," she moaned, fisting her hands in her lap. "I wish we could just morph ourselves inside." Thousands of fans lined the street. Cameras were flashing before the passengers were even unloaded.

Matt's jaw was tense, his eyes alert and watchful. Glancing at Jessie briefly, he grasped her hand and gave it a reassuring squeeze. "You're okay, kid," he said with a casual brush of his lips across her knuckles. "I've got your back."

Her small smile and the teeny light that appeared in her eyes at his words were welcome on this dark and difficult day.

"I know," she said as she thanked God for the presence of this amazing protector in her life. "Thank you, Matt. Really. For everything."

"'Course," he managed, his throat all of a sudden feeling a little thicker than usual.

Before Jessie looked away from his gentle gaze, she lifted their hands and held the back of Matt's fingers against her cheek, closing her eyes so she could soak up his energy. Inhaling for strength, she twisted around to her daughter. "Emily-Grace, honey, this is going to be a busy one. You need to stay with me. Hold my hand at all times, honey, unless Matt sees fit to carry you at some point. You got that?"

Anxiously watching the crowds, Emily-Grace had her head turned away from the church when local security startled her by whipping open her door. Unbuckling the seatbelt around the booster seat, she reached for the hand of the frightening man in the dark sunglasses and black clothing, but he grasped her waist instead of taking her hand, and set her on the ground.

Eagle eyes watching for signs of anything out of the ordinary, Matt moved quickly to make his way around the front of the vehicle. Jessie's door, too, had already been opened by local security. An imposing bald black man was offering her his arm.

Frowning, staring at the asphalt below her toes, Jessie stepped down from the big car and, watching as they pulled up behind, Josh couldn't suppress a grin. He could read Jessie's mind at times, and right now he knew damn well she was cursing the fancy heels on her feet and wishing for her usual brown boots or Converse Chucks. The grin disappeared quickly, though, when he saw fear cross her face as she grabbed their daughter's hand. She hated situations like these; the screaming, the chaos, the cameras flashing, were all reminders of how crazy their lives had become, how public and transparent and vulnerable all of them were.

Josh saw Jessie look anxiously towards his vehicle before he and Arnie jumped out and released Dylan and David from their car seats. Catching up to Jessie and Emily-Grace, he wrapped one set of fingers around Jessie's hand and carried David with the other arm. A quick glance to his right and he saw Arnie, with Dylan in his arms, jog up alongside.

Relieved at the comforting feel of her husband's warm fingers in hers, Jessie kept her head down.

Inside the church, everyone collectively inhaled and paused before they moved up the aisle to take their seats in a long wooden pew five rows from the front. Deirdre and Charles were already there with Jack and Lydia. Behind them were Steve and Charlie and their families. Kayla and Paul took up the rear. Arnie and Matt flanked Josh, Jessie and the kids, while Susanne, Dan and Ulysses, who accompanied Charles and Dee, took up posts in the church. The Sawyer family was to be well protected in this very public venue here today.

Arnie was on Jessie's right. Dylan was on her lap now, Emily-Grace on her left, and David next to his father, with Matt holding fort in the seat by the center aisle. Jessie exhaled slowly and wrapped one arm around her daughter's shoulders.

They settled just moments before the service started. Jacob, his father, grandparents, Talia's family, and a mournful parade of her cousins and aunts and uncles shuffled their way slowly up the aisle behind the exquisite virginal white coffin. Jessie forced her gaze towards the left, towards the sad procession.

In the center aisle, unable to help himself, as Jacob stumbled forward he scanned the assembled mourners for Jessie. Again, a surge of fury accosted him at the sight of her—with his son on her lap—but there, too, inherent in who Jessie was today, was the ugly mark Jacob had left on her face, which the longer lenses outside today were already digitally uploading to Twitter.

Confused and sorry and angry, he bit his lower lip and held her gaze as he drifted by, handsome in his expensively cut black suit, shaved for this weird day, but dazed and grieving and lost.

Jessie knew this about him; she wished to hell she could jump up and take Jacob's hand and walk him through all the pain of this bitter dimension they'd found themselves in, so he wouldn't look so scared and lonely.

Many of Jessie's recent moments had been infused with thoughts of leaving, considering Jacob's rage a few days earlier, and the muddled feelings Jessie had for him as a result. She had half-expected a directive to leave Nashville, one explicitly telling her she wouldn't be welcome at this memorial. Now, even, would Jacob holler out in his grief and rage and ask her to leave?

Deep inside, Jessie felt Jacob wouldn't do that. He wouldn't stoop so low as to humiliate and punish her any more than he already had. He wouldn't beg her to leave because he needed her with him today, five rows back and with another man, yet—here.

There were more in the Sawyer group who recognized Jacob's lonely posture and who ached to cease his pain. One was Kayla, who intentionally avoided her man's thoughtful eyes and instead sought out Jacob's, and who cursed under her breath when his only regard seemed to be for Jessie.

Josh and Matt fought to keep their tempers under control, drifting off long enough to miss a quick flurry of activity in their pew. Before either had a chance to react, Emily-Grace was up and gone, her wiry and thin ballerina body slipping past her brother and the men in the blink of an eye.

Gasping, Jessie half-stood and reached for her, but the child was at Jacob's side in a second flat, holding a hand up to him and waiting for him to take it. Jacob stopped moving and studied her, this little creature who really didn't belong to him, and whose mother continuously caused Jacob such intense heartache. A tiny upward curve formed on his lips and, for a moment, Jessie thought she saw a point of light flicker in the anguished eyes she adored.

Matt was standing now, reaching for Emily-Grace, but Jacob took the little girl's hand, moved her out of Matt's reach, and shook his head. Too, he let his eyes linger on Josh and then Jessie, each in turn. Gently scooping

Emily-Grace up in his arms, he slowly, silently, placed her on his left hip, and turned the middle finger of his right hand upwards at the same time that he started moving forward.

"Jesus Christ," Josh groaned. "Matt, go get her. What a fucking asshole."

Matt was only too eager to grab the child. He was exiting the pew when he heard Jessie call his name. Closing his eyes in frustration, he rotated his head around to see what he knew he would see, which was Jessie shaking her head slowly from side to side.

If I can't help him, at least my daughter can, she telegraphed to him across the wooden pew. As Matt cursed under his breath and sat back down, speaking in his wireless lapel mic to Susanne, Dan and Ulysses, who, because they were standing, could keep eyes on Emily-Grace, Jessie shifted her gaze to her husband, whose dark eyes, on her, were now flashing in anger.

Josh gritted his teeth at her in furious disapproval while, behind him, Kayla gloated and sent Emily-Grace a silent cheer.

The memorial was touching, but the Vancouver clan was tense throughout. Everyone was afraid to let his or her guard down, even for a moment. Past experiences had taught them that extra caution was called for in such vulnerable public events. And now, all through the readings, the music, and the videos of sweet Talia projected on a central screen, they had to worry about how to retrieve Emily-Grace from Jacob's grasp at the end of the service to maneuver her into the vehicle with Jessie.

Matt was incensed; even Jessie was afraid to look over at him because his cheeks were spotted with red, and his lips were pressed in a thin line when they weren't silently cursing and asking Dan and Susanne for updates on how Emily-Grace was getting along up front. Jessie wasn't worried. From where she was sitting, she could see her daughter's darkening-blonde ringlets snuggled into Jacob's shoulder.

Jacob's arm stayed around Emily-Grace the entire service, letting her know how much she was a genuine angel to him on the most difficult day of his life. Like her mother often could, the child had the ability to ease anger from pent up hearts. Also like her mother, most times at least, she had a power over Jacob that was calming, that could quiet his hurts.

Jacob made a point of walking down the opposite side of the large central aisle when he left the church, so nobody in the Sawyer party could access his girl, whose hand he held tightly as she padded along next to him. But he didn't count on Dan being outside, where Matt had ordered him to wait. The fans were mostly quiet now, respectful and watchful, but a low murmur started when Jacob appeared with Josh and Jessie's little girl alongside. Nervous, he picked her up and, flanked by Talia's imposing security, made his way towards a vehicle near the front of the line of shiny black SUVs.

Dan cut him off at the pass, halfway across the churchyard. "I'm sorry, Jacob, but I need to take Emily-Grace."

"No!" came an adamant squeal, half inaudible because it ended up buried in Jacob's chest.

"She needs to ride on a booster seat. Otherwise she could travel with you."

"It's a short ride, Dan," Jacob told him, fighting back the frustrated tears that had been threatening all day. "She'll be fine."

Dan played the illegal card. "There are cameras everywhere," he said quietly, reaching for the small waist. "She is not allowed to be driven in a vehicle without a proper restraint, without the proper seat. It won't look good."

"Do you really think I give a shit today about what looks good, Dan?" Jacob started to move away, but looked back over his shoulder at the church entrance as he did so. Jessie was standing at the top of the steps, watching him, ignoring Matt's urgent orders for her to move.

It was as if the world went silent then; all sound ceased, at least in Jessie and Jacob's messed up worlds.

You have my daughter, he thought he heard her say.

You have my son, Jacob sent back.

Beyond that, which wasn't malice as far as both understood, was something far deeper. It was about due diligence and responsibility, and a complete regard for the safety of the children in their care. And today Jacob was burying someone he loved who died in a car.

Aiming for his vehicle, he took three more steps as he considered that, while Dan asked Matt, via the lapel mic, how far he should go in this public arena towards getting the child back.

Jacob stopped.

With Matt's furious voice ringing in his ear, Dan moved in. This time, when the big man reached for Emily-Grace, Jacob let her go. His back to Josh and Jessie, he fought back an overwhelming urge to yell, to scream, or to crumple up in a heap on the pavement. Instead, he unleashed his sadness on Dan, whose heart ached for the kid despite what he apparently did to Jessie via that mark on her cheek and her swollen lip.

While Emily-Grace did the screaming and kicking for him, he said to Dan, "They have everything. They have my son."

"They're going out to Richard's too, Jacob. You'll see the kids out there."

Jacob waved a hand futilely in the air. His words were devoid of emotion, his eyes a blank stare. "So what's that give me," he asked as he backed away from the child screaming his name, "another hour? Maybe two? Then what?"

Dan overstepped his boundaries. But he knew this guy well, and he knew this shattered little girl in his arms well. "From what I hear, you're trying to step away anyway, Jacob. So what's the big deal?"

"I was trying to step away, I guess," Jacob agreed, pocketing his hands just before pivoting back around, "but that was when I still had hope that I'd be raising my own family. Did you know Talia was pregnant, Dan? You've got my permission to share that with Jessie, by the way. I just found out last night. Makes me want to give Jessie a bruise on the other side now to match the first. Even her up so she doesn't look so off balance. Wouldn't phase her anyway, cuz, you know, whores like her attract violence like honey attracts bees."

Jacob touched the corner of his right lip as Emily-Grace went silent, and Dan adjusted her in his arms so he could cover her ears. Jacob continued his damaging low-voiced rant. "Although I admit I'm surprised Josh hasn't left his mark and fixed the little bitch up already, for flying down to see me." To Emily-Grace he said, "You are welcome to come live with me any time, sweetheart. I wouldn't want a whore for a mother and a drunk for a father, either."

"I hope you didn't hear that," Dan muttered to Emily-Grace as, shocked, he watched Jacob stroll away alongside a female security guard, whistling, his head bowed down while cameras flashed around him.

The blood ran from Dan's face as he hurried towards Matt and Jessie. Instantly, both sensed that something more than they witnessed from afar had gone down. Emily-Grace kept her face buried in Dan's shoulder, but her body was trembling now, and she was sobbing her heart out.

"C'mere, baby girl," Jessie begged, reaching for her, but she refused to go to her mother.

Dan couldn't meet Jessie's eyes. Nor could he loosen the child clinging to his body.

"You'll see Jacob at the reception," Jessie tried. "Come on, Emily-Grace, Matt's having an apoplectic fit. People are taking pictures we don't want them to have."

Behind them, the boys already secured, Josh headed over to the vehicle. "What's the holdup?" he demanded. "We need to get out of here."

Matt answered brusquely, "Put her in her seat, Dan." He was holding the door open for Jessie. "You too, Jessie. In the car. Now."

Behind them, thirty feet away, something clanged heavily to the ground. Startled, everyone jumped. The barrier had come loose and was knocked over by the weight of the fans and paparazzi behind it. A surge of grieving people pushed through. By the anger in a few raised voices, some were clearly Jacob Ryan fans, and not Jessie and Josh fans.

"Dan, now," Matt ordered, the steady calm of his voice belying the fear underneath. Images of the Backstreet Boys on tour in Brazil snaked through his brain, their gridlocked vehicles being rocked by overzealous fans. "Get that child in the car. Jessie!"

Panicked, Jessie was reaching for her daughter when Matt grabbed her arm and shoved her inside, slamming the door behind her. Jessie screamed at him and pounded the door, but Josh was moving now too, and he roughly grabbed his daughter and yanked her away from Dan, which, despite Josh's fear-fueled adrenaline, still took him three tries to do.

"Jesus, Emily-Grace," he cried futilely, "get in the goddamned car!"

Dan jumped inside the second she was deposited, and Josh, with Arnie grabbing for his arm, was left behind the second he slammed the door, as Matt peeled away, tires screeching.

Susanne had jumped in Arnie's seat in Josh's car and, with the two boys already securely fastened in the back seat, was now skidding to a stop next to him and Arnie. Arnie whipped open the passenger door and Josh jumped in, and then Arnie vaulted into Kayla and Paul's vehicle when Paul, now behind the wheel, hollered at him.

In the lead vehicle, after twisting around to be sure Dan had her daughter securely fastened, Jessie pressed a hand to her forehead and collapsed back against her seat.

"Oh, Jesus," she moaned, then looked into the backseat again. Darting her eyes from the buckle upwards to her daughter, she was devastated to see that Emily-Grace had both palms pressed into her face, which was buried into drawn up knees, and was sobbing even more profusely. "Honey," Jessie tried, "I told you, you needed to stay with me. I'm glad you were able to help Jacob but in situations like this you gotta listen to me! And to Matt and Dan and Susanne and whoever, because it's their jobs to watch out for us and make sure we are safe!"

Her heart was racing, but they were now safely away from the crowds, escorted by motorcycle cops guiding them to the reception. Softening, Jessie reached for her daughter's hand but Emily-Grace refused to budge.

"Please," Jessie pleaded, "stop crying, honey. We'll chalk this up to learning, okay? We're all fine, it all turned out fine."

A low *harrumph* from Matt accompanied the remark, which earned him a nasty glare from Jessie.

When Jessie turned back to Emily-Grace she was relieved to see the little girl's sullen, angry eyes fixed on her, but the relief was short-lived when the child's next remark echoed the surly glare. "I hate you," she growled. "I hate you, I hate Daddy, and I hate Jacob. I want to go home."

Her heart crashing to her feet, Jessie gulped and watched her daughter curl back up into herself and turn her head sideways to stare out of the window. Jessie slid her gaze sideways to take in Dan, who sighed and looked away as well, and then she sat forward again and watched Matt's white knuckles grip the wheel in stony silence, his jaw working in helpless fury he knew he could not unleash.

"Well, then." Jessie, her face as pale as Dan's now, mumbled so the only person who heard her was Matt. "I know what I probably did, and I know what your daddy did, but I sure as hell don't know what has suddenly turned you against your beloved Jacob."

She answered herself. *You don't want to know.*

Jessie, too, twisted her head sideways and watched the city fly by.

Chapter Twenty-eight

*M*iles outside of Nashville, nestled amongst acres of luxury homes, they pulled into the circular driveway of a 20 000 foot grey stone English style manor house. Sitting on about four acres, they soon discovered that the terraced mansion, inside, featured crisp marble floors and soaring twenty-two foot ceilings.

At the reception, Emily-Grace clung to the only people she really felt secure around, and those were Charles and Dee. Her grandparents were always a shelter during the Sawyer family storms, but even they couldn't determine what hurt the child so that she didn't even seem to want to be with her cherished Jacob.

Josh stood in a small posse with Matt, Dan and Arnie, his feet planted apart, one hand pocketed, and one absently brushing the new whiskers on his chin, while Dan filled them in on Jacob's damaging words.

Standing apart from everyone, Jessie stood alone behind a gorgeous round antique mahogany breakfast table, in the shelter of a massive bay window, and watched Josh, knowing as she did so, that he was being beat up again as surely as if someone had set him up in front of a wall and was firing knives at him. She knew this because, as Deirdre walked Emily-Grace away, she had rousted Dan the moment she got out of the SUV, and so Jessie was well aware of how hateful Jacob had been towards her family. What he had done to Jessie a few nights earlier was unforgivable. But it was incomprehensible that he would abuse and hurt Emily-Grace in a very similar way, physical violence notwithstanding.

Josh turned at the waist and eyeballed Jessie.

He's wondering if I know, she thought. The favorite piece of rogue hair fell in front of his ear and landed on his cheek. *God, I love this man*, she sighed, aching to take him in her arms and beg him to fly them all home as fast as he could manage it. By all accounts in the press and media, Josh was a big tough guy capable of hurting his family, capable of playing, in the movie world, villains and heroes and spies and agents and cowboys. He was strong, he was physical; he was undeniably roguish, ruggedly handsome, and brave.

But inside, you are squishy and warm and sad, mused Jessie. *I love you and I miss you and I need you.*

As if he could hear her thoughts, Josh pawed a toe on the plush Turkish rug and nodded *so long* to the guys. "Thanks, Dan," he said as he turned. "You did what you could. My two girls are rebels, that's all. God help anyone who tries to stand in their way. It's just too bad they tend to get steamrolled in the process."

Matt grasped Josh's elbow as he moved to go. "We're going to have trouble getting Emily-Grace back into the car," he said. "Why don't we think about giving her a cooling off period with her grandparents tonight?"

"Yeah, that'll solve everything," Josh groaned, rolling his eyes. "Hell, yeah. She already hates me. What's one more day?"

"She'll come around," Matt determined. "She just needs some time to sort this out."

"Emily-Grace is far too young to sort out any of the shit that has come her way," Josh fired back, his face flushing red. "What she needs, it seems we are incapable of giving her. Seeing as I'm a drunk and Jessie's a—"

"Josh. No." Matt shook his head, a crisp warning flashing across his eyes.

"Oh, fuck off, Matt. Those aren't my words."

He left Matt seething with fury and remorse, and made his way over to his wife to try to ease her worry.

"Everybody's a mess today," he sighed, and pulled her into his arms so he could kiss the top of her head while she wrapped her arms around him. "And I have no idea how to fix things. I sure as hell can't take back hollering at Emily-Grace."

"Was Dan telling you what Jacob said to her?"

"Hell, yeah. I'm not gonna add, 'what the hell did you ever see in that guy?'"

"Um. You just did."

A low chuckle from Josh made her smile.

"Josh, Jacob's not exactly at the top of his game today. You know that, right? And if they were really fighting about me when their car got hit, then I'm surprised he's even allowing me in his company, even if it's fifty feet away at any one time."

"You know why he's keeping you in his sight, Jess."

The shoulders sank. "Yes. I suppose I do."

"Matt thinks we should let Emily-Grace stay with Grammie and Grampie tonight."

"Probably not a bad idea. Although I hate the thought of it."

"We'll be spending the evening calming down the other two anyway, after all the attention they're getting today."

"Not to mention sugar." Jessie dipped her chin sadly, and noted with mounting anxiety that one of Talia's nieces was, at that moment, feeding Dylan yet another double chocolate cookie.

"Shall we go? Have we been here long enough?"

"Yeah, I guess. I already spoke to Talia's parents. I guess I should just try to at least see Jacob before I go though, huh?" The thought made Jessie sick. Jacob's violent actions and angry words to Emily-Grace raced across her mind. She could feel a slow anger starting to build, but Jessie had to push her own feelings aside for now, and try to understand the torments fueling Jacob's despair.

Josh was silent, watchful.

"What?" Jessie asked.

"I don't get why you would even want to talk to him after what he did to you. And after what he said about us in the presence of our daughter."

And you don't even know the half of it, dear husband, Jessie caught herself thinking.

"I can't let him go with nothing but a wall of anger between all of us, Josh. There has to be a way to get through to him, to get past some of what's hurting him. Otherwise..." She let the sentence drift off into the dusky corners of the luxury home.

"Otherwise he'll ride out of your life on a dark horse and disappear, huh Jess?"

A lone tear pricked at the corner of one eye. "Y-yep," she managed, pressing a thumb against it to keep it from leaking out. "Us singer-types like to vanish on occasion. It's really a very romantic thing to do."

Josh's response was considered carefully before the words were spoken. "D'ya ever think maybe he needs to vanish? Out of your life, I mean? Out of ours? Permanently?"

Oh God, no. Never. But sense and reason took over. A quiet, slow nod accompanied Jessie's tiny, "Yes. I think maybe that would be a good idea, Josh." *Because I can't stay away from him,* she was thinking. *And because you'll kill him when you find out he forced himself on me.*

Josh saw the misery and sorrow bloom across Jessie's cheeks as that last thought passed through her mind. He frowned, and planted a hand on the mahogany table. Leaned on it. "There's more to this than you're telling me, Jessie." Her mouse-like response frightened him.

Sliding her hands under his suit jacket, resting them on his waist, she stared at his belt buckle and said, "Because you know I could never let him go before this, right Josh? So it must be bad."

Pausing, Jessie lifted a finger, which she trailed down the front of her husband's shirt as he stood stock-still, afraid of what she might tell him. The finger landed on his belt, her favorite spot. Jessie tucked her fingers in behind it and pulled him towards her. She looked up, and met his questioning eyes.

"Relax, cowboy," she said softly as Matt watched, hoping she wouldn't reveal her nefarious secret on this already out of control crazy day, "haven't we always said the past is the past and we need to let it go?"

"That was before Jacob hit my wife. And called her a whore."

The reminder chilled Jessie. Hearing her husband use that word while looking her in the eye was a lightning strike from her head to her toes. It sizzled inside her as she sucked in a breath and blinked back at him, trying not to let Josh see how much the nasty word hurt, even when he was simply repeating it.

The diaphanous eyes darkened. "Once a whore, always a whore," Jessie murmured, holding his gaze while she pushed her fingers down past the buckle. "Wouldn't you agree?"

"Jessie, what are you…? Jesus, people are watching us." Grabbing her wrist, Josh tried to remove her hand, but Jessie just slowly shoved it down further.

"That just makes it more fun," she purred, and something in her eyes disturbed Josh. The way she was looking at him…it was the old despair that, thankfully, Josh hardly ever saw anymore. Suddenly he had some idea of the game she was playing. It hit him like a brick dropped on his head from a twenty-story building.

His next words were barely there. Josh narrowed his eyes as he spoke them, forcibly removing his wife's hand from behind his buckle as he did. In a subdued tone, he asked blankly, "Did you have sex with Jacob in Florida?"

An icy chill took any warmth out of the liquid brown eyes Jessie loved.

She didn't answer right away. Jessie couldn't. But she couldn't look away from Josh, either. Her eyes were locked solidly in his, and the answer was a proud toss of her head and tears that started hopelessly dripping, communicating sorrow and failure with every drop. "Yes," she eventually whispered back. "I did."

To Jessie, it didn't matter that she said no to Jacob that day. It didn't matter that he was screaming at her while he throbbed inside her, that there was no pleasure in the violent way Jacob took her at the camp while Emily-Grace innocently dozed outside in the van. What mattered to her was that, at least at first, she wanted it.

Josh couldn't breathe. There were indeed people staring at them, celebrities and guests and, for God's sake, their daughter as well as the hapless Charles and Dee, who were barely warming back up to Josh after the last fiasco. There were, in the room, parents who just attended a funeral for their only daughter.

And there was also Jacob.

Jacob, who straightened now, wondering what the hell had just been said over there in the bay window. Jacob who, with a permanent scowl now, it seemed, had just ostracized the last Sawyer he loved dearly by calling the child's mother a whore, and her father a drunk.

By the window, Jessie was clutching at Josh's belt, begging him with a series of silent *please please pleases* not to walk away.

Josh was immobile, unable to move, to think, to breathe. "You promised," he whispered, eyes hurt and wide. "You promised you would not go there with him."

"Ah," she gasped between uneven, panicky breaths, "I did, indeed. And you and I both knew the stakes. You and I both knew how easy it would be."

"I hate his guts, Jessie. I hate his fucking guts. And right now…I kind of hate you too."

To the surprise and insatiable curiosity of everyone in the capacious formal room, with those final words, Josh stormed away. In the unreasonable silence that followed, Jessie aptly tried not to embarrass herself further, so she held the rest of her tears at bay.

In some ways, the reveal was actually a relief. In others, she was afraid it was another ending.

Josh grabbed Matt's arm as he passed. "Where the fuck were you in Florida?" he grunted. "Off with your own whore?"

"Jesus, you people," fumed Matt to Josh's disappearing back. "Come on," he said to Dan, Susanne and Arnie. "Round up this horse and pony show. We're out of here."

He moved to fill in Charles, Dee and Ulysses of the plan to exit, and of the wish for them to keep Emily-Grace for the night, but his heart was pounding. How much had Jessie told Josh? And how bad would the fallout be?

Everyone had mobilized by the cars before Jessie had the opportunity to catch Jacob alone. Unfortunately, her few brief moments with him were within sight of their entire group, as well as within sight of many others at the grand house that day. Jacob was standing at the top of the main stone steps, arms crossed, throat hurting at the imminent departure of people he loved, who he used to think loved him back.

Jessie made her way to him, teetering a little on the high heels she hated.

"Jacob," she started as, below, Josh leaned against his vehicle with Charlie and Steve alongside, and fired invisible bullets at the two of them, wishing he could run up the stairs and pound Jacob into the ground. "I don't want to leave you like this. With you hurting…with both of us angry."

Jacob blinked away the emotion that threatened to sink him, and gently reached out a finger to hold against the bruise on Jessie's cheek. His eyes followed it to her lip before drifting up to the pearlescent blues he adored. "I really hurt you," he murmured.

"Yep. You kinda lost it." She swallowed, and tried to keep her anger beneath the surface on this tough day, but bubbles of resentment blistered on her skin like burns. "You kinda suck right now."

"Did you tell Josh we slept together?" he asked her, the voice that sang ballads millions loved now gruff with grief.

She blinked. "We didn't sleep together, Jacob. You raped me. Technically."

He took a moment to process that before calling up his defenses and responding. "Ah. That's a big word for a whore." He leaned forward and whispered into her ear, as any semblance of light sank beneath the surface of his eyes, "Not sure it counts for whores."

"Seriously, Jacob? That's a bastard thing to say." Pinpricks of tears dotted Jessie's eyes.

Unable to find the words to respond, he shrugged.

"I could have charged you." Jessie took a step back. "I suppose I still could."

"But you won't, will you, Jessie? You know how I know that?"
She waited.
"Because you love me. Still. That's why. That's how I know."

"Well, you obviously don't love me back. A man who loves a woman would never hurt her the way you hurt me. Or my daughter." Her hands knuckled into white fists at her sides. Below, Matt went on alert. Josh took a step towards them. "I told you no, Jacob."

"You wanted it as much as I did."

This was a losing battle. Jessie folded her arms across her chest, swallowed, and looked away.

"Talia's dead," Jacob countered. "She's dead, and she's not coming back. You still want to talk about who hurt who the most, Jessie?"

"You can't blame me for what happened to Talia, Jacob."

"No need, right Jess? You're already busy blaming yourself."

"I don't want to. I'm trying not to feel responsible for how you feel about me, or what you may or may not have said to Talia about *me* to make her pull over."

"She called off the wedding, Jessie. She called off our fucking wedding, opened the door, and—" He couldn't say more. Jacob just made a strangled choking noise in his throat and looked away.

After a moment Jessie uttered the words that really did hurt both the most. The words stung like fire; they ate at them like acid. "We can't see each other anymore. It's over with us, Jacob. Our friendship, I mean. It's over. It has to be. Against my better judgment, I'm giving you a free ride on the nastiness of the other day because I admit I wanted it too, at least at first…and that scares the hell out of me. I don't want to be in that situation with you again. I can't be. So I'm done."

A nasty nausea worked its way up Jacob's body as he pondered the implications of that. "If you want to save your marriage, Jessie, then all the power to you. Be done." A rapid swallowing gave the fear beneath his attempt at a casual response away, though. A new question that was barely discernible escaped his lips. Jacob asked it by looking up at Jessie from underneath the long lashes that made him seem so sad all the time. "Do you? Do you want to save your marriage, Jess?"

She studied him before answering. "Are you asking me to leave him, Jacob? Because you know that's not an option. It will never be an option." Her arms dropped to her belly and squeezed it tight as her shoulders hunched over. Jessie kept her back to Josh and the others. But it didn't matter. She wasn't hiding a thing from them.

Jacob let all his worries hang loose the moment the anger finally dissipated and he crumbled. "You're gonna leave me here alone. With nothing. And nobody."

"John Paul and Katrine are here. And Charlene. You're not alone. The only time you will be alone will be when you choose to be."

He shook his head. "Not this time, Jessie. Not this time."

"It's such a mess now, Jacob. Everything's a mess. We fucked things up big time."

"It doesn't have to be," he said, reaching tentatively out to cup her sore cheek with his palm. "It doesn't have to be. Maybe it was a mistake, going back to him."

"You love me, yet you're so angry with me. I love you but I have to tell you, a part of me wants to hate you. What good would we ever be together now, Jacob? You hurt me in a bad way, because you blame me for what happened to Talia, to you and Talia. And the terrible things you said to Emily-Grace..." But Jessie laid her hand over his and leaned forward so that they were nose to nose. She couldn't help herself. Jacob was a drug, a long, slow puff of weed; he was heroin, a poison easing its way into her veins like a slithering snake.

"I know," he acquiesced, finally remorseful. "I know I suck. God, Jess! What did I do?"

Bending forward, Jessie brushed her lips against his cheek. "You lashed out at the one person who you knew could take it, that's what you did. I love you, babe," she said. "I'll always love you. But I can't be near you. What you did to me...it was like you just put a big exclamation mark on us. We're done, Jacob. I'm sorry about that, and I'm so fucking sorry about Talia." Jessie wrapped her trembling arms around his waist and buried her face in his neck.

"Take care of my kid," he begged, the old anger coming back to mask the heartsick wish for the world to open up and swallow him. Pressing her close, Jacob breathed in Jessie's lavender scent for the last time. Then, his shoulders shook.

Below, Josh was sick. He wasn't entirely sure what was happening up there, and he knew the universe, in some ways, had shifted underneath all of their feet again that day. It had started to shift, in fact, at La Casa on Boxing Day. Who was to blame, Jessie or Jacob? Or both?

Or me, he thought, remembering that Jessie and Jacob seemed happy when they were together in New York. *Or Morgan and Nadia*, he wondered.

He turned towards the car, leaned his arms against the roof and tried not to puke as, next to him, Steve laid a hand on his shoulder.

Matt saw what was happening. Clear as sin, he knew everyone in his care today was a mess, saying and doing things to hurt each other that only served to hurt himself or herself. While Jacob and Jessie were locked in their embrace at the top of the stairs, he decided he'd had enough. Jacob and Jessie were not good for each other, they were confusing the hell out of Emily-Grace, and it was agonizingly apparent that Josh now knew something that was tearing him apart.

Vaulting forward, Matt finally unleashed the fury that started dogging him the moment Jessie told him she was going to Florida in the first place. Sensing him fly by, Josh whipped around to see what the hell he was up to.

Matt took the stairs three at a time. At the top, grasping Jessie's arm, he wrenched her away from her old lover. "Get in the car," he demanded. "Go."

Stunned at his actions, Jessie backed up, but she didn't leave. Not yet. She heard every word Matt fired at Jacob that day. Matt started by grabbing Jacob by the throat.

Then he let loose.

"I am sorry for your loss, Jacob, I truly am. But it's no excuse to go beating up women, and it sure isn't cool to hurt the one person left who you know loves you the most. I can't tell you what it took for me to keep from driving out to your place and pounding you when Jessie came back from the camp. Actually, I can. It was her. And you know it was. As for Josh? You're just damn lucky he has her or he would've been down your throat too. Does he know you violently forced yourself on her? No. I doubt that's what she told him today. Again, how do I know? Because I know her. And because he would have killed you. Josh will never know unless Jessie decides to tell him herself someday. You should be charged but she refuses to sink you any lower than you've already sunk yourself."

Letting go, Matt backed away, shaking profusely, while Jacob grabbed his throat and gasped for breath.

"Don't ever let me see you near Jessie again," Matt demanded, "until you're ready to be the man we all love and admire. Because if I catch you anywhere near her before you get your shit together, I can't promise you that I'll be able to keep from strangling you with my bare hands. Do you understand me?"

Jacob didn't disappoint. He straightened himself up tall and shot right back at Matt, at a man he loved and respected beyond all others. He spoke with a cool veracity that stunned both Jessie and Matt for its simple power to destroy. The words were spat; they were poison.

"She got what she came for, Matt. Jessie likes it rough. She was bored of the old guy. She couldn't wait for a good fuck."

After the hateful words sank in, when Matt started going at Jacob with fists cocked and eyes blazing, Jessie cried out to him. "Matt, don't, he's just mad, and hurt, Matt, please!" Jessie was grasping at Matt now, grabbing his arms and trying to pull him down the stairs.

Matt's face was red, inflamed, as Dan and Arnie launched themselves towards the stairs. "I will chalk this up to your tragic loss, Jacob! As did Jessie when she cried herself to sleep the other night. But I beg you to ask yourself if the man standing before me is the man Talia thought she had. Because it's her memory you're dishonoring with this despicable behavior."

He backed away, Jessie pulling hard on his waist so that they both almost tripped. Dan and Arnie flanked Jacob and fired him warning looks.

Matt's last words were spat angrily at Jacob, fired in a slow staccato echoed by a trembling, jabbing finger. "Stay—away—from Jessie." Turning, he let Jessie guide him down the stairs.

On the ground below, as they moved away with one of her arms still around his waist, Jessie twisted around one last time to meet Jacob's tortured eyes and to plead with the universe to *Please let him be okay. Please.*

The folks congregated by the vehicles were standing in stunned silence, Josh included.

Matt stormed by Charles with two simple sentences. "You need to cut him loose, Charles. You need to take that sunuvabitch off your roster."

He hauled open Jessie's door and ordered her in. Shrinking from him, avoiding Josh altogether, she obeyed. It would only be the two of them in the SUV for the ride back to the hotel.

As Jessie watched Jacob disappear from view as he stood alone at the top of the stairs, he cut a lonely figure. She sank down in her seat, squeezed her eyes shut, and covered them with the heels of her hands.

Knuckles white, Matt drove in an unapologetic silence.

In Josh's car, with Arnie back at the wheel and the two boys drifting off to sleep in their car seats, Arnie laid a hand on Josh's shoulder.

"You okay, buddy?" he asked.

"No," was Josh's brief answer. The single word was followed by a simple sentence. "I need to go to a meeting, Arnie. Do you think we can find one?"

Arnie's laugh was a balm for Josh's tired soul.

"This is Nashville, Josh. I'll find us a dozen."

The sun was lowering in the sky by the time they reached the hotel, and the wind was picking up, bringing with it grey clouds with dark bellies. The forecast was calling for rain.

By eight o'clock, Nashville was soaked; people ran from their cars to their homes, and dogs and outdoor cats hid under low hanging foliage. Puddles the size of small swimming pools formed on the streets.

In the luxurious grand Hermitage and Renaissance Hotels, life went on via the children's routines and needs, but nobody was speaking except in hushed tones. It was as if an unscheduled blackout had been called. There was light, but in Josh and Jessie's suite, in particular, it seemed darker than pitch.

Chapter Twenty-nine

*J*essie was slouched on a chaise on the hotel bedroom's outdoor balcony when Josh went looking for her after rocking Dylan to sleep. Josh had been to an AA meeting and back with Arnie, and took Dylan from Jessie upon his return as if the motion could somehow renew his commitment to Jacob's biological son. David had been asleep for an hour already. The small guy was beat, but it was the littlest Sawyer who seemed to have the most energy and who always wanted to stay up til he simply couldn't stand to fight the sandman anymore. Emily-Grace was at the exclusive Hermitage with Charles and Dee, *currently in her room on an antique wingback chair, reading,* Dee texted to Jessie. The girl was barely speaking, even to her grandparents at the moment, with the exception of small grunts and the occasional whispered ask.

The Sawyer family had been back from the reception for a good few hours. Now it was time to sort some things out.

Josh found Jessie sitting tensely on the end of her outdoor lounger, wrapped in a blanket, but still shivering. Disappearing back into the bedroom, Josh came out with a second blanket, a thick brown microfiber something or other that he draped over her shoulders.

"Thanks," she mumbled. "Not sure I deserve that."

Straddling the chaise to sit behind her, Josh wrapped his arms around Jessie's shoulders and eased her body back against his chest. "I'm not sure what you deserve, Jessie. Don't even get me started on the 'I told you so's.' But I don't want you punishing yourself by sitting out here freezing. That would be much too easy."

"Ha. Glad to see you've retained your sense of humor." She paused. "Has Matt calmed down?"

"Last I heard, he was boxing at some bar with Arnie."

Jessie straightened.

"Kidding, Jess, relax. They just went for a drink. Coffee, in Arnie's case. I expect right about now they've turned the air blue over you and your shameless abuse of power and where it got you. Susanne had a nap but she's back here now until midnight, then Dan takes over. Susanne's outside in the hall," he added.

"That makes me feel even worse."

"They're all expecting World War III to break out in here. Nobody wants to be around for that."

"I don't know what to say, Josh." Jessie sighed, closed her eyes, and melted into his rigid but comforting chest. Before them, the lights of Nashville were spread out like stars, and from somewhere far below wafted the strains of an upbeat country tune. It would have been cozy if Jessie wasn't sick to death at the sight of Jacob standing alone at the top of Richard's grand exterior front staircase after Jessie turned him down—again. Worrying about Josh's capacity to forgive was also playing on her mind. Forgiving herself? Not really an option tonight. Tonight was about self-abuse and Jessie's bottomless pit of self-loathing.

Josh's chest was moving slightly as he breathed. Soaking him up, Jessie was glad for his presence there, and for his warmth, but she knew this was an illusion, an attempt on his part to create some semblance of peace in their suite both for the kids and for the hired security they counted on, whom had all over time become their very good friends.

Josh started on the tough stuff. "I've never been naïve enough to think you would just lose your feelings for him, Jessie, when you came back to me. You can't just turn that shit off. We're not light switches."

"You still think about Nadia."

"The Nadia I knew when we first got together. Not the one I found out about later."

"With Jacob there's always going to be a powerful connection, Josh. It's not just the music. It's everything about him. The way he moves, the way he looks at me, the way he dresses…it's everything."

"You stayed away from him before." Josh swallowed. "In Miami. I think."

"Yes, babe, I did. There was…one night. We got too close, on the bed. Just lying there, talking, sharing things, you know?"

"Lovely."

"Something could have happened that night but it didn't. We fought about stuff like that, even then. It was never easy being around him. But somehow we kept our distance, except for that one night. I think…Josh, I think I might have lost control that night if Jacob hadn't been the one to pull away. He knew better. He was wiser, then."

"I think I heard about that night. From Jacob, while you were missing. He can be pretty volatile when he's angry."

No shit. "You did good today, Josh. Really. I thought you would go after him with both guns blazing."

"I just might if I ever see him again. Today wasn't the day. But Matt… what the hell was that about? Why was he so angry?"

Jessie sighed. "Matt suffers a lot for me. He didn't like Jacob hitting me very much, he…He was the one who wiped up the blood, you know? And I guess the craziness of today just got to him, finally."

They were quiet for a moment, thoughtful. Six floors below, on the street, a bicycle swooshed through a series of puddles. The rider's vocal sheer joy at the childlike thrill traveled up to Josh and Jessie. But neither smiled nor laughed.

Jessie had a difficult question to ask. "You're not going to leave me, are you Josh? Because I wouldn't blame you if you wanted to."

Since he was behind her, she couldn't see his face or the way Josh squeezed his eyes tightly together and mouthed a silent prayer. But she could feel him press his body hard against her. Jessie relished the feel of his moist lips as he ducked his face into her neck.

"No," she heard him say, and the relief that ran through her body was liberating. But there was more. "I will never leave you, Jessie. I don't care how many other men you fall in love with. I'm the one who gets to hold you at times like this. I get to listen to you snore."

A tiny giggle warmed his heart.

"So glad, Josh. So glad. Maybe not the snoring part. Although I wouldn't be surprised if you thought about it. I need my ass kicked."

"You love him. I get that. I've always gotten that."

"There's never been anybody else. And there never will be."

"I honestly don't know if that makes me feel better or worse."

"I told him today, Josh, at the top of the stairs, that we have to stay away from each other. It's not even about hurting each other anymore, or about me hurting him when you and I got back together. It's more about us still being dangerous to each other. It's about all those pent up feelings and desires and missing the whole music vibe together. It's about not being able to completely let go."

"In a way, Jessie, I'm kind of glad you're finally being honest with me about Jacob. I've always known, but still…it means something to hear you say it."

"You don't need to be worried about me ever leaving you, Josh. You and me, always and forever, remember?"

"So I don't need to worry about you leaving me permanently, as long as you get the occasional sex in with him, is that it?"

Jessie groaned and buried her face in her hands. "I told you. I couldn't walk away," she lied.

"Where was our daughter when this was happening?"

This sucks. "In the van. Asleep."

"And Matt? Didya have another fun little threesome with Jacob?"

"Seriously, Josh. Matt was back at the rinky-dink redneck motel. I dumped his ass."

"Because you knew you wanted alone time with Jacob. He must have been thrilled. No wonder he's all roses and sunshine on this trip."

"Babe, please. Let's not do this. I told you Jacob and I won't see each other anymore. We just can't."

"What did he say to you at the top of the stairs today, Jess?" Josh was whispering again. He knew the answer would be sacred.

Jessie hesitated before answering. "He gave me the option to go away with him. I think he was hoping our honeymoon period—you and me—was over, you know?"

"Ah." A hot knife sliced Josh's heart in two like it was slicing through butter. "That scares the hell out of me."

"Me too."

"Did you think about it?"

"What? I…no."

"Even for a second?"

Jessie trained her eyes on a flashing green neon light in the distance. Its hypnotic pulse lulled her into a false zone, one that felt secure yet was as tenuous as a fairy's wing. She hung her head, and Josh clung more tightly onto her. Jessie felt him sigh against her as he buried his face in her hair.

"I will never let you go," he told her.

"I will never go," she said. And added, to herself, *But I thought about it. Just for a split second.*

Later, in bed, Jessie moved her body close to Josh and brushed back his hair. They had barely uttered a word since her unspoken admission. Some pain is meant to be shared, and some must be suffered alone. What a relief to Josh that Jessie was mourning the loss of Jacob publicly now, in front of him at least. Josh, who vowed on their wedding day that he would love every part of his wife *in good times and in bad,* came through for her now. It was a blow to his pride to know she still loved Jacob enough to feel his pain as deeply as she did; at the same time, it was a sweet, sweet blessing to have Jessie admit this and still want to hang on to their marriage.

Relief washed through Josh like the rain now falling softly outside. It only cleansed Jessie to a point, though. There didn't seem to be any sense at all in raising one unspoken issue, that nasty word, *rape,* since Jacob was no longer as of today going to be a part of Jessie's life.

There was, however, one last thing. Things. Children. A sad little girl, and a boy. Emily-Grace. Dylan. And sweet little David too, by association.

"She'll be okay," Jessie murmured in the dim light. "Once things settle down, Emily-Grace will adapt. She'll have to."

"How much do we tell her? How much do we tell Dylan?"

"We'll figure it out. One day at a time. Josh?"

"Um-hmmm?"

"What about Dylan?"

"What?"

"He's exhausting. He's a busy kid."

"Yes. That he is."

"He's not like the other two." She sensed Josh tense beside her.

"That's because he's got a few different genes running around his little body than they do. Jessie…you're still on birth control, right?"

"Yeah. I am."

"I'm exhausted. All of this is exhausting."

"Josh, I need to know one last thing. Since we're being open about shit."

A deep sigh came from his side of the bed. In the semi-darkness Jessie saw Josh raise his head up and rest it on an elbow. She stuck two fingers under the sleeve of his white T-shirt and took a deep breath.

"Do you ever think about Jacob being Dylan's father…I mean literally, biologically. Like on nights like tonight when he just won't settle down and you're beat, do you think about Jacob and curse at him and me?"

"I think about what Jacob's missing out on."

"It doesn't piss you off when you're tired and he wakes us up in the middle of the night? When he's whiny in the grocery store? When people look at you funny because he doesn't look like you?"

Josh was exasperated. "Jess, I took Dylan on when you were only a few months pregnant. Maybe what you should be asking is whether you like watching me raise him. Maybe you would rather it was Jacob. Maybe I'm raising your love child all wrong."

"Oh, for God's sake, Josh!"

"Look. I'm tired, okay? It's been a hell of a fucked up day. All of a sudden I've got a lot to process, Jessie. I need some sleep. Before Jacob's kid comes running in here and jumps on me before the crack of dawn."

Ouch.

Rolling over, Josh adjusted his pillow and settled into an attempt at sleep.

Staring at his back, Jessie groaned and slid out of bed. *I need to do some processing myself,* she was thinking, although a jaw-cracking yawn gave her a momentary lapse in which she considered climbing back into bed. She paused at the bedroom door where Dylan and David slept. David, the spitting image of his father, was sprawled out in idyllic slumber. Dylan was spending the night tossing and turning apparently, judging by the mussed up blanket wrapped around his knees.

Gently, Jessie nudged the blanket out from under him, and laid it back over Dylan's body. "I'm so sorry, baby," she told him, as the last wet tears of the day slid down her cheeks. "You won't get to know your father. Your biological dad, I mean. I don't even know if I should be telling you about him, or whether you'll remember the few times you did have some time with him. Dylan…just let me say one last thing about him and then that will be the end, okay? I want you to know that I loved him very much. I still do and I always will, even though he…he hurt me…in a bad way. I love him and I miss him and I will miss him every single day for the rest of my life. And you and me, kid, will have our times when we will go for walks or listen to music and you will wonder why I start to cry. I will never tell you why but somehow I think you will understand anyway."

Tucking his curls around her baby's small ears, Jessie had one last thing to add. "You look just like him," she murmured. "And you know something? I think that's what's gonna hurt the most."

She turned to go, then, and stopped suddenly. Josh was standing at the door to the bedroom. Feeling bad over what he'd said, he'd followed her. Now though, he wished he hadn't.

He swallowed, slapped the doorframe, and turned to go.

"Josh!" Jessie cried, suddenly feeling her stomach sink like a stone.

He stopped for a second, then, over his shoulder, tossed her a few final words for the day. "Maybe you should have gone, after all," he said. "And taken Jacob's son with you."

~⁓~

Jessie sat with Matt in the jet on the way back. She held Dylan on her lap for much of the flight, and she and Matt entertained him with blocks and stories and songs, some of which Jessie softly sang herself as she held her son close. Matt sat next to her in silent wonder at the impromptu concert he received from one of the world's biggest stars.

On the sofa at the back of the plane, Josh had settled next to Emily-Grace, who seemed to need his company today. David, constantly and adorably swiping long chestnut-blonde hair off his cheek, was across from them playing cards at a table with Charles, Dee and Dan. Ulysses and Susanne were deep in some philosophical conversation at the front of the plane, and Arnie, across from Jessie, Dylan and Matt, spent much of the trip picking up blocks that Dylan tossed, quite intentionally and with a loud holler each time, onto the floor.

Halfway through the trip, Arnie took Dylan walking up and down the interior of the small jet. At one point they ended up between the sofa and the table. When Jessie turned around to see how Arnie was getting along with the busy little guy, she was humbled to see Emily-Grace asleep, her head on Josh's lap, and his strong arm around her small body.

Josh didn't notice Jessie watching him at first. He was preoccupied studying the child Arnie was chasing around and around in circles. Dylan fell, and landed in a heap, all laughter and joy. The child looked up at Josh, and something in the serious, sad way Josh was studying him sobered Dylan. There was a suspended moment while Jessie held her breath as she watched some unspoken thoughts pass between them.

Dylan stood and walked over to his father's knees. Reaching out a hand, he simply said, "Daddy."

Josh turned his head away from Dylan and, with his left hand, used his thumb and forefinger to absently touch his nose and chin. When he looked back at Dylan, who was watching him with a curious innocence, Josh's eyes were moist. But he smiled, chuckled and nodded.

"If you say so," he agreed. "Daddy it is. C'mere. Give Arnie a break. I can hear the old man's knees cracking from here."

As he hoisted Dylan up under the crook of one arm so as not to disturb Emily-Grace, Josh caught Jessie's eye. He sobered, and snuggled Dylan up on his knee, under his arm.

Jessie sent him a small attempt at a smile, but it was hard fought, and landed flat. Josh turned his head away from her, and ran his fingers through Dylan's curls.

"Sleep, little buddy," he said, and helped him relax while Arnie retrieved a light blanket to lay over the two year old. "We're going home."

Chapter Thirty

*I*n two weeks, Jessie was expected in Brussels, Belgium for wardrobe fittings and camera testing. The Belgian bluegrass film would be going to camera on January 21st. The children and Josh would not be travelling with her. This was a solo journey, apart from Matt as her security, although during the six-week production run she anticipated at least one or two visits home, and a visit from her family when they came to Europe. Deirdre, and maybe Charles, would be by as well; Dee herself would be around for at least some of the shoot.

Dreading the idea of leaving the sullen and hurt Josh and the kids, and still agonizing over Jacob's violence—a secret she intended to keep forever—as well as the heartrending vision of Jacob alone at the top of the stairs, Jessie sank into a miserable depression as the clock ticked towards her inevitable departure date.

She was at La Casa, in her favorite spot at the kitchen island, fuming and twisting a pretty porcelain teacup around and around and around, when Matt wandered in and startled her by dropping his keys next to her cup.

He looked around. She was alone in her misery.

"Where is everyone?" he asked, sidling over to the large fridge and removing a can of beer. Pulling back the tab, he took a long drink as he placed his spare hand comfortably on his waist over the new leather bomber jacket.

Jessie sat back and appraised his impeccable good looks but didn't have the heart to provoke him as usual. "Does Charles know you keep the ordinary man's beverage in his exquisite cooling apparatus?" was the snotty answer instead.

"It's beer, Jessie, not cow urine."

"Well it ain't expensive wine or whiskey, is it? Charles must have had a heart attack when he saw *cans* in there."

"Someone's in a mood," Matt announced, leaning on his forearms on the island. "You'd think flying off to Belgium to shoot a film that pays a cool twenty million would actually make a girl happy."

"Ah, so I'm not only a whore, now I'm a spoiled ungrateful brat, too? So glad you're on my side, Matt."

"I came here to schedule your security for the shoot, Jessie. You've made the first part easy. I'll just take myself off the itinerary altogether, okay?" Lifting the beer to his lips, he paused. Across from him, Jessie was shoving the heels of her palms into her eyes. This was not a good sign, from his experienced perspective.

He grabbed one wrist and pulled it downwards. "Hey," he said. "I was kidding. I'll stick to you like bubble gum. What's going on?"

"Awww, well, let me see. Where shall I begin? Josh has turned into a stranger, seemingly overnight, Jacob is on his way out of my life forever yet I can't help but feel worried sick about him, Kayla's not speaking to me, even though I am financially supporting her workshops, and the only one of my children who *may* grow up anywhere near normal is, at this moment, asking if he can quit Junior Kindergarten and take up dance."

"Lots of men dance."

"David's four. And Josh is determined to see him in motocross, as far away from dance as possible."

"So Josh is still dealing with the fact that you were with Jacob?"

"Reeling, more like it. He tries, but it's hard for him. A constant reminder of my sexual liaisons with Jacob jumps on our bed daily, just after his early-bird brother, at the crack of dawn. I see in Josh's eyes now how hard it must have been for Wes to raise him. And Josh, at least, is trying." She peeked sadly up at her buddy. "Matt, I can't imagine what it must have been like for Josh as a kid. Wes pretty much hated him."

"Which is likely why Josh is trying so hard with Dylan, Jessie." Matt laid a hand over hers and gave the fingers a light squeeze. "But he still doesn't know about the—"

"I'd prefer to call it assault if you don't mind, and no, he doesn't. And he never will. He'd hunt Jacob down and shoot him. And he'd never look at me the same way again."

"Have you considered that it might actually ease things up at home, if Josh knew you tried to back away that night?"

"No, because I know my husband. He'd lose it, Matt. Kinda like you did, only a helluva lot worse." She froze. "Please tell me you're really coming with me to Brussels. I'm gonna need a friend."

Matt smiled warmly. It felt good to be needed, even though half the time Jessie just did what she wanted anyway. "Of course I am. For half of the time, at least. Julie's put in a claim on me for part of the shoot, so I think Arnie's planning to pop over for a bit to give me a break from the likes of you. He might bring his wife if that's okay, at least over a weekend."

Jessie rolled her eyes. "Twenty million. I think I can swing her trip. It's disgusting."

"Before taxes," Matt teased, shrugging and letting go of her hand. "You'll be giving a big chunk of it to the government."

"And to charity." Jessie sat back. "Nobody needs that kind of money."

"That's my girl."

Finally, a smile. Small, but the corners of her lips did turn up.

"You're doing the Grammys in February too, right Jessie?"

"Yep. Singing, watching, and maybe even winning. I think."

"With Jacob's song."

"One of them, yes. Musically, we're really great together. In real life, we suck, apparently."

"Charles says Jacob will be there too. At the Grammys."

"Nope. He won't." Jessie puffed up her cheeks like a blowfish, studied Matt's concerned gaze, and exhaled slowly so that she emitted a low whistle. "I had an email."

"So…Jacob is…"

"First of all, Charles is not letting him go. Yet. Despite your demands that he release him."

"I know that. I told Charles I was not in agreement with his choice."

"And?"

"And he wanted to know why. However, I was not able to break my promise to you and lie outright. So I had no real ground to stand on, seeing as Charles treats Jacob like a son and wants to retain that relationship, and that he chalked up Jacob's visible treatment of you to grief. Inexcusable, but grief all the same."

"And sexual frustration. You did get into that, right? And how I led him on and deserved to get nailed hard enough to slam my head into Timbuktu."

The image in Matt's head was sobering. He narrowed his eyes at Jessie. "I don't need a picture in my head of Jacob nailing you against your will, hard enough to send you to Timbuktu, Jessie. Not if you won't press charges against the bastard."

"I was talking about him hitting me."

"I—was not."

"I see. Matt, that's old news. Let's press on, shall we? Move ahead? Go forward? All that jazz?"

Matt waved a hand through the air. "Speak, She-Who-Must-Be-Obeyed. Don't let me stop you."

"Fine. Asshole. Second, Jacob is taking a break for a few months. A holiday of sorts. He cleaned his stuff out of Talia's place, moved it to one of his dad's houses down south—I have no idea which one—and took off. He's going sailing, apparently. Somewhere in the Caribbean."

"Jacob doesn't strike me as the kind of guy who sails. Has he ever sailed?"

"He met someone who knew someone who knew someone else who wants to sell an old boat, a 28 footer, he said. Wooden, I think. The guy is giving him lessons and Jacob is buying the boat. He plans to live on it."

"Sounds rather idyllic."

"Well, in the email he said it was either that or killing himself. I must say I'm rather relieved he chose the former."

"Josh must be glad he's gone."

"We no longer bring up Jacob's name in our household. I trashed the email after I read it ten or twelve times so I could memorize it."

"Jess…"

Raising a hand, Jessie held a palm out to him. "No, Matt. I have shed enough tears over Jacob to last me ten thousand lifetimes. I chose Josh, I will always choose Josh, and I will never say Jacob's name in his company again. I fucked up. It's over. I'm trying to mend fences."

"All right."

"Um, Matt…?"

"Still here, kid."

"Speaking of mending fences…"

"Mmmm?"

"I guess I'd better suck it up and start working on Kayla."

"I'm sure she would in fact appreciate that, Jessie."

Jessie sighed, and idly pushed her teacup towards the center of the kitchen island. "I've got a bit more time before I have to pick up Emily-Grace and David at West Point Grey. I'm going to drop by the workshop space and see if she'll talk to me."

"I thought the workshops weren't starting up again until mid February."

"They aren't. Josh said she's been down there a lot with Benjie from our old troupe, working out the choreography and doing admin for the spring tour. I'll take my chances."

"Josh has Dylan? You want me to come with you?"

"I'm fine. It's East Hastings, my old neighborhood. Every dark-hooded street resident has my back down there. If they didn't, Arnie'd chop them up and deposit the remains in Burrard Inlet. And yes, Josh has Dylan. They've been hanging out at Jack and Lydia's a lot. Josh works with Blue while Jack and Lydia spoil Dylan rotten. It seems to be a good arrangement. Charlie comes around a lot so Jane can stay home and snooze with their new little cowboy."

Wandering around the kitchen island, Jessie brushed her lips against Matt's forehead. He smiled, and a pink flush spread across his cheeks.

"You're blushing. I'm so glad you're coming with me to Europe, Spike. Just don't leave me alone with you. I don't trust myself," she winked.

"Go." Waving her away, Matt made an *ahhhh* fake-frustrated sound and chuckled. "You are one of a kind, Jessie. Stop worrying. Things will settle. They always do."

But he was wrong.

Twenty minutes later, at the workshop space on East Hastings, Jessie ended up having to use a spare key Kayla had given her, which in itself didn't surprise her all that much. It wasn't the safest area of the city in which to leave doors unlocked, especially if Kayla intended to spend any time there alone.

Locking the door quietly behind her, Jessie padded into the center of the space. The perimeter sconces were on, throwing a soft, airy light onto the tops of the walls and onto the ceiling. Since the lights were never on if nobody was in the building, Jessie made the assumption that Kayla, or maybe Mandy or Benjie if Kayla wasn't around, was in one of the offices.

Probably will scare whoever it is half to death if I don't call out, Jessie thought. *It's kind of creepy in here alone.*

Walking almost on tiptoe towards the office Kayla was using, Jessie called tentatively, "Hey! Anybody here?"

She halted abruptly at the sound of a male voice crying, "Shit!" and the accompanying rustle of bodies and clothing.

"Oh." Raising her eyebrows in curiosity, Jessie slurred flippantly, "Someone's getting in a little afternoon delight. What to do?"

She started singing to herself. *Should I stay or should I go, bomp bomp bomp bomp.*

"It ain't my business, I guess," she decided in the end, and turned to go. Just at that moment, though, a key turned in the main front door thirty feet behind Jessie, and a hand pushed it open. Kayla stepped into the space and stopped suddenly when she saw Jessie standing there looking rather tickled.

"What are you doing here?" she asked, aiming a serious scowl in Jessie's general direction.

"I was hoping we could talk, Kayla. Have some coffee or something. But someone…" Jessie half-grinned in amusement, "appears to be using your office. For some afternoon delight as they say. Some funky monkey business. Sex."

The color drained from Kayla's face at the same moment Jessie realized her error. Whoever was in the office was silent now. There was no more rustling, no more movement. But it would have to be someone with a key. And so that would have to be either Jack Deacon, the custodian, or Mandy.

"Oh, Jesus," Jessie gasped. "That better not be Jack."

Throwing her a nasty look, Kayla stomped forward and shoved open the door. Jessie peeked past her.

Mandy. And Mandy was with...Paul.

With a mighty scream, Kayla hauled off one boot and threw it at her man, who ducked and cried out. Mandy caught the heel of the other boot on her forehead, which immediately opened and started to bleed. Both were dressed now, at least mostly—their feet were still bare—but there didn't seem to be any effort underway to deny their afternoon activity.

"I left you to do paperwork!" Kayla was screaming. "Paperwork! You do that with paper! Or with computers these days!"

"Kayla! Cut it out!" Paul shrank from a stapler thrown directly at his face. It whizzed by and missed him by an inch. "This isn't helping any!"

Jessie grabbed a box of Kleenex from a bookshelf and jumped into the fray. "Here," she said to Mandy, who grabbed a few tissues and held them over the cut on her forehead.

"What is this, anyway?" Kayla stopped throwing things long enough to take in the sight of her live-in boyfriend and her borrowed assistant who, at the moment, were stealing glances at each other. "It better be love, because if it ain't you're gonna be sorry, Paul."

"Yes, you know what? He's the lawyer, Kayla." Mandy held out her bloody Kleenex.

"You can't throw me out for one indiscretion, Kayla." Paul almost spit the words out at her.

"The hell I can't! And if my instincts are correct, it hasn't just been this once. Do you think I left the two of you alone and then showed up half an hour after I left just for shits and giggles? Nuh-uh. Consider yourself out, you cheating bastard!"

A coffee mug went flying across the room, caught Paul on the edge of his hip, and smashed when it hit the wall behind.

Whirlwinds of emotions were flying through Jessie's brain. Kayla, her sister-in-law, with whom she was already on shaky ground because of her association with Jacob, had just caught her partner in a not-so-covert sexual liaison with her assistant. And had planned the consequences before pretty much knowing she would catch him.

No wonder you've been so pissed at me, Jessie thought, taking the bloody Kleenex from Mandy and handing her a few more. She wanted to say something to Kayla, to calm her down and encourage her to think things through, but there didn't seem to be much point. When she twisted at the waist to look at her, Kayla was standing alone in the center of the small room, tears streaming down her face, staring at Jessie as if this, too, were all her fault.

"I just don't get why people cheat on their partners," Kayla was saying sadly. "Why would you want to hurt the one person you supposedly love the most?" A small porcelain dancer statuette was in her hand. She let it drop to the floor. It splintered into a thousand tiny pieces. She turned back to Paul. "Get your stuff out of my place, you asshole, before I burn it. Or before I pull a John Denver and cut it all in half."

"Did he really do that?" Mandy asked. "Or is that just celebrity gossip?"

"Who cares?" responded Kayla. "Like, really Mandy. Who the fuck cares?"

Wheeling around on a low-slung suede boot, Kayla wiped sweaty palms on her leggings and spun away from the sorry sight of Paul's betrayal. He didn't even try to call her back, and tended to Mandy's cut instead.

Jessie followed the swinging blonde-blue ponytail out onto the street. "Let me drive you home, Kayla." She touched a shaking arm but Kayla threw her off.

"You're the last person on the planet I need consoling me, Jessie. And this was hardly a surprise, by the way, although I was praying and hoping my gut was wrong. Why don't you grab Paul and the two of you can take a long walk off a short pier. Bring Mandy and have a threesome, if you like. I hear you're into those."

Geez, I'll never live that down, will I? Jessie shrank into herself with dismay. Out loud she tried again. "You're in no shape to be alone right now, Kayla. Let me go with you, at least."

Two hands clutched her jacket at the shoulders and shoved her backwards, hard. Jessie's head hit the brick and she cried out.

Kayla's eyes were on fire. "You are forgetting how resilient us Sawyers are. We bounce back from the bad stuff without the likes of you dragging us down." Kayla started to back away, but she had one last stake to pound into Jessie's heart. "You know, I used to love and admire you so much. You sing all these songs about healing, and about loving each other, yet all you do is hurt people. If Josh knew what was good for him he'd throw your stupid ass out, and Jacob won't want you because you destroyed his chance at happiness with Talia. Or—oh, I know! You and Paul could hook up, hell, for all I know you probably already have, you slut! Stay away from me, Jessie. I neither need nor want any help from the likes of you."

The brick was scratchy and rough but, gasping for breath, her head now spinning, Jessie melted against it and watched Kayla stride angrily away. Moments later, the pink scooter zipped by, Kayla's middle finger proudly displayed for Jessie to see.

Paul slipped out from behind the glass door and stood next to Jessie.

"It's not love," he said. "It was just lust. That's all. Means nothing." Hands in his pockets, he looked over at Jessie. "How about for you?"

"Pain," she replied without a beat to even think about it. Sighing, she maneuvered her body back up the wall and started to slouch away. Over her shoulder she tossed her final words. "And that, Paul, in case you're wondering, is the definition of love and lust combined, with someone you're not supposed to be with. It's deadly."

At home later, Jessie approached Josh in the kitchen while the kids were playing nearby. "You need to call your sister," she advised him, a cautious air to her quiet words.

"I do? Why?" Josh turned away from dropping sliced green olives into a quinoa salad to consider Jessie's request. "Is she okay?"

"No. No, she's anything but okay." Jessie slid into a seat at the island opposite him and took his hand when he stopped working and faced her.

"You two had another fight."

"I suppose you could say that."

"What aren't you telling me?"

"Josh, she...uh, we actually, caught Paul and Mandy together in the Deacon space today."

Josh sucked on his lip for a moment before responding. A slow, "I see," eventually emerged from between his contemplative lips. His eyes never left Jessie's face.

"She's throwing him out."

"Um-humn. Well, shit. I like Paul."

"Josh, I…"

He air palmed her. "We're done talking about this, Jessie." Josh moved around the island and made his way to the back door, touching each of his kids' heads as he passed them and ignoring Dylan's cries of, "Daddy. Daddy, come see what I make!"

Following Josh, Jessie hooked her thumbs over her jeans pockets and called after him. "Where you going? Are you going to see Kayla? Josh, answer me. When will you be back? Talk to me!"

His black leather jacket was hanging from a hook near the door. He grabbed it, shuffled into its heavy warmth, and shoved his feet into motorcycle boots.

"It's freezing!" Jessie cried. "At least take the goddamned truck!"

"Momma, swearing is not nice," came from David's small lips as Emily-Grace, dressing a Barbie doll in a fashionable gown on the floor next to him, looked up, her eyes wide.

"Swear jar, Momma," she whispered.

"I'm sorry, kids, you're right," Jessie said as she dropped to the floor behind her children and pulled Emily-Grace and David close. "Momma is so careless."

At the sliding door, Josh stood and stared at the image of his family all together on the floor. They were perfect. They were real, broken, scared, needy, and perfect. They were here, in his home, under his care, all four of them. None were sick, none were missing, and none were beyond repair, as far as he was concerned.

He caught Jessie's moist and frightened eyes staring up at him, wishing, hoping, hurting. Screaming *sorry*.

"I told you," he said, his voice gruff with emotion. "I am never leaving you. And I will never let you go. But I need a drive right now. Okay, Jessie? Tell me you get why I need a fucking drive right now."

Jessie buried her face in her daughter's blonde ringlets. Her voice came out muffled. "I get it, Josh. I get it."

Josh reached for his black Harley half-helmet and slid the door open behind him.

He was gone before Jessie had the chance to say, "I love you."

The Harley roared to life moments later, announcing Josh's anger and frustration to the world as it thundered down the driveway and took a hard left.

Jessie took Emily-Grace's fully dressed Barbie in her hands, and ran trembling fingers over the soft red silk gown Deirdre had given the little girl for Christmas.

"She's lovely," she murmured. "Just lovely, honey."

"Maybe you could wear a dress like that one to the Grammys, Momma." Emily-Grace was hopeful, optimistic.

"Maybe I can, baby girl," Jessie replied with a forced smile. *Or maybe I will just melt away,* she thought. *And never sing again.*

Chapter Thirty-one

Half-packed boxes lay at Josh's feet as he sat, stony and silent, on Kayla's burnished red couch, her head on a pillow on his lap, his left arm securely around her shoulders. She was curled up into him, into the safety and unconditional love of her big brother on this, one of the most difficult days of her life.

Josh had arrived after a ponderous cruise up Cypress Mountain, where he had parked his bike and considered the lights of the city of Vancouver spread out before him. Who did they belong to, what did they mean? Were the people underneath those lights happy? Were their lives easy? Did they hurt each other?

On nights like this Josh wanted to slug back a few beers and throw the empties up into the seemingly limitless stars and their annoying twinkling inability to answer his questions, to take the ache in his gut away.

Kayla, the happy-go-luckiest of the Sawyers, everyone's sweet light, did not deserve Paul's treachery. In Nashville, on the way to the funeral, she had called Josh a doormat. Obviously she suspected at the time that something was amiss in her world. Did Josh deserve the hard lesson recently thrown his way too? Did anyone?

A few years ago I would have thrown in the towel too, he told himself. *But not now. Now I fight for what is mine. And that includes my wife, my kids, and my sister's happiness.*

Josh pantomimed tossing a beer bottle into the air. *Ppffffttttt* went the soundtrack in his head as the fantasy bottle flew end over end. In his mind, it arced above him and landed on the earth far below. Maybe on Paul's stupid head. Maybe on Jessie's.

Out loud he said, after the imaginary shattering of the bottle, "Jessie, I sure hope you can keep your promise to me. No more Jacob. No more temptations."

Dylan flitted across his mind. Jessie had been right that night, when Josh eavesdropped outside their sons' door at the hotel in Nashville. It wasn't going to get any easier as the boy grew into his father's—Jacob's—features. Even now, the curly dark hair was causing stares in the grocery store, backstage at Jessie's shows, on their film sets. Thanks to the media, everyone knew Dylan was Jacob's biological son. To Josh, it was still a knife twist to the gut when he allowed himself to think of what transpired back then for Jessie to end up pregnant with Jacob's baby.

But Josh had promised her—the day she told him, the day they got back together—that he would care for the boy as his own. And he had kept that promise. He would continue to keep that promise, even though...even though something had changed over the last few crazy weeks. No longer was Jacob a safe memory. In fact, Josh reminded himself, he was never a safe memory, in Jessie's eyes. In her eyes, Jacob was still someone she loved deeply, deeply enough to want to hold and love when he was hurting.

"But I'm not you, Kayla," Josh said to the cool wind and to the mysterious lights and to the earth grounding him into reality. "I can't let her go. If that makes me a doormat, so be it. I love her."

He pulled out his phone. Jessie had texted three times already. *Please come home Please come home Please please please come home*

A last heavy sigh, and Josh walked to his bike. Without responding to his wife, he piloted it safely towards Kayla's cozy tree-lined street, much to the annoyance of the quiet-loving neighbors, but to Kayla's tearful welcome.

Now, as he sat in silence on the couch, his sister all cried out and asleep in his care, Josh found his warring self at peace. He would put Jessie's revelations about Jacob behind him. Behind them. Because he had to, in order to move forward. Jessie would be leaving for Belgium soon, and by the time she got back Josh would be expected in Alberta to shoot the new series, finally officially named *Sacred Peace*, with Charlie. These were long-term gigs, and both would require separations, even if just for a few days at a time. Film sets came with temptations. There were always women willing to hide behind closed doors with a sexy male star. Hadn't Josh learned that the hard way, with Nadia? With the woman in Virginia all those years ago? Would two wrongs make a right?

No. He would have to be vigilant, wise and faithful. He would have to be a model husband to Jessie, so that she would never again have a reason to go running to Jacob.

He bent his lips to Kayla's ear. "Hey, sis," he mumbled, and she stirred. "I should probably go home. It's late. Are you gonna be okay?"

"Noooo," she answered, a weary downturn to her pale lips. "But I'll try to be."

A tiny curve appeared at one corner of Josh's lip. "Me too," he whispered. "Me too."

~ ~

At home, Jessie was surrounded by an unequalled love that made her heart swell in gratitude. She had broken a cardinal rule—after all, it was a school night—and brought all three of her babies into the big king bed for the night. They dozed around her now. Emily-Grace with her blonde curls fanning over her pillow, singer-dolly snug under one arm; David with Josh's beautiful fine hair and that odd piece that always wanted to go rogue; Dylan, the love child caught between two fathers, the one who Jessie cried for the most these last few weeks.

"My babies," she murmured, touching each lightly in turn, sending them hope and energy and strength for the days ahead, for whatever else life might toss their way.

Laying her head on the pillow behind Emily-Grace, she curled up around the slim body and refocused her gaze to the patio door, which led to the upper outside deck where, in the old days of nascent love, she often sat on Josh's lap, or between his legs, her fingers entwined securely in his, her head back against his strong chest and shoulder. In those days they would sit for hours, in love and happy, humbled at finding each other, grateful for the gift of touch, of the magic of making love, of becoming so fully a part of each other that it seemed their bodies and souls were one and the same.

That was before Deuce McCall. Before Jacob. Before Nadia and Morgan ripped Josh and Jessie apart in a horrifying way that sent Jessie running back to Jacob's soulful puppy dog eyes, his tender ballads, his sizzling lovemaking.

Jessie shivered, and buried her face in the pillow.

Oh, God, she moaned, thinking of Kayla out there suffering the worst kind of heartache; of Josh somewhere out there on his big Harley in the freezing cold, remembering the jagged edges of his own recent heartache; and of Jacob, alone and lost, their last connection a desperate plea to her from him—*please come with me.*

In a few short weeks Jessie would be leaving for Brussels, leaving Josh and her babies behind so the older kids could stay in school. Long days on film sets when you were in almost every scene were not ideal learning grounds or playgrounds for small kids. Would Josh be okay? Would he want to right her wrong with another wrong? Him being around Kayla at this juncture of her life, with the bitterness Jessie knew was already growing in Kayla's broken heart, would not help settle Josh's heart and mind.

A new sound started down the street, and made its way closer. It was low, insistent, rumbling, making its presence known. Like thunder.

The Harley.

Her heart racing, Jessie eased her tired mind and body off the bed, being careful not to wake the children as she moved. She covered them more fully, and her heart swelled with love again.

Leaving the room, she closed the door softly behind her, and padded quietly down the stairs, twisting a ringlet around and around her pointy finger as she did so.

Soon, the sliding door *whooshed* softly open, and Josh stepped inside. Drained and disillusioned, he exhaled as he placed his helmet on its shelf, and as he shuffed off the thick leather jacket.

Jessie made her way over to him, touched his bicep, and turned him towards her.

"Make love to me," she begged. "Please. Now. I need to feel you close to me again."

Josh didn't need to be encouraged any further. He pressed his lips to hers as he wrapped his arms around her, and lifted her. When he started up the stairs, Jessie stopped him.

"Our bed is full," she whispered as she bent to his ear to plant tender kisses behind the rogue hair before moving to the corner of his eye, his cheek, his mouth.

She could feel a sad smile below her lips. "The kids, I hope," he joked lamely.

"All three," she murmured.

They made love in the basement, in the blackness of the media room, where neither would have to read expressions or guess what the other was feeling. Touch was all they needed tonight; touch, and the open hearts to forgive.

Chapter Thirty-two

$\mathcal{S}$omewhere in the hot, stifling air of the Caribbean, under an endless indigo sky, Jacob set sail. His new ride was a fifty-year-old twenty-eight foot green-hulled wooden sailboat recently restored by a Halifax, Nova Scotia sailor ready to give up his solitary life on the sea for a woman who couldn't handle the carefree lifestyle.

The sailor, a thirty-two-year-old disillusioned musician, was taken aback when singer Jacob Ryan bought his boat but he, like most of the world by now, knew of Talia's unexpected death, and so he didn't ask questions. He took Jacob's money, the full amount he had asked for the creaky vessel, and he spent a week schooling Jacob on how to sail and care for her.

"She's my girl," the sailor had said, slapping the cabin rooftop with a firm affection. "Or, she was. Now she's yours. Take good care of her and she'll never let you down."

Just what I need, Jacob caught himself thinking. *A woman I can count on.*

The boat had a name and, in the interest of maintaining her identity as well as not spooking himself by bringing a curse aboard by changing the name, Jacob kept it.

Sarah May. Clean, short and feminine. Perfect. Stretched out on the deck or cruising the islands with a coffee in one hand and the tiller in the other, in the days and weeks to follow, alone at last, Jacob would reflect on the name. Who was Sarah May? Was she someone's true love? Did it last?

Jacob sailed with a red bandana tied around his head to keep the wind from playing in his hair and obstructing his vision. He knew the ports he visited were curious about his need for solitary venture but, for the most part, the locals had no clue who he was.

He wasn't pulling a Jessie, he told himself, running away and worrying people. In the interest of staying on someone's radar, anyone's, he had emailed his grandparents, his father, Charles Keating, and Jessie. In that order.

Apart from the usual worries about him sailing alone, all approved of his decision to take some time to recover from the loss of the woman he was meant to marry the day before he buried her. Jacob promised to check in from time to time, and to come home in a few months if he felt ready. In the meantime, Deirdre cleared his calendar and asked for a forwarding address so she could send him 'stuff,' she said.

He hadn't planned to email Jessie. It just seemed like the right way to say a final goodbye, and Jacob hoped Jessie would be wise enough to ditch the email before Josh could eyeball it. She wrote back almost immediately, concerned and sorry. Sorry for anything and everything he felt like blaming her for, he realized sadly.

I don't get it, he thought. *What I did to her in Florida was unforgivable. And why did I email her when she asked me not to?*

Because.

I want her to worry about me.

I want her to miss me.

I want her to love me.

Now, Jacob pointed *Sarah May* into the stiff breeze and hoisted her mainsail. It caught the wind with a mighty snap, and the boat started to coast forward. He wrestled with the jib until the boat was heeling thirty degrees starboard. As the waves started to slap the hull with a gentle ferocity that made his blood roil with anticipation, Jacob settled into the open cockpit and grabbed the tiller in one hand and a French-pressed coffee in a pottery mug in the other.

"Thar she blows!" he hollered, and raised the coffee like a trophy.

He sang a sad song as *Sarah May* cut through the waves.

If I needed you,
would you come to me,

would you come to me
for to ease my pain.

If you needed me,
I would come to you,
I would swim the seas
for to ease your pain.

The snap of the sails was intoxicating, the promise of obscurity powerfully liberating.

Ahead was open sea and a rising sun. Freedom, loneliness, and adventure. But above all…ahead was healing.

And ahead…was hope.

~ ~

The End.

~ ~

If I Needed You
Written by Townes Van Zandt
Featured in the 2012 film "The Broken Circle Breakdown"
Listen to it on my YouTube *Drifters* playlist **bit.ly/1QmQGBP**

Thank you!

Please remember to rate and review *After The Rain*—self-published authors rely on our readers to help spread the love!

P.S. You've made it this far…so you're officially a 'Drifterite!' Term coined by reader Amanda Grady of Ontario, Canada.

CLAIM your free excerpt from *A Song For Josh* by joining the Drifters readers' group at **www.susanrodgersauthor.com**

Happy reading!

Susan

www.susanrodgersauthor.com

Facebook: search **Susan Rodgers, Writer**

Twitter: **@srbluemountain**

www.bublish.com

email: **fatcat@pei.sympatico.ca**

About the Author

 Susan Rodgers' first novel *A Certain Kind of Freedom* was a Finalist in the Writers' Federation of Nova Scotia Atlantic Writing Awards for unpublished manuscripts. Her short story from the novel of the same name, published in two anthologies, has received rave reviews, as have the Drifters novels, Susan's all-time favourite books to write.

Owner/Operator of Bluemountain Entertainment, Susan is a 'Diploma With Honours' graduate of Vancouver Film School. She produces mostly documentary style client films and short dramas with plans to one day shoot a Feature Drama based on the novel Atlantic Blue.

Formerly a Museum Curator, in winter Susan lives with her partner Steve and her striped cat Oliver (Lucy Maud Montgomery once said the only good cat is a striped cat) in Summerside, Prince Edward Island, Canada. In summer, she hides in a small trailer in Darnley, P.E.I., where she writes novels, paddles kayaks, and crafts sandcastles on the beach. She makes frequent trips to Vancouver to visit her son Christopher, where she enjoys life in the hippie city while listening to great music and sipping on good espresso.

Books by Susan Rodgers

Drifters series:
A Song For Josh
Promises
No Greater Love
Riptide
Whispers of Home
And Then There Was Silence
Let the Music Cry
If I Could Sing You Home
After the Rain
Into the Blue
A Sacred Peace
Watch Over Me

Coming Soon:
A Certain Kind of Freedom
Seasmoke
Atlantic Blue

Feature Screenplays:
The Story of Jack & Emma
Atlantic Blue
Beautiful Jane
They Were Dreamers (adapted)

Short Stories:
S12
A Certain Kind of Freedom
A Gentle Peace